Steven kissed her with hot, sensuous lips. He bent her body backward until she felt the mattress of grass beneath her, and then his lips traveled from her mouth down along her throat to the first button that fastened her nightgown about her neck. Rebecca found herself surrendering to him, allowing him to do with her what he wished. She seemed to have no will of her own, but was subservient to his will, bending to his bidding like a slender reed in a strong spring breeze.

His graceful hands and agile fingers quickly and easily opened the buttons that held her nightgown closed, and suddenly she felt cool air on her naked, fevered flesh. His hand moved across her skin, cupping her breast, now warm and vibrant. He tenderly stroked the nipple with his thumb; the nipple was already swollen and straining to be loved.

Oh, yes, Rebecca thought hazily.

Steven stood up and began undressing slowly and deliberately before her wide, innocent, eager eyes. A moment later he too was nude, standing before her like a statue in the moonlight.

The sight of his smooth skin, rippling muscles, and obvious maleness aroused Rebecca to even greater heights of passion. He dropped to one knee, then placed a hand lightly on the inside of her thigh.

"No," Rebecca said, making one last, ineffectual plea, as much to herself as to Steven. "Steven, no, this isn't right!"

Steven didn't wait, but moved over her and then into her, and for the first time in her life, Rebecca was a woman being loved. . . .

Pinnacle Books by Patricia Matthews:

Love's Avenging Heart
Love's Wildest Promise
Love, Forever More
Love's Pagan Heart
Love's Daring Dream
Love's Magic Moment
Love's Golden Destiny
Love's Raging Tide

WRITE FOR OUR FREE CATALOG

If there is a Pinnacle Book you want—and you cannot find it locally—it is available from us simply by sending the title and price plus 50¢ per order and 10¢ per copy to cover mailing and handling costs to:

Pinnacle Books, Inc.
Reader Service Department
2029 Century Park East
Los Angeles, California 90067

Please allow 4 weeks for delivery. New York State and California residents add applicable sales tax.

_____Check here if you want to receive our catalog regularly.

Love's Sweet Agony

Patricia Matthews

PINNACLE BOOKS   LOS ANGELES

This is a work of fiction. All the characters and events portrayed in this book are fictional, and any resemblance to real people or incidents is purely coincidental.

LOVE'S SWEET AGONY

Copyright © 1980 by Pyewacket Corporation

All rights reserved, including the right to reproduce this book or portions thereof in any form.

An original Pinnacle Books edition, published for the first time anywhere.

First printing, May 1980

ISBN: 0-523-40660-6

Cover illustration by John Solie

Printed in the United States of America

PINNACLE BOOKS, INC.
2029 Century Park East
Los Angeles, California 90067

Love's Sweet Agony

Love is fire,
And love is magic,
Sometimes pleasure,
Sometimes pain.
Love is joy,
And love is tragic,
Sometimes mad,
And sometimes sane.
Love can bind,
And love can open,
Sometimes minds,
And sometimes hearts,
Love can find,
And then be broken,
Hurt can come
From Cupid's darts.
Love can bring you subjugation,
Love can make you wild and free,
I accept with jubilation
My love's own sweet agony.

LOVE'S SWEET AGONY

Chapter One

The March sun was distant and pale. A cold wind pulled at the spectators' clothing and reddened their cheeks. But even the midafternoon chill of this Illinois day could not dampen the spirits of the audience that crowded the railing of the track, cheering and urging on their favorites.

A few lucky viewers watched from the height of buggies, and young men and children crowded the roofs of nearby sheds. The spirit was one of holiday release, for this was fair time, one of the few times the hardworking farmers and merchants and their families could relax, and this was one of the favorite events of the fair, the sulky race.

Out on the track, the wheels of the lightweight sulkies were singing on the hard-packed dirt, throwing out rooster tails of dust behind them. The horses' hooves rose and fell in perfect rhythm; and as the nine pacers pounded down the stretch, one of them, its driver in cherry-red silks, moved slowly to the front.

At the finish line, Henry Hawkins, a small, wiry, peppery man of sixty-three, watched the stretch drive intently through a pair of field glasses. Those standing nearby could see his heavy, steel-gray eyebrows, which matched in color and density his thick thatch of hair, shining brightly in the afternoon sunlight. And though they couldn't see his snapping blue eyes, covered as they were by the glasses, they could see the humor and joy in a face which belied the fierce competitiveness and bulldog determination of the man.

"Come on, Paddy Boy!" he shouted. "Come on, Paddy Boy, show them what you're made of!"

Paddy Boy moved a full length into the lead, maintaining a gait which was so smooth and graceful that his body seemed not to move at all, only his legs and feet, flickering through the dust. His head was held high, as if to catch the wind. With the small driver perched precariously between the spinning, flashing wheels, Paddy Boy swept across the finish line a winner by a full length.

"Hot damn, you did it!" Henry Hawkins yelled excitedly, and jumped up and down with delight. He regretted his burst of enthusiasm almost immediately, for a jolt of pain shot through his side to remind him of the accident that had shattered a hip bone five years earlier, relegating him to a position at the rail, watching someone else drive his horse.

But even the nagging ache did not subdue the excitement, and holding his hand over the throbbing hip, as if by that action he could ease the pain, he moved with a quick, hopping gait over to the victory lane to greet Paddy Boy and lay claim to his one hundred dollar winner's purse.

The driver of the sulky turned the horse around, came back across the finish line, reached out and snatched the bright yellow purse that hung from the finish pole, flipped it to Henry Hawkins, and then left the track in the direction of the stables.

Once inside the stable the driver quickly unhitched Paddy Boy from the sulky, led him to a dim stall at the rear, unlatched the stall door, ushered the animal inside, and relatched the door securely. The driver then moved to a trunk in one corner of the stall and threw back the lid, exposing neatly packed women's clothing.

The driver whipped off the racing cap and the bandanna beneath it, shaking out shoulder-length black curls. She stepped out of the men's breeches and shrugged out of the sweaty red silk shirt. With a sigh of relief she unwound the cloth that bound her torso, and her small but well-shaped breasts sprang free. She rubbed them gently, wincing as she touched a tender spot. This was the part Rebecca Hawkins hated most, binding her breasts flat. Not only was it uncomfortable —particularly at times like this, just before her monthly—but it seemed to her to be a denial of her womanhood, which she was just discovering.

Her movements deft and practiced, she got dressed in a simple ankle-length green skirt and white blouse, then locked the trunk. Only then did she turn to Paddy Boy and begin rubbing him down, talking to him in a voice soft with love.

Back at the track, one of the track officials called down from the reviewing stand where he and the judges were sitting. "Paddy Boy just ran the fastest mile ever run in Alexander County Fair history, Hawk."

"What was the time?" Hawk asked.

"Two minutes, two seconds," the judge replied.

"Not bad. Not bad at all," Hawk said, smiling broadly and rubbing his hands together. "That was good time."

"Mr. Hawkins, pardon me, sir," a voice behind him said. "I'm Mr. Dennis, of the Cairo *Evening Citizen*. May I interview you for my paper?"

Hawk turned. Facing him was a small, ferret-faced man. Smiling proudly, Hawk said, "Of course, sir."

"Is this your first race in Illinois?" Dennis asked.

"No, no, we've been in four races at four different county fairs since coming into Illinois. And we'll race here again tomorrow afternoon."

"And have you been successful?"

"We've won two—three now, counting this one," Hawk said with a wide grin. "But this has been our biggest purse so far. The other races had purses of twenty-five and fifty." He shook the purse, and the gold coins inside jangled musically.

Dennis glanced around. "I hoped your driver would come back. I wanted a picture of the two of you together."

Hawk's glance slid away. "My driver is a shy one. He prefers not to have his picture took, or answer newspaper questions."

"But surely you have some influence over him? After all, he is in your employ."

"Yup, that he is. But he is stubborn about his privacy, and I've no wish to lose him. Best driver I ever had." Hawk laughed. "After all, I can no longer ride myself."

"Henry Hawkins! Of course!" Dennis suddenly said, pounding his fist into his hand. "I should have realized right off. You're *the* Henry Hawkins, aren't you?"

Hawk grinned. "Yup, as far as I know I am. At least, I am the only Henry Hawkins I know."

"You know what I mean," Dennis spluttered. "You are the Henry Hawkins who raced at the English Lord's Derby, in Epsom, England. You are the only American ever to win two races there."

"I've enjoyed some success, yes," Hawk said modestly.

"But I don't understand, Mr. Hawkins," Dennis said. "Why would a man of your background, someone as famous as you are, be racing at a nickel-and-

4

dime county fair? How could you have come so far down?"

The smile left Hawk's face and was replaced by an expression of pain. But only for an instant, and only noticeable by the most discerning, for he quickly erased the dour expression and addressed himself to the man's question.

"I rode the horses, son, but I didn't own them," he said. "I got the name, but not the money. I just made a living at it, and when I couldn't ride anymore, I didn't make a living anymore. It's that simple. So I bought a used sulky and a Standardbred who was past his prime. He won a few races for me, enough to keep me going, but he sired Paddy Boy, who is winning a few more."

"I—I'm sorry," Dennis apologized. "I had no right to pry."

"Of course you did, son. That's your job."

"Oh, here comes my photographer," the newsman said. "Perhaps you'd allow us to take your picture?"

Hawk saw the photographer approaching, and behind the photographer came his granddaughter, Rebecca.

"I'll allow your man to take my picture, provided my granddaughter is in it as well," he said. "I know your readers would rather see a pretty young girl than an ornery old codger like myself."

And indeed, Rebecca Hawkins *was* pretty. She was a slender girl of somewhat less than average height, with a mass of black ringlets that fell to her shoulders, framing a triangular face. Her face, fair and almost porcelain smooth, was touched with color only on the cheekbones and the mouth, and was set off by tawny eyes of a most unusual color, "like a sparkling glass of sherry," her grandfather was fond of saying.

These eyes were shining now, and her smile showed

5

small, even white teeth. The look she gave her grandfather was one of triumph.

"Come along, Becky," Hawk said. "Our picture is going to be in the Cairo newspaper. Ain't that dandy? Will it be in tonight's paper?"

"I'm afraid not, sir," the man replied. "It will be tomorrow before the woodcut can be made. Hold it, please."

Hawk and Rebecca stared into the tripod-mounted camera while the photographer crouched under the black hood. There was a loud click, then the photographer emerged from under the hood, folded up his camera and left.

"Thank you for the interview, Mr. Hawkins," Dennis said. "And good luck tomorrow afternoon."

"You're welcome, young fellow."

"Paddy Boy ran very well today," Rebecca said, as she and her grandfather left the track and strolled toward the stables. "He knows it, too, and is acting cocky."

"Oh, is he?" Hawk said. "And is the cockiness affecting Black Prince?"

"No," Rebecca said, laughing. "Prince is too fine a thoroughbred to be affected by Paddy Boy's carrying on. He's holding himself aloof, as usual. Though when I gave Paddy Boy his reward of sugar, Prince thought he should have some as well."

"You didn't give it to him, did you?" Hawk said with a scowl.

"Grandfather, how could I refuse him?"

"Oh, Becky, you are much too soft-hearted to be a good trainer. Black Prince has to learn that he is given his sugar only when he does something to earn it."

"But Grandfather, that isn't fair," Rebecca protested. "How do you think Prince feels standing by day after day? Paddy Boy wins races and receives his reward, while Prince has never even had his chance to compete. He *would* win if he ran in a race, you know he would."

"Of course he would," Hawk replied with a twinkle. "But darling, you know our plan."

"I know it, Grandfather. But does Prince?"

"Black Prince may well be the fastest thoroughbred in America, but we can't race him yet. We can't race him, because we must keep him a sleeper. Colonel Clark finally has the Kentucky Derby organized, and we're going to run Black Prince in the first race, come hell or high water. We'll wager all our savings on him, girl, and when he wins we'll have enough money to buy that thoroughbred farm we've been talking about," Hawk said, explaining the plan to Rebecca as if she didn't know it by heart, as if she hadn't heard these very same words hundreds of times during their years of travel from county fair to county fair, and from race to race.

"There they are," Rebecca said proudly, as she and her grandfather approached their two stalls in the stables. "My two beautiful darlings."

Both Black Prince and Paddy Boy heard her crooning voice, and turned their heads expectantly toward her. As Rebecca moved toward them, suddenly she heard the unmistakable sound of a horse neighing in pain, and the whistling, snapping sound of a whip being used.

"Grandfather, what is that?" Rebecca asked, gripping Hawk's arm tightly and looking down the long line of stalls in alarm.

"Sounds to me like some blackguard is beating his horse, girl," Hawk said angrily. "Here now!" he bellowed, hurrying toward the stall from which the sounds came. "You damned blackguard, stop torturing that animal!"

7

"Grandfather, be careful!" Rebecca called, starting after him on the run, frightened for him.

There was another popping sound as a whip snapped cruelly against horseflesh, and again the animal let out a bellow of agony.

"Damn you, sir!" Hawk shouted, jerking open the door to the stall and charging inside without regard to personal danger. "Stop abusing that animal!"

By now Rebecca had caught up with her grandfather, and when she saw the perpetrator of the cruelty, she gasped, feeling a chill pass over her body, for she had never seen anyone as evil and frightening in appearance as the man who stood before her, grasping the reins of a frightened horse in one hand and a whip in the other.

He was a big man, well over six feet tall and weighing easily two hundred pounds. His head was completely bald, so bald that Rebecca realized that he must keep it shaved. It was somewhat bullet-shaped, and his thick neck and bullish shoulders gave him the appearance of being carved from one solid block of granite. He was dressed all in black, but a closer examination of his clothing disclosed that it was of the finest cut and most expensive material. He had a vivid scar like a purple lightning flash on his left cheek, and as he looked first at Hawk and then at Rebecca, he rubbed the scar lightly with a fingertip, as if caressing it.

There were two other men outside the stall, one a small man, still dressed in yellow and black racing silks, whom Rebecca recognized as Timmie Bird, a driver, and another man she had never seen before.

"You are Henry Hawkins, aren't you?" the big man with the whip said. "Allow me to introduce myself, sir. I am Oscar Stull. I own this animal."

8

"That doesn't give you the right to beat it!" Rebecca said hotly.

Stull smiled at her coldly. "On the contrary, my dear young lady. It gives me a right to do anything I wish with the beast. Including killing it, if I should feel like it."

"Timmie," Hawk said, turning to the unhappy driver, "I've known you for a number of years. I've never known you to abuse a horse, or tolerate anyone who does."

"It's not my idea, Hawk," Timmie said miserably. His face clearly mirrored his fear of Oscar Stull. "But there was nothing I could do."

"You could tell this miserable scoundrel that you'll not ride or drive for him any more."

Stull laughed harshly. "No, Mr. Hawkins, he can't do that," he said. "For if he refused to ride for me, I would see to it that he never rode for *anyone* again."

"And how would you do that, you great bully?" Rebecca demanded. "Beat him with your whip, as you do your own horse?"

"Young lady, I don't make idle threats," Stull said with a cold sneer. "Mr. Mercy here has a way of seeing to it that my wishes are carried out without question. Don't you, my friend? This, by the way, is Mr. Mercy, my bodyguard. Unfortunately, I have need of one from time to time."

"I can well imagine," Rebecca said in disgust.

She looked at the man Oscar Stull called Mr. Mercy. He was the one she had never seen before and, she decided, she could do quite nicely without ever seeing him again.

He wasn't very large at all. In fact, he was quite small when compared to Oscar Stull, and at first the idea of Mr. Mercy being Stull's bodyguard seemed ludicrous. He had a gray, almost sickly pallor to his skin which was accented by the colorless, drab clothing he wore. His eyes were gray, too, but they made an immediate, shocking impression. They were like blocks of ice, and Rebecca, staring into them, saw not the slightest flicker of feeling or compassion.

It was, she imagined, like staring into the face of death. If any man in the world didn't fit his name, it was Mr. Mercy.

"Why are you whipping this poor creature?" Hawk demanded of Stull.

"Why? Because *he* was beaten, Mr. Hawkins. But, ah, you know that well enough, don't you, sir? It was your horse that did the deed."

"And you're lashing your animal for that?" Hawk said in disgust. "Good Lord, man, I've lost two out of the last five races. Do you think I would beat Paddy Boy because of that?"

"You have your training methods and I have mine," Stull said blandly.

"And as you can see, our training methods work," Rebecca added.

"So do mine, young lady, more often than not," Stull retorted. He stared at her with eyes which, for the first time, really appeared to see her.

Rebecca had learned to recognize lust in men's eyes. No one had ever explained it to her, and she was certainly innocent of any experience by which to judge; but she was a bright and intuitive girl, and she had learned the facts of life from practical exposure in the form of horsebreeding. Therefore, her innocence was not confounded by ignorance.

Rebecca was twenty years old, and sometimes, when she thought of the mating process as it applied to humans, she felt a certain pleasant speculation. But the thought of such a thing with this man who was staring at her with such a devouring look made a chill race down her spine, and she shivered involuntarily.

"However," Stull was going on, "I can see that my training methods, effective as they may be, are disturbing to you, so I will cease." He said it as if granting a great favor.

He smiled again, another smile without mirth, and handed the whip to Timmie Bird, who took it with a sidelong glance of shame toward Hawk and Rebecca, then scurried out of the stable.

"Mr. Stull, in every race, only one horse can win," Hawk said. "Surely, sir, you can accept racing for the sport that it is?"

"I am afraid that I'm not a man with a temperament for losing," Stull replied. "And, as you say, though there are losers in every race, there is also a winner. I prefer to be the winner."

"Hello!" a man's voice called from outside the stable. "Mr. Hawkins, are you around?"

Hawk and Rebecca walked back out the door of the Stull stall and looked toward their own, to see who had hailed Hawk. A tall, slender young man with sandy-blond hair stood outside their stall, peering in at Paddy Boy and Black Prince. He was well dressed, too well dressed to be an ordinary working man, Rebecca thought, and he looked rather like a dandy. He was reaching up to pat Paddy Boy affectionately, smiling and talking to the horse in a soft, lilting Irish brogue.

"Yes," Hawk answered, going toward him with Rebecca on his arm. "I am Henry Hawkins. What may I do for you, sir?"

"Ah, Mr. Hawkins!" the young man said. "I am Gladney Halloran, sir, and I've come to buy your supper for you."

"You're going to buy Grandfather's supper?" Re-

11

becca said in astonishment. "Why on earth should you do that?"

Halloran glanced at her, and his grin widened. It was, she noticed, a crooked grin, as if his jaw had been slightly misaligned in a brawl of some kind; though, other than the crooked smile, there was nothing else about him to suggest a brawler. So why did the idea of a brawl come to mind? Rebecca wondered. Then, as she studied him more closely, she realized why. His eyes, which were flashing merrily at her, also showed a flash of something else, something that hinted that he was a man quick to anger, a man prepared to defend his position, right or wrong. What she had mistaken for slenderness from a distance was now revealed as a wiry muscularity. Unaccountably, Rebecca began to feel ill at ease.

"And you would be his granddaughter now, lass? Sure, and it'll be a pleasure to buy supper for you as well, for 'tis that flush I am, thanks to the pair of you."

"Thanks to us?" Hawk asked dryly.

"Aye, the two of you, and the gentleman here with the fine Irish name of Paddy Boy. 'Twas the Irish name, I must admit, which led me to wager on him in the first place. And he paid very, very well, that he did, so the least I can do is feed the two of you."

"Thank you, Mr. Halloran, but that won't be—"

"We'd be delighted to accept your offer, Mr. Halloran," Hawk said, interrupting his granddaughter and shaking the young man's hand.

"Grandfather!" Rebecca exclaimed in dismay.

"Well, why not?" Hawk said. "After all, letting the man buy our supper will save us the price of a meal. I see nothing wrong in that."

"You should listen to your grandfather, lass. 'Tis a good head he has on his shoulders."

Oscar Stull had come out of his horse's stall when

12

the Hawkinses left to speak with Gladney Halloran; and when he did so, he spotted Black Prince. He moved over to stand by the thoroughbred's stall. He examined him with a great deal of interest and a clear knowledge of horseflesh.

"Mr. Hawkins, will you be racing this horse on the morrow?" he asked.

"No," Hawk said shortly.

"No?" Stull looked at Black Prince more carefully, paying particular attention to the depth of his chest and his long graceful legs.

"Would you be interested in a match race then? Just your horse against mine? The winner to take the other's horse?"

"No, I think not," Hawk responded.

"Don't answer hastily, sir, not until you see my animal. She's a magnificent filly, out of Lazy by Virgil, same as William Astor's gelding, Vagrant. And Vagrant has already won the Alexander Stakes, the Belle Meade Stakes, the Sanford Stakes, the Colt Stakes, and the Colt and Filly Stakes at Lexington."

"I know of Vagrant," Hawk said interestedly. "What of your horse?"

"Stull's Pride by name," Stull said. "She's run fairly well, nothing I could brag on. From the looks of your horse, though, she wouldn't have to run more than fairly well to win," he said condescendingly. "He looks good for nothing, save as a stud, for breeding purposes. And I would use him for that, if I won. I certainly wouldn't be interested in racing such an unpromising-looking animal."

"I wouldn't be so blasted sure of that," Hawk said huffily. "Black Prince just might surprise you."

"Black Prince, you call him? Quite a noble name," Stull said sneeringly. "If your horse was as noble in bloodline as in name, now . . ."

"You have yourself a race, sir!" Hawk said explosively.

"No, we do not have a race," Rebecca broke in. "Grandfather, whatever has come over you?"

"Becky, you heard what the man said about Black Prince! It's insulting! Who does he think he is?"

"He's just trying to goad you," Rebecca said.

Hawk sighed, scrubbing a hand down across his face. "Perhaps you're right, girl. I lost my head there for a minute. I'm sorry, Mr. Stull. There will be no race."

"No race?" Stull said harshly. "But you have already agreed to it!"

"Well, now I'm disagreeing," Hawk said easily. "There will be no race, sir. Black Prince isn't ready yet, and I'll not take a chance racing him too soon."

"Mr. Hawkins, you are a man with a well-respected reputation, sir. You have won victories in England and all over America, and yet you let a slip of a girl dictate to you? What man with any pride would do that?"

"The girl was but reminding me of my own decision, made long ago," Hawk said patiently. "And she was quite right in reining me in. I fail to see why you are so riled, sir. I have said that there will be no race, and that is how it shall be."

"I am not a man to be balked this easily," Stull said menacingly. "I'm warning you, sir!"

"Warning me? Are you threatening me, Mr. Stull?" Hawk said, bristling.

"No, no, of course not," Stull said hastily, backing off slightly. "But I am not a man to—"

"You are not a man who is welcome here," Gladney Halloran suddenly spoke up. He had been stroking Paddy Boy's nose all the while, saying nothing, and seemingly paying no attention. He continued to caress

14

Paddy Boy, and spoke the words as casually as if he had just been asked the time of day.

"What did you say?" Stull reared back, his eyes cold with rage. "What business is this of yours? You have no stake in this!"

"I'll not be speaking for these nice people," Gladney said, indicating Hawk and Rebecca with a flip of his hand. "But Paddy Boy here, for whom I have developed a special affinity, has just told me that you're not welcome around him. He says that you are disturbing him with your loud mouth and rude manners. And he told me to tell you to hightail it."

"Why, you insolent ape!" Stull sputtered angrily, his cold eyes narrowing. "I ought to thrash you within an inch of your life."

Gladney gave Paddy Boy a final pat on the nose, then stepped away from the stall. He stood easily, poised lightly on the balls of his feet, with his arms hanging by his sides, his hands not clenched into fists but curled loosely. His body seemed to grow taut, not in a tight, anxious way, but in the manner of a tiger about to spring or a race horse about to dash forward. He smiled at Stull, a wide, easy, crooked grin, and then he raised his left arm, palm up, and began motioning with his fingers, curling them inward.

"An inch of my life, is it?" he said placidly. "Come ahead, Mr. Stull."

Stull took one step toward Gladney, then seemed to think the better of it, stopped, and forced a strained smile onto his face. He reached up and fingered the scar on his cheek.

"No," he said. "No, I think not. After all, why should I concern myself with you, when I have Mr. Mercy? I pay *him* to see to it that people like you don't trouble me."

"Aye," Gladney said easily, smiling still. "You run

along now to your Mr. Mercy like a nice gent, and leave Paddy Boy and me in peace."

"Mr. Hawkins," Stull said, "We'll be meeting again, you may be sure." He looked at Rebecca with the strained smile still upon his face, bowed slightly, insolently at her, then withdrew.

Rebecca shivered. "That man gives me a chill."

"Mr. Halloran, from the way you handled Stull, I'd be honored, sir, if you would let me buy *your* supper," Hawk said, laughing, as Stull stalked away out of sight.

"No, sir," Gladney replied. "'Tis the victory of Paddy Boy we're after celebrating, and not the exposure of a bully boy for what he is. I'll be doing the buying, sir, from my winnings." Gladney glanced around the stable. "But in truth, Mr. Hawkins, the driver deserves my gratitude as well, for 'twas indeed a fine race he drove."

"Yes," Hawk said, "I agree to that."

"Then he'll join us?"

"I'm afraid not, Mr. Halloran. He's a very shy young man, and can scarcely stand to meet strangers."

Gladney laughed. "Sure, and it's a rare man who don't take his just rewards for a job well done. Especially as there are so many willing to take rewards not due them."

"You'll respect his wishes then?"

"Of course," Gladney said. "Though I'd like to leave the price of a dinner for the young man, so that he can dine alone sometime."

"Believe me, that won't be necessary."

"Well then . . ." Gladney shrugged, then rubbed his hands together in anticipation, looking from Hawk to his granddaughter. "We'll be off then?"

"Becky, you've no objection?" Hawk asked hopefully.

Rebecca had been studying Gladney Halloran as the young man and her grandfather conversed. There was something about him that disturbed her. It wasn't the fear that Oscar Stull evoked in her. Her fear of Stull was generated by a sense of foreboding caused by his mere presence. Her feeling of apprehension about this young man was quite the opposite for, inexplicably, she felt a strong attraction toward him. His manner was charming, and that of course could account for some of it. But there was a physical attraction as well, and in truth, Rebecca was without experience in such feelings, and didn't understand them. *That* was what she feared . . . the physical attraction that she couldn't understand. And in addition, she was curious about him, and that proved to be the dominant factor in her deliberations. She put aside her reservations, at least for the moment, and smiled; and by that smile, nearly dazzled Gladney Halloran.

She said, "Mr. Halloran, if you wish to buy our meal, sir, then I shall offer no objections."

"Wonderful!" Gladney beamed.

"Oh!" Rebecca gasped suddenly, her glance going past him. She clapped her hand to her mouth, and her eyes grew wide in sudden fright.

"What is it?" Gladney demanded.

Rebecca pointed to the corner of the stable building. "I thought I saw that awful man again, that Mr. Stull."

Her grandfather snorted. "Well, our friend Mr. Halloran here ran him off once, I guess he can do it again." He winked at Gladney.

But Rebecca still stared into the darkness.

"What is it, girl? There's nothing to worry about. He's a great bully, to be sure, but like most bullies—"

Rebecca stopped him by putting her hand on his arm. "But Grandfather, I'm sure he had a gun. I saw it shine in the light from the window!"

Chapter Two

Damn the woman, Oscar Stull thought, jerking his head back out of sight as he heard Rebecca Hawkins call out. He did have a gun in his hand, and he quickly dropped it now, kicking loose hay and horse dung over it. Then, taking his riding quirt in the same hand in which he had held the pistol, he stepped around the corner, as if nothing had happened.

Gladney Halloran had responded to Rebecca's warning, and was already striding forward as Stull rounded the corner.

"What were you doing lurking back there?" Gladney demanded angrily.

"I beg your pardon?" Stull said blandly. "What do you mean? I have horses stabled here. Who has a better right than I to be here?"

"You have no right to skulk about with a gun," Gladney snapped. He advanced menacingly.

"A gun?" Stull replied. He held his coat open. "Do you see a gun on me? What the hell are you talking about, fellow?"

"I thought I saw one," Rebecca said faintly.

Stull looked at the bright metal handle of his riding quirt, and laughed. "My dear young lady, you undoubtedly saw this." He held the quirt out handle first.

His ruse worked, for some of the anger in Halloran's

19

eyes abated, and he looked at Rebecca questioningly. "A quirt, is it? Is that what you saw?"

Rebecca wasn't certain. She could have sworn she saw Stull holding a pistol—but it was only a fleeting glance. It *could* have been the quirt.

"I . . . I don't know. Perhaps it was," she admitted grudgingly.

"I assure you, Miss Hawkins, that it was," Stull said. "None of you are in any danger from this quirt, and I apologize if you were frightened by it."

"No," Rebecca said in a quiet voice. "It is I who should apologize to you, Mr. Stull. I obviously made a mistake."

Stull laughed, the same, flat, mirthless laugh Rebecca had begun to associate with him, and he rubbed the lightning-flash scar with a perfectly manicured finger. "We all make mistakes, Miss Hawkins. Think nothing of it."

Gladney had been listening, and while some of his anger had abated, he was still far from appeased. Something about this man Stull aroused antagonism in him, and he voiced it now.

"Sure and there's something queer going on here, Stull, and I'm not being taken in by your smooth manner."

"Mr. Halloran, I assure you that your fears are groundless," Stull said.

Gladney grinned sourly. "Oh, I've no fear of you, Stull, you can count on that. Nor liking for you, either. Now, we'll be on our way, but I'll not be forgetting your skulking, so don't be trying anything."

The scar on Stull's cheek flamed deep purple, and a blood vessel in his temple throbbed like a writhing snake, all the more visible because of his total baldness. But he managed to hold his tongue while the three took their leave. He watched them go with a baleful gaze, then let out a long breath of air. He should have known better than to return with the pistol. Deeds of that sort he left in the hands of Mr. Mercy. But Mr. Mercy had been sent on an errand; and such was Stull's anger and humiliation over Halloran's insolent defiance of him that he didn't take time to reason. He knew only a white, hot fury and blood lust, and that was what had motivated him to hurry to his carriage, remove a pistol from the boot, and come back in the hope of catching Halloran alone. Halloran was a known gambler and confidence man, and had undoubtedly made enough enemies, so that any of a dozen people could have cause to kill him.

It had been Stull's intention to shoot him dead and then leave him there for someone else to discover. But that damned girl and her grandfather had spoiled his plan. And she had nearly exposed him!

Stull thought of the girl long after she was out of his sight, and a picture of her flashed across his mind's eye. It was a most delightful picture, in which she was naked and bound before him, gagged so that she couldn't cry out, but without a blindfold so that he could look into her eyes, which were wide with terror. A quick, flaring heat built in his loins, and it burned away the unbridled anger he had felt toward Halloran, so that all he could feel now was a hunger for Rebecca Hawkins, a hunger that he could satisfy only in his own particular way.

For Stull's way with women was colored by his cruel nature. He delighted in trifling with them, causing them pain and humiliating them until they begged him to let them please him. He could only achieve sexual gratification by reducing a woman to the lowest level of degradation. Obviously, there were few women who were willing to participate in Stull's brutal sex play. Those who did were usually prostitutes, who demanded a heavy payment and afterward, invariably, refused to return. It didn't matter all that much to Stull that they never returned, for the variety of new women was a stimulant in itself, and added a certain fillip to his sexual activities. But not until this moment did he realize what an exquisite sensation it would be to subject an innocent girl to his whims. What a delight it would be if Rebecca Hawkins were that girl! How he would love to humiliate and brutalize her!

And it would serve her right, too, he thought viciously. She and her grandfather, the Hawk. They had never heard of him until today, but Stull knew of them. He knew that Henry Hawkins was one of the best-known names in American horse racing, and had, in fact, been awarded a charter membership in the Louisville Jockey Club and Driving Park Association, the sponsoring organization for a new race to be called the Kentucky Derby.

The Jockey Club had been founded just this year. Its chief organizer, M. Lewis Clark, had visited England to study the British Lord's Derby, and he returned to Louisville determined to start the Kentucky Derby, fashioned after that race.

Racing was at a low ebb at the time, having deteriorated to country fairs and match races. There were only a half-dozen tracks of any consequence in the entire country, and they sponsored races only sporadically. Kentucky thoroughbred breeders were seriously considering closing their stock farms because yearlings were selling for a mere hundred dollars or less. So, to create a demand for the thoroughbred, Clark had formed the Jockey Club, hoping it would demonstrate the superiority of Kentucky horses and create a demand for them.

Clark approached the most respected names in racing and lured them into his organization. But he did not approach Oscar Stull. In fact, when Stull applied for membership, he was told that the subscription list had been filled.

Stull was infuriated by the snub. He tried first to buy his way into the club, and when that didn't work, he tried to worm his way in through blackmail and coercion. But that didn't work either, so he found himself on the outside, looking in.

The members of the Jockey Club were not restricting Stull for petty or prejudicial reasons, but to protect the avowed purposes of the club. Already the Kentucky Derby, not yet run, had created great interest throughout the country, and it was felt that everyone associated with it must have impeccable background credentials. Stull simply did not qualify. He was well known for his ruthlessness and his anything-to-win tactics. In short, the members of the Jockey Club considered themselves gentlemen, and it was universally agreed that a gentleman Stull was not.

However, they would not be able to prevent him entering a horse in the Kentucky Derby, provided that he paid the nomination and entry fee and met all the other qualifications. So now it was Stull's burning ambition to enter the first race, which was to be held on May 17, 1875, and win it. In that way he would be vindicated for the snub.

It was typical of Oscar Stull that he would react to their snub just as he had reacted to Gladney Halloran's challenge, and to Paddy Boy's victory over his horse. In fact, it could be said that Stull's entire life was a reaction to outside stimuli.

Stull had been born forty-five years earlier in the waterfront district of Boston. His mother was a tavern wench, and his father a sailor—though which one of the hundreds of sailors who visited his mother, he never

23

knew. He was named Oscar, because his mother remembered that "one of the sailors around that time told me that his name was Oscar," and Stull, because across the street from the hovel where she lived, a large sign said: "Stull Warehouse and Supply."

Stull's mother drank herself into insensibility every night that he could remember, and by the time he was seven years old, Stull was totally independent of her, stealing or begging his food. He found her dead in a noxious alley during the winter of his fifteenth year, and he stood gazing down at her with as little sorrow as if she had been a stray cat or dog, run over by a drayman's wagon.

Shortly after that, Stull began to get more from his life of crime than mere survival, and by the time the Civil War started, he had become one of Boston's leading underworld figures. And that came close to being his downfall, for with his notoriety came recognition. Thus, when he killed a money messenger during a robbery, he was recognized and had to flee for his life.

The Federal army was a good place to hide and, for Stull, a fortunate place to be. Shortly after joining up, he was assigned to a small commissary detail to transfer one hundred thousand dollars in gold from one location to another. The detail was attacked by a Confederate patrol, and though the Federal troops beat the attack off, Stull's commanding officer was killed and the other three men wounded. Stull, recognizing his chance, finished off the three wounded men, hid the gold, and then reported that the Confederates had taken off with the money.

After the war, Stull returned to the spot where he had hidden the gold, retrieved it, and moved to Kentucky to begin living the life of a gentleman. And yet, despite the money, despite the distance between his

24

criminal life in Boston and Lousville, Stull had never really been accepted as a gentleman.

It was then that Stull recognized the importance that horses played in Kentucky life. He bought a string of race horses, in the hope that by racing them he could win the respect he hadn't earned. However, Stull never recognized that the intent of the Sport of Kings was indeed the sport of it. He was obsessed with the idea that through winning he would gain the acceptance he so longed for. To this end, his credo became victory at any cost. He bought the finest horses he could find, hired the best drivers and jockeys, and cheated when he found ways to do so.

Stull was hard on jockeys, seldom keeping one for any length of time. But he was even harder on horses, beating them unmercifully as part of his "training," and venting his ire on them when they lost. And, because he made many enemies by his behavior, he found it necessary to hire Mr. Mercy.

Mr. Mercy could frighten even Stull, because he was a man capable of anything. Stull reacted emotionally to most situations, letting his anger rule him; but Mr. Mercy was cool and calculated. He could, and did, kill without compunction. He neither liked nor disliked anyone, and never smiled nor frowned. Very little pleased him, and very little made him angry. Stull knew that he had Mr. Mercy's loyalty only so long as he paid for it.

Not even Stull knew Mr. Mercy's first name. In the beginning Stull had asked, and the man had replied, "Mr. Mercy is sufficient. No other name is necessary."

Even as Stull was thinking of Mr. Mercy, the gray man appeared, moving quietly out of the lengthening shadows of the approaching evening.

"It is done," Mr. Mercy said quietly.

"Done?"

"The thing you told me to do."

Suddenly Stull remembered. In his rage at Gladney Halloran, he had momentarily forgotten that he had dispatched Mr. Mercy on an errand. Now he smiled broadly. "Good, good!" He massaged the purple lightning flash on his cheek. "Hawkins spoke of the *sport* of racing today. Now we'll see how much he enjoys it tomorrow, after he loses."

Gladney Halloran had rented a carriage so he was able to drive Rebecca and Hawk into town in grand style. He found a place to leave the carriage on Water Street, overlooking the Ohio River, and he tied the team to the hitching rail, then helped Rebecca down from the carriage.

"Oh, look!" she said, pointing to the river. "Isn't it lovely?"

The Ohio River had caught the last, slanting rays of the setting sun and was now a stream of gold. Half a mile downriver it joined with the Mississippi, and the Mississippi, being muddier, refracted the sunrays in such a way as to look silver. The currents of the two rivers made a very discernible line of demarcation, so that in the quickly fading light, there was one stream of molten silver, creating a picture which could not have been made more colorful by Currier and Ives.

There were several riverboats tied up along the bank, but one of them, the *Ohio Queen,* stood out from all the others. It was a large, multi-tiered stern-wheeler, painted white with blue trim. The paddle wheel, paddle box, and connecting rod were all painted red. As the sun had nearly set by now, the boat was already ablaze with its evening dress of lights, and yellow squares of illumination shone from every window and door, while golden lanterns glowed from every pillar and post.

"That's where we'll be eating," Gladney said, noting that Rebecca was staring at the river craft with something like awe.

"We're going to eat on a riverboat?"

"Aye, that we are," he said. He smiled the same crooked grin again. "Tell me, now, have you never heard of the quality of the food to be got on a riverboat?"

"Yes, of course," Rebecca retorted. "But how are we going to manage it? We aren't passengers. Do they serve just anyone?"

"Not just anyone, lass," Gladney said. "But sure and they'll serve Gladney Halloran and his friends. Come along now."

Rebecca and her grandfather followed Gladney toward the gangplank of the boat, picking their way across the cobblestones which had been put in place to reinforce the levee against the frequent floods. Gladney offered her his hand, but Rebecca disdained it. She regretted it immediately, because she slipped on a slickened cobblestone and nearly fell into the river. Gladney caught her arm just in time.

He chuckled. "I'm not too proud to offer my assistance again," he said easily, "if you aren't too proud to accept it."

Without answering him directly, Rebecca gave him her hand, steadying herself, until the gangplank was reached.

A huge black man was winding a coil of rope at the top of the gangplank. When he saw Gladney, he dropped the rope and let out a whoop, grinning widely.

"Mista Gladney, what a sight for these old eyes!

Welcome back to the *Queen*. You-all going all the way to N'Orleans with us?"

"Hello, Big Sam," Gladney said, smiling in delight. "You mean Captain Jenkins hasn't sold you off yet?"

Big Sam laughed uproariously. "Mista Gladney, you know they ain't no more slavery. Can't nobody sell Big Sam, if'n he don't want to be sold."

"Nobody could sell you anyway, Big Sam. You're not worth a wooden nickel, and that's a fact. You know why? Because you're too puny, that's why. Sure and my sainted old grandmother could whomp you, you're that puny."

The big black man bellowed with laughter. Then, still laughing, he picked up a section of iron rod from the deck. Under Rebecca's awed gaze, he began bending it around into a complete loop. As he did so, the huge muscles of his arms, shoulders, and neck bulged powerfully.

"Mista Gladney, could your old sainted grandma do that?" he asked. "Tell the truth now."

"Aye, that she could, and with one hand behind her as well," Gladney said with a straight face.

Big Sam said fondly, "You-all a funny man, Mista Gladney. I like it when you come around the *Queen*."

"Is that old riverpirate, Jenkins, on board?" Gladney asked.

"Yes, suh, he is," Big Sam answered. He straightened the rod, which Rebecca later learned was used to help anchor the deck cargo, then pointed with it toward the stern of the boat. "Fact is, I just saw Cap Jenkins down by the paddlebox not more'n ten minutes ago."

"I think I'll have a few words with him," Gladney said. "Think you can see that no harm comes to my friends meanwhile?"

"Mista Gladney, should the devil himself come up out of this old river, I'll do battle for your friends if

I have to," Big Sam said solemnly. "I ain't never forgettin' the day you saved my hide."

"Aye, and it was a worthy hide to be saving, too, old friend," Gladney said, throwing an arm around the big man's shoulders and giving him a quick hug. "I'll be back shortly," he said to Rebecca and Hawk.

Gladney walked briskly along the deck of the *Queen,* running his hand lightly over the polished rail. It was less than a year ago that he had boarded the *Ohio Queen,* intending only to go from St. Louis to New Orleans. He ended up staying on board for three months, as a favor to Captain Jenkins. Now Jenkins owed him a favor in return, and Gladney hoped to collect it tonight.

Captain Jenkins was nearly seventy years old. He was tall and thin, and had a long white beard which curled forward on his chin. He was leaning over the rail staring at some mechanism in the paddle wheel when Gladney spotted him.

"What's the use in studying it, Cap? 'Tis more than the likes of you can figure out, that's for sure."

Jenkins gave a start, looking around with a glower. Then his face broke into a smile of recognition. He stuck out a long bony hand, and took Gladney's in a surprisingly strong grip.

"Cut the Irish blarney, Glad," he said. "You've no one to con here."

"Yeah, I guess you're right," Gladney said somewhat sheepishly. The Irish brogue suddenly fell away. "Force of habit, I guess. But I'm working the fair here, and when I slip into my brogue, it's damned hard to come out of it."

"Your tongue is going to lock around your Black Irish words one of these days, and you'll forget the King's English. Then where'll you be?"

"Sure, and 'twould be a fine thing, I'm after thinking," Gladney said, slipping easily back into his brogue. "For what's a fine, upstanding Irish lad like me want with the King's English, anyway?"

"Especially when you're working the easygoing, dumb Irishman act, eh, Glad?" Jenkins said.

Gladney grinned. "The really greedy ones, the ones who are quick to take advantage of someone they think they can beat, take the bait a little quicker if they feel superior to me."

"Gladney Halloran, a con man with a mission in life," Jenkins said, laughing. "Glad, I don't know how you manage to survive, I really don't. You've too soft a heart, and too high principles, to be a good con artist."

"Did you ever stop to think that that's what makes me good at it? I did all right by you, now didn't I?"

"You did that, Glad. You did indeed," Jenkins agreed. "Those fellas had their teeth into me, and they were going for blood. I would have lost my boat, and everything else I won, if you hadn't come along when you did and outsmarted them at their own game. It was a pleasure for these old eyes to watch."

"I consider that one of the highwater marks of my illustrious, if illicit career," Gladney said gleefully.

"Tell me, Glad, how did you happen on board? Going down to New Orleans with us?"

"Not this time, though I must confess that the idea has its appeal," Gladney replied. "I came close to contracting a case of homesickness for this old bucket when I tramped on deck just now."

"So you just dropped by for a visit. That's mighty nice of you, Glad."

"A visit, yeah, but a little more than that," Gladney said. "I have two friends with me, and I'd like to treat them to the finest supper along the Ohio. That means

30

the dining saloon here on the *Queen*. If we're welcome, that is."

"Of course you're welcome. Any time, you know that," Captain Jenkins said warmly. "And you'll be at my table besides. Who are your guests?"

"Henry Hawkins, for one and his granddaughter, Rebecca."

"Henry Hawkins? Haven't I heard that name somewhere? It seems to stick in my mind."

"It could well be. He made a name for himself as a jockey a few years back, both here in the States and in England."

"Of course! The Hawk! I've won a dollar or two betting on him. And his granddaughter, you say?"

"As lovely a creature as you'll ever see anywhere, anytime, Cap," Gladney said, his voice ringing with sincerity that surprised even him.

"Oho!" Jenkins said, roaring with laughter. "I dare say she must be a beauty. She sure as hell seems to have captured your fancy."

"You could be right." Gladney felt color rise to his face. "But you can see that I want the supper to be nice." He grinned almost bashfully. "Nothing but the best for the Halloran and his friends."

"It will be, Glad. You have my personal word on that. I'll have a private word with the cook."

"Oh, and Cap, you'll not be commenting on my brogue now, will you? As a favor to me? Sure, and 'tis the only way they've heard me speak. And I'd not be wanting them to know different, not for a spell."

"Good Lord, Glad, you're not working a con on them?" Jenkins said in alarm. "Don't know as I can allow that on the *Queen*."

"No, no," Gladney assured him hastily. "The truth

is, I won a goodly sum betting on their horse in the sulky race this afternoon, and this supper is my way of saying thanks to them. But I'm intrigued by them as well. There's something about the pair of them that aroused my curiosity, and I'd like to find out the mystery. For one thing, their driver seems a bashful one, and most drivers I've ever met are just the opposite. So, to that degree, Cap, I *am* working a con. You won't give me away, I hope?"

"I wouldn't think of it, lad," Jenkins said, a twinkle in his eye. "Now you go fetch your guests to the saloon, and I'll make certain sure they get the royal treatment. But," he held up an admonishing finger, "if you try and pay for this, I'll have Big Sam toss your arse into the river."

"You don't need to threaten me with Big Sam. Have you ever seen me spurn a free meal?"

"Say," Jenkins exclaimed, glancing at his pocket watch, "there'll be music tonight, too." He cocked an ear, and Gladney could hear faint strains of music coming from the dining saloon. "The entertainment has already started."

"Cap," Gladney said, seized by an idea, "have the band play 'My Old Kentucky Home' when we come in, will you?"

Captain Jenkins chuckled. "My fine Irish bucko, I hope the old man knows what he's doing, letting you around his granddaughter." He left, still chuckling, to take care of the arrangements, and Gladney hurried back to Hawk and Rebecca. He found them listening to a story by Big Sam.

". . . yes, ma'am, I could feel that rope round my neck," Big Sam was saying. "Fifteen or twenty whites had it in their heads that I was goin' to hang for somethin' I didn't do. I tried to tell 'em, I wasn't even in their town the night before, I was workin' on the

32

Queen. But they said that the one that killed that white lady was a big nigger, and I was the biggest they'd seen.

"Then, just afore they put the whip to the hoss that was going to jerk that buggy out from under me and leave me dancing at the end of the rope, Mista Gladney, he come runnin' up with a bundle of dynamite, the fuses sputterin'. He said he was goin' to blow everybody to Kingdom Come if they didn't let me go. He told them like I'd told them, that I didn't do it."

"What happened then?" Rebecca asked, enthralled.

Big Sam smiled. "All of them white men was scared even whiter by that Mista Gladney and the dynamite he was holdin' in his hand. They ran in every direction and left me there. Mista Gladney, he just strolls calm as you please over to the buggy and takes the rope off my neck, still holding onto the dynamite as if it weren't no more dangerous than a lit cigar."

" 'Gentlemen,' he says, 'back off and let me and my friend here get on back to the boat where we belong, or I'll blow all our heads off.'

"Now, I don't mind tellin' you, ma'am, I was getting plenty scared myself by this time, that dynamite burnin' down! But Mista Gladney didn't seem none worried. Finally, I says to him, 'Mista Gladney, ain't you-all held onto that dynamite long enough?'

"Mista Gladney, he just laugh and says, 'Big Sam, this here ain't nothin' more than some chunks of rope tied up in a bundle, made to look like dynamite.' And he laughed till he just about to cry, over how he tricked them white men."

"You've got to admit, Big Sam, they were a funny sight, standing around waiting to be blown up," Gladney said, stepping out of the shadows where he had been waiting for the story's conclusion.

"Mista Gladney, I was just tellin' your friends how you-all saved my life."

"I heard," Gladney said dryly. "Wait until they learn what a great liar you are, Sam Tally."

"Now, Mista Gladney," Big Sam said, unabashed. "I had to keep your friends entertained, didn't I?"

"Aye, Big Sam, and I'm beholden to you. Now, Mr. Hawkins, Miss Hawkins, if you will come along, I've made arrangements with the captain for our supper."

Rebecca said, "Was he lying to amuse us? Or was he telling the truth?"

Gladney grinned engagingly. "So long as it kept you amused, what difference does it make?"

Rebecca watched the man who led them along the deck with a new interest. The story of his rescue of Big Sam, as told by Big Sam—and she suspected that the tale was true, if embroidered—was one of a man of courage, to be sure. But there was more than courage to a man who would bluff fifteen armed men with pieces of rope, passing them off as a bundle of dynamite. There was foolhardiness as well—almost a disdain of personal consequences. This Gladney Halloran was a most intriguing person.

"What do you think?" Gladney asked, as they stepped into the saloon.

Rebecca had never been in the grand saloon of a luxury riverboat before. She had crossed the river many times on ferry boats, and she had gone to England in comfortable, if not luxurious accommodations, yet she had never seen anything to match this. The grand saloon was a large room, larger than any room in any house she had ever seen. Half a dozen crystal chandeliers hung from the ceiling, and another dozen lanterns burned brightly along the paneled walls. The floor was covered with a deep, rich, blue carpet, and on all the tables there were settings of the finest china, crystal, and silver.

Then a strange thing happened. At the far end of the saloon the orchestra, which was in the middle of another piece, suddenly stopped playing that number and started playing "My Old Kentucky Home." The other diners glanced toward the three newcomers, then began to applaud.

"What is this?" Rebecca asked, glancing at Gladney in some confusion.

"Sure, and 'tis no more than Paddy Boy's due, for winning the race this afternoon," he said. "And 'tis only the respect due to a man who represented Kentucky so well on the racing tracks of the world."

Rebecca peered at him, to see if it were possible that he was making sport of her grandfather. But his praise seemed genuine, and Hawk beamed under it. All at once it made her glow as well. She knew that somehow Gladney had stage-managed this whole thing, and she liked him for it.

"Good evening, Mr. Halloran, sir," the head waiter said, as Gladney ushered Rebecca and Hawk to their table.

"The captain's compliments, sir, and he has taken the liberty of ordering for you." The head waiter snapped his fingers, and a bucket of chilled champagne appeared as if by magic. "Enjoy," he said.

And enjoy Rebecca did. Never, in all her twenty years, had she known such luxurious service or tasted such exquisite cuisine. It all seemed a dream to her, a golden fantasy come true. She was overwhelmed, made dizzy, by the champagne and by what was happening. Although she conversed with Gladney, and laughed at all the proper times, she really had no idea what they said or did, for she was totally lost in the glory of this magnificent wonderland.

But all too soon, it seemed to Rebecca, there were signs that this marvelous evening was drawing to a close. Her grandfather began yawning, an obvious indication that he was tired. And when his yawns failed to produce the desired effect, he cleared his throat loudly several times. Finally, he just spoke what was on his mind.

"Becky, it's getting late and I'm tired, girl. It's been a long day."

"All right, Grandfather," she said.

"Wouldn't you like to take a turn around the deck before we call it an evening?" Gladney asked hopefully.

"Oh, yes!" Rebecca said. "Grandfather, may we?"

"You two youngsters go ahead," Hawk said grumpily. "I'll just sit here and wait for you."

"Are you sure you don't want to go with us, Grandfather?"

"I'm sure," Hawk said. He took a case from his inside coat pocket and extracted a cigar. "I'll just have me a smoke. Go on now, young people, and enjoy yourselves."

It was cool and dark on deck, and Gladney and Rebecca strolled arm in arm, gazing out over the black, twinkling river. Someone was playing a banjo nearby, and the thrumming music reached Rebecca's ears only as a pleasant sound. They moved to the rail and stood there for a moment without speaking. Rebecca shivered.

"Are you cold?" Gladney asked solicitously.

"Not terribly."

Gladney took his coat off. "Here," he said, "hold this over your shoulders. It will warm you."

Rebecca turned to face him as he put the coat around her shoulders. She looked up into his face. Suddenly she realized, without knowing how, that he

36

was about to kiss her. And, even more startling, she realized that she wasn't going to resist it.

Gladney pulled her close to him, bringing his mouth against hers. At first the contact was tender, almost hesitant, but as Rebecca made no effort to pull away, the kiss grew bolder. His arms wound around her tightly, pulling her body against his. Abruptly Rebecca realized what was happening, and she began to struggle in surprise and fear. But the harder she struggled, the more determined he became to hold her, until she abandoned the struggle and let herself go limp in his arms.

Then a strange thing began to happen. The surprise changed to surrender, the fear to curiosity and then to sweetness. A strange pleasure stole over her, and when Gladney opened his lips on her lips and pushed his tongue against hers, it was shocking and thrilling at the same time. An involuntary moan escaped her throat. Her blood felt as if it had changed to honey, and her body was warmed by a heat that she had never before experienced. The kiss went on, longer than she had ever imagined such a thing could last, and her head grew so light that she abandoned all thought, savoring this newfound pleasure.

Finally Gladney broke off the embrace, leaving Rebecca limp as a rag doll.

"I'm sorry," he said breathlessly. "Please, lass, forgive me for taking advantage of you like that. Sure, and I don't know what came over me."

"I . . . I don't know what came over *me*," Rebecca said, breathing deeply and trying to quiet the racing of her heart. "I know that a proper lady should scream, or something . . . but I guess I'm not a proper lady. Please, Mr. Halloran, take me back to my grandfather now."

"Of course," he said. "Come along."

"Captain Jenkins!" someone yelled from the lower deck. "Captain Jenkins, come quick!"

"What is it?" Rebecca asked in alarm. "What's that man shouting for?"

"I don't know," Gladney said. "Shall we go find out?"

They went quickly down the stairway to the lower deck. Rebecca stopped as she saw something lying on the deck, something in the shape of a man. Whatever it was had just been pulled from the river, because it was wet and dripping.

"Rebecca, don't look!" Gladney suddenly said, trying to shield her.

But she had already seen too much. "You needn't bother to protect me," she said in a dead voice. "I know what it is. I even know *who* it is. It's Timmie Bird, Oscar Stull's driver. He's dead, isn't he?"

Chapter Three

Rebecca slept fitfully that night. The image of poor Tim Bird's body lying on the deck of the boat, with river water dark as blood staining the wooden planks, remained with her, and she was unable to tell when she was awake, thinking of it, or asleep, dreaming of the horror. The result was a night with little rest, and by morning she was much more tired than she had been when she went to bed the night before.

Despite this, she was glad to see the new day arrive, because in the light of day the horror began to fade. So as soon as it was full light she was up and about, tending to Paddy Boy and Black Prince.

There were several others out in the gray light of morning—trainers, riders, drivers, and owners—and they were all talking about the violent death of Timmie Bird. There was no doubt that it had been murder, since it had been learned that the back of his head had a gaping bullet wound.

There was a sense of outrage that one of their own had been shot and thrown into the river like a piece of driftwood, and all agreed that "somebody should do something," without specifying who should do what. People who had known Bird and those who had barely known him spoke glowingly of him and mourned his demise.

Of course, Rebecca knew, they weren't really

mourning Tim Bird at all. They were frightened by the heightened awareness of their own mortality, and it was this new awareness and their inability to express it which gave birth to the spurious eulogies, at least for most of them.

The incessant talk about the subject was nearly as depressing to Rebecca as her fitful dreams had been, so when she saddled Black Prince and took him down to the track to exercise, it was as much for her benefit as for the animal's.

Black Prince was a beautiful horse. His coat was a glistening ebony in color, his unusually long tail somewhat lighter. He was just under sixteen and a half hands at the withers, and a model of conformation, completely blemish free. These traits were readily apparent even when Black Prince was at rest. But it was when he was in motion that his qualities really came through. At a walk he attracted attention, but at a gallop he commanded awe. He could produce amazing speed with arrogant ease, with his graceful legs stretching into astonishingly long, high strides, while his powerful hindquarters drove his well-balanced body forward with blinding quickness.

Rebecca could feel the horse quiver between her legs, and knew he was aching to run full out. He was holding back only because she restrained him. His sleek muscles trembled and strained to be set free.

"Prince, darling, I know you want to run," she said, reaching over to pat him lovingly on the neck. "But we can't. Not just yet. You know the plan. I've told it to you often enough."

Black Prince blew, as if he understood but was voicing his disapproval. He tossed his head once, impatiently.

Rebecca glanced around the track. She and Black Prince were the only ones about that she could see, and they were a fair distance from the stables, so that there was little chance of being observed from there.

"Oh," she said impulsively, "why not? There's no one to see, and Grandfather isn't around to know. Come on, Prince, let's have a nice run!"

She guided Black Prince to the starting line, turned him to face down the track, then sat for a second, getting ready. In her mind now, this wasn't a county fair track in Cairo, Illinois, but the new track at Churchill Farm, in Louisville, Kentucky. The railing around the track was crowded and the grandstand now being built in Louisville was completed and packed with roaring spectators.

She reached down again and stroked the horse lovingly. Then she said in a low, carrying voice, "Let's show how it will be, Prince!" She slapped her legs against his sides, and they were off.

"Go, Prince, go!"

The animal burst forward like a cannon ball, reaching top speed almost immediately. Rebecca bent low over his withers, holding him close to the rail, laughing into the rush of wind with the pure thrill of the run, feeling as if she and Black Prince were one, sharing the same muscle structure and bloodstream. They flashed around the first turn with Black Prince's hooves drumming a steady rhythm, kicking up little spurts of dust behind him. On the backstretch she urged him to an even greater speed, and for a few dizzying seconds, she had the fantasy that he was going to take off and fly!

A young man leaned against a railing post, partially hidden by the morning shadows. He had been watching Rebecca work with Black Prince. He was fairly tall and slender, but with disproportionately broad

41

shoulders. His eyes were large and dark and shone with a brilliant light. His hair was also dark, and straight, and he had long sideburns that framed a handsome, dark-complexioned face. His hands were strong and well shaped, his fingernails were manicured, and at the moment his hands held a stopwatch.

Steven Lightfoot had been watching the rider working the horse with only idle interest. It was the kind of interest any good horseman had in watching another work: an objective analysis of the rider's technique, and a genuine appreciation for the beauty of the animal. But Steven's interest heightened into curiosity when he saw the horse at top speed. For even from this distance, he knew that he was watching an exceptional horse.

He punched the stopwatch as the great black horse passed a furlong pole and timed the animal as it blazed down the backstretch, hurtling like a comet, brushing close to the earth. At a quarter of a mile Steven punched the watch off, then looked at the time and whistled in disbelief. Twenty-four and three-fifths for the quarter mile! That was fantastic time for a casual morning run.

Who was that horse? And, maybe just as important, who was the rider?

As Rebecca and Black Prince came around the third turn, she saw the man watching them, and she realized with dismay that he was timing Black Prince. She had no idea what his time was, but she was sure that it was probably very close to Black Prince's best ever. And his blinding speed was a secret that she and her grandfather wanted to preserve at all costs.

She pulled back on the reins sharply, and by the

42

time Black Prince rounded the final turn, he was doing little more than an easy lope. That meant that whoever was timing Black Prince wouldn't have gotten a time for the entire distance.

"Why did you pull him in?" the stranger asked, walking out onto the track as Rebecca trotted Black Prince across the finish line.

She swung down out of the tiny saddle and began walking the horse. She was dressed in riding breeches and a jockey's jacket, with her hair twisted up under a cap. She removed the cap and shook her head, letting her hair hang free.

His mouth dropped open. "My Lord, you're a woman!"

"Half the people in the world are," Rebecca said tartly. "Why are you so surprised?"

"I've never known a girl who could ride the way you were riding," Steven said. He looked at the stopwatch in his hand. "I was trying to get a time on you. Do you realize you covered a quarter of a mile in just over twenty-four seconds?"

"Did I?" Rebecca said innocently. "Goodness gracious, that's quite fast, isn't it? I didn't realize I was going so fast. No wonder I was frightened."

Steven laughed. "Miss, I don't know what game you're playing. Whatever else you were, you weren't frightened!"

"Oh, but I was. That's why I slowed down. Anyway, if Grandfather found out that I ran Prince as fast as all that, on his bad foot and all, he would be simply furious with me. You won't tell him, will you?"

"That horse has a bad foot?" His look was incredulous. "Good Lord, if he can run like that on *three* good feet . . . ! As for my telling anyone anything

. . ." He spread his hands. "I wouldn't even know who to tell. Who are you, and who is your grandfather?"

"I am Rebecca Hawkins, and my grandfather is Henry Hawkins."

"Henry Hawkins? The Hawk?"

"Yes. Do you know him?"

"I know of him, as do all lovers of horse racing," Steven said. "I've never had the pleasure of meeting him, but I would like to do just that. I'll tell you what. You introduce me to the Hawk, and I shall guard your terrible secret forever."

"How can I introduce you, sir? I don't even know your name," Rebecca said, falling in with his facetious manner and relaxing a bit. Perhaps it was going to be all right.

Steven smiled sheepishly. "Well now, that's true, isn't it? I'll just have to plead guilty to being so surprised by your being a girl, and so taken by your beauty once I made that discovery, that I simply took leave of my manners. Please forgive me, madam."

He coughed, took one step back and made an elegant bow. "Miss Hawkins, I am Steven Lightfoot, your humble servant. I'm sorry that I have no calling cards on my person, but I shall bend every effort to remedy that when next we meet."

Rebecca had to smile, hastily hiding it behind her hand, and suddenly she realized that she was attracted to this man. It was very odd that in the short space of two days she had met two men, both of whom attracted her. Of course, she *was* twenty years old. Perhaps it was time she took notice of men, as the few women friends she had were always telling her.

She gave herself a mental shake. She had more important things than men to concern herself with.

"Are you a native, Mr. Lightfoot?" she asked, breaking the awkward silence.

"Do you mean am I from Cairo?"

"Yes."

"No, I'm from Louisville, Kentucky. I'm here to ride in the race this afternoon. But, to be truthful in answering your question as to whether I am a native, I must confess to being one-half Indian. I hope that doesn't frighten you?"

"Of course not. Why should it?"

The easy smile left Steven's face, and for a moment his features hardened into an expression of bitterness. When he realized what had happened, he quickly erased the flash of bitterness with another smile, genuine, though touched with a bit of long-suffering patience.

"There are places I can't go," he said. "There are people who would rather not associate with me, because I'm a half-breed. And legally I can't even buy a drink. I find that particularly ironic," he added with a self-deprecating laugh.

"Why not?" Rebecca asked. "How are you different from anyone else?"

It took Steven a moment to realize that Rebecca had asked the question in all innocence, and he began to laugh. In fact, he laughed so heartily that she became upset and showed her displeasure.

"Miss Hawkins, don't be offended," Steven said, wiping the tears of laughter from his eyes. "I meant no harm, and I wasn't laughing at you. It is just refreshing to see someone so innocent of prejudice that they should ask such a question. Clearly, you aren't aware that it is against the law to sell or even give alcohol to an Indian, half or otherwise. Would that all people were like you. I'm sorry if you misunderstood my laughter."

"Very well, Mr. Lightfoot, I accept your apology," Rebecca said. "And you are right, I didn't know—"

"Becky!" a voice called, and they looked toward the stables to see Henry Hawkins limping toward them.

"Is that your grandfather?"

"Yes," she said. She looked at him with a plea in her eyes. "Please say nothing of seeing me run Prince."

"You have my word," Steven said easily. "Introduce me to your grandfather and your secret is safe with me."

"You're spending too much time with Black Prince and not enough with Paddy Boy, girl," Hawk said in a scolding voice as he neared them. "After all, Becky, it *is* Paddy Boy who is racing, and not Black Prince."

"You have another thoroughbred?" Steven said in astonishment.

"We have a pacer we use for the sulky races," Rebecca said hastily. She saw her grandfather studying Steven with some suspicion. "Grandfather, this is Steven Lightfoot. He claims to be a wild Indian."

"Wild Indian, is it? That's a claim I'd be careful of spreading about," Hawk said.

"Your granddaughter is making sport of me, I believe," Steven was smiling. "I merely mentioned in passing that I am half Indian. And a full-blooded horseman," he added with pleasure. "That is why I am so pleased to meet you, sir. I have heard a great deal of the Hawk, sir."

Steven extended his hand, and so genuine was he with his enthusiasm that there was little room for suspicion of his motives. Hawk accepted the outstretched hand and they shook warmly.

Steven said, "A pacer, you say? Then you'll have a horse in the harness race, as well as the thoroughbred race today?"

"No," Hawk said quickly. "That is to say, we will

46

have an entry in the sulky race, yes. But that is all. We have no entry for the thoroughbred race."

"What of this magnificent creature?" Steven asked, indicating Black Prince. "He is a fine-looking animal. In fact, I would dearly love to challenge you to a match race, but I'm afraid that I would lose, and thus forfeit my own thoroughbred."

Hawk laughed. "Exactly. That's why I will not enter Black Prince in a match race," he said. "He is a young horse, and may someday be good. But I wouldn't consider risking him yet. Racing him too soon might cause an injury."

Steven turned his head aside to give Rebecca a wicked, knowing look. Her face reddened and her glance skipped away.

Hawk was saying, "I take it you will be riding in the race this afternoon?"

"I will indeed," Steven said enthusiastically. "I'll be on my thoroughbred, Bright Morn. If you'd care to wager a dollar or so, I think I can promise that you won't be disappointed. Bright Morn will win."

"Well!" Rebecca said. "You don't lack for conceit, do you, Mr. Lightfoot?" It was an uncalled-for remark and she knew it, but she had to get back at him for that wicked grin.

"It isn't conceit at all, Miss Hawkins. It's confidence in Bright Morn that makes me boast. It has nothing to do with me personally. I hope you've taken no offense."

"Of course not," Hawk said sharply. He glowered at Rebecca. "Girl, you should know the difference between personal conceit and a man's confidence in his horse. You should know that as well as anyone."

Rebecca felt a tide of color rise to her face. Her grandfather was correct; she had spoken out of turn. But her remark hadn't been motivated by a desire to get back at Steven Lightfoot as much as a reach for something to say, an attempt to establish some sort of contact with him. She had tried too hard and ended up by saying the wrong thing.

"I'll walk Prince back to the stable," she said stiffly. She looked shyly at Steven. "I'm sorry that I spoke out of turn. Yesterday, I met a most disagreeable man, a man who is full of conceit, and I reckon this may have caused me to see it in others, when there is none."

"Who is this man?" Steven asked. "Perhaps I should take pains to make his acquaintance."

"I wouldn't advise it, he is most unpleasant." Rebecca made a sour face. "His name is Oscar Stull."

"Oscar Stull? Yes, I've heard of him, though I have yet to meet him. His reputation, if you excuse the expression, Miss Hawkins, has a stench. The driver who was murdered last night . . . didn't he work for Stull?"

"He did," Hawk said.

"I thought as much. I hear that Stull has already hired a new driver for the race today. It's a mystery to me how he found someone new so quickly. Who is your driver, Mr. Hawkins?"

"We have a young man," Hawk said. "A real shy young man, who doesn't like to see or talk to anyone on race days."

"Sounds unlike most horse people I know, but that is his right, of course," Steven said. "You might wish him good luck for me. In the meantime, I've my own horse to attend to." He bowed to Rebecca. "I hope I shall see you both later."

Rebecca and Hawk watched Steven Lightfoot walk away, then they led Black Prince back to the stables.

"He seems like a very nice young man," Hawk observed.

"Perhaps a bit forward."

"Look here, did the young jackanapes try something he shouldn't?" Hawk said tightly.

"No, no," Rebecca said quickly, laughing at her grandfather's indignation. "He wasn't offensive, Grandfather. Truly, he wasn't."

"All right, if you say so," Hawk said doubtfully. "Look! Isn't that Gladney Halloran?"

"Where?" Rebecca asked, turning.

"Over there, at that table near the end of the stable. I wonder what all those men are doing around him?"

"Grandfather, why don't you see to Prince and Paddy Boy?" she asked, handing the reins to Hawk. "I think I'll go over and thank him for that lovely supper last evening."

"Dandy. Go ahead, girl. But don't forget that our race will be run early this afternoon. Our driver must be ready."

"*He* will be," Rebecca said, smiling.

Hawk led Black Prince back to the stables, and Rebecca walked over to Gladney Halloran, who was standing behind a small folding table, talking to the men grouped around. He didn't notice her and she was just as glad, for this would give her the opportunity to observe him without his knowledge.

"Now, me lads, who would be wantin' to place a wee wager? Sure, and 'tis a simple thing. All a man has to do is find this wee little pea under the shell, and you win. One dollar can win you two, lads," Gladney was saying.

"You mean all it'll cost me to win two dollars is one dollar?" one man asked.

"Faith, and that's what I'm saying. I'm a bit of a fool, you see, givin' such odds on such an easy game to win."

49

All the while Gladney was talking, he was moving the three half-shells around. Now and then, he would pick one up to show the pea, then put it back and start all over again.

Rebecca stood on the edge of the group, angry and appalled. The last thing she had expected to see was Gladney Halloran running a common shell game! The sight of him at such an activity had shattered her illusions. The day before, Gladney had become almost a hero in her eyes by challenging Oscar Stull in so bold a fashion, and then being treated with so much respect on board the *Ohio Queen*. Big Sam's tale of Gladney's exploits had only reinforced her image of him, and then she had even let him kiss her!

Now, learning that he was little more than a fair-grounds confidence man, his larger-than-life image was deflated. She wanted to walk away from the scene; for in truth, she was embarrassed by it. Yet, strangely, even under these circumstances she found that there was still something about the man that drew her.

So she remained to watch.

"You, lad," Gladney said, speaking to a youth of about sixteen who was standing in the front row. "You've the look of a lad with sharp eyes. Show them how 'tis done."

"I don't have any money," the boy replied.

"'Tis no never mind, me boy," Gladney said smoothly. "I'll just use you as a demonstrator, and if your eyes are as sharp as they appear to be, you'll win yourself a quarter. Now, you can't beat that for a bargain, can you lad? 'Twill cost you nothing."

"I'll give it a try," the boy said eagerly.

"Now that's a good lad," Gladney said approvingly. He put the pea on the table, and held up one of the walnut half-shells. "Now keep your eyes peeled, lad."

Gladney began moving the shells around swiftly, his supple hands deft and sure. After a few seconds he stopped. "Which one, lad?"

"That one," the boy said promptly, pointing to the shell in the center.

Gladney raised the shell, and there was the pea. "You win!" he exclaimed. "You have grand eyes, lad."

"That wasn't any great shakes to my way of thinking," a well-dressed, fat man said scornfully. "I knew where the damn pea was all the time!"

"Did you now?" Gladney said with a straight face. "Would you care to play the game, sir?"

"Nope," the fat man responded. "I'll just watch for a while, if you don't mind."

"I never mind an audience," Gladney said. "It's good for my business. Who among you would like to play?"

"I'd like to." A tall, gaunt man dressed in coveralls and a red flannel shirt stepped forward. His face and hands showed the wear and tear of years of hard labor.

"Sir, I can tell that you are a working man," Gladney said. "A dollar, now that's a dear thing. Are you sure you want to risk it?"

"I'm sure," the man said. "I been waitin' all year long for this fair, and I aim to whoop it up a bit. I figure one dollar ain't goin' to do much in the way of whooping, but for three, I can have me a fine time." He laughed, and the other men laughed with him.

"You're sure, is it?" Gladney said, looking closely at the man.

"What's the matter, are you afraid my eyes are

too quick for you?" the man asked, and looked around for the expected laughs.

"All right, my friend," Gladney said. "Put your dollar on the table and keep your eye on the pea. Sharp now!"

Oh, Rebecca thought, *surely he isn't going to take what is probably that poor man's last dollar! If he does, I'll tell him what I think, right here and now!*

Gladney moved the shells around, then looked up at the bettor with a questioning expression on his face.

"There!" the man said triumphantly, pointing to the shell on the left with a long, calloused finger.

Gladney picked up he shell, and there was the pea. The men oohed and aahed in appreciation, and general glee was expressed over Gladney's loss.

"You, too, have exceptionally good eyesight. Aye, that you do," Gladney said with a sigh. He handed over two dollars.

"Thank you, mister," the bettor said, beaming proudly at the money. "I'll have me a high old time with this, I'll tell you." He put the money into his pocket and pushed his way out of the crowd.

"I knew where that one was, too," the well-dressed fat man said.

"Ah, did you now. Then would you care to place a wager, sir?"

"No," the fat man replied.

But another man played the game, winning one, losing the second. The crowd laughed when the player lost.

"He got you that time, Pete!" someone called.

"He didn't get me," the fat man said pompously. "I knew where that pea was all along."

Gladney ignored him this time. He just put the pea under a shell, and began moving them around quickly. This time there was no bettor. Gladney's hands moved so swiftly they were little more than a blur. Finally he stopped and started to turn the shells over.

"Wait!" the fat man shouted. "Before you turn them over, I'd like to place a bet."

"You should have made your bet before I began," Gladney said worriedly.

The fat man smiled triumphantly and looked around. "Now," he said smugly, "you are all going to see how to beat a con artist. You see, when no one is playing, they leave the pea under the shell, to make it look easy. When someone is betting, they cheat."

Gladney drew himself up indignantly. "That is an insulting accusation, sir!"

"If this fella has been cheatin', he's not doing such a good job of it," one man said. "He's paid out more money than he's won, that's for danged sure!"

"All a come-on. I'm telling you, he's cheating," the fat man insisted. "And I can prove it right now."

"How you gonna do that?" another man asked.

The fat man looked at Gladney, smiling slyly. "Because if he ain't cheating, he'll let me make a bet right now."

Gladney wore a look of dismay. "That isn't the way the game is played. You have to place your bet before I start."

"That's because I've caught you out," the fat man crowed. "You didn't think anyone would bet, so you left the pea under a shell instead of palming it. I know where it is. Hell, anyone knows where it is. So if you're running an honest game, you'll let me place my bet!"

"All right," Gladney spread his hands in defeat. "Put your dollar on the table, friend."

"No, sir," the fat man said, shaking his head vehemently. He had the grin of a hungry wolf. He reached into his inside coat pocket, took out a thick roll of bills and peeled off several. "I want to bet a hundred dollars!" He slapped the money down onto the table.

"One hundred dollars!" a man gasped. "On a shell game?"

"One hundred to your two hundred, that's the odds you offered the others," the fat man said. "Is it a bet?"

"I don't know," Gladney said with a worried expression. " 'Tis a small game I run here, for light entertainment only. No one can get hurt too bad with such low stakes, and even if they lose, there's the fun of playing. You'd be after takin' the fun out of it with such a large wager, sir."

"Either you accept my wager," the fat man challenged, "or you stand exposed for the cheat that you are!"

"Then it seems you leave me no choice," Gladney said resignedly. "Which shell is the pea under, sir? Make your choice."

The fat man looked at the others with a smirk. He drew himself up and without hesitation pointed a finger at the end shell on the right. "That one, it's under there!" As Gladney reached to turn over the shell, the fat man knocked his hand aside. "No, you don't. I'll pick up the shell!"

He scooped up the shell and turned without even looking under it for the pea, facing the onlookers for his just plaudits.

But to the fat man's dismay, the crowd didn't cheer, they gasped. He swung his head around and saw that the pea wasn't where he thought it should be.

"What the hell!" he blustered. "You palmed the damn pea then. It ain't under any of the shells!"

Arms crossed over his chest, Gladney said coolly,

"If you would kindly pick up the middle shell, sir?"

With trembling fingers, the fat man turned over the middle shell, and there was the pea.

Jeering laughter ran through the crowd. Gladney raised his voice. "Is it agreed that the bet is mine?"

"Hell, yes! You won fair and square!"

"And punctured the wind from old lard gut here!"

"Thank you, friend," Gladney said, scooping up the money from the table.

Livid with anger, the fat man pushed his way through the crowd, pusued by catcalls and raucous laughter.

Glancing over the heads of the crowd, Gladney saw Rebecca for the first time. "Gentlemen, it has been a pleasure to while away the time with you this morning, and I thank you for coming around. But the game's closed for now, for the harness races will start soon. I'll be looking them over so as to place a wager or two, as I'm sure you all will. And my special thanks to the large gentleman," he smiled broadly, "who was so generous."

As the crowd dispersed, Gladney crossed to Rebecca. "And how are you this fine, bright morning, Mistress Hawkins?"

"So," Rebecca said. "*This* is how you make your living?"

He looked at her amusedly. "Could it be, lass, that I detect a note of disapproval in your voice?"

"You do indeed!"

"And would you be tellin' me why?"

"Why? Why do I disapprove? It should be obvious, shouldn't it? I've seen men like you at every fair and race meet my grandfather and I have attended. I've seen poor people come to the fair and lose money to the shell games, the hoopers, the wheels, and the numbers, and I've never had anything but disgust for the type of men who would stoop so low, taking money from people who can't afford to lose it. Now I learn that *you* are one of those men."

"How are we so different, you and I?" Gladney said. "Are you so naive as to believe that no one has ever lost money betting on your horse? Probably a lot more money than they would ever lose to any game of mine."

"I'll tell you how it's different. With a horse race the bettor at least has an honest chance. A con man *controls* his games."

"That's so terrible, is it? You saw the old farmer. Don't you think his day is a little brighter because of me? If I couldn't control the outcome, there is a chance he would have lost his dollar."

"Then you *admit* it?" she said, staring.

"Aye, lass. I admit it. And do so without burning shame."

"Then I am ashamed for you," Rebecca said, lips compressed into a thin line.

"Lass, lass, don't waste your shame on me," he said with a patient sigh. "There may come a time when you need it for yourself. I'd hate to think that it was all squandered on the likes of me. I scarcely deserve it." It was a statement clearly made with tongue in cheek, and Gladney smiled widely, but Rebecca didn't think it was humorous at all, and she told him so.

"Listen please, lass, accept my apology," he said. "For I have no wish to offend you. I want us to be friends. Can that not be?"

She gazed into his face, at the flashing eyes and the beguiling, crooked grin, and she could no longer hold the edge to her anger. She relented, and returned his smile reluctantly. "I don't approve of what

56

you do, I will never approve," she said, "but I see no reason that we can't at least be friends. I see no harm in that."

"Now that I most heartily approve of!"

Rebecca had been curious as she had watched his manipulation of the walnut shells, and she was still curious. "Gladney . . ."

His face lit up brightly upon hearing her use his Christian name. "Aye, Rebecca?"

"How did you do it? How did you fool that fat man, pompous idiot that he was?"

Gladney threw back his head and laughed, a sound of pure delight. "Sleight of hand, my darlin', sleight of hand," he finally said and would offer no further explanation. He took out his pocket watch. "It's not too long until the harness races. Come along, I'll lay down another hefty bet on Paddy Boy, then we'll get us a good position by the finish line and watch him run."

"Dear God, the race!" Rebecca's hand flew to her mouth. "I nearly forgot. I have to go."

"Go? Go where?" Gladney demanded. "Can't you watch the race with me?"

"No, I can't," she said nervously. "I have to go get the driver ready."

"Get the driver ready? What do you mean, get him ready?" He stared at her in bewilderment. "Can't he get ready himself? Is he all that helpless?"

"As Grandfather told you, he's a very shy person. If anyone besides Grandfather or me comes around, he gets upset. Too upset to drive well."

"Lord above, such a driver I've never heard of, but what the devil. He's your driver. You tell him to drive well, because I'm going to put everything on Paddy Boy to win."

57

"Gladney, please no, don't do that," she said. "I don't want to feel responsible for you losing all your money, if Paddy Boy doesn't win."

Gladney dismissed her worry with a careless flip of his hand. "Rebecca, don't be after worryin' about the Halloran. I've been broke before and I'll be broke many times again. It's what makes the in-between times more fun, makes life worth the livin'. Aye, that it does. You go see to your driver now, and if you can join me to watch the race, fine. If not, perhaps afterward we can celebrate the victory together."

Rebecca started to turn away, then faced around. "Tell me something. Gladney. Your brogue. You don't always speak it. Why is that?"

"It's an affliction I have, darlin'," he said solemnly. "It comes and goes. I have no control over it."

As Gladney and Rebecca went their separate ways, in another corner of the fairgrounds a meeting was taking place between Oscar Stull and his new driver, Red Parker. Parker was an exceptionally small man with close, beady eyes, a malevolent stare, and flaming red hair like a rooster's comb. His nose was hooked like a hawk's beak, and his mouth was a thin, nearly lipless line. He was always angry with the world because he was so small, and this anger was the dominating factor of his personality.

"Remember," Stull was saying, "contact must be made, or the wheel may not come off. You've got to get in close enough to bump into the Hawkins sulky, but without getting yourself tangled up. Can you manage it?"

"I can do it, Mr. Stull," Parker said cockily. He examined his dirty fingernails carefully, as if the task Stull had set for him was a simple one.

"You'd better be damned certain," Stull snarled.

"I'll not be beaten by Hawkins's animal a second time."

Parker smiled, and the smile, rather than softening his features, gave him a vulpine look. "Don't fret, Mr. Stull. Hawkins's driver is going to find himself sitting on his arse in the dirt, trying to dodge a half-dozen speeding rigs at once. I hope he has a thick hide, 'cause one hoof is all it'll take to crack his head open like a melon!"

Chapter Four

Right across the street from the racetrack stood a hotel that had gained national prominence during the Civil War, when it was used as General Grant's head-quarters. Now that Grant was president of the United States, his one-time occupancy of the hotel made it a popular place with visitors to Cairo, and it was always the scene of bustling activity. But it was even busier during the three days of the Alexander County Fair, since it was here that most of the jockeys, driv-ers, trainers, and owners stayed.

It was eleven in the morning, and the crowd was very large. Men and women were packed into the lobby, and the noise level was so high that normal conversation was next to impossible. Everyone yelled at everyone else in order to be heard, which only in-tensified the bedlam. Men waved drinks and cigars and even hands full of money as they tried to place last-minute wagers on the races that would begin soon. Women, too, were caught up in all the excite-ment, and were no less vociferous than the men, so that occasionally a high-pitched shrill of laughter would ring out above everything else.

Only the drivers and jockeys were quiet. They were already dressed in their brightly colored silks, and they stood out in the crowd like gay flowers among cabbages. Like all athletes since the time of the Roman

Games, they were introspective before competing; alone with their thoughts, they prepared themselves mentally and emotionally for the contests that lay before them.

But not all the drivers were in the lobby. Some were still getting dressed, including the driver for the Hawkins entry, Paddy Boy. The cherry-red blouse which was the Hawkins color lay across the bed, and the driver, in trousers, sat on the edge of the bed pulling on a pair of highly polished boots. Then, with the boots on, the driver walked to the dresser and stood in front of the mirror.

Rebecca Hawkins smiled at her reflection. "I wonder what would happen if I showed up at the race like this?" she mused aloud. She giggled at the idea. "I bet I would create such a furor that I'd win handily. Perhaps we'd better save this idea for the Kentucky Derby." She laughed, making her breasts jiggle, and she laughed even harder.

On the dresser in front of Rebecca was the winding cloth which she used to bind her breasts for the races. She had to conceal her true identity when she drove, because the rules and by-laws of all the races specifically stated that the drivers and jockeys must be men. If her true sex were discovered, she would be disqualified. Of course, she and her grandfather could hire a driver, but the expense of that would erode their winnings, and the winnings were very necessary if they were ever to buy their own thoroughbred farm.

When they first began racing, Rebecca had talked Hawk into the subterfuge, and he agreed reluctantly, but only until they could afford a driver. From time to time he still threatened to hire a driver, but Rebecca knew that he never would—unless she was found out. For Rebecca was better than any driver they could find; even her grandfather admitted that.

Still, it was not right that she should be forced to masquerade as a man.

Though the reasons were clear enough to her, the whole thing seemed terribly unfair to Rebecca. For while other drivers were able to reap the rewards of public acclaim for their victories, she had to be content with the secret knowledge of her successes. It was also unfair, she decided now, that she should have to hide her true sex from Gladney Halloran and Steven Lightfoot during the times she drove.

Rebecca frowned, puzzled. Now why had *that* thought popped into her head? She had been thinking of the race and the eventual farm that she and Hawk hoped to buy, and logically there was no reason to think of Gladney or Steven. And yet, suddenly and inexplicably, she had thought of them.

Her face flushed red. She was angry at herself for allowing such unwelcome thoughts to surface. And yet she didn't know what to do about it.

She also didn't know what she could do about the way she was reacting to such disquieting conjectures. For she felt a lightness in the pit of her stomach and a strange, warming sensation lower down. She thought of Gladney's kiss the night before, and her reaction to it, and the feeling of giddiness intensified.

Rebecca studied her image more closely, paying particular attention to her breasts. She felt a heightened sensitivity in them. The two mounds of flesh, which had been little more than an annoyance to her in the past, suddenly took on a new perspective. She studied them now not as something which had to be covered to enable her to drive the sulky but as evidence of her womanhood.

She knew that men liked to look at women's breasts for she had seen them do so. Did they like to touch them, to caress them? And if so, what did it feel like to them? And what would it feel like to her, if a man did touch them?

Rebecca touched one breast lightly, hesitantly, embarrassed by the act. There was a strange, flaming heat flowing from her flesh, and she could feel it in her fingers. That was odd, very odd indeed! She had touched her breasts many times in her life, but never before had she noticed such a phenomenon, although, she realized, never before had she touched them in such a deliberate fashion.

She moved her finger along the pale, rising mound, stopping just outside the aureole. There was a tingling sensation there, and she noticed that her nipple had drawn into a tight rosebud. Daringly, she stroked the nipple, and was amazed and a little frightened by its sensitivity. She wished that Gladney had touched her there last night, when he kissed her. It would have been interesting to see what happened. She wondered if Steven would touch her there, if he ever kissd her. Did he want to kiss her?

Abruptly, Rebecca squeezed her eyes shut and put both hands down on the dresser, gripping the edges tightly. What had come over her? What was happening to her, that she could allow these thoughts to hold sway over her mind? She reminded herself angrily that she had a race to drive, and there was no time for such distracting fancies.

When she opened her eyes again, Rebecca began to bind her breasts slowly and deliberately, wrapping the band around her tightly until her torso was a smooth, unbroken line from her shoulders to her waist. Her breasts were no longer visible even in profile and her disguise would be effective. But this time she was aware, as never before, of the heat and mass of the flesh she had bound, as her breasts strained to be free.

Only two rooms down the hall from Rebecca, a woman was experiencing what Rebecca was thinking about. Her name was Stella—the only name she had given Steven Lightfoot. She was small, with long black hair and an elfin figure. From a distance she looked astonishingly like Rebecca Hawkins, and it was for this reason that Steven had been drawn to her. Stella was a business lady, she had told him, plying her trade among the prosperous men drawn to the fair. She had quoted a price, and Steven hadn't quibbled. Now they were in his hotel room, nude together upon the bed, and Steven was tracing his fingers lightly across her skin, across her breasts, and stroking down across the taut satin skin of her stomach.

"Ummm, that feels good," Stella murmured, looking up into his eyes.

"Close them."

"Close what?"

"Your eyes."

"Why?"

"Because you have beautiful eyelashes, and I like to look at them."

Stella did have beautiful eyelashes, but that wasn't the real reason Steven wanted her to keep her eyes closed. They were blue, while Rebecca Hawkins's eyes were gold. And when Stella's eyes were open, he couldn't hold the image of Rebecca in his mind's eye.

Stella pulled his mouth down to hers and they kissed, long and deep. One of his hands nestled in the small of her back, just above the sweet rise of her buttocks. The other moved up to cover her breast and closed gently around it, skillfully kneading the nipple.

Stella arched under his hand. "Ohh!" she said, when finally the kiss had ended. "Oh, my! I'm glad everyone doesn't make love like you do."

"Why?" he asked, puzzled by the rather strange remark.

She smiled shyly and winked. "Because if they did, I'd do this for free, and then I'd probably starve to death."

Steven had to laugh. Then he kissed her again, as he moved over her. He continued to touch her with skilled, tender strokings, feeling his own blood run hot now, as the woman boldly, hungrily returned his caresses with her own, just as eager.

Either she was eager for him or she was a damned good actress, he thought. He was not a frequenter of whores, so he had no yardstick by which to judge. Yet he was sure that this woman was not acting—her passions were aroused. This pleased him enormously.

"Ah, yes, yes!" she cried out. "Now! I'm ready for you! Hurry, lover!"

Steven entered her with gentleness, but Stella would not have it that way. With a moaning sound of pleasure, she surged to meet him and urged him to greater effort with hands and mouth. He buried his face in her hair and felt her responding to his quickening strokes with obvious delight. All his senses were engaged in the ecstasy of the moment, and when he felt her quivering beneath him in a shuddering release, he could hold back no longer.

Still, even in that moment of supreme pleasure, his thoughts were of Rebecca Hawkins.

* * *

There was a huge crowd attending the harness races. Three races already had been run, but this one, billed as the "race of champions," featured only those entries that had won at least one previous race during the three-day meet. There were seven entrants, and Rebecca and Paddy Boy were in the number four position, with three horses on either side. She sat poised and ready to go, holding the reins loosely, confidently, waiting for the crack of the starter's whip. Her hair was tucked securely under her cap, her breasts were carefully bound, and she was dressed in the trousers and cherry-red silks of a driver. No one, not even the drivers on either side of her, knew that she was a woman.

Rebecca had learned that there was little danger of her being recognized as a woman before or during a race. Each driver had other concerns, and concentration on the race to the exclusion of everything else was the mark of a good driver. It was only after a race that she had anything to worry about.

The number two horse suddenly bolted forward a few yards, and there was some delay while the embarrassed driver brought the animal back into position.

"Gentlemen, are you ready?" the starter shouted. "Let us try and have a good, clean start."

There were seven affirmative nods, and the muscles in men and beasts tensed as they waited.

The starter's whip popped behind them with the report of a pistol shot, and the seven horses surged forward almost as one.

The horse in the number two position took the lead, and Rebecca steered Paddy Boy into the hole behind him, but another horse and sulky moved alongside her. She suddenly found herself hemmed against the rail, followed very closely by a trailing horse and unable to go forward because of the lead sulky. She was in what was often called the "parked" position, an uncomfortable and often hopeless place to be.

Then she noticed that the driver to her right was crowding dangerously close. She glanced over and saw that he was wearing the yellow-and-black stripes of Oscar Stull. He was an ugly little man with a hawk nose and bright red hair peeking out from under his cap. He was grinning evilly at her.

"You're crowding me!" she shouted.

The little driver never lost his evil smile, and now he moved even closer to her, until their wheels bumped slightly.

Rebecca realized that he was doing it deliberately. He had to be!

The first bump had been light, but now there was another bump, and finally a third, much harder than the first two.

And that was when it happened. Under the impact of the third and final collision, the axle on Rebecca's sulky gave way. She watched with a sickening, frightened sensation in her stomach as the right wheel snapped off and that side of the sulky fell.

The crowd gasped, and some of the women screamed as they saw what had happened. The jagged edge of the sulky dug into the turf, spewing dirt behind, and finally spilling Rebecca out. She hit the ground right in front of a cluster of three sulkies which were close behind.

Though unhurt when she struck the ground, Rebecca knew there was a great danger of being run over, and she held her breath as the other horses flashed by, one pair of hooves pounding the turf mere inches from her head. The entire incident had taken but a few seconds, yet while the hooves thundered past her it had seemed an eternity.

Several people ran onto the track toward her, and Rebecca hastily checked her riding cap to ensure that no errant falls of hair were loose to give her away. She sat up, a little shaken but otherwise unhurt.

"Are you all right, bub?" the first man to reach her asked.

"Yes, I'm fine."

Getting to her feet, she looked across the track and saw the pacers running down the backstretch, with the Stull sulky leading by nearly a length. Paddy Boy hadn't given up; he was struggling along, trailing the field, with the damaged sulky bouncing and weaving behind him. Rebecca winced, praying that he wouldn't injure himself. She hurried across the grass infield and towards the finish line.

"Do you need a doctor to check you over?" one of the track officials called over to her.

"No, thank you, I'm not hurt," she replied, keeping her voice low.

She reached the finish line just in time to see the Stull sulky flash across, the driver still smiling the same chilling smile he had worn when he made Rebecca crash. Paddy Boy, dragging the ruined sulky behind him, finished last, then pulled up just beyond the pole.

She hurried to him. "Good horse, Paddy, good boy. You tried, didn't you? Are you hurt?" she asked anxiously, fearful that the bobbing, bouncing sulky might have struck his legs.

She ran her hands up and down them and felt nothing amiss. There was no blood, and the horse didn't flinch away from her touch. She breathed a sigh of relief. Nothing appeared to be wrong.

The sulky wasn't so fortunate. In addition to the lost wheel, the ordeal of being pulled the entire distance with one wheel turning and the other plowing in the dirt had twisted the rig frame all out of shape.

It was obviously damaged beyond repair, and they would definitely have to buy another one in order to continue racing.

Rebecca sighed. How quickly their fortunes had changed! This might have been one of their most successful meets ever, but suddenly it was the most disastrous. For not only did they lose today, they would have to use yesterday's purse to replace the destroyed sulky. That meant that the entire three days had ended up costing them money.

Rebecca disconnected the sulky and left it in a wrecked heap alongside the rail, with instructions that it be taken away. She saw Hawk limping forward and motioned him away. Then she climbed up onto Paddy Boy's back and morosely rode him to the stables. She rubbed him down, and then hurried to the hotel to discard her disguise.

She had sustained very little personal damage during the fall, nothing she wasn't able to wash away in a hot bath. She had a bruise on one thigh and another on her right shoulder, but they weren't too painful. She credited her good fortune to the fact that much of the force of the fall had been absorbed by the sulky frame itself, and she had not lost her seat until the side of the sulky had already dug into the dirt. Then she had just flipped off, and rolled along the ground in such a way as to lessen the severity of the impact. Her only real danger had been the possibility of being run over by the following sulkies, but by a stroke of great fortune that had not happened.

No thanks to the Stull driver, she thought grimly.

It was nearly an hour before Rebecca, bathed and soothed, returned to the track from the hotel. Inside the stables she found her grandfather talking to

70

Gladney and Steven. At first she was a little surprised at finding the two young men together, but then she realized that they both must have come to check on Paddy Boy, and in so doing met one another.

"Ah, Becky," Hawk said, giving her a searching look. "I was getting a bit worried, girl, wondering where you were."

"I'm fine, Grandfather," she said. "I was just making sure that our driver wasn't injured. You've checked Paddy Boy?"

"He's fine and dandy," Hawk said. "Gladney and Mr. Lightfoot were worried too, and were kind enough to drop by and check on him."

"It's nice of you both to be concerned," Rebecca said.

"How is your driver?" Steven asked. "He looked like he took a nasty spill, but by the time I made my way there he was already gone."

"He's fine," Rebecca said. "He just needs a little rest, is all. He'll be ready for our next race." She looked sidelong at Gladney. "I hope you didn't really bet everything on Paddy Boy."

"Ah, but I did," he said cheerfully.

"Then you've lost your money," she said in dismay. "I *am* sorry." Gladney shrugged, and his blue eyes flashed merrily. "Ah, it wasn't really mine anyway. Paddy Boy just let me use it for a day. Didn't you, Paddy Boy?"

"It isn't the first time Glad has lost everything on a horse," Steven said dryly. "And I'm sure it won't be the last."

"Oh! You two know each other?" Rebecca asked in surprise.

"Aye, that we do," Gladney said.

Rebecca was a little disappointed by this informa-

71

tion, but she couldn't put her finger on the reason why. Somehow, she had hoped that she had been the catalyst which had caused them to meet.

"You are friends then?"

"You might say that," Gladney replied. "Let's say that I prefer his company to many I've met. But when it comes time to lay claim to something, I will claim it without regard for friendship. And I'm making that claim now."

"Claim? What claim are you talking about?" Rebecca asked innocently.

Steven threw back his head and laughed. "Glad, my friend, it would appear that the young lady in question does not recognize your claim."

"Oh, but I recognize it," Gladney said. "Make no mistake about that. And she will too, in time."

Belatedly, Rebecca realized what their banter meant, and she felt herself flush. What right did Gladney Halloran have to make such a statement? She opened her mouth for a cutting remark, when Hawk said suddenly, "It seems we have company."

Rebecca and the others turned to look in the direction Hawk indicated. Oscar Stull and his henchman, Mr. Mercy, were approaching.

"Unwelcome company, if you ask me," Rebecca said angrily. "It was his driver who crashed into our sulky hard enough to snap off the wheel."

Stull was close enough to hear her words. "I'm sorry about the accident," he said suavely. "I do hope your driver wasn't hurt?"

"The driver is fine, Mr. Stull," Rebecca said hotly. "No thanks to you however. I'm certain that you told your driver to crash into the wheel."

"Told my driver to crash into the wheel? I don't know what you're talking about." His smile was superior. "My dear young lady, you do seem to be prone to making false accusations. First you said I had a gun yesterday, and now this."

"I'm not wrong this time."

"Can you prove it?" he challenged.

"No, how can I? But I saw it happen!"

"That is far from proof. It was an accident, nothing more."

"What do you want here, Stull?" Hawk demanded.

"Oh, I simply wanted to check out a theory of mine," Stull said.

"A theory? What theory is that?"

"It is my belief that people enjoy winning more than losing or . . . playing the game. You've just lost a race, Mr. Hawkins. Are you as good a sport as you were yesterday? How do you feel about losing?"

"I feel dandy," Hawk growled.

"Do you know? I wonder. Is racing still a high and noble sport to you? Or do you feel the bitterness of losing?"

"I never feel bitterness over losing," Hawk said, "as long a race is honest and aboveboard. I would resent having the outcome of a race decided by trickery, such as deliberately crashing into another sulky in order to break a wheel off."

"It seems your granddaughter has poisoned your mind as well." Stull's short laugh was contemptuous. "Again, I say *prove* it was intentional. Mr. Hawkins, when two sulkies come together in a race, it is as dangerous for one as it is for the other. Certainly it is not something to be done by plan. My driver could have just as easily lost *his* wheel. Now, wouldn't you agree to that?"

"I suppose you're right, Stull," Hawk said with a sigh.

"But in answer to your question, sir," Steven said unexpectedly, and everyone looked at him in surprise,

73

"The question of what it feels like to lose can be better answered by yourself after this afternoon's thoroughbred race. I will be astride my horse, Bright Morn, and I fully expect to win. Therefore, as you will also have a horse entered in that race, it means you shall lose. Then we'll see how you feel, Mr. Stull."

Steven's bold statement took Stull aback. "Just who the devil are you, sir?" He fingered his scar.

"My name is Steven Lightfoot."

"Oh, yes, I've heard tell of you. The half-breed Indian who calls himself a gentleman," Stull said in a jeering voice.

Steven's fists doubled and he took a step forward. Gladney placed a restraining hand on his arm. "Easy, fellow, easy." In a steely voice he said to Stull, "Speaking of gentlemen, a gentlemen would know when his presence is not wanted. I'd suggest you leave."

"A con man and a half-breed." Stull's sneer was a little forced. "A fine pair indeed! Neither of you would know a thoroughbred from a jackass!"

Steven shook Gladney's hand away. "I will answer that on the track this afternoon. I intend to beat your horse soundly!"

Stull's face flamed and the vein in his temple throbbed dangerously. His eyes glowed with an intense light for a long moment, but then he managed to regain control of himself.

"That remains to be seen," he said stiffly. "By the way, as you may have already heard, I have posted a reward for any information leading to catching the murderer of Timmie Bird. If you hear anything which might help the police in finding the guilty person, please tell me at once. In the meantime, I bid you good day."

He clicked his heels and bent forward slightly from

the waist. With a curt nod to Mr. Mercy, he strode away, Mr. Mercy a gray shadow by his side.

"That gentleman is a most disagreeable gent," Hawk said tightly.

"That disagreeable gent is no gentleman," Gladney said.

Hawk frowned at him. "Gladney, did you really lose all your money on Paddy Boy today?"

"I'm afraid I did," Gladney said with a shrug. "I failed to follow my own rule, and I paid for it."

"What rule is that?" Hawk asked curiously.

"Never get too greedy. Greedy people are what keeps me in business. Today I was so certain that Paddy Boy would win that I wanted to make a killing. I thought it was a good wager."

"Perhaps it would have been, if this sulky hadn't been tampered with." This came from Steven. He had walked over to examine the ruined sulky, which had been dragged into the stable and left there.

"What are you talking about?" Hawk said.

"The axle was cut."

"No," Hawk said emphatically. "You're wrong there. Believe me, the first thing I did was check it thoroughly. If a file or saw had been used, part of the break would have been clean and smooth, the rest jagged." He walked over to the sulky. "As you can plainly see, that's not the way it is."

"I didn't say that a file or saw had been used," Steven said. "I just said it was cut. The axle was cut with acid."

"Acid!" Hawk exclaimed. "Now just how can you tell that?"

Rebecca and Gladney joined them, and they watched as Steven pointed down at the broken axle.

"See how the metal has darkened here, and here?

And there it has bubbled up, like melted candle wax. It has been soaked with sulphuric acid. That made it snap like a dry stick when the other sulky wheel struck it."

"Then I was right!" Rebecca said. "Stull's driver did crash into our sulky on purpose."

"You're probably right, Rebecca. He knew that it would only take a jar or two to snap it right off."

"But we still have no proof that Stull was behind it," Hawk said glumly. "We all know it was Stull, but how could we prove it to anybody's satisfaction?"

Gladney squatted on his heels beside the sulky. "Steven, my friend," he said, looking up with a shadow of a smile. "My guess is that the man with the bald pate doesn't much like to lose. If I were you, I would be on my guard this afternoon."

"Don't worry, I fully intend to be," Steven said stoutly. "You may be sure of that!"

Gladney stood up, stretching lazily. "All this thinking on an empty stomach is bad for me. I suggest we all go somewhere for a bite to eat."

"No, Gladney," Hawk said quickly. "I'll buy our meal. After all, you treated us last evening. And now you're busted, besides."

"That's no problem." Gladney grinned laconically. "The hotel doesn't know I'm busted. I'll just put it on my bill. And you're not in such good shape yourself, Hawk. You're going to need a new sulky."

"I'll manage. I insisted that it's our turn to buy, don't you agree, Becky?"

Rebecca was still piqued about Gladney's stating his "claim," and she just shrugged in reply.

"Of course," Hawk said awkwardly, "Becky and me may be taking up too much of your time. You likely have better things to do than dine with an old man and a young girl."

76

"Sure, Mr. Hawkins, and what better thing could there be for a young Irish lad like meself than to spend time in the company of two such darlin' people as you and the charmin' lass who is your grand-daughter?"

"Are you working another con, Mr. Halloran?" Rebecca said tightly.

"No, Miss Hawkins," Gladney said, dropping the brogue. "You and your grandfather *are* two lovely people, and I *am* Irish. And believe it or not, until I worked hard to overcome it, such a brogue was my natural way of talk. Because of that, I sometimes slip back into it. I meant no offense by it, and I hope none was taken."

"I . . . I guess not." Rebecca said, disarmed once again by his candor and sincerity.

"But Hawk, you must agree to allow me to repay this debt when I am with funds once more."

"We'll see," Hawk said.

"Mr. Lightfoot, would you join us?" Rebecca asked.

"I wish I could," Steven said. "But I have a race to ride this afternoon and there are some things which need my attention beforehand."

"Oh, that's really too bad, old friend," Gladney said, pulling a long face. "I'm certain you would have made a contribution to our group." He chuckled. "But I shall endeavor to see that Miss Hawkins doesn't give you a second thought. You may have no worry on that score." He offered his arm to Rebecca.

Rebecca evaded him, took her grandfather's arm instead, and noticed Steven's sudden smile. Rebecca was somewhat embarrassed by the rivalry that had sprung up between the two men. It was evident that they were competing with one another, and it was equally clear that her favor was the prize. She could only pretend to be innocent of any knowledge of what

77

was going on. But secretly she was very aware, and she found it most satisfying.

The hotel restaurant was crowded, like every other eating establishment in town during the fair. In fact, it looked as though they might not get a table.

"Maybe it won't be so crowded after the thoroughbred race," Hawk said. "We could come back then."

"Wait a minute," Gladney said. "Let me see what I can do."

He excused himself and vanished into the crowd. A few minutes later he returned with the head waiter, who led them over to a corner where a potted plant was being removed to make a place for another table.

"I hope you and your party find this suitable, Mr. Halloran," the head waiter said.

"It will do nicely, thank you," Gladney replied.

He fetched a chair for Rebecca while the waiters were busy placing two more chairs around the table. Gladney appropriated the one in the middle, closest to Rebecca, for himself.

"How did you manage this?" she asked.

"It's like the shell game," he said with a conspiratorial wink. "I can't give away all my secrets now, can I?"

The head waiter returned to their table, carrying an envelope on a small tray.

"Mr. Hawkins?"

Hawk glanced up. "Yes?"

"This message is for you."

Hawk looked surprised, but he took the envelope and started to leave a tip, which the head waiter declined. He opened the envelope and quickly read the note.

"What does it say, Grandfather?"

"The track commissioner has asked that I join him in his private dining room, here in the hotel."

"Oh, how nice of him!" Rebecca said. "You are going, aren't you?"

"I should," Hawk said. His face lit up. "It would be rude to turn him down. It even could be that he's learned, some way, that Oscar Stull was responsible for the sulky's so-called accident. You sure you wouldn't mind, you two?"

"No, of course not," Rebecca said.

"Gladney?"

"Mr. Hawkins, you go on along and enjoy yourself," Gladney said soberly. "I'll do my best to look after your granddaughter for you."

Hawk looked from Gladney to Rebecca and smiled. "I reckon you will at that, Gladney. Leave it to an old man for not seeing things more clearly. You two have a nice time."

Rebecca watched her grandfather leave. She was secretly pleased that he had been summoned, leaving her alone with Gladney. She wanted to be alone with him. She enjoyed his company, even if she didn't approve of his profession, and she was certainly in no danger of being kissed here, in the crowded restaurant, so she could quite easily control the situation.

Gladney spoke at that moment, interrupting her thoughts. "Where will you and your grandfather be going from here?"

"Paducah, Kentucky. We have a race down there two days from now."

"What an interesting coincidence," he said. "I, too, will be in Paducah in a couple of days."

"Really?"

"Really," he said cheerfully. "Unless, of course, you decide to go somewhere else. Then I shall be *there*."

"What are you saying? It doesn't make sense!"

"Doesn't it now?" He reached across the table and took her hand in his.

"Doesn't it show?" he said dramatically. "This wild, insane attraction I feel for you cannot be contained. I am mesmerized by your beauty, dazzled by your charm. I am a fly caught in your web, and I shall follow you to the ends of the earth!"

"Stop it! Stop your Irish blarney," Rebecca said, laughing helplessly. "You're attracting attention. Everyone is staring at us!"

"Becky, my dear, are you so innocent, so unaware of the power your beauty has over men, that you can't realize that everyone is *always* staring at you?" he asked in a quiet, serious voice.

He was still holding her hand, and when his mood turned from humorous to serious, Rebecca became acutely aware of it. She was also aware of a strange melting warmth in her body, a warmth that seemed to start at the point of his touch, then flow through every part of her. How, she wondered, could she feel a weakness in her knees, when he was simply holding her hand?

"Would you care to order now, sir?" a waiter suddenly asked from behind Rebecca, startling her. She jerked her hand from Gladney's grasp and gazed down at the table with her cheeks flaming in embarrassment.

"Yes," Gladney said, leaning back. "We'll have whatever is today's special. Unless, Rebecca, you'd care for something else?" he asked, looking over at her.

"No, no, that will be fine," she said hastily.

"I'm sorry he came when he did," Gladney said, after the waiter had left. "I was enjoying holding your hand."

"Did it ever occur to you that I might not have been enjoying it?"

He looked at her with his crooked grin. "I don't

think I believe that, Rebecca. If you weren't enjoying it, why did you allow me to hold it so long?"

"I just didn't know how to withdraw without embarrassing both of us, that's why!"

"Oh? Well, in that case, it's a good thing the waiter provided you with the opportunity, isn't it?"

"Yes."

"And if he hadn't appeared, I suppose you would have let me hold your hand for the rest of the afternoon?"

Exasperated, Rebecca snapped, "I don't wish to sit here and discuss holding hands with you, sir!"

"Very well, what shall we discuss?" He leaned back, one hand resting negligently on the table. "The kiss last night! That's a subject I wouldn't mind discussing. Have you thought about that today?"

"I most certainly have not!" she said sharply. "And if you were a gentleman, you wouldn't bring it up."

"I make no claim to being a gentleman, never have," he said calmly. "Not to you, not to anybody. A gentleman would never be in my line of work."

"Your line of work," Rebecca said through gritted teeth, "is another subject I don't care to discuss. I should think you'd be ashamed to even mention it."

"You keep on, darlin', you're going to leave us with nothing to talk about."

"There are other, more proper subjects . . ."

"Such as?"

"We could talk about the weather, the lovely autumn colors, the race meet . . ."

"Or the way your lips shine in this light," he interrupted. "The way your hair falls to your shoulders in a soft, dark cloud. The way your brows arch so charmingly over your eyes. The way those eyes leap out and grab a man's heart, and hold it captive with their beauty."

Rebecca knew that she was blushing furiously. No man had ever spoken to her in such a manner, and she found his words, spoken with that soft Irish lilt, utterly charming and exciting, almost as exciting as last night's kiss had been. And yet, she knew that she should stop him. She shouldn't sit here and listen to him go on this way. It just wasn't proper!

"Don't," she said in a whisper. "Please, Gladney, don't speak to me this way."

"All right," he said with a straight face. He looked at her without speaking, holding the gaze so long and with such intensity that Rebecca became nervous.

"And don't look at me like that, either," she said. "Please!"

He sighed softly. "Well, it seems I can't talk to you, and I can't look at you. I guess that leaves only one thing."

"What?"

"This," he said in a tender voice.

Before she could divine his intent, he leaned across the table and kissed her. As had happened on the riverboat the night before, the kiss took her breath away, driving from her mind the time and place and circumstances, so that she found herself responding to it, kissing him back with fully as much ardor as he was kissing her.

Once, when Rebecca was a little girl, she had fallen from a tree and the breath had been knocked from her body. It had been a strange, frightening, reeling sensation, lying there not knowing quite what had happened, or where she was, or if she would ever breathe again. And now Gladney's kiss brought much the same sensation flooding through her.

"I do hope I'm not intruding," a man's cold voice said behind her.

Rebecca started, sitting back in a state of utter confusion. She glanced around and was dismayed to see Steven Lightfoot behind her, his dark face scowling.

"Mr. Lightfoot! What are you doing here?"

"Why shouldn't I be here? This *is* a public eating establishment, I believe." He was staring icily at Gladney. "Although it's a little hard to be sure, with what I've just witnessed."

The realization of what she had been doing in a room crowded with people struck Rebecca belatedly, and she gasped, putting her hand to her mouth. Dear God! She must be losing her mind! Her face flamed nearly as scarlet as the cherry-red silks she wore when driving the sulky.

"Steven, what are you doing here?" Gladney said in a disgruntled voice. "I thought you were preparing for your race. I must say that you chose a most inopportune time to pop in."

"So I noticed," Steven said. "I do apologize. If you weren't quite finished, I could go out and come back in a few minutes." His voice dripped with sarcasm.

"That might not be such a bad idea," Gladney said.

"No!" Rebecca said. "Now just stop it, the two of you. I'm embarrassed enough as it is. Please don't humiliate me further."

"You're right, Rebecca. I came to see your grandfather," Steven said, formally. "The track commissioner knows of a good sulky he can buy cheaply and I thought he might be interested in it."

"I'm sure he would be, but he's . . ." She broke off, frowning. "That's strange. He's with the track commissioner now, in his suite here in the hotel."

"I agree, Rebecca, that is strange," Steven said, "since I just left the commissioner not twenty minutes ago."

Rebecca was more mystified than ever. "I . . . I don't understand. The commissioner sent Grandfather at note here at our table, inviting him. Isn't that right, Gladney?"

Gladney was looking down at the table with one hand over his eyes, as if shielding them from her.

"Gladney?"

"I think I'm beginning to get the picture," Steven said grimly. "Tell me, Rebecca, did the head waiter deliver this note?"

"Yes, he did."

"And did Mr. Halloran have an opportunity to speak privately with the head waiter before the note was delivered?"

"Well . . ." Rebecca hesitated. "Yes, he did speak to him but to get us a table."

"Still using that old ruse, huh, Glad?"

"Gladney, what *is* he talking about?" Rebecca exclaimed.

"Nothing," Gladney said quickly. "He isn't talking about anything at all, Rebecca. He's just trying to stir up trouble."

"Something is odd here," she said, "and I want to know what it is."

"You're a victim of one of Glad's old tricks, Rebecca," Steven told her. "He paid the waiter to slip your grandfather a note, telling him that the track commissioner wanted to eat with him." He laughed. "Once Glad even got a girl's father out of the way by having the poor man think that the President of the United States wished an audience with him. Your grandfather, Rebecca, is no doubt up in some room right this minute, wondering why the track commissioner is so late. And the commissioner is over at the track, because he knows absolutely nothing about any of this."

"Is that true, Gladney?" she demanded.

"Rebecca . . ." Gladney sighed in resignation. "I

84

just wanted a chance to be alone with you for a little time." He managed to look forlorn. "There was no harm done. Not really. Hawk will probably get tired of waiting shortly and come back down."

Rebecca stood up abruptly just as the waiter returned, carrying two plates. "Steven, will you take me out of here, please?"

"With the greatest pleasure."

"Are you leaving now, madam?" the waiter asked, as he placed the plates on the table.

"Yes," she said curtly.

"But madam, what about your food?"

Rebecca gazed down at the plates of roast beef, peas, mashed potatoes and gravy, and gave a sudden smile. "Mr. Halloran will take care of it, I am sure," she said sweetly.

She picked up her plate and turned it upside down on Gladney's head. The brown gravy ran down into his eyes. Gladney simply sat, eyes closed, without moving or saying a word.

"Mr. Lightfoot, if you please?" Rebecca said, head high.

Face grave but with eyes dancing with laughter, Steven extended his arm. Rebecca took it and they swept out of the restaurant, as laughter at Gladney Halloran's predicament began to rise behind them.

Chapter Five

Steven made good on his promise to win the thoroughbred race and Gladney, wagering money he really didn't have, won back all he had lost on Paddy Boy. He showed up at the stables later that afternoon, holding a fistful of money and in a happy mood. He wanted to take them all out to supper, even including Steven in the invitation. Implied in the extravagant gesture was an apology to Rebecca and her grandfather for the trick he had played on them.

"How do we know that you don't have some other trick up your sleeve, even now?" Rebecca asked suspiciously.

"You're right, Rebecca," Steven said. He was flush with his victory and obviously enjoying Rebecca's displeasure with Gladney. It was clear that he intended to take full advantage of it.

"You keep out of this, Steven," Gladney said dourly. "I don't see that it's any of your concern."

"Oh, but it *is* my concern. I consider Rebecca and her grandfather friends of mine, and I can't stand idly by and watch you con them."

"Thank you, Steven," Rebecca said, "for your concern."

"What?" Gladney said angrily. "Dammit—Excuse me, Rebecca, but can't you see why he's doing this? Talking about somebody doing a con job!"

87

"Doing what? Steven hasn't done anything except be a perfect gentleman," she said spiritedly. "You're the one who tricked me."

"Now, Becky," Hawk said tolerantly. "Don't be so hard on the young man. It was an innocent enough shenanigan, the kind any young man might pull to be with a young girl."

"Shenanigan!" Rebecca said with an unladylike snort. "You've taken to talking just like him!"

"Besides," Hawk said as if she hadn't spoken, "I was the one who ended up by myself, not you. And if I'm not mad about it, then I don't see why you should be."

"Mr. Hawkins, thank you, sir! At least *someone* is on my side! And please do accept my apologies. I'll make it up to you in some way, my word on that."

"There's no need, Gladney," Hawk said with a chuckle. "I told you, I understand. Becky, what do you say? Forgive and forget? Come on now, girl."

"I wouldn't trust him, Rebecca," Steven said. "That Irish brain of his is wickedly devious. Don't say I didn't warn you."

"Rebecca, can't you see what he's trying to do?" Gladney exploded. "He's doing everything he possibly can to turn you against me!"

"And why shouldn't she?" Steven said, a touch complacently. "She knows you're up to no good. She doesn't want to talk to you, now or ever again. Why don't you just stop annoying her? Come along, Rebecca, you and I will go to supper. Just the two of us."

He had gone too far, and Rebecca whipped around at him with flashing eyes. "Steven Lightfoot, you don't make my decisions for me! If I want to see Gladney again, I will. And as for going out with you, just the two of us, the answer is no."

"At least I wasn't selfish about it," Gladney said. "I included everyone in my invitation."

"So you did," Rebecca said. She put her finger on her chin and studied both young men with a twinkle in her eye. "I know! We will *all* go out. On a picnic!"

"Right!" Gladney said happily. He would much rather have dined alone with her, but at least he wasn't being left completely out in the cold. He and Steven would go to the picnic on equal terms. Inwardly he sighed with relief, and he made up his mind right then and there that if he ever tried one of his "tricks" again, he would make damned sure Rebecca didn't catch him at it.

"A picnic, you say," Hawk said dubiously. "Where?"

"Down at Fort Defiance," Rebecca said. "I heard someone talking about it. It's the spit of land that juts out where the Ohio and the Mississippi meet. It's very pretty, I understand, and a perfect spot for a nice picnic."

"I can think of dandier places to have a picnic than an army fort," Hawk said.

Rebecca laughed. "It isn't really a fort, Grandfather, not anymore. It was fortified during the Civil War, but there is nothing there now."

"That sounds like a grand idea," Gladney said, rubbing his hands together. "Don't you think so, Steven? We'll all have a great outing!"

Steven gave him a sour look. "Yeah," he said flatly. "We'll have a marvelous time, I'm sure."

"We'll have to get horses," Rebecca said, enthusiastic now. "And have a picnic basket made up."

"We won't need horses," Gladney said, a little nervously. "I can rent a buckboard."

"Oh, no," Rebecca said. "There's no road into the place, so I was told. We'll need horses to get in and out."

"Of course there's a road," Gladney said. "There has to be."

"How do you know? Have you been there before?"

"Well . . . no," he said. "But there must be a road in, especially if it's a popular picnic spot."

"Well, I've heard differently," Rebecca said firmly. "At any rate, horses will be more fun. Let's use horses."

"No," Gladney said again.

She stared at him. "Why not, for heaven's sake?"

"No reason, really," Gladney muttered. "It just seems foolish to me for us to all ride horses, when we could go in comfort on a buckboard."

"I agree with Rebecca," Steven interjected. He was puzzled as to the reason Gladney was so insistent on a buckboard, but his instinct told him that this was an advantage he should seize. "It would be better to rent four horses. That way, we could take a moonlight canter along the river's edge. You certainly couldn't do that in a buckboard."

Rebecca exclaimed in delight. "You're right, we couldn't!"

Gladney said resignedly, "Since you're so determined on the damned horses, I'll tell you what. You three go ahead and get the horses, and I'll take a buckboard. That way, I can take the picnic basket, blankets to spread out, and some bottles of wine."

"Oh, don't be silly," Rebecca said crossly. "All those things can be toted just as easily on horseback. Now, it's three to one. You've been outvoted, Gladney. We're going on horseback, and that's final!"

Suddenly, Gladney slapped his forehead with the heel of his hand. "What the hell! Here I've been arguing about all this when I just remembered that I can't go anyway. I've got something I have to do."

Rebecca said, "What could be so important that

you can't celebrate your good fortune today by going with us on a picnic?"

"It's just something I forgot about, is all. So I reckon I won't be able to join you. But I hope you all have a nice time."

Rebecca was looking at him intently. Something didn't ring true about his excuse. He seemed oddly embarrassed, and she could see no reason for that. And then with an intuitive leap she knew. "Gladney, what is it? You have some other reason you don't want to go, don't you? Now what is it?"

"Nothing," Gladney said defensively. "Nothing but what I told you. I just remembered something, that's all. You go on, you can have just as good a time without me."

"Oh, we will, Glad," Steven said triumphantly. "Much better, probably."

Rebecca said, "It's the horses, isn't it, Gladney?"

He gave a start. "The horses? No, of course not. Why should it have anything to do with horses?" His voice was unconvincing.

"It *is* the horses," she said. "Don't tell me you can't ride a horse!"

"Well, I'll be damned!" Steven burst into laughter. "That's it! Of course that's it! Come to think of it, I've never seen you on a horse, Glad! Not ever!"

"Hush now, Steven," Rebecca scolded. "Don't make sport of him."

"I can ride a damned horse," Gladney said. "I just don't care to, if I can help it."

"I don't believe you," Steven said.

"Steven, now stop it!" Rebecca rounded on him.

He held up his hands, struggling to control his mirth. "All right, all right!"

She turned back. "Gladney, why didn't you just come out and say so? It's no great crime not to be able to ride a horse well. I know people who wouldn't get on a horse if their life depended on it."

"I know, but it's not something a man can be proud of." He laughed at himself. "They're such fickle creatures. I don't think they like me. I love to wager on them, I like to be around them, like Paddy Boy there, but whenever I climb on board one, disaster strikes!"

Steven was still enjoying his rival's discomfort. He saw a groom he knew slightly, riding past. He hailed the man, who drew his mount up. Steven strode over to him and asked the loan of his horse for a few minutes. "Sure, Mr. Lightfoot. I reckon I can trust the man who won the thoroughbred stakes today." He got down, and gave the reins to Steven.

Steven led the animal over to Gladney. "Here," he said. "I know this horse. He's gentle as a kitty cat. Why don't you show us that you can ride?"

"I don't have to prove anything to you, Steven!"

"Which is the same as admitting you can't."

"I admit to no such damned thing!" Gladney said angrily. "But I'll be damned if I'll let you goad me into something, just to prove it to you!"

Rebecca had walked over. "Now this has gone far enough. Gladney's right, Steven. He doesn't have to prove anything to us."

"He does to me." In a taunting voice Steven added, "Maybe you could use a sidesaddle. That's how women ride."

"Damn you, Lightfoot!" Gladney said through gritted teeth.

He snatched the reins from Steven's hand, and in one supple motion he vaulted into the saddle.

Steven knew that this particular horse was especially trained to work with thoroughbreds, and it had taken on many of their characteristics. It was sensitive and moody, familiar with the weight, feel, and smell of the groom who normally worked with it. The people around it now were unfamiliar, and it sensed the tenseness and anger in Gladney's voice. Thus, when Gladney swung onto its back so abruptly, its reaction was instinctive.

"Gladney, look out!" Rebecca screamed, as soon as she saw the animal's reaction.

Her warning came too late. The instant the animal felt Gladney's weight upon its back, it exploded into action. Stiff-legged and wild-eyed, it seemed to go straight up into the air, coming down with a force that threw Gladney's body forward so that his head almost touched the animal's neck. As he grabbed the saddle horn, the horse reared, and Gladney was thrown backward, his hat swirling away to land in the dust as the frightened animal pawed the air.

Gladney let out a shout. He hung onto the saddle horn as if his life depended upon it, and perhaps it did. The horse bucked again, twisting its body, and Gladney felt himself leave the saddle, only to hit it again with painful force when the horse's feet again hit the ground.

Then in an instant his ordeal was over, for as the animal bucked again, Gladney's grip on the horn was broken, and he sailed over the animal's head, landing heavily on the ground near the paddock railing.

Rebecca ran to him, calling his name. "Glad, are you hurt?"

Steven had started laughing the moment the horse started bucking. Now he stopped, and hurried over to Gladney with a concerned look.

"Is he all right?"

Gladney raised his head, and said shakily, "I . . . I think so. I'm not sure."

"You damned idiot," Steven said, angry now. "You shouldn't have leaped on him like that. You don't do that to a strange horse. Any fool knows that!"

"Gladney, you're bleeding!" Rebecca exclaimed. She took a perfumed handkerchief from her dress pocket and dabbed at his lip where it was bleeding.

"I think I did that when I hit the ground." He sat up, glaring at Steven. "You set me up for that whole thing!"

"No, I didn't, friend. Certainly I didn't want this to happen. You could have been badly hurt," Steven said.

Walking over, Hawk said, "Boy, you've got a lot to learn about horses. Steven is right, you shouldn't have landed on his back like a tiger. And you were leery of him. An animal can smell that. Then he got spooked, because he didn't know what you were going to do."

"All right," Gladney said sourly. "You're all right. I can't ride a horse. Now laugh!"

"We're not going to laugh, Gladney," Rebecca said soberly.

"Well, your friend there is." Gladney pointed at Steven.

Hawk said, "Glad, I don't know anybody who can't ride."

"Well, you do now," Gladney said glumly. He climbed to his feet, dusting his trousers.

"How the devil did a man in this country ever get full grown without learning to ride? How do you get around?" Hawk asked curiously.

"I travel about in a buggy, that's how. And I was brought up in New York. Only the society folk ride, for pleasure in Central Park. There were always the horsecars when I needed to go somewhere. Or trains, or boats, or stagecoaches. I never had the opportunity to ride a horse when I was a kid, nor the desire to ride one when I grew older."

Steven shook his head pityingly. "You know what they say about getting thrown from a horse, don't you?"

"No, what do they say?" Gladney took Rebecca's handkerchief from his lip and examined it. There was not a great deal of blood.

"Why, once you are thrown, you should climb right back up again."

"I believe I'll forego that pleasure, thank you." Gladney glanced venomously at the horse, which had calmed down and was being led away by the groom. "They're stupid beasts, horses. Aye, that they are."

"You're not the man I thought you were if you don't get back on it at once."

"I said no," Gladney said curtly. "And I'm warning you, stop clacking about it."

"Oh, you're warning me, are you?" Steven laughed. "Should I tremble in my boots?"

"That's enough, Lightfoot," Gladney said dangerously.

"I'll tell you what," Steven said, still in that taunting voice. "Try it sidesaddle. Maybe you'll—"

Before Steven could get all the words out, Gladney's fist lashed out, catching Steven squarely on the jaw and knocking him to the ground, in almost the exact same spot where Gladney had landed after being thrown from the horse.

"Why, you Mick bastard!" Steven said angrily, and he started to get up, but the moment he regained his feet, Gladney hit him a second time, sending him to the ground again.

"Stop it!" Rebecca screamed. "Will you two stop this nonsense?"

Gladney got in one more solid blow before Steven

managed to scramble along the ground until he was far enough away to get to his feet, just in time to set himself for Gladney's headlong charge.

Gladney was moving too fast, and his foot skidded in a pile of horse droppings. Arms windmilling, he almost fell. Stepping in quickly, Steven took the advantage offered and smashed his fist alongside Gladney's cheek. The blow sent Gladney reeling back against the paddock railing. He came off the railing roaring with rage, and the two men stood toe to toe, hammering at each other.

"You two . . . *children!*" Rebecca said, close to tears. "You can fight it out until doomsday as far as I'm concerned! Come, Grandfather, let's leave."

So saying, she spun on her heel and walked away, leaving the two men brawling. Hawk looked from Rebecca's retreating back to the two combatants. He spread his hands, shrugged, and limped after his granddaughter.

Neither Steven nor Gladney took note of the departure of Rebecca and Hawk; they were too intent on each other. With neither man having the advantage of surprise now, they were just about an evenly matched pair. They were of approximately the same size, both were quick and strong, and both had a punch that would have quickly put away an average man. When they fought each other, it was something to behold, and already a crowd was gathering to watch and cheer on one or the other.

Gladney's lip, which had been cut when he was thrown from the horse, was now swollen from the blows Steven had landed there. One of Steven's eyes was puffy and blackened. They were both still on their feet, warily circling each other with mutual respect, fists cocked, waiting for the right opportunity. The rain of blows they had landed on one another early on had been punishing, and they had abandoned their wild onslaughts as their anger cooled slightly. Now each sought an opening.

In truth, with their anger cooling, the primal urge to do battle had subsided. As they circled each other, holding their fists up, they noticed for the first time that a crowd had collected in a loose ring around them.

"She's gone," Gladney said suddenly.

"Who's gone?"

"Rebecca."

Steven glanced around. "Well, I'll be goddamned! So she is!" He stepped back, lowering his guard slightly.

Gladney said, "And she's the reason we're taking our licks at each other. Right?"

"Right."

"Hit 'em!" someone in the crowd called. "Go on, Glad! Hit 'em a good lick, he's wide open!"

"Do we really want to give these bloodthirsters a free show?" Gladney said with a slight smile.

Steven smiled back. "No," he said. "At least I don't. How about you?"

"Hell, no."

Steven dropped his hands. He took a step forward and held out his hand. "Then let's stop this foolishness."

"No!" another spectator shouted. "Don't stop now! It's just getting good."

Gladney looked at the outstretched hand. Grinning his crooked grin, he clasped it in both of his.

"There is one thing I do want you to know, though," Steven said.

"What's that, my friend?"

"To my way of thinking, Rebecca is unclaimed territory. I've got as much right to court her as you do."

"But I saw her first, you know I did!"

"That may make you a front runner, but that's all," Steven said. "And I've dealt with front runners before. What's the matter, are you afraid of the competition?"

"Competition, is it? Why don't we put it this way: may the best man win!"

"I agree, since that means that I am assured of victory," Steven said, laughing.

"And let us remember that other old saying. . . . All's fair in love and war."

"Oh, I'll keep that in mind, knowing you as well as I do." Steven glanced around. "I see we've lost our audience, as well as the Hawkinses. I suppose that means that our picnic is off."

"Yeah, I would imagine so. They're probably halfway to the Cape by now," Gladney said negligently.

"The Cape?" Steven said quickly. "What do you mean?"

"Nothing," Gladney said, his glance sliding away. "It was just an expression."

"You mean Cape Girardeau, right? That's where they're racing next, isn't it?"

"Now, how would I know where they're racing?" Gladney said innocently. "Even if I knew, you think I'd tell you? So we've declared a truce. That doesn't mean I'm helping you, for God's sake!"

"But you've already let it slip!" Steven crowed. "Cape Girardeau, that's where they're going. The Southeast Missouri District Fair is being held there, starting tomorrow. They'll be racing there! And so will I, thanks to you, old friend."

Gladney was shaking his head. "Nope, you're wrong. The fair at Cape Girardeau isn't until next month. But if you don't believe me, go find out for yourself. And good riddance."

98

"Excuse me, Mr. Lightfoot . . ."

They both turned to see the groom who had loaned Steven his horse. Steven said, "Yes? What is it?"

The groom looked at Gladney, scrubbing at his chin in some embarrassment. "I hope you're not upset with me, sir, about the horse throwing you. But you scared the critter. He meant no harm, he was just reacting."

"So everyone has been carefully telling me. No, I'm not upset with you. I'd just as soon forget it."

The groom nodded, relieved. "That's good. Now if you gents will excuse me, I have to go help load Mr. Stull's horses on the boat." He turned away.

"Just a minute!" Steven said quickly. "Did you say you were helping load Oscar Stull's horses on a boat?"

"Yes, sir. He's got the two pacers, and a thoroughbred, you know, and he's leaving this evening."

"Leaving for where?"

"Why, over to Cape Girardeau, Mr. Lightfoot. The fair there starts tomorrow."

Steven grinned widely. "Thanks for telling me. It seems I've been getting some wrong information here."

Gladney turned aside, kicking the dirt as though disgusted with himself. The groom touched his cap and hurried off.

"So," Steven said, "the Cape Fair isn't until next month, huh?"

"I guess I was mistaken," Gladney mumbled.

"Sure you were. Glad, you'd better get into another line of work. Your cons seem to be backfiring on you."

"Could be you're right. I'll have to ponder on it." He brightened. "At least I was lucky today. I won enough on that thoroughbred of yours to make up for what I lost on Paddy Boy, and enough to retrieve my diamond stickpin from that bloodsucking money lender."

Steven laughed. "You mean you had to borrow on that again? It's going to get worn out, passing back and forth so many times."

"It's my ace in the hole." The diamond stickpin Gladney was talking about was a large, perfect, four-carat stone, set in a solid gold pin. He enjoyed wearing it, and he was careful to wear clothes to set it off. But his real reason for having it was as a sort of emergency fund. It was easily worth five hundred dollars, and he had found that money lenders were willing to loan half of its value when he needed it. There had been many times in the past when he had to fall back on such loans, but always, as this time, he had managed to scrape up enough money to redeem it.

"Where is it?" Steven asked.

"At the Cairo Bank. A man I know there lent me money out of his own pocket, charging me an arm and a leg in interest, but it was worth it."

"Let's see now . . ." Steven pursed his lips. "It's in the bank, and the bank is closed until the morning. Which means that you won't be able to leave for the Cape until after the bank opens tomorrow."

"That's the way it is," Gladney said gloomily. "Not if I want my stickpin back, and I sure as hell do!"

"And that means I'll have nearly a full day's start on you." Steven was smiling with wicked delight.

"You think I don't know that? Why don't you wait around until tomorrow, and we'll make the trip together? I have an idea that could make us both some good money."

"I'm not interested in any of your schemes, Glad. I don't have a diamond stickpin," Steven said dryly.

100

"If you were a fair man, you Indian bastard, you'd wait for me!"

"You said it yourself a few minutes ago. All's fair in love and war."

Gladney heaved a lugubrious sigh. "Then would you at least give Rebecca a message for me when you see her?"

"That depends. What's the message?"

"Tell her that I'm sorry for the trick I played on her. Tell her I won't do it again."

"That kind of promise from you, Glad?"

"Just pass on the message, will you, and never mind the sarcasm."

"Oh, I'll give her a message, never fear," Steven said blandly. "Now why don't you come along and see me off on the boat to the Cape?"

"Thanks a lot," Gladney said sourly.

The riverfront was a busy, exciting place. There were three packet boats tied up at the wharf, which was alive with the hustle and bustle of river commerce. One boat was bound south for New Orleans, with stops in between. Another was headed up the Ohio for Cincinnati, calling on all the Ohio River ports. The third, the *Maypole*, the one Steven would be taking to Cape Girardeau, was actually bound for St. Louis.

Gladney stood by while Steven supervised the loading of his thoroughbred, Bright Morn, on board.

Then, as they stood saying their farewells, a familiar and unpleasant voice spoke from behind them. "So the pair of you are heading for the Cape as well, eh?"

They turned around to see Oscar Stull behind them, flanked by the silent Mr. Mercy.

"No," Gladney said, "I'm just here to see my friend off."

"Yeah, I'm going," Steven said, smiling tightly. "I

101

can't pass up an opportunity to beat your horses again, Stull."

The blood vessel began to jump in Stull's bald temple, but he held himself in check, managing a slight smile. "You are beginning to annoy me, Mr. Lightfoot." He massaged the purple scar on his cheek. "And I find it hard to put up with such annoyances for long, especially from a half-breed."

Steven jerked his thumb. "Your pet rat there looks hungry. Why don't you give him some cheese to gobble? And you'd better tell him to watch it. These riverboats are stocked with cats to keep them clean of rats."

The expression on Mr. Mercy's face remained unchanged. That, more than anything else, sent a chill down Gladney's spine. If the man had changed expressions, or made some remark, even a threat of some kind, it would have been less intimidating than that emotionless face.

Oscar Stull was rhythmically striking his thigh with his riding quirt, his gaze riveted on Steven. Then he motioned with the quirt. "Come along, Mr. Mercy."

The pair marched up the gangplank and onto the *Maypole* without once looking back.

"Steven, those two scare the hell out of me," Gladney said. "You'd better keep a watchful eye out on that boat, or you'll end up with your ass buried deep in Mississippi mud!"

"You don't have to tell me that," Steven said. "After I beat his horse today, he gave me a look, and as the saying goes, if looks could kill . . ."

The whistle of the *Maypole* blared, the sound rolling across the waterfront in warning.

"Well," Steven said, "I see it's time to go." He grinned at Gladney. "What was the message to Rebecca you want me to pass on?"

"Never mind," Gladney said grumpily. "You probably wouldn't get it right, anyway."

"You're probably right."

Behind Steven the gangplank slowly elevated, and the *Maypole,* whistle still shrieking, began to inch away.

"Friend," Gladney said urgently, "you'd better hump it, or you're going to be left behind!"

"You'd like that, wouldn't you?" Steven laughed. "It'll never happen."

The water under the stern boiled white as the paddle wheel churned the river, pulling the boat away from the wharf. The distance widened. Steven, still laughing, ran lithely down the cobblestone levee. He crouched slightly, then leaped gracefully across the widening span of water and landed with sure feet upon the lower deck. He turned and waved, shouting something that was lost in the night.

Another warning whistle sounded, this time from the Ohio River packet. Gladney smiled, then laughed aloud.

He delved into his trouser pocket for the diamond stickpin and pinned it to his vest. He had lied to Steven. He had borrowed money on the stickpin, true, but from a local moneylender, not the banker, and he had retrieved the stickpin immediately after collecting his winnings from the thoroughbred race.

He took out his boat ticket for Paducah, Kentucky, and hurried along the levee toward the Ohio River packet. By the time he had boarded and made his way to the bow of the boat, the *Maypole* had made the turn from the Ohio to the Mississippi, heading north.

He doffed his hat at the dwindling lights of the *Maypole,* and said aloud, "Like I said, Mr. Lightfoot, all's fair in love and war!"

Chapter Six

Rebecca stood at the window of their Paducah hotel and watched the rain. It had started during the night and was still continuing, softening the early morning light with its veil so that now, even after sunrise, the room behind her was dark.

There was a knock on the door. She opened it to admit her grandfather.

"It'll be a slow track today," he said. "But I was just outside. It should soon clear up, I hope."

"Poor Paddy Boy. He hates weather like this."

"Who does like it?"

"I certainly don't."

Hawk chuckled. "Me too, girl." They walked over to the window together. Hawk groaned, massaging his hip. "It's weather like this that makes my hip begin to ache. Then I remember London."

The rainy weather had made Rebecca pensive. Staring out the window, she said, "Grandfather, tell me again about Mother and Daddy before they got married."

"You like that story, don't you, Becky?" His smile was indulgent. "All right, I'll tell it again." His eyes grew blurred as he looked back through time and his voice became tinged with melancholy. "Your ma was Harriet Stanford then. Her pa owned a large tobacco plantation next to Oak Valley farm, where I was overseer. It was a thoroughbred farm, and I was trainer and jockey for all the horses. The farm and horses belonged to Owen Johnson." He laughed proudly. "Wasn't a horse within three hundred miles that could beat any of our horses."

"And Grandpa Stanford never let any of his horses race against the ones you trained."

"Lord, no! Your Grandpa Stanford thought racing was a sinful waste of time. Idle foolishness, he liked to call it. In fact, he would get furious with Harriet when she sneaked over to watch our animals, and he caught her at it."

"And yet you say she always kept coming back. She must have already been as crazy about horses as I am."

"I'm not sure it was the horses so much. She came more to see your daddy, I'd say. Bart was a handsome devil then, and almost as good a rider as I was. And how he liked to show off for your mother! Hell, I could be in the barn or off somewhere, and know that your mother was around without my seeing her, just by the way that boy rode!"

"Tell me about when they eloped," Rebecca coaxed. She had heard the story numerous times, but it always fascinated her, and was one she enjoyed hearing again and again. And what better way was there to spend a rainy morning than listening to her grandfather's stories?

"Mr. Stanford, like I said, considered horses nothing but beasts of burden. Using them for racing, or show, or for anything other than work animals, was all foolishness to his way of thinking. So he considered anyone spending their time training horses for any other purpose just plain fools. That included just about anyone around, especially myself or your father.

"So, when he found out that Harriet was spending

time around Bart, and even worse, getting serious about him, he raged and ranted. He laid down the law to the poor girl, ordering her to never go over there again."

"But she did," Rebecca said.

"Oh, that she did, you can bet on it! She came as regular as rain, sneaking over whenever she could. We all conspired to protect her. If we saw her father, or anyone from her daddy's farm, we'd pass on a warning to her, so she could hide away somewhere until they'd gone."

"Good for you!"

"But we'd all reckoned without Stanford's determination to put a halt to it. When he found out he couldn't stop it any other way, he bought the Johnson place. Owen Johnson was getting on, and willing to sell to him at a good price. Stanford, he not only bought the place, but sold off every racehorse on it."

"That must have been awfully hard on everybody."

"Well, he did offer nearly everyone a job on his own place, I'll grant him that. But that didn't include me and Bart. After all, that was the prime reason he bought out Johnson, to get rid of us."

"So what did you do?"

"Colonel Clark and some others had been considering sending Kentucky horses to England to race them there. They were hoping to get the British interested enough to buy Kentucky thoroughbreds. So they hired me, and in the end that worked out just dandy for me."

"What about Mother and Daddy?"

"Bart found a job on another horse farm, and the first chance they had, Harriet ran off and they got married."

Rebecca laughed. "And that made Grandpa Stanford really furious."

"Oh, you can bet on it! I understand he almost got a stroke, but there was really nothing he could do about it. Your mother was of age, and they *were* married. The only thing he could do to get back at Bart and your mother was to swear that from that day on, your mother was no daughter of his."

"I know from a few things Mother said that she was hurt deeply by that," Rebecca said sadly. "Why do you suppose Grandpa Stanford didn't ever forgive her?"

"Who knows, girl?" Hawk put his arm around Rebecca's shoulders and pulled her against him. "It was a bad thing to do, and it did hurt your mother very much. To my way of thinking, it may have even helped to kill her. Anyway, by acting like he did, old Stanford missed out on getting to know his granddaughter, and I've got to say that his loss was my gain. You've been a joy and a comfort to me, Becky. More than you'll ever know. It was a happy day for me when your mother brought you to London."

"I remember very well when mother took me to London," Rebecca said musingly. "You'd been over there for ten years, which was from before I was born, so I'd never seen you. But Daddy had been killed at Gettysburg during the war, and Mother knew even then that she was dying. And so, with nowhere else to turn, she took me across the ocean to London to be with you, rather than go the short distance to Louisville to be with Grandpa Stanford. I suppose she had no actual choice, since he would have turned us away."

"And I'll always be grateful for that," Hawk said. "I don't mind telling you, I was getting mighty lonesome in London. Oh, I had friends, other jockeys, trainers, and the people I met as the sales agent for the Kentucky Breeders. But I was awful anxious for a face from home. I reckon I would have lit out for home, but the war came along, and when I heard that Bart was dead, I lost heart. I even gave up riding for a spell, just didn't care one way or t'other.

"Then you and your mother came, and that brought me back. Though I must admit that the first time I saw Harriet's face, it wasn't all that joyful for me. I had no idea she had been sick, and seeing that once beautiful face pulled and wracked with pain just about broke my heart."

"Mother was sick all the way over," Rebecca said. "I guess it was a miracle she lived those last few days after we came to you. You know, it was as if she clung to life by sheer will power. She stayed alive long enough to get me to you, because she felt it was her duty. And then, when that duty was done, she just gave up and went to sleep."

"I know," Hawk said softly. He squeezed Rebecca's shoulder, started to speak, and seemed to choke up. He coughed behind his hand and quickly left the room. Rebecca was sure that there were tears in his eyes, even though the room was too dim to tell.

She continued to stare out the window at the softly falling rain, and thought about her mother. It had been a day like this when Harriet Hawkins died . . .

"Mother, I had no idea London was such a big town," Rebecca said.

Theirs was an attic room, and from the dormer window Rebecca could look out over the roofs of the city. For as far as she could see, stretching off into the rain-dimmed distance, there was nothing but buildings. It was a city of such enormous magnitude that it was a little frightening to a ten-year-old girl.

"It is a big city, Rebecca dear," Harriet Hawkins said from the bed. "But you needn't worry your head

109

about how big it is. Your grandfather is here, and he will take good care of you."

There was an ominous sound to the statement, and Rebecca, even at ten, had enough insight to be frightened by it. She left the window, with the rain beating against the pane, and stepped quickly to stand by her mother's bed. Her mother had one arm folded across her forehead, and never had Rebecca seen her face so drawn and pale. She had lost a lot of weight on the voyage over, and her thin hand seemed almost transparent, its only color the prominent blue veins.

"Mother, why did you say Grandfather would take care of me? Aren't you going to take care of me?"

"I've done all I can, everything in my power," Harriet said. "I'm tired now. I'm so terribly tired."

"Rest, mother," Rebecca said. She put her small hand in her mother's and the older woman tried to squeeze it, but there was no strength left.

". . . tired," Harriet said one more time.

She died in her sleep sometime during the night, and Rebecca began a new way of life, a life that was to be hers from that time forward.

Horse racing was truly the Sport of Kings in England during the latter half of the nineteenth century, and the events were so crowded with titled gentry that many referred to them as "Royal Affairs" or "Affairs of State." With the arrival of his granddaughter, Henry Hawkins felt renewed interest in life, and he began riding more, taking the girl with him everywhere he went. He became one of the most popular riders in the events. He was an American, and that set him apart. He was also a great jockey, and that earned him respect and fame. And since he represented the Kentucky Breeders' hopes of selling thoroughbreds in England, he raced only the finest animals his Kentucky backers could send him, and that made him a consistent winner.

Rebecca loved all of the racing scene. Since she was the only girl around and the Hawk's granddaughter to boot, she was treated with respect and affection— "spoiled rotten" was the way Hawk put it when he was exasperated with her.

Rebecca learned quickly what it meant to be a winner. She basked in the glow of popularity that surrounded her grandfather, and she kept a scrapbook of newspaper accounts of his feats. Young as she was, she was very impressionable, and much more taken with her grandfather's fame than he was. It wasn't long before she decided, secretly of course, that she would ride herself someday, and enjoy the same success her grandfather enjoyed.

Then, during the summer of Rebecca's sixteenth year, her life changed again. While riding in a steeplechase, Hawk fell under his mount when it went down, and his hip was crushed, ending his riding career forever.

It had long been Hawk's dream to return to Kentucky and buy a horse farm of his own, and perhaps he would have been able to, given a few more years of racing. But he didn't have the money at the time of the spill, so he saw no choice but to return to the States and try to raise the needed money in some other way.

That way proved to be one which thrilled Rebecca. Shortly after they returned to Kentucky, Hawk began training her to drive a sulky and to ride. They trained for an entire year. Rebecca, who had a burning desire to excel, was able to match that desire with a natural athletic ability. She was agile, with excellent reflexes, and Hawk knew before the year was out that she could be one of the finest drivers and probably one of the greatest jockeys he had ever known.

It was too bad that she was female, but he eventually came to terms with that. She was so good that it would be a waste of time cursing the fact that she had been born a girl—he just disguised her, and thus avoided the obstacle of her sex.

They had been racing for four years now, but in truth the expenses of their nomadic existence seemed to eat up so much of their winnings that their dream appeared no closer. Then Hawk's old friend, M. Lewis Clark, formed the Louisville Jockey Club and Drivers ~rk Association, and came up with the idea of Kentucky Derby. Already the Derby was beginning to take on all the trappings of America's greatest thoroughbred race. Now their plans hinged upon entering the Derby and winning. Upon that goal hung their dream of the horse farm and their future.

Rebecca thought of the farm often. She could close her eyes and see a green valley and white fences, a large white-columned house, a red barn, and fields of beautiful horses, each one a champion racer, with her their rider. For she had no intention of *ever* giving up riding.

"It looks like the rain is letting up," Hawk said behind her, "just as I predicted."

"What?" Rebecca said with a start. So engrossed had she been with her remembrances and dreams that she hadn't heard him re-enter the room.

"I said the rain appears to be slackening off," Hawk said again. "We'd better hustle down to the stable to see to our animals, especially Paddy Boy."

"Yes, you're right, Grandfather." She added musingly, "I wonder if Steven or Gladney are here yet."

"Why should you care?" he said dryly. "Weren't you upset with the pair of them for acting like children? I seem to recall you saying something like that."

"Yes," Rebecca said. "And I had a right to be upset." She laughed at herself. "But when they aren't acting like children they can be . . . most charming. At least things are never dull when they're around."

"Careful, Becky," Hawk warned in a teasing voice. "First thing you know, you'll be forced to make a choice between them."

"Good heavens, Grandfather! I just remarked that they can be charming. That doesn't mean I'm losing sight of the fact they can also be childish! Imagine, fighting like that!"

"Many women would think it dandy to have two men fighting over them."

With a shake of her head, Rebecca marched out of the room.

Still, despite her protestations to the contrary, it was apparent to Hawk that Rebecca was happy to see Gladney Halloran waiting at Paddy Boy's stall when they reached the stables. Hawk grinned to himself as he watched her struggle to conceal her delight.

"Well!" she said coolly. "Have you and Steven finished fighting?"

"Yep." With a sheepish grin Gladney touched a finger to his lip, which was still swollen and puffed. "I reckon we both owe you an apology for that."

"Well, I should think so. It was embarrassing, as well as humiliating."

"It won't happen again, I promise you."

Curiosity prompted her to ask, "Which one of you won?"

"Neither. I'd call it a draw."

Rebecca glanced around. "I would feel much better about it if I heard that promise from both of you. Where is Steven?"

"Oh, he's sorry he couldn't be here," Gladney said

offhandedly. "He went down to Cape Girardeau. He's entered the thoroughbred race there."

"But why? The purse is just as large here."

"Who knows what goes on in an Indian's head?" Gladney said, spreading his hands. "Besides, who needs him around?"

"For my part, I don't need either of you around," she said hastily. "It just seems . . . well, strange that he should enter Bright Morn there, instead of here."

But deep inside, Rebecca did experience a pang of disappointment that Steven had chosen Cape Girardeau over Paducah. Though she would not admit it to anyone, she had come to revel in the attention of the two young men.

Steven Lightfoot was indeed in Cape Girardeau, and mad as a hornet. He hadn't been there very long before he realized that somehow Gladney Halloran had managed to outwit him.

Immediately after he had registered for the thoroughbred race, he inquired where the pacers were registered.

"Right here," the man behind the desk said. He picked up a tin can and squirted a stream of brown tobacco juice into it, wiped his mouth on his sleeve, then plunked the can back down. "You got a pacer, too, have you?"

"No," Steven said. "I just wanted to know if a friend of mine has registered yet."

"Who might that be?"

"Henry Hawkins."

"The Hawk? Nope, he ain't registered."

"But he must be!" Steven said in dismay. "He left on an earlier packet. He should have been here long before me."

"I know the Hawk well," the man said. "Not only

ain't he entered, he ain't even in town. If he was, I'd've heard by now."

"You're wrong, you must be. But I wonder why he hasn't registered yet. How much longer does he have?"

The man pulled a watch from his vest pocket and consulted it, wiping the glass over the face of the watch with the same sleeve he'd used to wipe his mouth. "He's got exactly seventeen minutes. Anyone who ain't registered by that time ain't gonna be able to enter."

"Henry Hawkins will not be entering this race," said a voice behind Steven.

Steven faced around to see Oscar Stull and the stone-faced Mr. Mercy. "How do you know that?"

Stull smiled unpleasantly, "I make it my business to know such things. I find it always helps to know who you're racing against. Hawkins has entered the three-day meet down at Paducah."

Steven cursed under his breath, knowing then that Gladney had conned him.

"Mr. Mercy," Stull said. "Will you see to the entry requirements? Mr. Lightfoot, I would like a private word with you."

"Talking in private to a half-breed?" Steven said tightly. "Doesn't that go against the grain? I started to say against your principles, forgetting for the moment that you have none."

Stull's eyes flashed in momentary anger. Then he smiled without mirth. "When it comes to business matters, I will deal with the devil himself."

"I can well believe that."

Stull drove on, "I have a proposition you may find to your liking. It could be mutually beneficial."

"Stull, I can think of nothing to do with you that would be mutually beneficial. I knew of your reputation long before I met you. You will do anything to win, and that I detest in any man. So what could we possibly have in common?"

"The Kentucky Derby," Stull said.

Despite himself Steven knew that he showed a sudden flash of interest.

"I see," Stull said, smiling triumphantly. "It appears that we *do* have a common interest."

"I am interested in the Kentucky Derby, yes. I can't very well deny that. It will be the greatest horse race ever run in America, and I intend to be in it."

"As do I," Stull said, "As do I. But I also intend to win, and there you can help me."

"Apparently you didn't understand me, Stull. I told you I plan to enter the Derby. So why the hell would I help *you* win it?"

"Because it would be well worth your while to see that I win."

"Are you saying . . ." Steven stared. "You would *pay* me to lose?"

"Yes," Stull said. "And consider a possible side benefit, if you will. Our Mick con man no doubt will bet rather heavily on your horse. If your horse loses, he will also lose. As you two appear to be rivals now for the attention of Miss Rebecca Hawkins, this would give you a decided advantage."

"You're incredible, you know that, Stull? How about the other horses? McGrath has a couple of pretty good thoroughbreds, Chesapeake and Aristides. And don't forget Volcano, that's Rice's horse, and he's beaten Bright Morn two times out now. Do you intend to buy off everyone in the race?"

"Of the horses you mentioned," Stull said stolidly, "I fear only Chesapeake." He got a distant look in his eyes, massaging the scar on his cheek. "I shall see to it that he is no problem."

116

"What can I say to penetrate that thick hide of yours? A simple 'no' probably won't do it. What if I put it this way? No amount of money would even tempt me to lose that race on purpose! Bright Morn will beat your horse—again!"

"I've heard Indians are stupid," Stull said with a sneer. "But I thought, being only part Indian, you'd be only half stupid. It seems that I was wrong."

Rage boiled up in Steven thick and hot, and he ached to smash his fist into that sneering face. He took a steadying breath and said, "You disgust me, Stull. Without a doubt you are the most disgusting man I have ever known." He turned on his heel and walked away.

A red mist obscured Stull's vision as he watched Lightfoot walk off. Lightfoot was like all the rest of the Kentucky gentlemen—too good to associate with Oscar Stull. And this one a half-breed!

Well, he would show the breed. He would show all of them, *after* he had won the Kentucky Derby.

How sweet that victory was going to be! The Kentucky Derby, a race sponsored by gentlemen, and run by gentlemen, would be won by a man with whom none of those gentlemen would associate. Oh, how he intended to make them eat crow!

It was at least four hours until post time for the first thoroughbred race, and Stull went back to his hotel room to wait. He lay on his bed; his fury was so hot that his blood seemed to boil.

In an attempt to dampen his anger, he entertained himself with thoughts that brought a smile to his face. In his mind he could see Colonel Lewis Clark, H. P. McGrath, and General Abe Burford, gentlemen all and organizers of the Kentucky Derby, groveling on their knees before him, all begging him to show them mercy. They were soon replaced with images of Henry Hawkins, Gladney Halloran, and the arrogant half-breed, Steven Lightfoot.

And Timmie Bird.

Timmie Bird, who had had the audacity to come to him and tell him that he had discovered Mr. Mercy treating the axle of the Hawkins sulky with acid. Then, when Stull had informed the jockey that Mr. Mercy was merely following instructions, Bird had threatened not only to quit, but to expose Stull and Mr. Mercy to Henry Hawkins and the track officials. Stull was left with no choice but to have Mr. Mercy dispose of Timmie Bird. In fact, it made things simpler all around, because Stull had already been thinking of hiring Red Parker to replace Bird. Parker was a man after Stull's own heart. Bird, like too many others in the business of racing, had been a "gentleman." Stull was only too happy to be rid of him.

Timmie Bird wasn't the first person Mr. Mercy had disposed of at Stull's orders. There had been others. Several others, in fact. Including several women.

Not all of the women Stull used in his particular sexual activity could be hushed up with a bonus payment. Some had been so outraged by his brutal treatment that they had threatened to go to the police. Of course, as they were mainly whores, the police might not have lent a sympathetic ear to their pleas. Still, it was not worth the risk. It was much easier to have Mr. Mercy deal with the problem.

And in this one thing, Mr. Mercy's usual stoic nature seemed to desert him. For quite accidentally, Stull had discovered the only thing in which Mr. Mercy took pleasure. Mr. Mercy killed men indiscriminately and without emotion, but he actually enjoyed killing women. He took immense pleasure in it, the way another man took pleasure in a woman's

118

flesh. To kill a woman was, for Mr. Mercy, the ultimate sexual experience.

As was often the case when Stull was thinking violent thoughts, he became sexually aroused. The images of the torture and degradation of his enemies were replaced by images equally as brutal of women. His breathing became labored and sweat poured off him.

"Mr. Mercy!" he called.

The door to Mr. Mercy's room swung open, and the gray man stood there in answer to Stull's summons.

"Get me a woman, Mr. Mercy."

Mr. Mercy stared at Stull with his usual lack of expression.

Stull felt his need growing very strong, and with it his lust for an experience of exquisite sadism. "And this time, Mr. Mercy, when I am done with her, you may have her, to do with as you wish. Call it a reward for services well rendered."

Then Stull saw something few men had ever seen. He saw Mr. Mercy smile.

There were three days of racing planned for the Southeast Missouri District Fair, with the final race on the third day to be the race of champions. That race carried a very large purse, and it was naturally the ultimate goal of all the participants.

All except Steven Lightfoot. Steven had already purchased a ticket on the afternoon packet boat for Cairo, where he would change boats, then proceed up the Ohio to Paducah. He didn't intend to give Gladney any more advantage with Rebecca than he could help. But as he would be unable to leave before late afternoon anyway, Steven thought he might as well participate in the first race of the meet.

Ten horses were at the starting post, including Oscar Stull's entry, Bold Diablo, ridden by the monkey-faced little jockey.

"You got lucky in Cairo," Stull's jockey told Steven as they waited for the snap of the starter's whip. "But you won't be so lucky here."

"Gentlemen, ready your mounts," the starter called.

Steven reached down and patted Bright Morn's neck, then balanced himself in the saddle.

The whip popped behind them and the ten horses exploded forward. Suddenly, the rider alongside Steven veered his horse into Bright Morn, nearly knocking Bright Morn off his feet. Steven thought it was an accident, and gave way to give the other jockey a chance to steady himself, but the rider, this time with obvious intent, came at him again! In the meantime, Bold Diablo had taken a two-length lead.

So, Steven thought, *it isn't an accident!* The rider was on a horse that evidently had no chance of winning, and he had sold out to Oscar Stull.

Steven pulled to the outside of the track, running away from the horse trying to throw Bright Morn off his pace. As Bright Morn was by far the superior animal, it was a simple matter to avoid any further contact, but in so doing he lost ground. By the time Bright Morn was out of danger, Bold Diablo had gone eight lengths in the lead.

Now they were pounding around the second turn, going into the backstretch, and Steven bent low over Bright Morn's head, urging the horse on. The field was strung out from Bold Diablo on back. Steven began passing them one by one, until he was second only to Stull's horse as Bright Morn streaked by the half-mile post.

Under Steven's firm but gentle persuasion, Bright Morn unleashed a tremendous burst of speed, closing fast on Bold Diablo. Coming around the far turn, Bright Morn drew even with Stull's horse, and they went into the stretch neck and neck.

Stull's rider was whipping his animal, laying on the lash as hard as he could, and when he glanced over and saw Steven even with him, he slashed out with his whip, catching Steven in the eye. The pain was sudden and sharp, and Steven closed both eyes involuntarily. Thus, he was riding blind for the last half furlong, bent low over his mount's neck, trusting the instincts of Bright Morn to carry him across the finish line. He opened his badly watering eyes just as they crossed the wire, and saw that Bright Morn had won by a neck.

He let Bright Morn run another furlong, gradually slowing him, before he swung the horse around and returned to pick the winner's purse from the hook on the pole at the finish line. His eye was smarting; it was the same eye that had been blackened by Gladney's fist. Anger coursed through him, and he glanced around for Stull's rider, fully prepared to stomp him into the ground for what the man had done to him. Hell and damnation, he could have been permanently blinded!

One of the officials trotted over. He said admiringly, "Mr. Lightfoot, I do believe that's one of the fastest finishes I have ever witnessed. I'll be looking forward to seeing your horse race for the next two days."

"This is the only race I'm riding here," Steven said, still looking around for Parker. "I'm leaving this evening for Paducah."

"Paducah?" the official said in surprise. "But our purse here is the same. And it is an honor to have your animal as an entry. Surely you can be persuaded to change your mind?"

121

"I'm sorry, sir. I appreciate the compliment, but I have urgent business in Paducah."

"Well, we'll be sorry to lose you, Mr. Lightfoot. At least may I wish you good fortune in the Paducah races."

"Thank you." Steven gave the man a half-salute and kneed Bright Morn, about to head to the stable. That was when he saw Parker, sitting negligently on Bold Diablo, as if mocking Steven, daring him to act.

Later, Steven realized that he should have been suspicious, since Parker was nowhere near the stables. Instead, he was on the opposite side of the track, and he seemed to be taunting Steven to come to him. Steven threw all caution aside and sent Bright Morn galloping around the track toward the Stull horse. His only thought was to catch Parker and give him a sound thrashing. He was halfway to the other horse before the grinning little jockey made a move. Then he turned his horse and started down a dirt lane leading toward a thicket of trees.

"What's the matter, Parker?" Steven called. "Afraid to take what's coming to you?"

The other man just rode on, and Steven followed him into the trees. Then he saw that the narrow lane ended abruptly and he laughed aloud. He had him now! There was no place for Parker to go. To get out of the trees he had to turn his horse and ride back this way.

Apparently Parker recognized this as well. He halted Bold Diablo and kneed him around.

Steven was puzzled to see the man smiling widely and gloatingly, and a wind of caution blew through his fevered mind. He reined Bright Morn in. But he was too late. He had brought his horse to a stop underneath a huge oak, and a rope suddenly came down like a writhing snake. It looped around him, snapped tight, and Steven was jerked from his saddle.

He landed on his feet, but the rope was still around him, pinning his arms to his sides. He struggled to free himself, but again he was too late. Four big men in rough clothes converged on him, seemingly from all directions.

One of them said cruelly, "Mr. Stull says you need to be taught a good lesson, and we're just the buckos that can do a good job of that."

Stepping close, he aimed a punch at Steven's face, clearly assuming that Steven would be an easy target. But the rope had gone slack around Steven, falling down around his ankles.

Steven blocked the blow easily with his left forearm and drove a crushing blow of his own, aiming at the thick neck and the Adam's apple of his attacker. His aim was accurate, and the big man reeled back, grabbing at his neck. His face contorted with agony, his mouth opened and closed soundlessly as he struggled for breath.

Steven whirled lithely, catching a second man flush on the nose. He was gratified to feel cartilage crush under his fist. Bright red blood spouted down across the man's mouth and over his receding chin.

Steven's triumph was short. By this time the other two had closed in. A stunning blow caught Steven high on the temple, and another split the skin on his cheekbones. The man he had caught on the nose waded in again, roaring with pain and rage.

Steven reeled back under a rain of blows. He tried to fight back, but the odds were too much. After a few moments he was hammered to the ground. Landing on his hands and knees, he tried to summon the strength to get back onto his feet, but his knees felt weak as water and there was no strength in his arms. Then a boot caught him in the side, and he was spun over onto his back. The pain in his ribs was like a knife thrust.

A succession of kicks landed on his head and sides. By now he was numb and felt little pain. His consciousness was going. He ceased trying to struggle and gave in to it.

Just before blackness finally claimed him, he heard a high keening sound, and knew it must be a cackle of triumph from Parker.

Chapter Seven

The new sulky was heavier and not as well balanced as the one that had been wrecked in Cairo, and the track was muddy and slow. Paddy Boy didn't like the sulky, and he didn't like the track. As a result he and Rebecca made a poor showing in the first race, finishing third. That was good enough to qualify them for the consolation race to be run the final day, but the remaining qualifying races were closed to them. The purse for the consolation race was not a large one, yet it was big enough to offset the expenses of the meet, so Hawk decided that they might as well stay around and try for it.

Because they lost the race on the first day, Rebecca was free on the second day to enjoy the fair, and Gladney was more than willing to show her around. Although Rebecca had been a part of the fair circuit for years, it was as if she were seeing a fair for the first time. She and her grandfather came to the fairs only for the races, and their world was the world of the racetrack. They shared common ground with the fair workers, but nothing else.

"Have you ever visited the street?" Gladney asked.

Rebecca knew that he was talking about the row of wagons in which the carney people lived. The wagons were actually homes on wheels, and the carney people lived in them when they were working, and quite often between fairs as well.

The wagons were set up just behind the midway, shielded from the fairgoers by colorful canvas signs and stalls. They were placed in neatly ordered rows, and though hundreds of people came to the fair, only the insiders ever ventured behind the signs to wander up and down the "street," as it was called by the carney people.

"I've seen them, of course," she said, "but I've never walked there."

"Come along," Gladney said. "It's an experience you shouldn't miss."

It could have been a quiet street in any community. Clean laundry hung on lines strung between two adjacent wagons. Children laughed and ran and played, as children did everywhere. A very muscular man in pink tights, wearing a walrus moustache, sat calmly on a keg, eating an apple and reading a book. A large poster on the wagon identified him as "the world's strongest man." Beside him, sleeping peacefully on a blanket in the sun, was a baby.

"They have their own little community here, as you can see," Gladney said.

"Our paths don't cross that often," she said. "I guess that's because Grandfather and I always stay in a hotel, while they live out here all by themselves. I've often wondered about that."

"Don't you know? Don't you really know?"

She frowned at him. "No."

"Rebecca, in nine towns out of ten, there are city ordinances against renting rooms to carney people. Many places won't even serve them a meal."

"I don't believe that," she said stoutly. "We've never had any trouble getting a room anywhere."

"You're not carney people," Gladney explained patiently. "You just come to the fairs to use their race-tracks. That exempts you from the stigma."

"How about you? You're a carney person, aren't you? But you stay in the finest hotels and eat in the best restaurants."

"Ah, but you see, love, the people need me," he said with a wry smile. "I fulfill dreams for them. They can win money off me, and if they don't make me acceptable, then they can't make winning money off me acceptable."

"And yet, when you think of the seamier side of a fair, you think of the con artists," she said. "Gladney, how can you live such a life?"

Gladney was saved an answer by a voice hailing him, "Gladney, are you going to pass right by an old friend without speaking?"

They turned. On the steps of a wagon stood a tall woman with dark, flashing eyes. She wore clothing that looked strange to Rebecca—a long dress of many colors, a bright scarf binding her hair, and red boots peeking out from under her long skirt. Amber-colored earrings dangled from her ears and her long fingers dazzled with rings.

"Tanya!" Gladney exclaimed. "I hadn't heard you were in Paducah."

"I arrived too late last night to set up for business." The woman's dark eyes were on Rebecca. "Aren't you going to introduce me to your friend?"

"Ah . . . yes." Gladney seemed strangely nervous. "Tanya, this is Rebecca Hawkins. Her grandfather follows the racing circuit."

"How do you do, Miss Hawkins," Tanya said in her throaty voice. "You are very attractive." Her full lips curved in amusement. "But then Gladney is well known for having an eye for the ladies."

127

Gladney took Rebecca's elbow. "We must be going, Tanya. We'll . . . uh, see you later."

"Oh, I'm sure you will, Glad."

Tanya's rich laughter pursued them.

As Gladney hustled Rebecca off the street, steering her back toward the midway, Rebecca looked back over her shoulder. Tanya was still on the steps, hand on one hip, staring after them.

Rebecca said, "And who is Tanya?"

"She's one of the carney people. She tells fortunes," he said curtly.

"You seem to know her quite well."

"Nothing strange in that. I know most of them."

"Is that the only name she has, Tanya?"

"Far as I know it is."

She looked at him, but he refused to meet her eyes. "I don't know much about fortunetellers, but I understand they use crystal balls. Don't tell me that you use her crystal ball to place your bets. No wonder you always lose!"

He relaxed with a laugh. "Of course not. I may be a crazy Mick, but I'm not *that* crazy!"

They were back on the midway now. It was crowded with hundreds of fairgoers, all with smiling faces and looks of eager anticipation.

"Look," Gladney said, seizing on an opportunity to distract Rebecca from thoughts of Tanya. He pointed to one of the booths.

It was a game of chance that featured a large wheel with several numbers. The wheel was given a quick spin by the wheelman, and then a pointer clicked against the pins protruding from the wheel. Gradually, the wheel slowed down, and when it stopped, whichever number the pointer landed on was the winner.

"This particular game is not gaffed," Gladney grinned. "That means it isn't rigged. When someone is cheated, basically it is because they have cheated themselves."

"How do you explain that?"

He grinned crookedly. "A good con game will work only if the person being conned is greedy, as I may have mentioned a time or two. On the wheel, for example, the numbers are arranged in such a way as to give natural odds. If the odds are twenty-five to one that a certain number will show up, the player bets a nickel and has a chance to win a dollar. Admittedly, that slants the odds slightly in favor of the game, but that is only fair. But there are always people looking to make a killing, and they are the ones who can be had."

Gladney indicated a couple of young men in the crowd. They were standing one to each side of a man who looked decidedly more prosperous than the rest of the crowd.

"Those two are 'sticks,'" Gladney said. "They've found a mark in the prosperous-looking gent. Now they'll go to work. They are going to convince the mark that the wheel is gaffed, and that they know a way to beat it. They can't do it themselves, they'll tell him, because the operator knows them, so they need a local who's willing to help them break the wheel, and they'll split the winnings three ways. They warn him that it's dishonest, but there's a chance for a lot of money in it for him."

"Then what?"

"They convince him to wager heavily on a number where the odds are a hundred to one or better in favor of the wheel. The wheel is honest, so ninety-nine times out of a hundred, the wheel is going to win, and the player is taken for his poke."

"But that's dishonest!" Rebecca said, shocked.

"Dishonest, is it? It can only work if the man being taken has larceny in his heart."

"In other words, you're saying you can't cheat an honest man," Rebecca observed.

"That's one way of putting it." Gladney laughed.

Even as Gladney was explaining the operation of the game to Rebecca, the prosperous-looking gentleman began nodding and smiling. Then he took a thick wad of bills from his pocket.

"Now, the next step is, they'll give him a sheet of paper with instructions on it how to meet and split up the money the player is going to win," Gladney said. "Then they leave him alone, so the wheel operator won't spot them. Or so they tell the mark. Watch what happens next."

The two sticks gave the man a piece of paper, as Gladney had said they would, shaking hands to seal the bargain. Then they faded back into the crowd. The man watched them for a moment, long enough to be certain that they were out of sight, then crumpled the piece of paper up and tossed it to the ground without once glancing at it.

"He threw it away!"

"Naturally," Gladney said. "If they hadn't thought he would throw it away, they'd never have given it to him. This gent is thinking, 'Why should I meet them later and split any of my winnings?'"

Rebecca watched, fascinated that she was privy to what was unfolding before her eyes. The player was unaware that he was being watched and that his every move had been anticipated in advance. She laughed.

"Funny, is it?"

"You probably won't understand, Gladney, but I feel a little . . . I don't know. Privileged, I suppose, at knowing something is going to happen before it does."

"Yes, I know the feeling," Gladney nodded. "It's a little like sitting on a cloud with God, isn't it?"

His remark had exactly captured Rebecca's feeling, and she looked at him a bit strangely, startled by his perception.

"It isn't a unique feeling," he said with a faint smile. "In fact, it may be one of the attractions of this profession of mine."

"How did you get into it, anyway? Were you always a con man?"

"Sure, and for an Irish lad growin' up in New York, there was a need for muscle or wits. I chose the latter as bein' the more desirable of the two, if you catch my meanin'," Gladney said, suddenly slipping into his Irish brogue.

"But you're out of New York now," she said passionately. "You could find honest, decent work."

"Decent work, is it? Doing what?"

"I don't know," she said. "But there are many things you could do, I'm sure. Clerk in a store or bank, work on a boat or a railroad, be a farmer, there are any number of things I can think of."

"Of all the things you mentioned, only one would hold my interest."

"Which one is that?" Rebecca gave him an amused glance. "Work in a bank, I suppose? You'd probably like that, you'd be around money all the time. And you'd probably figure out some way to get some of it for yourself."

"I'll admit, there is that pleasant aspect to the thought of banking. But, believe it or not, I'd really like to farm."

Rebecca said incredulously, "You, an Irishman from New York, would like to farm?"

"Maybe it *is* the Irish in me," he said defensively.

131

"All my ancestors back in Ireland were people of the soil. It's the only thing that would allow me to be my own boss. That's what I like about my life now. I'm free to go to this fair or that one, get up in the morning or sleep late, work or not, as the mood suits me. And I have to answer only to myself."

She shook her head disapprovingly. "If you had that kind of an attitude in farming, you would never make a success of it."

"I assure you, Rebecca, I wouldn't make it in the profession I have chosen either, if I didn't work at it. But the whole point is, I have only myself to answer to and no one else. And though there can be some pretty compelling reasons for working, such as eating three good meals a day, still there is no one to push me into doing anything I don't want to do."

"I can understand that," Rebecca said thoughtfully. "I know that the life Grandfather and I lead now is a difficult one, travelling around from here to there. But I honestly believe that he prefers this life to the life we led in England, despite the position he held there. And that is because he was always taking the orders of the Kentucky Breeders who were sponsoring him."

"Rebecca, would you like a doll?" Gladney said suddenly.

He pulled her to a stop in front of a booth that offered dolls as prizes to any marksman who could put three shots in a dot half the size of a man's thumbnail.

"What makes you think you'll win?" she said tauntingly.

"I don't know that I will," he replied, "but you pay your money and you take your chance."

Gladney paid not for three shots but for six, and his first shot was way off the target, into the white at the side of the dot.

"You're going to have to do better than that," she chided him.

He merely smiled and squeezed off another shot. It too was way off target, striking almost on top of the first one. His third shot was no better.

"Great marksman you are," she said. "I thought you were supposed to shoot at the black dot in the center of the target?"

Gladney looked over at her and winked. "Have you got a doll picked out?"

Rebecca looked at the top shelf and saw a beautiful doll there. It had been years since she had owned a doll, and she had certainly never had any as beautiful as this one.

"As a matter of fact, I do see one I like." She laughed self-consciously, then added, "But I don't see how I'm going to get it, if you can't shoot any better than you've just demonstrated."

"Which one is it? Point it out."

"That one," Rebecca said, indicating the doll. It had shining golden hair and a dark blue dress.

"Get it down for her, Jack."

And to Rebecca's astonishment, the booth operator reached up for it and handed it across the counter to her.

"But you haven't won it, Gladney—"

She was interrupted by the crack of the rifle as Gladney took the first of his second round of three shots.

"Oh! You hit it!" she said excitedly.

Gladney shot twice more, shooting as rapidly as he could pull the trigger, and all three bullet holes looked like one, plunking dead center into the black dot.

Grinning, Gladney put the rifle down, then walked away from the booth with Rebecca proudly clutching the doll. A crowd had gathered as Gladney shot, and now they pushed up to the counter to take their turns.

"The first three shots were merely to see how the rifle was sighted," Gladney explained. "Most people only invest in three shots at a time, and give up in disgust. That is the edge that the operator has. While a customer is shooting his three shots, the operator is busily loading another rifle. If the customer pays for a second round, the operator hands him the second rifle he just loaded. It makes it look like he's simply saving time, but what he's doing is giving the shooter a new rifle with a new sight pattern. That way, the shooter never learns how that particular rifle shoots. After three or four different rifles, each one with a slightly different sight pattern, he generally gives up. He hasn't been cheated, exactly, but the operator has maintained an edge."

"Thank you for the doll, Gladney," Rebecca said. She hugged it to her as if it were a baby. "I've never had one this lovely."

"A beautiful doll for a beautiful lady," Gladney said gravely.

"Wait a minute!" She skipped to a stop, glaring at him. The meaning of what he had told her had just penetrated. "That shooting booth is . . . what was the word you used? Gaffed, that's it!"

He blinked at her. "What are you talking about?"

"It's rigged in favor of the operator!"

He said disgustedly, "Oh, for God's sake, Rebecca! Grow up!"

"And not only that." She glanced back at the shooting booth, which was doing a brisk business now. "You were acting as a stick, attracting a crowd!"

"I was not, I swear that was the furthest from my mind!" he said indignantly. "I was doing nothing more than trying to win a doll for you!"

"You—you're hopeless!" she said angrily. "You'll never change!"

His own temper igniting, he said cuttingly, "Change? Why should I change? And why is it that a woman feels she always has to change a man before she'll marry him?" He crossed his arms over his chest, glowering at her.

"Marry? *Marry!*" For a moment she was rendered speechless. "Of all the gall! To think that I would even consider marrying you! Who cares if you ever change, Gladney Halloran? I certainly don't."

She turned on her heel and stormed off. Almost immediately she was swallowed up by the crowd.

Suddenly, Gladney laughed explosively, struck by the irony of the fact that, angry at him as she seemed to be, she had marched off with the doll still clutched protectively to her breast!

Probably if Gladney hadn't been angry at Rebecca, he would not have made his way to Carney Street. For he did know Tanya, he knew her quite well. He had pleasured himself with her many times in her bed.

Most people thought that Tanya was of gypsy blood, a myth she did nothing to discourage. In fact, she had been born Bess Armstrong, on a worn-out farm in Indiana. Having little liking for the hard work of farm life, and certainly with no desire to end up a farmer's wife, she had escaped as soon as she could and become a "gypsy" fortuneteller.

Despite the aura of mystery she provided in her fortunetelling tent, Tanya was an earthy, uncomplicated person at heart, with a hearty appetite for the sensual side of life. She was bawdy and uninhibited in bed. What Gladney liked about her was that she made no demands other than sexual ones. She welcomed him into her bed, they reveled in their pleasure, and then they went their separate ways until their next sexual encounter.

Tanya opened the door to her wagon at his knock, and he slipped inside. It was dim, with only an incense candle guttering in one corner. Tanya had changed into a floor-length wrapper. Her own body scent mingling with that of the candle stirred Gladney's senses, and his pulse accelerated immediately.

"I've been waiting for you, Glad."

"Pretty sure of yourself, aren't you?" he said huskily.

"You're here, aren't you? We haven't been together in . . . what? Two months. I figured you'd be randy."

"There are other women around, you know."

"None that gives you what I do." As she spoke, Tanya opened the wrapper. She was naked underneath, her flesh full and voluptuous. "Certainly not that la-de-da young lady I saw you with." She let the wrapper fall around her feet.

Gladney wanted to scold her for her comment about Rebecca, but his throat closed up at the impact of her body. He took two steps and folded her into his arms. Her full breasts pressed against his shirt front, and he could feel them moving, probing his chest like small, curious animals.

Gladney kissed her, deep and long. Her mouth still fastened to his, she began undressing him. He tried to help, but his fingers were thick and clumsy as sausages.

Shortly, they were nude on the narrow bed together, locked body to body. Both were ready for what was to follow, and no further preliminaries were necessary. At Tanya's throaty urgings, Gladney rose over her. She sighed gustily as he went into her, and drove her hips against him with a powerful surge. He thrust deep inside her.

136

"Ah, Glad!" she murmured. "I've missed this!"

Their lovemaking was violent but prolonged. Finally Tanya cried out stridently as rapture took her. Her outcry and her trembling body were enough to bring Gladney to the moment of shuddering release.

After a little he disengaged himself, and although the bunk bed was narrow, they managed to lie side by side, one of Tanya's legs thrown over his. Head propped on one elbow, she combed her fingers through the moist hairs on his chest.

"Now, wasn't that nicer than what the racing lady could offer you? Of course, from the looks of her, I doubt very much that you've bedded her. Or ever will."

Gladney raised his head to growl, "I'll thank you to watch your tongue when speaking of Miss Hawkins!"

"Oho!" She arched an eyebrow. "Kinda touchy, aren't you? This can't mean that Glad, the free-and-easy Mick, has finally lost his heart? Now that bit of news is going to break women's hearts all over the fair circuit!"

"Tanya, you're beginning to irritate me. You're messing into something that's none of your affair!"

He got out of bed and began to dress.

It was late afternoon when Gladney, feeling male-happy but also a touch guilty, walked into the stables and approached Paddy Boy's stall. His step quickened when he saw Rebecca talking to a slender, dark man by the stall.

As Gladney came up, the man was saying, "Ain't Paddy Boy running today, Miss Halloran?"

"He lost yesterday, Ted," Rebecca said glumly. "He won't get a chance to run again until the consolation race tomorrow."

"Yeah, I know how you must feel," Ted said. "I lost over in Cape Girardeau yesterday, so I thought I'd wander on over here and try and enter one of the races tomorrow, hoping maybe somebody might drop out."

"You were over at Cape Girardeau?"

"Yep."

Rebecca saw Gladney, and her glance passed over him as if he didn't exist. She said to the slender man, "Who won the thoroughbred race at Cape Girardeau?"

"Bright Morn, ridden by Steven Lightfoot."

"He would," Gladney said dryly. "He's one of the luckiest men I've ever known."

"I wouldn't say he was all that lucky," Ted said. "Not after what happened to him."

Rebecca said in alarm, "What do you mean?"

"Well, I'll tell you. Some queer goings-on over at the Cape yesterday. First there was this girl, and then him."

"This girl and then what?" Rebecca demanded. "What girl are you talking about?"

"Oh, I don't know the girl's name," Ted said. "Some say she was a . . ." He gulped, then said, "No other way to put it, she was no better'n she should be. A girl often seen around the hotels. Anyways, they found her dead, beaten to death."

"Dead!" Rebecca exclaimed. "But what in heaven's name does that have to do with Steven?"

"Nothing, actually," Ted said quickly. "No direct connection that anybody knows of. But he was near beat to death, just like the girl was. He's laid up in his hotel room now, I understand, busted up something awful."

"But how did it happen, and why?" Gladney asked.

"Nobody seems to know for sure," Ted said. "My suspicion is robbery. He won the race, did Lightfoot, and he came back to take the purse from the pole. The purse was seventy-five dollars. The next thing is, they found him down in a clump of trees, t'other side of the racetrack, fairly beaten to a pulp, his pockets empty. His horse was still there, grazing. I guess he was lucky they didn't take his horse, too."

"Oh, Gladney!" Rebecca admitted to his presence for the first time. "He can't just be left alone there, beaten up and everything. Who knows how bad it is?"

"Oh, you're speaking to me again, is it? What do you want of me?"

"Well, somebody should go fetch him. It wouldn't look right, me being a woman . . ." She blushed in confusion. "You know what I mean!"

"Yeah, I can guess." Gladney smiled at himself, remembering the reason for Steven being in Cape Girardeau in the first place. Again it seemed that one of his sly maneuvers had backfired. "So I'm elected, am I?"

"Please, Glad? I would appreciate it so much!"

He eyed her speculatively, thinking of a question to ask her: just how *much* would she appreciate it? But he had the good judgment not to voice it.

"Steven will appreciate it, too."

"Oh, I'm sure he will."

The Cape Girardeau Fair was already breaking up by the time Gladney arrived. One of Stull's horses had won the race of champions on the last day, and it was the subject of general conversation in the first tavern Gladney entered. Some said it was the fastest horse they'd ever seen run, and indeed the animal had set a new track record. But a few others insisted that the Lightfoot horse, Bright Morn, could have beaten the Stull entry, if Lightfoot had not been injured and unable to ride.

Gladney nursed his drink and listened to the conversation long enough to learn which hotel Steven was using. When the talk switched to speculation about the murdered prostitute, Gladney scooped his change from the bar and went directly to the hotel.

The desk clerk at the hotel smiled broadly and turned the register toward him as Gladney approached the desk. Only twenty-four hours before, Gladney knew, this same clerk would have been surly. Yesterday, every room was filled, and there would have been people milling in the lobby, desperately bargaining for rooms. But now, with the fair over, the clerk undoubtedly had an almost empty hotel, and once again a patron was to be greeted with a pleasant smile.

"I won't be needing a room, thank you."

The smile disappeared. He said sourly, "I see."

"I'm sure you do. After all, why waste all that good cheer on someone who doesn't want a room?"

"What can I do for you, sir?" the man said frostily.

"I'm here to see Steven Lightfoot. I'd like his room number if it's not too much trouble."

"I'm not to give that information out, sir. Mr. Lightfoot left orders he was not to be disturbed."

"Not to be disturbed, is it?" Gladney leaned on the desk on his hands, and thrust his frowning face at the clerk. "I am with the state attorney general's office. I believe the young lady who was found dead was murdered here in the hotel?"

"There's no proof of that!" the clerk said, intimidated.

"Also, Mr. Lightfoot was severely beaten, and there is every possibility there is a connection between the two crimes. Now I find that the hotel is hampering my investigation." Gladney took paper and pencil

140

from his pocket and held the pencil poised to write. "May I have your name, please?"

"There is no need for that, sir. I certainly have no wish to hamper an official investigation. You misunderstood, that's all." The clerk's manner was now servile. "Mr. Lightfoot is in Room 205. The second floor, third door on your right at the top of the stairs."

Keeping a straight face, Gladney nodded officiously. "That's better. I will enter into my report that I received full cooperation from your hotel."

"Thank you, sir. I would appreciate that."

But Gladney was already heading toward the stairs. He was grinning to himself as he went up. If that dummy had asked for identification, he thought, he'd have been up the creek.

He rapped on the door of Room 205. A muffled voice said, "Who is it?"

"It's your old friend, Gladney."

"Gladney? What the devil? Wait a moment."

Gladney heard dragging footsteps, then the noise of a bolt being slid back, and retreating footsteps. By the time Gladney had opened the door and entered, Steven was back in bed.

A facetious remark died on Gladney's lips when he saw Steven's condition. One arm and his head were bandaged, and his lips were almost swollen shut. Both eyes were puffed, and bruises stood out lividly on his face.

"Try not to say anything funny," Steven said. "It hurts like hell when I laugh. Not that I've been doing much laughing."

"Good Christ, man! I heard you'd been beaten up, but I didn't expect anything like this. Any idea who did it?"

"You must already know. You called it when you told me to be on my guard."

141

"Stull did this? Stull and his henchman, Mr. Mercy?"

"Not personally, neither one. But Stull ordered it done. One of his bruisers who worked on me admitted that Stull had sent them. One of them won't be singing in any more church choirs. I smashed his Adam's apple good." He smiled, and winced with pain.

"How badly are you hurt, Steven?" Gladney said with concern.

"Bad enough. I'm not dead yet, but I won't be riding for a while. The doctor told me I had some cracked ribs."

"Hell and damnation! I *am* sorry, friend, believe it or not. If I hadn't sent you off on the wrong scent, this might not have happened."

"Don't think that hasn't crossed my mind, and some of the things I've thought about you would have blistered that tricky hide of yours. But what the hell! It was stupid of me to fall for it." He frowned, peering at Gladney through the slits left by the puffiness around his eyes. "Come to think of it, why are you here? You're the last person I'd expect to see."

"You won't believe me."

"Try me and see."

"Rebecca sent me after you, the minute she heard about the beating."

Steven laughed aloud this time, ignoring the pain. "So the time with her alone didn't do you much good, did it?"

"Oh, I was doing great until she heard about you," Gladney said casually. "You sure you didn't arrange all this just to lure me away from her?"

"I'd hardly go *that* far." Steven tried to sit up, groaned, and slumped back onto the bed, his face suddenly gray.

"What the hell do you think you're doing?" Gladney said in alarm.

"Didn't you say that Rebecca sent you for me?"

"Well . . . yes."

"You found me, so I'm ready to go."

"Ready? Steven, I had no idea you were stomped on this badly. Neither did Rebecca. I think you'd better stay here until you heal up more."

"Oh, no, you don't. You'd like that, wouldn't you?" Steven said stubbornly. "Hand me my clothes."

"Steven, I'm serious. I'm not trying to con you now. You're in too bad a shape to travel."

"Glad, help me out of this damned nightshirt, and give me my clothes. I'm going even if it kills me."

"It damned well might, you know."

As Gladney hesitated, Steven sat up, swung his legs off the bed and stood up, swaying. He took two steps toward his clothes folded across a chair, then groaned, his eyes rolling up in his head. He began to fall, and Gladney had to move quickly to catch him before he hit the floor.

Chapter Eight

Rebecca's new sulky, which had been a problem during the first race, was even more of a problem during the consolation race. The right wheel had a tendency to grab, forcing the sulky out toward the center of the track and causing Rebecca to continually give ground. The recalcitrant wheel was added to the unfavorable weight and balance of the rig, so that the race was run under the most trying conditions imaginable.

Despite this, Rebecca refused to give up, and her superior driving skills, plus Paddy Boy's competitive heart, paid off. Paddy Boy managed to win by a slight margin. However, the victory was a hollow one, for a close examination of the sulky after the race disclosed the fact that the frame had been badly twisted at one time, and a proper alignment would be impossible. The sulky they had paid good money for in Cairo was worthless.

"What are we going to do now, Grandfather?" Rebecca said, in near despair.

"There's only one thing we can do, Becky, and that's buy a new one."

"Do you have any idea where we can find one?"

"Yes," Hawk said. "I'm going to Cincinnati. There's a company there that builds them to buyer specifications, and I'm going to have one built." He added grimly, "I'm going to have us a dandy one built this time, hang the expense."

"But how long will that take?"

"Two, three weeks," Hawk said. "We'll have it in time for the Lexington Stakes."

Rebecca sighed. "That means we'll miss the next two meets. And we could certainly use the money."

"No help for it, girl." His smile was spare. "Besides, you can only get money by winning, and there's no way of doing that with this sulky."

Rebecca gazed at the sulky. It was painted a brilliant red and the frame was a gracefully curving bar. Its beauty was considerable, belying the flaw in its construction.

"I suppose you're right," she agreed.

"Besides, with a new sulky and with Paddy Boy getting a couple of weeks' rest, he'll be in top condition in time for the Lexington Stakes. And their purse is high enough so that we could recoup everything we might have lost. If we win, of course."

"You're right, of course, Grandfather. Anyway, as you say, there's no help for it."

She walked over to the stall and smiled at Paddy Boy. Paddy Boy's neck was hanging out over the stall's gate, and he had been watching Rebecca and her grandfather closely, as if he understood everything they were saying.

"Well, Paddy, are you ready for a little rest?"

"I don't know about the horse," a voice suddenly said. "But I certainly am."

Rebecca whirled about in surprise at the sound of the voice and saw Steven Lightfoot standing before her. He had a bandage around his head and one arm, and his face was bruised and cut.

"Steven! Dear God!" She clapped a hand to her mouth. "You look terrible!"

146

He grinned wanly. "Thanks," he said. "That really cheers me up."

"Oh, I'm sorry!" she said contritely. "You know what I mean." She went to him quickly, and impulsively kissed him on the cheek.

"Well now, that was almost worth getting beaten up for," he said, smiling painfully. He touched a finger to the cheek she had kissed.

Hawk said, "What *did* happen to you, boy?"

"Let's just say I ran afoul of some poor sports," Steven answered with a shrug. "But at least they taught me a lesson. I have definitely decided that I need to start being more careful of the company I keep. So here I am, in the best company I know of." Steven smiled warmly at them.

"We're glad to see you back, Steven," Hawk said. "Though, from the looks of you, I wonder if it's wise for you to be up and around like this. I think you should hole up somewhere and rest for a few days. Maybe even a week or two."

"That is exactly what I have in mind. The doctor said it would be at least two weeks before I could ride again. In fact, that's one reason I dropped by. I want to invite you both to come down to the farm with me for a week, for as long as you'd care to stay."

"The farm?" Rebecca asked with quickened interest.

"Yes," Steven said. "Oak Valley."

"Oak Valley farm?" Hawk said with raised eyebrows. "Doesn't that belong to a man named Stanford?"

"It did," Steven said, "but my father bought it from Stanford recently, and he's turning it back into a thoroughbred farm. So you've heard of the place?"

Rebecca was bursting to tell Steven that her father had been born there, but Hawk warned her quiet

147

with a fierce glare. He said quietly, "Yes, I've heard of Oak Valley."

"It's a beautiful place," Steven said enthusiastically. "You'll love it. I understand it was once one of the finest thoroughbred farms in the country. Then Stanford bought it and began raising tobacco. Can you imagine? But he had two bad crop seasons in a row, and had to sell off the property. My father then bought it, and we're well on the way toward restoring it to what it once was. That's why I want you to come with me, to see it."

"Oh, Grandfather, can we?" Rebecca said, her eyes dancing with excitement.

"I don't see how we can, Becky," Hawk said gruffly. "I've got to go up to Cincinnati to get the new sulky. I told you."

"But Oak Valley is on the way, isn't it? Couldn't we at least spend a few days there? Besides, we'll have to do something with Paddy Boy and Prince." She glanced at Steven. "Could we board Paddy Boy and Prince at Oak Valley, while we're in Cincinnati?"

"We'd be glad to oblige," Steven said.

"Appreciate the offer, boy, but it's quite impossible for us to spend any time there."

"But Grandfather, I should think you of all people would want to—" Rebecca began, but Hawk turned a baleful glare upon her.

"I don't care to discuss it," he said stiffly.

Of course! Rebecca realized that she was stupid for not remembering. Oak Valley held nothing but sorrowful memories for Henry Hawkins.

"Very well, Grandfather," she said meekly.

"But," Hawk said, relenting slightly, "we can at least drop our animals off there. I do accept your kind offer to board Black Prince and Paddy Boy. I was a mite concerned about leaving them in the care of strangers."

"Good!" Steven said happily. "That way, at least I know I will see you again, because you'll have to come back for your horses. Come, we must get them loaded. I've already booked passage on the afternoon packet. For," he smiled shyly, "all three of us, hoping you'd agree."

"Where is Gladney, do you know?" Rebecca asked. "He did come after you, didn't he?"

"Oh, yes. He found me in bed in the hotel room, revived me when I fainted, then helped me get dressed, and even went so far as to bed me down on the packet."

"But didn't he come back on the boat with you?"

"Nope." Steven was grinning.

"Then where is he?"

"Did you mention something to him about racing in Clarksville, Tennessee?"

"Yes, the Montgomery County Fair is opening there, but we won't be going there," Hawk said. "We intended to go there before the Lexington Classics. But," he waved his hand disgustedly at the sulky, "this piece of junk isn't fit to race anywhere. We'll just have to skip that race, along with others. We won't race again until Lexington."

Steven threw back his head and roared with laughter, stopping only when his cracked ribs began to pain him.

"I fail to see the humor in our sulky falling apart," Rebecca said severely.

"Forgive me, Rebecca," he gasped out. "Of course it's unfortunate that you will have to buy a new sulky. I wasn't laughing about that. It's Glad. This time he's outfoxed himself. When he put me on the packet, I asked him where he was headed, and he told me Clarksville. He said, and I'll try to quote him exactly, 'I know you'd like to see Rebecca alone, and I reckon I can trust her with you in your condition.' He said this, figuring all the time that he'd be seeing you in Clarksville. Oh, I can just see his face when you don't show up!"

"I see," Rebecca said. Her face was stormy. "That young man does assume an awful lot. Perhaps this will be a good lesson for him."

In point of fact, there was another reason Gladney Halloran was willing to allow Steven some time alone with Rebecca. Of course, the fact that Steven was practically a cripple had some bearing on his decision not to accompany him back to Paducah.

But he wanted some time in Clarksville before Hawk and Rebecca arrived. He had made arrangements for something special in Clarksville, and he wanted it kept a secret from Rebecca, at least until it was an accomplished fact.

He sat looking through the window of the day coach as the green Kentucky fields rolled past the train, and thought of Rebecca Hawkins. What a change she had wrought in his way of life! Of all the women he had known, a not inconsiderable number, never had one affected him quite like Rebecca had. And he kept asking himself why.

She was pretty, there was no denying that. But the world was full of pretty girls, and he had been able to have his share. So it had to be more than that.

She was a woman of independent nature, and he liked that. She was unusually bright and witty, and that too counted heavily in her favor. But again, he had known witty, independent, pretty women in the

150

past, and they had not completely disrupted his thinking, as Rebecca had.

What was it about Rebecca that intrigued him so? He smiled to himself. Perhaps this was the thing that poets wrote about. Only a poet with great command of the language could express the inexpressible or fathom the unfathomable. It was certainly beyond Gladney's power to understand why, but he knew without doubt that he was deeply in love with Rebecca.

"Sure, and what right would the likes of you, Gladney Halloran, have to love a lass so fine?" he demanded of his reflection in the coach window.

He had spoken softly, but now, realizing that he had spoken aloud, he looked around quickly to see if anyone had heard him. Fortunately, no one had, for the other passengers in the car were either engaged in conversation or lost in their own private thoughts.

Yet the question Gladney asked of himself was a valid one. For he was the son of an Irish immigrant, come to New York to escape the potato famine which devastated Ireland in 1845 and 1846. The promise of wealth in the new land never materialized for Pottor Halloran, and he died of overwork, trying to scratch out a living for his family. His wife took in laundry to make enough money to feed her three children. Gladney, anxious to ease the burden on his mother, left home at fourteen.

He joined the New York Irish Brigade as a drummer boy, and went off to fight in the crusade to make all men free. The Civil War was a terrible war for anyone who took an active part in it, but for a fourteen-year-old boy, it was a shocking awakening to the brutal facts of life. He saw men suffering unspeakable horrors and committing unpardonable sins. But he also saw man at his most noble. He witnessed acts of compassion and unexpected examples of courage. He saw honor, truth, and valor. He witnessed men of faith as they cursed God, and he saw atheists fall on their knees begging His protection. Gladney had examined his own conscience, discovering that he was more religious than he thought he was, though less than he felt he should be.

By the time the war ended he had been commissioned a lieutenant, a promotion earned during the fires of battle. He was only eighteen years old, but he had come to an accommodation with life that was normally found only by the far, far older. That was because the crucible of war aged a man. There were times when Gladney had thought that a particular day would be his last on earth. That he was still alive at the war's end, he considered, was a miracle of sorts, and for that reason Gladney refused to take his life too seriously, and lived each day as if it were a bonus.

It was because of this philosophy of life that he had never taken any woman seriously. But now all that had changed. Rebecca had changed it. A measure of how seriously he was taking Rebecca was the fact that he had wired money ahead to Clarksville for the express purpose of buying a horse.

Gladney was going to learn to ride. No matter if he broke both legs and both arms, he was going to learn!

"I wired ahead that we would be on this boat," Steven explained to Hawk and Rebecca, as they stood with several other passengers on the deck as the packet approached the dock in Louisville. "If they got my telegram, there should be someone here to meet us."

"Your father?" Rebecca asked.

He laughed. "No, I hardly think so. My father will be too busy with his bourbon."

"Oh," Rebecca said in a subdued voice. "You mean he drinks?"

"Yes, of course, he . . . Oh, wait a minute. Do you mean is he a toper?"

She said hesitantly, "Well . . . yes."

Steven laughed again. "No, my dear Rebecca. He *makes* bourbon. My father owns the Kentucky Home Bourbon Distillery."

"Kentucky Home? That's a very large company, isn't it?" Hawk said. "I've seen that brand all over."

"It's the second largest distillery in America." Steven smiled gently. "Now, Rebecca, can you understand what I meant when I said that I consider it ironic that I can't buy a drink in many places? I can sell it to *them*, but they can't sell it to *me*."

"Why, Steven, you must be rich!" Rebecca said in sudden realization.

"Rich? Yes, I suppose I am. At least my father is. I've never really given it that much thought. You see, I'm gone from home most of the time, following the fairs and the racing circuit, and I live on just what I earn. I only come home when there's a long period between races, and I never ask Father for money. It's a point of pride with me."

There was a slight bump as the packet boat captain pegged the boat to the dock, then blew his whistle. The shrill note of the whistle made Rebecca cover her ears with her hands. A white cloud of steam drifted across the decks, then broke up.

"There," Steven said, pointing. "There's Jims, come to pick us up now."

Rebecca looked in the direction indicated and saw a beautiful, highly polished phaeton standing by the curb of the brick street that ran down to the river's edge. It was being driven by a stately looking black man and pulled by a team of black horses.

"Oh, how lovely!" she cried.

"Not as fast as a sulky, perhaps, but a lot more comfortable," Steven said in a teasing voice. "Come on, I'll check if our horses and luggage are being attended to. I'm anxious to show you Oak Valley."

He hurried them down the gangplank and over to the phaeton. The driver smiled broadly when he saw Steven, and he hopped down from the driver's seat to embrace him. Steven quickly introduced Hawk and Rebecca.

"Your daddy, Mister Steven, say the first thing I'm to do is to give you and your friends a mint julep, to welcome you-all to home," the driver said. He walked around to the back of the carriage and opened the lid of a trunk. "I got all the fixings right here."

And true to his words, inside the trunk there was crushed ice, bourbon, water, sugar, mint, and three silver cups.

"Jims has been with the family as long as I can remember, and he's like a second father to me," Steven said in a low voice.

"I was trying to explain once to my British friends what a mint julep is," Hawk said. "But though I had the exact recipe in mind, I never was quite able to put a good one together."

"Jims makes the best I've ever tasted," Steven said. "Jims, tell Mr. Hawkins your secret."

"I be glad to tell him, but that don't mean he's gonna know what to do."

"Tell him anyway," Steven said, grinning.

"Well, suh, you start off with the mint leaves. They has to be fresh and tender, you see. Then you have to press them leaves against a goblet made out of coin-

154

silver, usin' the back of a silver spoon. But you'll only bruise the mint leaves gently now." He demonstrated the procedure as he talked.

Rebecca watched Jim's demonstration, and marveled at the graceful manner in which he handled the mint leaves and the silver.

"Now," Jims went on. "Once you got the leaves bruised real gentle-like, you take them real careful out of the goblet, leavin' just the juice in. Next, you put in the cracked ice, but no more'n half full. Now, you take the finest mellow bourbon you can find," he smiled broadly at Steven and held up a bottle of Kentucky Home, "and this here is the finest, aged in oaken barrels just like it's supposed to be, and you pour just a jigger in, allowin' it to slide real slow down through the ice."

Now Jims had the three silver goblets prepared. He continued with his instructions. "Next, into another, bigger crystal goblet, you got to mix granulated sugar, real slow, into cooled limestone water. You got to make a silvery mixture, as smooth as the rarest oil from old Egypt, and then you pour that on top of the ice.

Jims poured the liquid into the goblets, very carefully measuring each portion. As he did so, beads of moisture gathered on the burnished exteriors of the silver goblets. Next, he garnished the brim of each goblet with choice sprigs of mint.

"Now, young miss, you first," Jims said, handing the silver cup to Rebecca with a slight nod.

Rebecca took it, relishing the goblet's coolness and savoring the bourbony-mint odor of the liquid. Her grandfather was next, and then Steven.

"What shall we drink to?" Steven asked.

"How about drinking to fast tracks?" Rebecca suggested.

"An excellent toast," Steven agreed. He held his cup out, and the other two clicked their goblets against his.

"To fast tracks," Steven intoned.

"Ummm, absolutely delicious," Rebecca announced, after taking her first sip. "Jims, Steven is right. You *do* make the best mint julep I've ever tasted."

"I'll second that," Hawk said.

"Do you-all know where the first mint julep came from?" Jims asked, beaming from their praise.

"No, but I'd like to know," Rebecca responded. "Where did it come from?"

"It come from a river boatman," Jims said. "He left the river to go lookin' for some spring water to mix with his bourbon, and he found some fresh mint growin' alongside this spring. So, he thinks to himself, 'I do believe I try that mint and see what it taste like with the bourbon.' So, he try it, and he like it, and that's where mint julep come from."

"What a wonderful story!" Rebecca said, clapping her hands together, knowing it was the reaction Jims expected. But whether a myth or not, it was an interesting little story.

"Has anyone come to see to our things?" Steven asked. "And to our horses? Along with Bright Morn, the Hawkinses have two horses on board the packet."

"Yes, indeed, it's all took care of," Jims said. "You-all just climb into the carriage and enjoy your mint juleps, whilst I give you a nice, easy ride out to Oak Valley."

It was a pleasant, almost giddy feeling to be sipping a mint julep and riding in such luxurious style. Rebecca leaned back to enjoy it fully. The way to Oak Valley took them out Grand Boulevard, and Steven pointed out the Louisville Jockey Clubhouse. Next to the clubhouse was a new grandstand, with a spire at each end and in front a new racetrack.

"I suppose you know what that is, Hawk," he said.

"You're damn right I do," Hawk said. "That's where the first Kentucky Derby is going to be run."

"Grandfather is a member of the Association," Rebecca said with some pride.

"Of course you are, Hawk!" Steven said, slapping his forehead. "I'm sorry. I feel foolish, pointing it out to you of all people!"

"Don't feel foolish, boy," Hawk said. "It's dandy seeing it again."

There were two horses working out on the track, and Steven asked Jims to stop the carriage for a moment so they could watch. The horses were running nearly neck to neck; one was a small chestnut, the other a larger black. The black was clearly the stronger horse, and gradually began pulling in front, so that by the time they crossed the finish line, the black was nearly two lengths in front of the chestnut.

"Do you know those two horses?" Hawk asked.

"Oh, yes. They both belong to McGrath. The black is Chesapeake and the chestnut is Aristides."

"Chesapeake looks like a dandy horse," Hawk said, with a tinge of envy in his voice.

"Most people say he will win the Kentucky Derby."

"I imagine there are a few who might have something to say about that," Hawk said dourly.

"I'm sure there are." Steven motioned for Jims to continue on. "I'm hoping Bright Morn figures in it. And I'm sure you have the same thoughts about Black Prince."

"Black Prince?" Hawk said, scowling. "Now what gave you the notion I have any intention of running Black Prince in the Derby?"

"Why, I . . ." A quick glance at Rebecca showed him the look of concern on her face, and he remembered belatedly that he had promised not to give away

157

her secret. Somewhat lamely, he said, "I suppose I just assumed. Being the fine horse that he is, I was sure you'd be racing him in the Derby."

"It never pays to assume anything, boy," Hawk growled. He relaxed a trifle. "But I reckon you're right. It's just that I haven't made the decision to enter him just yet." He leaned forward suddenly, squinting. "I see that your daddy has changed the color of the barn."

Rebecca hadn't realized that they were nearing the horse farm. Having never seen Oak Valley, she gazed about with interest.

"You've been here before?" Steven asked in surprise.

"Yes," Hawk said, without elaborating. He looked around the farm, at the neatly kept buildings, well-constructed stone fence, good roads, and fields of green grass. "I'm glad your father bought it, Steven. This is the way Oak Valley was meant to be."

"There's the house," Steven said. He pointed to a large, two-story brick house, rising majestically from the top of a hill. A long, curving, chipped marble driveway led up to it, and the carriage turned onto it from the main road.

"Steven! Oh, Steven, you're back!" a young woman screamed, rushing out to meet the carriage. She came to an abrupt stop when she saw Steven's bandages. "Oh, you're hurt!"

"Nothing to it, just a scratch or two," Steven said, and leaped lightly out of the carriage to show that the injuries weren't severe, though Rebecca could see in his face, hidden from the girl, a grimace of pain. He turned around and gave the girl an affectionate hug, and Rebecca felt a twinge of jealousy.

The girl was about Rebecca's age, with soft ringlets of brown hair and flashing blue eyes. She was a very pretty young lady.

158

Rebecca and Hawk both disembarked from the carriage, and they stood awkwardly by while Steven and the young woman embraced. Then the girl saw Rebecca, as if noticing her for the first time, and she stepped back from Steven and looked at him questioningly.

"Jean," Steven said, "I want you to meet Rebecca Hawkins, and her grandfather, Henry Hawkins. Rebecca, Hawk, this is my sister, Jean."

The unexpected jealousy burning in Rebecca subsided immediately and she felt ashamed of it. Now she smiled graciously at Jean Lightfoot.

"Jean, how nice to meet you," she said warmly.

"Steven, how pretty she is!" Jean said enthusiastically. "And how nice it is that you brought house guests home with you. Especially now. Steven, you don't know it yet, but I have the most wonderful news! I'm getting married, right here next week!"

"Now, that is wonderful news!" He leaned forward to kiss her on the cheek.

"Rebecca," Jean said, looking past her brother, "I do hope you will stay for the wedding, and be one of my maids of honor!"

"I'm afraid we can't do that," Hawk said. "We have to get on to Cincinnati."

"But couldn't you postpone it?" Jean asked.

"I'm afraid not," Hawk said.

"Who is the lucky man, as if I didn't know?" Steven asked.

"Paul, of course," Jean said. She looked at Rebecca again. "I do hope you and your grandfather will at least be able to take supper with us. I want you to meet my fiancé. His name is Paul Stanford, and he lives on the Stanford farm, which is right next to ours."

"Who did you say?" Rebecca asked in disbelief, as

a grunt of astonishment came from Hawk. She caught his hand and equeezed it.

"Paul Stanford."

"He's the grandson of Thomas Stanford," Steven was saying. "He is the man who owned Oak Valley before my father bought it."

"Yes, I . . . I know," Rebecca said quietly. She looked at her grandfather. His face had lost color, and he suddenly looked older.

"Grandfather," she asked anxiously, "are you all right?"

"I'm fine, girl." He was frowning at Steven. "There's something you should know, Steven, about the Stanfords."

"Paul?" Jean asked apprehensively. "Is something wrong with Paul?"

Hawk smiled at her. "Nothing to fret about, girl," he said. "Put your mind at ease. But Steven, I haven't told you everything I know about this place. You asked if I had been here before, and the answer is yes. I used to be the foreman here, before Stanford bought it. He bought Oak Valley because his daughter was in love with my son. He was trying to break them up. But he didn't do it. They got married anyway, and they had a child. A girl."

Steven sucked in his breath, and stared at Rebecca in dawning comprehension.

"Yes," Hawk went on. "Becky is that child. It would appear that she is this Paul's first cousin."

Jean laughed in delight. "But that's wonderful! Then we will soon be kin. Oh, and you can tell me all about Paul, Rebecca! About when he was a little boy. It will be wonderful to hear stories about him."

"I'm afraid I can tell you nothing at all about him," Rebecca said slowly. "You see, I've never met him.

More than that, I didn't even know he existed until this minute."

"You've never met your own cousin?" Jean asked incredulously.

"I'm afraid not," Rebecca replied. "Nor my Grandfather Stanford, either."

"Oh, but you should!" Jean said. "You must! Mr. Stanford is really a very nice man," she laughed charmingly. "He doesn't understand why we turned this place into a thoroughbred farm, but since my father makes whiskey, he believes he can't be all bad. Besides, they say he's mellowed some in his old age."

"If he's mellow now, I would hate to have been around him when he was young," Steven said.

"Well, he *is* mellow now," Jean said stoutly.

"Are you sure that you're not seeing him through a rosy glow, now that you're going to be related to the old curmudgeon?"

"Hush now, Steven!" Jean's color rose. She said to Rebecca, "Are you really serious? You've never met him?"

"No, I never have. Like Grandfather said, my mother ran off to get married, and he disowned her."

"Then you should stay one more day at least," Jean insisted. "For he and Paul's folks are coming over tomorrow night."

"No, I . . . I don't think that I care to," Rebecca said.

"I think you should," Hawk said suddenly.

"What?" Rebecca stepped back in surprise. "Grandfather, do you realize what you are saying?"

"I know, girl, and I know the things I've said before." He put his hand affectionately on her shoulder. "Becky, I have loved you from the moment I first slapped eyes upon you. It was as natural as rain, because you were my granddaughter. But I've felt guilty about it too, all these years, because I knew that I had no right to keep you all to myself."

"You had every right, Grandfather," she said spiritedly. "Mother chose you, and, after all, she was Grandfather Stanford's daughter. *He* disowned her, not the other way around!"

"Still, it's not right," Hawk said stubbornly. "The bad feeling was between your mother and her father, and you had nothing to do with it. You have a right to meet your maternal grandfather, and he has a right to meet you." Hawk glanced over at Steven. "Steven, you invited us to stay at Oak Valley. Suppose I go on to Cincinnati alone? Would it be all right to leave Becky here with you? I could meet her later in Lexington, for the Lexington Stakes. After all, I don't really need her to buy a new sulky."

"Would it be all right? It would be more than all right!" Steven said fervently. "I can't think of anything that would make me happier!"

"Good, it's settled then. That's the way we'll do it."

"Grandfather, can we talk alone for a few minutes?" Rebecca said.

He looked over at her, and sighed. In a gentle voice he said, "Of course, Becky. Will you excuse us for a minute?"

Motioning for Rebecca to follow, he walked toward a large, spreading oak tree near the corner of the house.

"Grandfather, I don't think this is the right thing for me to do," she said, once they were out of hearing distance of the others.

"It is right, girl," Hawk said firmly. His face wore a look of melancholy. "The only thing wrong with it is that it should have happened long since. I should have brought you here to meet your mother's father when we first came back to the States. I was just being selfish, that's all. But it's always made me feel guilty, and I haven't always thought too highly of myself because of it. Now it's time to put things right. How do you think Stanford would feel if he learns you were here and ran off without seeing him?"

"I don't much care how he feels!"

"Yes, you do, Becky," he said softly. "I know you better than that."

"If I meet him, I might hate him!"

"Hate him? Now why would you do that?"

"For what he did to Mother."

"Child, that was a long time ago, and that was between your mother and him. There are two sides to every story, you know. After all, your mother was just as stubborn and headstrong as he was, or she would have gone to him when she got sick. Now, I won't allow you to carry this any further without at least seeing him, now that the opportunity has come. Think about it now. If you don't, you may come to regret it in the future. Don't forget, he's old now, older than me by a number of years."

Rebecca looked deep into her grandfather's eyes and glimpsed the pain he was going through. Her heart went out to him. She threw her arms around him, and was embraced by him in turn.

"I love you, Grandfather," she said, deeply moved. "I loved my mother and my father, too, but I haven't missed them so much as I might have. You've been the family that I might have missed."

"Bless you, girl, for saying so," Hawk said.

When they separated, both had tears in their eyes. Rebecca laughed shakily. "Aren't we a fine pair now?" she said. She looked toward the house.

"Wait," Hawk said. "Let's wait a spell before we walk back. I've no wish for Steven or the others to see me with tears in my eyes. It wouldn't be manly."

163

"I find them very manly," she said, and kissed her grandfather on each eyelid, tasting the salt of his tears and feeling a lump in her throat as she thought of how much she adored him. "But if you want to wait a little, we'll wait."

"Mr. Hawkins," a man's voice called. They looked toward the house to see a man in his late fifties striding toward them. He was an older, somewhat heavier version of Steven, though still, Rebecca noticed, retaining Steven's good looks.

He approached them with a smile and an extended hand. "I'd like to welcome you to Oak Valley. Or, since my son just told me that you were once foreman here, perhaps I should say welcome back. Anyway, come in and make yourself at home. My home is yours." He grinned. "I'll pour you a tot of Kentucky Home, sir, the finest whiskey man ever made."

"That sounds dandy to me. Come, Becky," Hawk said.

Rebecca held back for a moment, looking up the rise at the big house, and then around the farm. She knew that she was seeing the same sight her mother had seen more than twenty years ago, and somehow she felt as if her mother was with her now. Then a cloud passed under the sun, plunging her into shadow, and she shivered, hugging herself.

"Becky?"

"I'm coming, Grandfather."

Chapter Nine

It must be one o'clock in the morning, Rebecca thought, and she was still unable to get to sleep. Perhaps it was the idea of being in a house which had played an important part in the lives of her father and mother. Perhaps it was the thought of meeting her grandfather Stanford for the first time. Perhaps it was just being on this beautiful farm in such close proximity to Steven. But for whatever reason she tossed restlessly for hours after retiring.

The rest of the house was very quiet, and Rebecca was confident that everyone else had gone to sleep hours ago. She wished that she could be as fortunate. She sighed, fluffed up her pillow, tried to find a more comfortable position, and closed her eyes.

No good. Within a moment, the position was uncomfortable again, and the pillow had mysteriously grown hard. She sighed, fluffed the pillow once more, and repositioned herself. But still sleep would not come.

Finally she sat up. A bar of soft moonlight streamed in through the window, painting dappled shadows on the wall. Rebecca got out of bed and walked over to the window, opened the curtains and looked outside.

The dappled shadow came from a large magnolia tree which stood just outside the window. Its dark, shining leaves moved softly in the gentle night breeze, catching the moonbeams in scattered bursts of silver. The moon was so bright that Rebecca could see for miles, far across the rolling hills of Oak Valley farm. The landscape was delineated in shades of silver and black. She felt that she had never seen anything quite so beautiful.

On impulse, she pulled a wrapper around her; then, barefooted, she stepped cautiously out of the room. The hall was thickly carpeted, and she could feel the carpet's rich texture beneath her feet as she walked silently down the length of the corridor. As she passed the various bedroom doors, she could hear snoring or soft, even breathing, and she was certain that she was the only one awake.

The house was dark, but a splash of moonlight coming in through the glass door at the foot of the stairs acted as a beacon to guide her. She moved slowly and silently down the stairs.

As she reached the landing, she was startled by a sudden clicking noise, followed by a whirring sound. Rebecca froze as she felt her hair prickle, and she grabbed at the bannister in sudden, numbing fear.

Dong!

Rebecca relaxed with a soft laugh. It was only the hall clock, which proved her right about the hour.

By the time she was at the bottom of the stairs, the moonlight was bright enough for her to be able to see quite easily. She opened the front door without difficulty; then, making certain that she wasn't locking it behind her, she stepped through it and closed it after her.

She crossed the veranda and after a moment's hesitation went down the steps. The grass felt soft and cool, and she raced across it like a child, her hair, wrapper, and nightgown streaming out behind her.

Finally, out of breath, she reached the other side of the grass, and collapsed on the low stone fence.

The gentle breeze was still blowing, and it felt good as it moved through her hair and touched her skin. The breeze carried with it the aromatic perfume of magnolia, honeysuckle, and sweet shrubs.

Rebecca became aware of a bubbling, splashing sound, and she got up to walk toward it, to discover a swift-flowing brook. Beside the brook there was a small glade of grass and moss, sheltered by a rock overhang.

Rebecca felt drawn to it, and she walked over to sit on the grass and gaze up at the moon. She pulled her knees up, and as she did so her wrapper and gown fell back to expose her legs. They shone white in the silver light. She wrapped her arms around her legs and rested her chin on her knees. The position was very comfortable, and the breeze felt marvelous. She smiled to herself, because she knew that the pose was probably unladylike, yet she didn't care. In fact, she had a strong, inexplicable notion to take off all her clothes. It was a wicked thought, but one which, strangely, caused a rush of pleasure through her.

"It *is* a beautiful night, isn't it?"

Rebecca gasped as a man's voice broke into her reverie, shattering her mood and making her suddenly aware of her attire. She glanced around and saw Steven standing behind her. He was smoking a cigar, and the ash on the end glowed red as he took a puff.

"I'm sorry," he said easily. "I didn't mean to frighten you."

"I'm not frightened," Rebecca retorted. "I was just startled, that's all."

She made no effort to cover her legs, or change her

position. She knew that she probably should, it was the proper thing to do, but she was enjoying the feeling of the breeze across her legs. Steven was the intruder, after all. And, though she knew it was really wicked of her, she was also enjoying the idea of Steven seeing her this way.

"I saw you running across the lawn," Steven was saying. "You looked so beautiful, so . . . so released from something, I couldn't resist coming out here."

"What were you doing up so late?"

He shrugged, blowing smoke. "I just couldn't sleep. That often happens to me when I come back after being away for a while."

"Nor could I." Rebecca sat unmoving for a moment, with her head resting on her knees. Then she spoke again. "Oak Valley is as beautiful as *Grandfather* told me it was."

"This place has a special meaning for you, doesn't it?" Steven asked. "Something that you haven't told me about?"

"Yes," she said in a low voice. "It is where my mother and father met and fell in love."

She told him the story then, quietly, but with deep feeling. She had heard it from her grandfather many times, and had thought of it often, although, she realized with surprise, this was the first time she had told it to anyone else. Yet it was a story that begged to be told, and in the telling, Rebecca was able to relive the story of the ill-fated lovers.

"That's a beautiful story, if a little sad," Steven said when she had finished. "I'm glad you're here to see Oak Valley. And I'm glad you shared the story with me, Rebecca."

"What about you, Steven?" Rebecca asked, head tilted to one side. "What is your story?"

"Nothing as dramatic as yours." He laughed quietly,

then held his hand out, indicating the farm. "You see it right here. I told you that my father made his money in whiskey. Buying this farm was little more than a whim to him, a sort of a sideline."

"And yet you ride in the races, instead of remaining here. Why is that?"

"Because it is something I love," he said. He butted his cigar, flipped it away, then came to sit on the ground beside her at a respectable distance. "Besides, it may be that I'm rebelling."

"Rebelling against what? Everything here is so lovely, you have so much . . . What could you possibly be rebelling against?"

"*A-yuh-wi-wa- Gi-Ga,*" he said.

She reared back. "What?"

"That's Cherokee for Indian blood," he explained. He looked at her and smiled a sweet, sad smile. "You said today that you have never seen your grandfather Stanford. Well, I too have a grandfather I've never seen. Nor have I ever seen my mother."

"How can that be? Did she die giving birth to you?"

"No," he said. "For all I know she may be alive today, somewhere."

"I don't understand."

"My father once tried a noble experiment," Steven said with a bitter twist in his voice. "He hired Indians to help with the corn distilling. After all, who knows more about corn than an Indian, isn't that right? There was a young Indian woman who caught my father's fancy and, as sometimes happens, she and my father fell in love. Or made love," he added. "In any event, the end result was the same. I came along. And when I was born this young Indian girl put me in a sack and left me on my father's doorstep. To put it bluntly, Rebecca, I am a bastard, and a half-Indian one at that."

169

She made a sound of sympathy. "But your father took you in, didn't he? I mean, obviously he did, and acknowledged you as his son."

"Yes," Steven agreed. "He took me, and acknowledged me as his own as soon as I was old enough to know about such things. And when he married my stepmother, Jean's mother, she treated me as if I were her own child as well. When she died, I felt her loss as keenly as I would have had she been my real mother."

"Then I don't understand, Steven. What is there to rebel against?"

"Just this," Steven said. "I have a white man's name, I was raised as a white man, and half the blood that flows in my veins is white man's blood. Yet my Cherokee mother, the woman I have never seen, has left her mark on me. No matter my background, no matter my education, no matter my father's wealth, what it all comes down to is this—I am a breed. I can't assume my rightful place in society, because as a half-breed I have no rightful place. Therefore, I rebel. I follow the fair, and there I'm only as good, or as bad, as my last race."

He fell silent, and Rebecca could think of nothing to say in reply.

After a moment he said, "As for my father accepting me as his son, I'm not so sure he would have if there was another son, if Jean had been a boy instead of a girl."

"I'm sorry, Steven," Rebecca said, deeply touched. She stared into the night and was silent for a moment. "I guess I'm not the only person with a difficult family relationship in my past."

Rebecca glanced into his eyes, and their gaze held for a long moment. Then Steven made an inarticulate sound deep in his throat, and moved close to her.

170

Hesitantly, he put his hand to her face, let his fingers linger for a moment, and then pulled her into his arms, pressing his lips against hers.

A tide of feeling, bewildering and frightening, swept over Rebecca. She had been kissed before, by Gladney, and she had experienced the quick flash of heat before. But those times there had always been in the back of her mind the awareness that nothing could happen, that she was safe. The first time had been on board the riverboat and the second time in the restaurant and both situations had been self-limiting.

But here she was alone. It was the middle of the night, they sat on the soft grass, the very air was scented with romance, and she was nearly undressed. It was a frightening situation and yet, more than fear, she experienced want, and more than caution, she knew desire, desire that seemed to grow with each passing second.

Steven kissed her with hot, sensuous lips. He bent her body backward until she felt the mattress of grass beneath her, and then his lips traveled from her mouth down along her throat to the first button that fastened her nightgown about her neck. Rebecca found herself surrendering to him, allowing him to do with her what he wished. She seemed to have no will of her own, but was subservient to his will, bending to his bidding like a slender reed in a strong spring breeze.

His graceful hands and agile fingers quickly and easily opened the buttons that held her nightgown closed, and suddenly she felt cool air on her naked, fevered flesh. His hand moved across her skin, cupping her breast, now warm and vibrant. He tenderly stroked the nipple with his thumb; the nipple was already swollen, and straining to be loved.

Oh, yes, Rebecca thought hazily.

171

And she remembered, for a passing instant, the moment she had spent before the mirror in the hotel room in Cairo, fantasizing about this very thing. She had wondered then what it would feel like, and now, having it actually happen to her, she could almost hear her nerve endings singing with delight. Never had the sense of touch been so exquisite, the pain of wanting so sweet.

Yet she knew that this was wrong. She had no right to be doing this, no right to experience the pleasure of the moment as intensely as she was. She tried to utter a soft cry of protest, but the sound that emerged from her throat was not protest—it was ecstasy. All her feelings and emotions were trapped by his touch, and the sensations his touch was evoking. She had no thoughts which could be sustained for more than a second, could start no positive action to prevent what was happening; and a moment later, she discovered that even the questionable protection of the nightgown had been removed, leaving her completely naked. She was surprised because she was not aware of the moment the garment left her body, but she was thrilled, too, for the soft breeze caressed her bare thighs, making her all the more aware of her nakedness.

Steven stood up and began undressing slowly and deliberately before her wide, innocent, eager eyes. A moment later he too was nude, standing before her like a statue in the moonlight.

The sight of his smooth skin, rippling muscles, and obvious maleness aroused Rebecca to even greater heights of passion. He dropped to one knee, then placed a hand lightly on the inside of her thigh. Beside them the silver water splashed and sang, producing music to accompany them, from the tenor rush over the larger rocks to the soprano trill of the brook breaking into the white water over the polished stones.

"No," Rebecca said, making one last, ineffectual plea, as much to herself as to Steven. "Steven, no, this isn't right!"

"It is right, Rebecca, and you know it. You feel it as much as I do. What else can it be but right, when we both feel the way we do?" His voice deepened. "I've been thinking of this very moment since the instant I first saw you. You must have thought of it, you must have!"

"Well, yes, I admit that I . . ." She let her voice die away, realizing that her words were not merely an admission, but permission for him to proceed.

Steven didn't wait, but moved over her and then into her, and for the first time in her life, Rebecca was a woman being loved.

She felt his weight and breathed the male scent of him, tobacco and leather, bourbon and horseflesh. There was a small, stinging pain when he first began, but swiftly the pain left to be replaced by the overwhelming sensations which rushed through her body like liquid fire.

Gone now, as he thrust into her again and again, was all thought of right and wrong. Rebecca knew only the moment, and the pleasure of the moment, and she rose up against him, giving him all that was hers to give.

Then it started—a tiny, tingling sensation which began deep inside her, pinwheeling out, spinning faster and faster, until every part of her body was caught up in a whirlpool of pleasure. Her body was wound like the mainspring of a clock, tighter and tighter, until finally, in a burst of agony which turned miraculously into rapture, it attained the release and gratification it yearned for. There were a million tiny pins pricking her skin, and involuntary cries of pleasure poured from her throat. She felt as if she lost consciousness for just an instant, and lights sparkled before her eyes as her body gave its final convulsive spasm.

They lay together for several minutes afterward, while Rebecca floated with the pleasant sensations which stayed with her like the warmth that remains after a fire burns low.

Steven put his hand gently on her hip. She could feel the coolness of his palm as it lay across the sharpness of her hip bone and the soft yielding of her flesh. Somehow, that solitary move, even more than the pleasure they had just shared, seemed a possessive gesture. And in that moment, Rebecca felt as if she belonged to him.

It was late in the morning when Rebecca awoke the next day. She felt a small heavy ache in her loins, and instantly remembered what had transpired the night before. Though there was no one to see her, her cheeks flamed red with the memory, and quickly she pulled the bed covers up to her neck and lay there, bathed in the golden sunshine, trying to untangle the disjointed thoughts which flooded through her mind. She had lost her virginity in the hot darkness of the night before. She knew that she should feel shame, but instead she felt a still-lingering sense of pleasure; and a quick, flaring heat seared her body as she recalled the primitive passion that had swept over her during her moment of surender.

There was a quick knock on the door, and Rebecca heard Jean's voice call softly to her.

"I'm awake, Jean. Come in," she said.

The door opened and Jean swept in, vibrantly alive and smiling. "It's a lovely day outside," she said breathlessly. "It would be a shame if you missed most

174

of it by staying abed. I know it's rude of me to wake up a guest like this, but I didn't want you to miss it."

"No, it's my fault," Rebecca said. She sat up and stretched, yawning. "What time is it?"

"It's nearly noon."

"Noon!" Rebecca gasped. "Good heavens, of course I should be up! Grandfather, has he—?"

"He left hours ago," Jean said. "He said you needed a good rest, so he wouldn't disturb you, and told me to tell you goodbye for him."

"But I should have been up when he left," Rebecca said slowly. She felt a sudden sense of loss and desolation. Since that long-ago day in London, they had rarely been apart for more than a few hours at a time, and now she wouldn't see him for several days, perhaps a week.

"Would you like some breakfast?"

"No, Jean. Thank you, but I'll eat with everyone else when you have your dinner."

"Steven told me you were a good rider, Rebecca. So, if you've no objections, you and Steven and Paul and I are going riding today. I want to show you Oak Valley."

"Yes," Rebecca said, her enthusiasm kindling. "Yes, I would like that very much."

"Good! I'll see you downstairs shortly. Paul is already here. I told him about you, Rebecca. He is very anxious to meet you."

When Rebecca came down the stairs a half hour later, wearing a woman's riding habit, there were two men in the drawing room. They both rose to greet her. One was Steven and the other, she knew, must be her cousin, Paul Stanford. It felt strange to meet a kinsman of hers. Except for her mother, father, and grandfather, Rebecca had never seen another member of her family.

175

Paul was taller than Steven and nearly as dark, though his eyes were blue, where Steven's were brown. He had a full moustache, which he touched nervously with a fingernail as he was being introduced.

"I knew that you existed, of course," Paul said, "but I never really thought I'd ever have the pleasure of meeting you."

Rebecca studied him for a moment, then smiled in genuine pleasure. She held out her hand. "I'm just happy my period of isolation has come to an end."

Paul took her hand in both of his and smiled, more at ease with her now. It was a friendly smile, and Rebecca felt immediately drawn to him. Perhaps her grandfather was right. Perhaps it was time to end the feud begun by her mother and Grandfather Stanford. Besides, Paul certainly didn't have anything to do with that.

"You haven't forgotten me, have you, Rebecca?" Steven said in a teasing voice.

She looked quickly at Steven and felt a flush rise to her cheeks. She feared that anyone who looked at the two of them now would guess their secret. There was a gleam in Steven's eye.

Of what, she wondered. Of a secret shared? Of a desire for more dalliance? Of conquest? It was somewhat unnerving, and her glance jumped away, unable to hold his gaze.

Jean had just come in, and her glance darted from Rebecca's face to her brother's, and then back to Rebecca. Rebecca thought that she saw a look of comprehension cross the other girl's face but, thankfully, there appeared to be no hint of condemnation.

"Shall we go for our ride now?" Jean said, providing Rebecca with a way out of the situation.

"Yes, let's," she said hastily.

* * *

Paul and Jean were obviously in love, and as the four rode across the green valleys and through the shaded draws of the farm, they had eyes only for each other. They carried on conversations that made no sense whatsoever to Rebecca—a whispered word, a suggestive laugh, an eyebrow held just so, or lips pursed in a special way, and there would be complete understanding between them.

Rebecca wondered if this was the language of lovers, which she had heard so much about. Were two people who were in love so closely attuned to each other's thoughts and emotions that they didn't need conventional language to communicate? She was intrigued by it, and somewhat envious of them.

Another thought intruded into her mind. Were Paul and Jean lovers in the way that she and Steven had been last night? Had they lain together, had they experienced pleasure in each other's bodies?

There was another exchange between the two of them which meant nothing to Rebecca, but which must have been a challenge to a race, for Jean, laughing joyously, slapped the side of her horse and the animal sprang forward. Paul was right behind her, and very quickly the distance between the two young lovers and Rebecca and Steven widened, leaving Rebecca and Steven relatively alone.

They rode along together for several minutes in a companionable silence. It was a most pleasant day, and Rebecca was struck by the beauty of the place. Last night, under the silver moon, it had taken on the aura of a land of enchantment. Today, under the bright, golden light of the sunshine, it was less a land of enchantment and more a tangible example of what Rebecca really wanted. This was what the county fairs, the small stakes races, the travel, and the no-

177

madic existence were all about. It was truly her dream come to exciting life. How she would love to live out her life on a place like this!

As though reading her thoughts, Steven said, "What do you think of it?"

"It takes my breath away, it's so lovely," she said. "I don't think I can really put it into words."

"My father owns four other farms, you know."

"Like this one?" she said in astonishment.

"Oh, no," he said with a chuckle. "They are row crop farms, raising corn mostly. Did you know that before Kentucky became famous for its bourbon it was known for its grain crops? But my father discovered that shipping corn back east to market cost so much that it wasn't very profitable. Then, when someone got the idea of making whiskey from the corn, and shipping it that way, corn suddenly became more profitable. That was when Kentucky became a leading whiskey-manufacturing state. My grandfather was one of the first, and he passed it on to his son, and I suppose eventually it will be passed down to me."

"Why do you just suppose? Is there any doubt?"

Steven looked grave. With a sigh he said, "Not really, not insofar as my father is concerned. I know that he would prefer that I not travel around, entering the horse races. Yet he isn't that adamant about it. In fact, since he bought Oak Valley, he has become quite interested in racing. Did you know that he offered Hawk his old job back before he left this morning?"

"No, I didn't," Rebecca said, interested. "Of course, I overslept this morning, and Grandfather had already left. He really did offer him the job?"

"Yes, he did. He and your grandfather hit it off quite well. My father suddenly had the notion that with your grandfather as foreman and trainer, we could produce champion thoroughbreds here."

"I'm sure that Grandfather could," Rebecca said. "What did he say? Did he turn the offer down?"

"Not entirely. He left the door open. He said a lot depended on you."

"I see," Rebecca said slowly. "Although I'm not sure why he said that. Grandfather is his own man, and is quite capable of making up his own mind without any help from me."

"There's something else that definitely depends on you," Steven said boldly.

"What would that be?"

"My future."

Rebecca laughed. "How on earth could your future depend on me?"

"Because it does." He reached across and took the reins to her horse, stopping it, and reining his mount in beside hers. He turned in the saddle to look directly at her, and Rebecca could hear the leather of the saddle squeak as he did so.

"Because I want you to marry me," he said simply.

"You . . . you want me to marry you?" She was stunned by the totally unexpected proposal.

"Yes."

"Steven, I . . . I don't know what to say," she stammered. "I didn't expect this."

"You could say yes," he told her. "You *have* to say yes. Especially now."

"Why especially now?" she said, puzzled.

"Because of last night," he said diffidently. "After last night . . ."

She straightened up in the saddle. "You mean last night makes me a soiled woman?"

"No, no! Don't be ridiculous! I meant nothing of

179

the sort, and you know it. I just meant that . . . Well, last night was special for me, and unless I'm badly mistaken, you felt it, too. I felt something much deeper than the moment, and I know you did too."

"That's true, I did," she said in a low voice.

His voice quickened. "Then that means that you love me?"

"I—I don't know," she answered. She looked at him in confusion. "Steven, I'm just all mixed up right now, that's all. This is much too sudden. I need time to think about it."

"Good," he said, smiling broadly.

She stared. "Good?"

"Good that you didn't say no right off. At least now I can keep alive the hope that you will eventually say yes. And whatever I can do to convince you, I will do. But I don't want to wait forever, Rebecca. When will you decide?"

Rebecca put her hand on his. "Let me at least wait until after the Kentucky Derby. I'll tell you then, I promise."

"Why then?" he said in bewilderment. "What does the Derby have to do with us?"

"Because the dream my grandfather and I have had for so long is dependent upon the Kentucky Derby."

"Rebecca, don't you see?" he said intensely. "You won't need the Kentucky Derby now. You and your grandfather can come here to live. You told me this is everything you would ever want, right here. Why worry about the outcome of the Kentucky Derby?"

"It wouldn't be the same thing," she said quietly. "I want to know if Grandfather and I could have realized our dream on our own. Your way, we would never know. And I'm sure Grandfather feels the same." For a dangerous moment she thought of telling Steven that *she* was the mysterious Hawkins jockey, but it

180

wouldn't be fair to Hawk. Instead she said, "You think that I'm not tempted by what you offer?"

"Then say yes," he said with a laugh. "As Glad might say, faith and begorra, lass, 'tis good for the soul to yield to temptation once in a while."

Gladney! She hadn't thought of him in—how long? To conceal the conflict that Gladney's name set up within her, Rebecca said hastily, "No, I can't. It's too quick, Steven, too soon. I have to know that when I say yes, I mean it beyond a doubt. I mean, that I'm saying yes to *you,* not this farm, or because," she turned her face away, "because of last night."

"You *did* enjoy last night?"

"You know I did," she admitted. "So much that I can't help but feel sinful."

"Rebecca, there is nothing sinful about it, believe me. What took place between us was beautiful. And I'll not have the memory of it spoiled by your feeling guilty, do you understand?"

"I understand," she said meekly, her face still averted.

The drumming of hoofbeats brought her head around, and she saw Paul and Jean galloping back toward them. She took her hand from Steven's, though not with a quick, embarrassed motion as she might have done a few days ago.

After all, compared to what she and Steven had so recently shared, holding hands was innocent enough. And right. Especially if she was soon going to become Mrs. Steven Lightfoot!

Chapter Ten

As the blue hills of Oak Valley turned purple in the evening shadows, the guests began arriving. Phaetons, broughams, landaulets, and rockaways, luxurious and graceful carriages all, moved majestically along the tree-lined, curving drive. They deposited their occupants under a portico where uniformed black servants greeted the arrivals and escorted them into the house.

Music, provided by a formal chamber orchestra especially hired for the occasion, spilled out of the house and rolled across the wide expanse of lawn to welcome the arriving guests. But the music of the orchestra was nearly drowned out by chatter and laughter and the clink of glasses, as the partygoers got into the spirit of the occasion.

Inside the house the party ebbed and flowed with bursts of laughter. Steven Lightfoot stood near a large French door, watching the crowd under the pinpoints of light from the glistening candle chandeliers.

"Steven, why are you standing over here all alone?" Jean asked, walking up to him. "This is my official engagement party, and you've spoken to practically no one."

"Why hasn't Rebecca come down yet?" Steven asked anxiously.

"You mean she hasn't?" Jean glanced around the room.

"I certainly haven't seen her. Have you?"

"No, but I just assumed that you would have her off somewhere all by yourself."

"Well, I haven't seen her, and I'm getting a little worried," Steven said. "You don't suppose I could talk you into going upstairs and checking on her, do you?"

"Of course you can," his sister said fondly. "You know you've always been able to talk me into almost anything."

"It's just that, well, maybe she's too nervous about meeting a newly discovered grandfather. Anyway, she should be here, and I'm concerned."

Jean looked out over the throng, looking for Thomas Stanford. As she did so, she took idle note of the dozens of lovely young women in their butterfly-bright gowns and sparkling jewelry.

"I think I know the problem," she said with a frown. "It was stupid of me not to realize."

The sounds of the party reached Rebecca's ears in her room upstairs, reminding her that she had already delayed her appearance far too long. But she couldn't help it. She had a problem.

She had already taken her bath and fixed her hair, and now she stood by the bed, examining with a critical and frustrated eye her two best dresses—actually, her *only* two dresses. One was red and the other green, and neither of them would do for the party.

Clothes had never meant very much to Rebecca. She wore dresses only because as a woman it was expected of her. She much preferred the convenience of the riding breeches and shirts she wore when she was driving in a race. But here, in the elegant surroundings of Oak Valley, she realized for the first time the poverty of her wardrobe. In fact she was

184

seriously considering feigning some illness in order to avoid the embarrassment of appearing downstairs so shabbily dressed.

There was a light knock on the door.

"Yes?" she called out.

"It's me, Jean. May I come in for a minute, Rebecca?"

Rebecca stared at the dresses on the bed. She didn't want Jean to see how scanty her wardrobe was, so she drew the counterpane over them, then stood back, her chin up.

"Yes, Jean," she said. "Come in."

The door opened and Jean made her usual sweeping entrance. Over her arm she was carrying a golden silk gown, pinched in at the waist and flaring out into many tiers.

"Men don't seem to understand that a lady never travels with her best clothes," she said breezily. "I happened to notice that we were the same size, Rebecca, and I thought you might like to wear this." She held the dress in front of her and turned slowly.

"Oh, Jean!" Rebecca said, touched by the generous, understanding gesture. "You don't have to do this."

"I know I don't have to, but I want to." Jean smiled impishly. "After all, we are going to be inlaws, aren't we?"

Rebecca tensed. "Inlaws?"

"Yes. I'm marrying your cousin."

"Oh."

Jean laughed infectiously. "Don't worry, Rebecca. I'm not trying to push you into marrying my brother. I imagine he's taking care of that himself."

"He is," Rebecca admitted.

"I'm glad!" Jean said. "Are you going to marry him?"

"I don't know!"

"Do you love him?"

"I don't know that, either. How can I be sure of that? I've only known him a few days."

"I knew the instant I saw Paul Stanford," Jean said blithely. "I knew I was going to marry him, no matter what!"

Rebecca laughed. "What if he hadn't felt the same way?"

"It wouldn't have mattered. I would have convinced him in the end."

"There's that much of Steven in you, anyway," Rebecca muttered. At Jean's questioning look, she shook her head and said ruefully, "I'm sorry, Jean. I guess I'm not giving you very good answers, am I?"

"Yes, you are, Rebecca." She put her hand lightly on Rebecca's arm. "It would be all too easy for a girl to be so swept up that she might make a rash decision. There have been times I thought I might be rushing into something, but the more I know Paul, the more certain I am that we are right for each other. But it's good you're keeping a level head. Whatever you decide will be fine with me. We'll always be friends. Won't we?"

"I certainly hope so."

Jean smiled brilliantly. "And we will still be kin. Now, there is a selection of jewelry in that box on the dresser over there. Wear this dress and pick out jewelry to match, so you'll be absolutely beautiful. I want everyone to see how lovely you really are. But I don't mind telling you now that if Paul wasn't your cousin, I wouldn't dare allow you to come down looking so beautiful, for I would turn absolutely green with jealousy!"

"Jean, I don't know what to say," Rebecca gestured helplessly. "I've never had a friend like you. Her life had been centered around the racing circuit for so

186

long that there had been no opportunity to make friends.

"You don't need to say anything," Jean said. "Just come down to my party and enjoy yourself."

A short time later, Rebecca stood nervously at the top of the stars looking down. She had never seen so many people at a private party before. The ballroom, which was visible from the top landing, was a kaleidoscope of color and texture. And she had never seen so many beautiful gowns! She had the sinking feeling that people would guess that she was wearing a borrowed dress.

Over in a corner, she saw Steven talking to a distinguished-looking gentleman with snow-white hair and a goatee to match. Rebecca sucked in her breath and held onto the bannister for a moment. Something told her that the man with the goatee was her newly discovered grandfather. Finally, she squared her shoulders and walked slowly down the stairs, descending into the milling throng as a bather into water.

She glided gracefully through the partygoers until she was just a few feet away from Steven and the man with the goatee. She said softly, "Steven?"

Steven looked around at her, and the expression on his face sent a quick thrill through her. She had examined herself critically in the mirror before coming down, inwardly pleased with what she saw, for this elegant dress of Jean's brought out her beauty. Now the expression on Steven's face confirmed that.

"Rebecca, my God!" he exclaimed. "I knew that you were beautiful, but I had no idea how ravishing!" His voice was hushed with awe.

"Then you . . . you are Rebecca Hawkins," the white-haired man said. His voice was tight with emotion, and he seemed to have difficulty speaking.

Rebecca studied him closely. Yes, she could see the resemblance to her mother, especially the eyes. And those eyes, she noticed, were suddenly moist with tears.

"Dear God, girl, can you ever find it in your heart to forgive a stupid old man?" he asked in a choked voice.

"Grandfather!" Rebecca said, all reservations swept away.

She threw out her arms and ran to him. She felt his arms go around her, and when he pulled her to his chest she could feel the beating of his heart. "Please, Grandfather, don't ask me to forgive you. It is I who should have come to you. I'm sorry, I'm so terribly sorry!"

"At last," Thomas Stanford said. "I've seen my baby girl's daughter at last! I was afraid I would die without ever seeing you!"

"I'll see you as often as possible now, Grandfather, I promise you," Rebecca said fervently.

Finally, after a long embrace, Stanford let her go and stepped back to look at her. He managed a smile, though his eyes were still moist. "Oh, yes," he said. "You were right, Steven. You *are* beautiful, Rebecca. If I may say so, just like your mother."

Uniformed servants began circulating through the crowd at that moment, ringing tiny bells and calling the guests to the banquet table. Rebecca, escorted by Steven on one side and her new grandfather on the other, started into the dining room. There were tables set up all through the house, but the guests of honor were seated at the dining room table.

The meal was the finest example of Kentucky gourmet banquets. There was chicken soup with rice, fried Ohio River catfish, bacon, cabbage, beans, barbecued lamb, roast duck, applesauce, roast turkey, cranberry sauce, roast beef, broiled squirrel, leg of bear, baked opossum, sweet potatoes, roasted ears of corn, hominy, boiled potatoes, stewed tomatoes, hot cakes, corn dodgers, and a large assortment of beverages, including Kentucky Home bourbon. But the most popular dish was clearly burgoo.

Rebecca had tasted burgoo a few times, but never had she eaten any as delicious as this. Burgoo was a rich stew, made from beef, lamb, pork, chicken, beans, onions, potatoes, apples, peppers, and a generous portion of cayenne. It was a Kentucky tradition, and the recipes for it were carefully guarded secrets. Rebecca learned, not to her surprise, that this particular burgoo had been prepared by Jims, who had made the mint julep.

The subject of conversation at the table eventually turned to racing, and that was understandable, since two of the honored guests were Colonel M. Lewis Clark and H. P. McGrath, founding members of the Louisville Jockey Club and instrumental in organizing the Kentucky Derby.

"It is only right that Kentucky resume its rightful place as the queen of American thoroughbred racing," Clark was saying. "After all, the first circular track west of the Cumberland was in Kentucky."

"Where was that, sir?" one of the guests asked.

"It was at Crab Orchard," Clark explained. "Close to one hundred years ago, Colonel William Whitlet laid out a course. Unfortunately, he was a man ahead of his time, for racing fell on hard times after that and his track was closed."

"But there are more races now than there have ever been," another guest said. "Every little fair today seems to have one."

"That's my point," Clark said. "And as long as racing stays in the realm of fairs and small race meets, the sport will never attain the prominence it has gained in Great Britain." He glanced over at Rebecca and smiled. "But you don't have to take my word for that. I'm not the only one at this table who was thrilled by the Lord's Derby. You saw it too, didn't you, my dear?"

"Yes," Rebecca said, nodding.

"Then I take it you will agree with me that there is no comparison between the sport as we practice it here today, and the way it is practiced in England."

"Racing is much more grand in England, I can't deny that."

"And she should know, as her grandfather—" Clark looked at Thomas Stanford with an apologetic smile. "Pardon me, Mr. Stanford, I mean her *other* grandfather, was a well-known jockey in England. But now, with the Kentucky Derby in our own country, hopefully we'll have a race which is just as glorious, right here in America."

"And I shall participate in that race," McGrath said.

"*You* are going to ride?" someone asked incredulously, and there was general laughter, for H. P. McGrath was a man of considerable girth.

"No, no, of course not," McGrath said, laughing along with the others. "No, I have two jockeys, a colored boy by the name of Oliver Lewis, who'll be riding Aristides, and a white man, Joe Henry, on Chesapeake. Chesapeake is the better horse, but it won't hurt any to have two horses entered. It'll improve my chances of winning by a great deal."

"Chesapeake is a fine horse," Rebecca said. "I watched him run yesterday."

"Will Hawk be entering Black Prince?" Clark asked.

"I don't know for certain," she said cautiously. "We certainly hope to enter him."

"I can tell you that Bright Morn will be entered,"

Steven said. "And I understand that Oscar Stull intends to enter one of his horses, Bold Diablo."

"Oscar Stull," Thomas Stanford said with a distasteful curl of his lip. "Gentlemen, your operation would be greatly enhanced if you could ban that scoundrel from entering."

"I heartily agree," Clark said. "But there seems to me little we can do about him at this point. We have managed to prevent Stull from having any influence in the organization, but I fear it will not be possible to bar him from participating in the Derby, if he meets all the requirements and pays the fees."

"Nonetheless, he is a man without scruples," Stanford said.

"What about you, Mr. Stanford? You've not attended the races up until now," McGrath said. "Will you be there on Derby day?"

"Yes," Stanford said, looking over at his granddaughter and smiling. "I've been an old fool long enough. It is high time I started making amends for mistakes made in the past."

After dinner the table was cleared away and moved back to make room for those who wished to dance. Steven asked Rebecca for the first dance and she readily agreed.

"Have you given any thought to my proposal?" he asked.

"Steven, I told you! I'll give you an answer after the Derby," she said with a frown.

"I know you did, but I invoked special magic tonight, and I hoped that it was working," Steven said with a mischievous grin.

"Special magic?"

"Yes. It's an old Kentucky custom. I held an apple under my armpit until it was warm, then I ate it. That is supposed to give me special powers over you."

"I'm afraid it didn't work." She laughed at his downcast expression. "And what other magic tricks do you know?"

"I don't know any others. I wouldn't have known that one if Jean hadn't told me. She believes in all of them. I hope you don't disappoint me on this one." He added hopefully, "Maybe it just hasn't had time to work yet."

"We shall see," Rebecca said.

A short while later, during a break in the dancing, Jean came up to Rebecca carrying a small silk bag suspended from a gold cord. "Wear this," she said.

Rebecca looked at the bag with suspicion. "What is it?"

"It's the tomato seeds from tonight's dinner."

"What!"

"Wear it. Tomato seeds from a wedding or an engagement dinner will help you to attract the man you love."

Rebecca dissolved into laughter. "You mean the way the apple helped Steven?"

"He told you about that?"

"He did."

"The rat!" Jean peered at her anxiously. "But did it work?"

"Not so far as I can tell." Rebecca laughed again. "I don't know, Jean. I do know one thing. I don't need to attract another suitor right now. I have one too many as it is. You see, there's not only Steven, there's another man to consider. His name is Gladney Halloran."

"Oh," Jean said disappointedly. "So your real problem then is in deciding which of the two is right for you."

"Well, I didn't really realize that I had a problem, but I suppose you could put it that way."

Jean smiled knowingly. "I know how to take care of that as well."

"All right, how? Not that I believe any of this for a minute, you understand!"

"But it works, Rebecca, believe me. Do you know how I knew Paul was the man for me?"

"How?"

"By having a backward supper."

"A *what?*"

"A backward supper," Jean explained. "You get several girls together, who are dear friends, and you fix a supper. It is a very special supper, and no one is allowed to say anything while it is being prepared. Also, the whole meal is cooked backwards. You not only walk backwards, you mix the ingredients backwards, you do everything backwards. Then you'll get a sign that will tell you. When I was having my backward supper, Paul's carriage was passing by outside on the main road, and the axle broke. He had to stop here to repair it. Now, wouldn't you call that a sign?"

"Honestly, Jean!" Rebecca was laughing helplessly. "Well, I certainly don't intend to do anything as elaborate as preparing a backward supper, just to find out which of the two is for me!"

"You don't have to," Jean said. "There are other ways. For instance, tonight before you go to bed, all you have to do is swallow a thimbleful of salt. Then you are sure to dream of your intended."

Still amused, Rebecca said, "What if I dream of the other one, not Steven? Wouldn't you be disappointed?"

"Oh, I'm sure it would be Steven," Jean said confidently. "But if it isn't Steven, then perhaps it shouldn't be. Don't you see? What I want most of all, Rebecca, is for *you* to be happy. Do say you will take some salt tonight. Please?"

"You're sweet, Jean, but I just don't believe any of this!"

"Please, Rebecca, for me?" Jean pleaded. "Just try it. What harm can it do?"

"Oh, very well," Rebecca said, weary of the discussion. "I'll try it. But it would be my luck to dream of someone like Oscar Stull." She shivered. "And that wouldn't be a dream; that would be a nightmare!"

The dancing began again, and Rebecca promptly forgot her promise to Jean. She was claimed, not by Steven, but by one of the other young men present. That young man was followed by another, and still another, until Rebecca lost count. Never, in her whole life, had she enjoyed such a delightful time. She was sorry when, shortly after midnight, the party finally broke up.

She went to bed with visions of the party still dancing in her head. She was almost too excited to sleep, and she couldn't get the melody of the last song out of her mind. In bed, she turned over once, and noticed a thimble sitting on the dresser. She was sure it had been placed there by Jean after their talk. Rebecca laughed to herself.

"All right, Jean, you win," she said under her breath.

She got out of bed and padded barefoot across the room to pick up the salt-filled thimble. She looked at it for a second, then as if it were a dose of bitter medicine, she put the thimble to her mouth and swallowed with a toss of her head.

She coughed and nearly gagged. Quickly she poured herself a glass of water from the pitcher that stood on the dresser.

A flicker of red light passed across the mirror, and she looked around in alarm, wondering where it had come from. She heard a horse whinny. It was a soft whinny, as if the animal were merely curious. Then

194

she heard another whinny, this one shrill and laced with fear.

Rebecca ran to the window and jerked the curtains aside to look out. Her glance went to the barn, and she saw a soft, flickering, orange glow. The barn was on fire!

Her heart climbed up into her throat. Paddy Boy, Black Prince, and almost a dozen other valuable horses were in that barn, she knew, including Steven's horse, Bright Morn.

"The barn is on fire!" she screamed out the window.

Without waiting for a response or taking time to put a wrapper on over her nightgown, she raced out of the room, down the stairs, and out into the yard, shouting the alarm over and over.

The fire was growing minute by minute. As she headed toward the barn at a dead run, she heard Steven's voice calling. Without slackening her pace, she looked back and saw him leaning out an upstairs window.

"Rebecca! No, don't go in there alone! The horses will be terrified, you won't be able to handle them alone!"

"I've got to get them out," she called back over her shoulder, racing on.

"Wait, wait for me!" Steven shouted frantically. "I'm coming right down!"

There were other shouts from the house now, but as yet Rebecca was the only one outside. She feared that no one else would make it in time. If the animals were to be saved, it seemed it was up to her to do it. She reached the barn in a few more steps and, disregarding all thought for her own safety, pulled open the door and ran inside.

She was dismayed at the amount of smoke already collected. It billowed and swirled like an eye-stinging

195

fog, and she couldn't see more than a few feet in front of her.

"Paddy Boy! Prince!" she cried.

The horses were screaming in their terror, and she heard the banging of hooves against the sides of the stalls. Suddenly, there was the sound of wood splintering, then the drum of hoofbeats as a horse pounded toward her. It materialized right in front of her, out of the smoke. The animal's nostrils were distended, the eyes were wide with terror, and the lips were drawn back over yellow teeth. For amoment Rebecca almost bolted—it looked for all the world like the devil's own fiery steed.

She got a grip on herself, yelling, "Easy, boy, easy!"

The horse bolted past her as if she weren't there, screaming wildly in its dash for freedom. It brushed so close to Rebecca that it knocked her to the ground. Her head struck the side of a water trough, and she knew no more.

A short distance from the burning barn, hidden in a grove of trees, Oscar Stull said to Mr. Mercy, "Wasn't that the Hawkins girl who just ran into the barn?"

"I believe it was," Mr. Mercy replied, his voice equally soft.

Stull rubbed his scar vigorously, and an evil grin lit his face. "Well, well, well! What do they say about two birds with one stone? I came here to eliminate the Lightfoot horse from competing with me, and I get an unexpected bonus. This is truly a most fortunate evening for me. Keep your eyes open, Mr. Mercy, while I see to it that Miss Rebecca Hawkins remains with the horses she loves so much."

Stull slipped out of the trees, moving catlike through the night shadows until he reached the corner of the barn. A quick glance showed him that as yet no one else was coming from the main house. He ran down the side of the building and quickly slid the large, two-by-four bar lock into place. The glow from the fire made his shadow dance along the ground like a capering demon.

A shout from the house alerted him, and he shot a glance back over his shoulder. He scurried down the side of the building and back to where Mr. Mercy waited.

Let them get there, he thought gleefully; *it'll be far too late to save the girl! That barn will be a raging inferno before they can reach her!*

Chapter Eleven

Steven ran across the lawn toward the barn. He was worried about the horses, but the important thing was to get Rebecca the hell out of there! Damned foolish woman, running into a burning building like that!

When he reached the barn, he was stunned to find the heavy double doors were barred from the outside.

"Rebecca!" he shouted. "Are you in there?"

"Yes," came the faint reply.

Steven began to struggle with the heavy bar. Smoke was pouring out of the cracks in the burning building, making it hard to breathe and harder to see. How could the door have become barred from the outside?

As he strained to lift the bar, he heard the sound of a gunshot, and saw wood splinter as a bullet slammed into the door only inches from his head.

"What the hell!" He spun around in the direction of the gunshot.

He was just in time to see two muzzle flashes from the grove of fruit trees on the low hill. A pair of bullets hit the door behind him. Instinctively, Steven dropped to the ground, only to have another bullet kick up dust in front of him.

"There's a woman trapped in here!" he shouted furiously. "What the hell are you doing?"

Error199

"Steven, what is it?" Roger Lightfoot called from the house.

"Dad, bring a gun, quick! There are two men in the fruit orchard shooting at me, and Rebecca is locked in the stable!"

The front door of the main house crashed open and several men ran out. There was enough light to show Steven that at least two of them had rifles.

His glance jumped back to the grove of trees, and he saw two shadowy figures running in the opposite direction. Evidently, they had spotted the rifles also.

Steven jumped up and attacked the barn door again. He couldn't budge it. Somehow the wooden bar had become wedged so tightly in the slide that it was impossible to move. He took a step back and glared at the thick, heavy door with anguished frustration.

Rebecca was in there, and there was nothing he could do about it!

Inside the barn the noise, the heat, and the smoke had become almost unbearable. The horses screamed in panic and agony as the smoke began to clog their nostrils. They kicked the walls of their stalls in desperation as the fire roared and snapped like a snarling beast.

Rebecca tried to stand, but dizziness overtook her and she fell back to her knees. Although she didn't realize it at the moment, it was the best thing she could have done under the circumstances, for the air was still breathable close to the ground.

"Rebecca!"

"Yes," Rebecca answered, her voice stronger. "Steven, I'm here. Help me get the animals out."

"Forget about the horses," he shouted back. "Get yourself out of there."

"No, I've got to get the horses out," she said doggedly.

"There's no way! Rebecca, listen to me. The barn door is jammed shut and I can't get it open. You've got to find another way out of there!"

"Jammed shut?" She looked around dazedly.

"Yes. Now get out of there. Right now!"

What had been fear in Rebecca quickly turned to sheer terror. She fought a rise of hysteria. She couldn't lose her head now, but if the door was jammed shut, how was she going to get out?

There was a sudden sound of crashing wood, and Rebecca looked around to see that another horse had kicked the side out of its stall. Suddenly she got an idea. Grabbing a saddle blanket, she doused it in the horse trough and then, crouching low, she ran over to the horse and threw the blanket over its head, blinding it. Talking soothingly, she led the animal over to the stable door. There she turned it around and abruptly jerked the blanket away.

The sudden removal of the blanket terrified the horse, and it acted instinctively, lashing out with both back legs. There was a splintering noise and the door flew open, crashing back on its hinges.

Steven's voice sounded right behind her. "Thank God, Rebecca, now get out of there!"

"Not without the horses," she said, and holding the wet blanket she ran back into the roiling smoke.

But now Steven was able to come in with her, along with his father and several other men. They all ran into the burning building, squinting through the smoke. They groped their way to the stalls.

"Cover their heads!" Steven yelled. "Cover their heads, or you will never be able to lead them out!"

Black Prince was the horse most on Rebecca's mind,

and she darted back to his stall. By the time she started out with him she saw thankfully that someone else had grabbed Paddy Boy and was leading him to safety. A few minutes later nine horses had been led out of the burning barn, and counting the two that had escaped earlier, eleven had been saved.

Only two horses remained inside. Rebecca stood shivering in the night air as she watched the burning building. The fire created a glowing circle of light in the darkness. Darting in and out of the hellish glow like so many moths were farmhands carrying buckets of water. They splashed them ineffectively onto the conflagration to little avail. The fire sent tongues of flame out of every crack, and the roof was now blazing in several places.

"It's no use, men," Roger Lightfoot finally said. "It's too late to save it. It would be better to wet down the buildings close by, to make sure that a spark doesn't set one of them afire."

"Right, Mr. Lightfoot," the leader of the bucket brigade said, and the men started throwing water on all the adjacent outbuildings.

"Are you all right?" Steven said, and it wasn't until he spoke that Rebecca realized that she had been standing in the circle of his arm.

"Yes," she said.

Under her horrified gaze the barn roof caved in, flames shooting high. A horse screamed inside—a high, piercing, shuddering cry of agony. Rebecca closed her eyes, and turned her face into his shoulder. "Oh, Steven! Those poor creatures! Why couldn't we have saved them all?"

"I'm sorry about them, too. But I'm thankful that we saved as many as we did. And if it hadn't been for you, Rebecca, we wouldn't have saved any. You're a brave woman, did you know that?" His voice swelled with pride for her.

"Not really," she said. "I was scared to death all the time I was in there."

"What do you think bravery is? Bravery is overcoming your fear, and still doing something. A person who is without fear isn't brave, he's stupid. No, you were very brave to do what you did."

"How do you suppose the fire got started? Did someone leave a lantern burning?"

"No," he said, his smoke-blackened face set in grim lines. "I'm afraid I know how the fire got started, and it was no accident."

"No accident?" She stared up at him. "You mean it was set on purpose?"

"Yes."

"But who would do such a thing?"

"The same person who tried to kill you."

"Kill me?" She gasped. "Steven, what in the world are you talking about?"

"Rebecca, after you ran into the stable, the door was shut and barred from the outside."

"Maybe the wind blew the door shut."

"Then how did the wooden bar get into place?"

"Maybe it fell into place by accident."

"It couldn't happen that way, not the way it is designed," Steven said positively. "The wooden bar has to be lifted into place. No, it was deliberate."

"How can you be so sure?"

"Because something else happened. While I was trying to open the door, someone shot at me from those trees over there." He pointed. "Several times."

Rebecca paled. "Who was it?"

"It was too dark to tell. All I saw were two shadowy figures. But I can make a good guess."

Rebecca shivered again, but this time it wasn't from

the cold. Although she already had an inkling, she asked anyway. "Who do you think it was?"

"Oscar Stull and his ever-present sidekick, Mr. Mercy."

"He's an evil man, I know that, but what reason would he have to do such a thing?"

"To eliminate Derby competition. Bright Morn was in the horse barn, as well as Black Prince. If he had his way, he'd like to run in the Derby all alone. That way he'd be sure to win."

Rebecca said, "Shouldn't we report it to the police?"

"And tell them what?" Steven shook his head. "That two shadows fired several shots at me? That our barn was fired, and I *think* Stull and Mr. Mercy did it? I can't prove a thing, Rebecca, and until I can it would be a waste of time to go to the authorities."

"You think he'd burn a dozen horses to death, just to eliminate two?" she said in disbelief.

"I'd believe anything of that man," Steven said grimly. He told Rebecca then of Stull's attempt at bribery on the day he, Steven, received the beating.

"But he doesn't even know that we're entering Black Prince. He did try to set up a match race between Black Prince and his horse, but Grandfather wouldn't do it."

"Has he ever seen Black Prince run?"

"Not to my knowledge."

"But I saw him run, remember?" Steven pointed out. "And if I happened to see it, there's every reason to think that one of Stull's minions saw you working the horse at some time or other, and reported back. And that would be enough to alarm him. From what I saw of Black Prince that one time, I consider him as good as any horse around, and that includes Bright Morn and McGrath's pair." He grinned suddenly. "Don't misunderstand now. I think Bright Morn can beat yours. But I welcome competition, and Stull doesn't."

"Thank you, Steven." She smiled wanly and touched his hand. "If we do run Black Prince, and I'm sure we will, may the best horse win."

Steven's father walked over to them. "Young lady, we certainly owe you a vote of thanks," he said. "Both for giving the alarm, and for helping us save the animals."

"I'm only glad that I saw the fire in time."

"Son, she shouldn't be out here like that, she'll catch her death of cold," the older Lightfoot scolded. "Take her back inside."

It wasn't until then that Rebecca remembered that she was wearing only her nightgown, a thin cotton garment. Ordinarily, it would have been long enough and opaque enough to preserve her modesty, but in the breeze, the thin cloth was molded to her body.

"Here," Jean said, coming up with a blanket to wrap around her. "I'll take her up."

"Thanks, Jean," Rebecca said gratefully, flushing. "Everyone must think I'm shameless, being out here in my nightgown. But I completely forgot."

"Everyone thinks you are wonderful," Jean retorted. "And everyone is right. Now, come on back to the house, and let's put you to bed."

As they walked along, Rebecca gave a little laugh. "You know, if it hadn't been for you, I would never have seen the fire."

"Me? What did I have to do with it? I was sound asleep, and it was almost over before I woke up. I understand some shots were fired, but I didn't hear them."

"It was the salt," Rebecca said. "I saw the flames when I went to the dresser to swallow the thimble of salt."

"My goodness! There I'm even more glad that you got out of the barn safely," Jean said. "For if you hadn't, I would have never forgiven myself."

"Don't be silly," Rebecca said easily. "But for that salt, all the horses might be dead."

"I suppose you're right," Jean said, with a shiver. Then she smiled. "Did you swallow the salt?"

"Yes," Rebecca said.

"Then you shall dream of your own true love, I promise you."

"I hope you're right," Rebecca said. "Otherwise, I fear I shall have only nightmares about the fire, and I don't wish to relive *that* again!"

They had just reached the steps to the veranda, and Rebecca turned to look back toward the barn. The structure of the stable had already collapsed in on itself, and only a few blazing timbers still pointed toward the night sky. Burning bits of straw drifted high into the blackness, carried aloft by the rising columns of heated air, and billows of orange and brown smoke boiled up. Rebecca thought of what Steven had said about the door being barred from the outside, and then quickly closed her eyes tightly to force the sight of the ruined stable out of her mind.

Jean, apparently sensing how she felt, said, "Would you like to sleep in my room with me tonight?"

"No," Rebecca said quickly. "I wouldn't want to put you out. But you are sweet for thinking of it. Thank you, Jean."

Suddenly, Rebecca wished that Steven had been in a position to make the same offer. Not for sexual reasons, but because she knew that with him by her side, she would fear nothing—not even Oscar Stull. The possibility that Stull might be lurking out there in the night somewhere made her skin crawl.

* * *

Gladney did not become a good rider. In fact he became a barely adequate rider, but he did manage to conquer his aversion to the beasts, and the gut-wrenching fear he experienced every time he climbed onto the back of one.

He rode triumphantly down to the railway station to greet the train that brought the jockeys, drivers, and horses who had run in the Paducah races to Clarksville, Tennessee.

It was not the best idea he'd ever had. For, though he had it in his mind to be regally astride his horse when Rebecca and her grandfather arrived, the horse was spooked by the train. When the train stopped with shrieking brakes and billows of steam, the horse snorted, rearing.

Gladney kept his saddle the first time the horse reared, but he didn't even try for the second time. As soon as the horse's forelegs hit the ground again, Gladney jumped off. He glanced around in quick embarrassment, but saw, thankfully, that since everyone was so intent on the arrival of the train, few paid any attention to him.

Because of the crowd, Gladney was unable to get close to the train when it began unloading, and he supposed that was the reason he didn't immediately see Rebecca or Hawk. But when he watched the horses being unloaded, he didn't see Paddy Boy or Black Prince, either.

A small man, a sulky driver Gladney knew slightly, was examining the shoe of one of the horses, and talking to a man Gladney assumed to be the owner of the horse.

Gladney walked over to them. "Excuse me, do either of you know Henry Hawkins, or his granddaughter, Rebecca?"

"Sure, know 'em both," the driver said.

"I was supposed to meet them at the train, but I don't see them anywhere."

"Ain't surprised," the sulky driver said. He continued to examine the horse's hoof as Gladney talked, and didn't look at him once. The owner was staring at Gladney, but he didn't speak.

Gladney gave an exasperated sigh. "Well, would you mind telling me why you 'ain't surprised'?" Gladney said sarcastically.

"Because they ain't on the train," the driver said. He straightened and laughed heartily at his own joke.

Gladney wanted to ask the man if he knew where they were. But he refused to give him the satisfaction. He stalked away in anger.

A jockey had just climbed on his horse nearby. As Gladney started past, he said, "You want to know where Hawk and his girl are?"

Gladney's head came up. "Are you talking to me?"

"I am if you want to know where the Hawk is."

"Hell, yes, I want to know."

"They're in Cincinnati."

Gladney frowned. "Cincinnati? What kind of race is in Cincinnati?"

"No race in Cincinnati," the jockey said. "Ain't nothing much in Cincinnati."

He smiled broadly, enjoying his brand of humor fully as much as the sulky driver had. At least, Gladney thought, the jockey's sense of humor was easier to take, since he was conveying information.

"Leastways, I never heard of any race in Cincinnati," the jockey continued. "But even if there was a race, that ain't why the Hawk went there. He went there to buy a new sulky, the way I get it. The one they had, it ain't worth a tinker's damn, I heard the Hawk say."

208

"They're buying a sulky in Cincinnati? Where in Cincinnati?" Gladney demanded.

"Why, at the sulky-buying place, where else?" the jockey said. He slapped his horse on the neck and rode off, laughing to himself, leaving Gladney grinding his teeth in frustration.

Could Steven be behind this? He wouldn't put it past Steven to have done something to Hawkins's sulky, just so they couldn't make the Clarksville race! He had a sneaking hunch that wherever Rebecca was, Steven was around.

Before the next train left, Gladney finally learned which "sulky-buying place" Henry Hawkins was going to. According to one of the other owners with whom Hawk had discussed his problem, the new sulky was to come from the Cincinnati Carriage Company.

Gladney thanked his source of information, returned his rented horse to the livery stable, and took the night train to Cincinnati.

Gladney had ridden many trains in his life, including several freights where his presence was unknown and unwanted. He liked trains, and he had made a study of them. He had even found a way to win money from his fellow passengers, on those occasions when he saw the opportunity. It was a simple trick, but one which never failed to amaze his victims, often eliciting a genuine laugh of surprise over his accomplishment and a good-natured parting with their money when they lost the wager, especially as Gladney was careful always to keep the stakes low.

It was a simple wager. Gladney would bet that he could accurately guess the speed at which the train was traveling. The accuracy of his estimate could be proven by timing the passage of the mileposts, but he didn't need the mileposts for his estimate. Some of his victims insisted that he close his eyes, others would attempt to confuse him by purposely starting him in between two mileposts, but no matter how they did it, he was always able to guess the speed of the train within twenty seconds.

Gladney smiled now as he thought of it, and looked around to see if anyone in the coach might be a potential mark. There was one old couple, a young woman and two children, one middle-aged woman, and a man dressed in the somber clothes of a minister. No likely prospects.

That was a shame, he thought. He knew that the train was now traveling at forty-two miles an hour.

Gladney never revealed his method, but it was a secret he had learned once from a friendly freight conductor who welcomed the company of freight riders like Gladney. All that was required was to count the number of clicks the train wheels made per twenty seconds. The number of clicks per second was equal to the number of miles per hour the train was traveling.

Forty-two miles per hour, Gladney thought. And the fastest race horses turn a quarter of a mile in approximately twenty-four seconds. Gladney worked that out in his head, and realized that at top speed, a race horse was running just under thirty-eight miles an hour. But even if a horse could hold his top speed for one hour, which he couldn't, of course, the horse would still be four miles behind this train, which was running at a relatively modest speed. Some trains out west, Gladney knew, traveled at close to sixty miles an hour.

He smiled to himself. So what if he wasn't a good rider? It should be obvious to anyone with any sense that the days of the horse as a means of transportation were limited. If a way was ever found for trains, or some similar means of travel, to run without tracks, the horse would be finished.

But not horse racing, he mused. Despite his personal aversion to riding the creatures, he had to admit that a thoroughbred at full gallop was one of the most beautiful sights on this earth.

He settled back in the seat and slept until they reached Louisville. There he had to take a ferry across the Ohio River, and then board another train which would take him on to Cincinnati.

While crossing on the ferry, there was a stir of excitement when one of the passengers pointed out what appeared to be a fire about three miles downriver.

Gladney studied the clouds, lit from below by orange flames, and for a moment he fancied he could almost smell the fire. During the war he had seen many houses and barns burned, smelled the smoke and burned wood—and too many times the stench of charred human flesh. From that time he never witnessed a building ablaze, that those grisly recollections didn't come to mind. He felt compassion for the unlucky victims of this particular fire, and was only happy that he was no closer to it.

Gladney Halloran was a man accustomed to travel, and within minutes after he had boarded the train on the Indiana side of the river he was asleep again. He didn't wake up until the conductor came through the coach announcing their arrival in Cincinnati.

It was close to ten o'clock in the morning when Gladney stepped through the front door of the Cincinnati Carriage works, and before he even had time to ask about Hawk or Rebecca, he spotted Hawk.

Hawk was standing next to a new sulky, eyeing it in open appreciation. The wheels of the little racing carriage were nearly as tall as Hawk himself. They were very thin and light, rimmed with rubber tires. The frame of the sulky was a gently curving arc, with a tiny seat perched on top.

"Good morning, Hawk," Gladney said as he approached.

Hawk looked up and smiled broadly. "Look at this, would you, Glad? Have you ever seen anything so beautiful?" he said eagerly, speaking as though there was nothing at all unusual about Gladney's sudden appearance.

"Aye, she's a pretty lass," Gladney said drolly. "But a bit flimsy for my tastes, I'm thinkin'. Are you sure she's strong enough?"

"Hell, yes, it's strong enough." Hawk pounded on the frame with his fist. "This is Bessemer steel," he announced proudly. "There's nothing stronger in the world." He stepped back and looked at the sulky for a long, admiring second. "Nor is there anything as beautiful."

"I'm afraid I can't quite agree with you there, Hawk. To my way of thinking, your granddaughter is a sight more lovely."

Hawk looked startled, then laughed heartily. "You've hit upon the weak spot in my argument, Glad," he said. "I can't find fault with that statement, since I too believe Becky to have the best of it there."

"What does Rebecca think of your new sulky?" Gladney asked casually.

"She hasn't seen it yet."

"Oh? Knowing her, I should think she would be down here first thing, gazing at it with a critical eye, searching for every possible flaw."

Hawk was grinning. "You know Becky well enough, that's for sure. And she would be doing just that if she was here."

The statement caught Gladney by surprise, and he

looked at the older man with a puzzled expression. "You mean she isn't here in Cincinnati?"

"Nope," Hawk said. "She was going to come, but she decided to stay at Oak Valley with the Lightfoot family for a few days."

"What?" Gladney gasped. "You mean she's staying with Steven Lightfoot, and you *allowed* it?"

"Not only allowed it, but encouraged it."

Gladney was taken aback. "I see," he said in a subdued voice. He sighed. "You're right, of course. Naturally, as her grandfather, you would be more interested in seeing that she was being courted by a man of means, rather than a man like me . . ."

"Now whoa up, Glad! Don't be getting the wrong idea," Hawk said sharply. "And don't feel sorry for yourself."

"If ever there was a reason for a man to feel sorry for himself, it would be now," Gladney said disconsolately. "To see such a girl taken away from me . . ."

"I told you not to go getting the wrong idea, boy. I encouraged her to stay at Oak Valley so she could meet her grandfather."

"Her grandfather? You're her grandfather. I don't understand."

Quickly, and without embellishments, Hawk told Gladney the story of Rebecca's mother and father, and the part played by Thomas Stanford.

"That's a touching story," Gladney said when Hawk was finished. Then he grinned slyly. "And one which I can take as an inspiration as well, for I see myself as being like Rebecca's father. I should think that would put you on my side in this situation, Hawk."

Hawk shook his head, grinning. "Bart was an excellent rider, as is Steven. Bart lived at Oak Valley, as does Steven. And yet you say the story makes you feel akin to Bart?"

213

"The horses have naught to do with it. It's because my position would seem to be the least favored now."

"You're impossible, Gladney!" Hawk shouted laughter. "But you know, in a crazy way I think I can see your point. And you're right. Although I think Steven is a fine young man, I somehow find myself on your side. But don't ask me to explain why. God only knows, I sure don't."

This time it was Gladney's turn to laugh. "There's an old Kentucky expression I heard once," he said impishly. "It's said that you must bait the cow to get the calf, not that I consider you a cow, Hawk, but you know what I mean. And now that I've got you on my side, let's see how I do with the calf!"

The subject of their conversation was only that moment waking, having slept late for the second morning in a row. Rebecca seemed to have an unusually bad taste in her mouth this morning, and she went to the wash basin to brush her teeth. She poured a small amount of tooth powder into her palm, wet her brush, and scrubbed her teeth vigorously.

It wasn't until she was done that she remembered why there was such a terrible taste in her mouth. It was because she had swallowed a thimble of salt last night.

She smiled as she remembered Jean's words. Had she dreamed last night? She stood still for a moment, thinking hard, trying to recall whether or not she had dreamed.

Yes, she had! She remembered it now. It was difficult to focus on it, because now there was only a fleeting shadow, whereas a moment ago there had been form and substance. Who had been in her dream? That was the important question.

Suddenly, as if he were standing right before her,

she saw the handsome, smiling face of Steven Lightfoot. He had been the man in her dream. Yet it
seemed to her that she had also dreamed . . .

As if the thought of Steven had conjured him up, he
knocked on the bedroom door. "Rebecca, it's Steven.
Are you up?"

"Just a minute, Steven," she answered.

She looked around the room quickly, then slipped
on her wrapper. She walked over to the door and let
him in.

"How did you sleep?" he asked as he stepped into
the room. He was smiling, as if privy to some private
jest.

"I slept very well, thank you," she said somewhat
primly, remembering her dream.

"Any dreams?" Steven asked. His smile grew.

Rebecca flushed crimson. "Jean told you about the
salt, didn't she? That was sneaky!"

"Then you did dream," he said. "And it was about
me, wasn't it? Tell the truth now."

"Well, yes," she admitted reluctantly. "At least, I
seem to remember doing so."

"Rebecca, that's wonderful!" He brought his hands
together sharply.

"Steven, surely you don't place stock in such a
thing as that?"

"Why not? After all, I'm part Indian, and Indians
believe in dreams. Half their life is guided by their
dreams. Besides, if you dreamed of me, it only confirms what I've been telling you anyway."

"It confirms nothing! Besides, you promised," she
said, trying to make her voice severe. "You promised
not to press me."

"But I didn't promise not to do this," he muttered.
He seized her and kissed her full upon the mouth.

"Steven, please!" she said, pulling back when she

had recovered the strength to do so, for in truth the suddenness of the kiss and her own quickly aroused response to it had rendered her defenseless for a moment. "Someone will see us! You're not even supposed to be in here!"

"Who is there to see us?" he asked. "Jean is spending the day over at the Stanford place. My father has gone into Louisville, taking Jims with him. Everyone else is down at the barn, trying to salvage what they can."

"Oh, the horses!" she said, seizing on the excuse to forestall him.

"The horses are fine, all grazing in the pasture as if nothing had happened."

"They were fortunate."

"And you were fortunate," Steven said. "But I was the most fortunate of all. I would have gone mad if I had lost you."

He put his arms around her again, and this time she made no effort to pull away. As he spoke to her in soft, endearing terms, she could feel his breath on her ear, and it was a thrilling feeling. She leaned into him, pressing her body ardently against his. Her heart began to pound as she felt the hardening of his manhood against her.

"I love you, Rebecca," he murmured. "I love you, and I want you. Now!"

"I want you too, my dear, but we shouldn't. Not here, not now."

But even as Rebecca protested, she knew that her newly awakened sensuality was overcoming her resistance. Besides, she told herself, what difference did it make? She had been intimate with him once. A bell rung cannot be unrung, so there was nothing to be gained by the pretense of propriety. She surrendered to his kiss with a sigh, returning it with an ardor to match his.

There was no further conversation; there was no need for it. The bridge had been crossed, and they were communicating on a level beyond words. Gently, Steven removed her wrapper and nightgown, and Rebecca felt her body tremble as his fingers brushed it. A moment later she was nude and stretched out on the bed. Steven leaned down to kiss her breasts, and the touch of his tongue to her nipples sent shudders of pleasure rippling through her.

Now he stood back, looking down at her body as he undressed. Rebecca felt his languid appraisal of her body without embarrassment. In fact, she took pleasure from his slow, hot gaze, tingling everywhere his glance lingered, as though he was actually touching her there.

When he got into bed with her, Steven caressed her with skillful, tender supplication. He explored her body with the easy confidence and expertise of an experienced lover. Soon the flood of passion, so recently discovered by Rebecca, swept her along until she was returning his caresses with unchecked desire.

Steven finally entered her, gently, and with a moan of pleasure she rose to meet him. She locked her arms around him, drawing him to her and burying her head in his neck, murmuring as he thrust into her again and again. Then, quite inexplicably, Rebecca thought of the kiss she and Gladney had shared on the riverboat. And as she did so, last night's dream became crystal clear, and she realized that Gladney Halloran, as well as Steven, had been in her dream.

What would Jean make of that?

As Rebecca's pleasure mounted to a painful pitch, she knew in a small corner of her mind that it was a matter she would never discuss with Jean. A full-throated cry escaped her, and she rose and clung to Steven with all her strength.

Chapter Twelve

Gladney and Henry Hawkins were waiting at the Lexington train station, where Rebecca and Steven Lightfoot were due to arrive on the three o'clock train, known locally as the "Louisville Flyer." Gladney and Hawk had come to Lexington the day before, and had arranged for stalls for the horses and rooms for themselves. Gladney noticed that Hawk booked only two rooms, one for himself and one for Rebecca. He did not make arrangements for the driver.

Gladney thought about that for a spell, and then as they waited at the station he finally gave voice to his suspicions. "Rebecca is your sulky driver, isn't she, Hawk?"

"What?" Hawk said, blinking. They had been silent for a long time, and Hawk had nearly gone to sleep, sitting there in the early afternoon sun.

"I said, Rebecca is your driver."

Hawk stared at him for a moment, then looked off. "Now, why would you say a thing like that, boy?"

"Because I have finally figured it out. No matter how often I asked to meet your driver, I was always turned down. Then I wondered why the driver wasn't with you in Cincinnati to help you select your new sulky. And I wondered why he wasn't here now to meet you, and why he hasn't come around to inspect the sulky."

"How do you know that he hasn't come around to see it? How do you know he hasn't already driven it to see how it handles?" Hawk challenged.

"Because I tied a string around the wheel," Gladney said, smiling. "If that sulky had been driven, that thread would have been broken. But it's still in place."

"Clever young whippersnapper, aren't you?" Hawk said sourly. Then he sighed. "All right, Gladney, you're right. Becky is our driver."

"Why have you tried so hard to keep it a secret from me?"

"That should be plain enough. Because if anyone learns of it, we would be disqualified."

"Hellfire, Hawk! Do you think that I would want to get Rebecca disqualified?"

"No, I'm sure you wouldn't," Hawk said. "But it's better to be too safe than sorry. You know what they say, when three people know a secret, it's no longer a secret. I'm sure you understand."

"Yes, I can understand. At any rate, don't worry, your secret is as safe with me as it ever was. Does the Indian know?"

"No," Hawk said. "At least I don't think Steven knows. Unless Becky has let it slip this past week. We've gone to great pains to keep the secret, and if you hadn't been the clever nosy bastard you are, you wouldn't know."

"If I can find out, Hawk, others will eventually," Gladney said. "But if they do find out, you can be certain that it won't come from me."

"I don't know as that's true," Hawk said grumpily. Then he gestured sharply. "Ah hell, boy, why lie to you? I'm scared spitless all the time that someone *will* find out, and I'll be without a driver. Sure, I could find one, but none as good as that girl! She's a dandy!"

Gladney nodded. "I agree. Watching Rebecca drive when I thought *she* was a *he*—"

"The Louisville Flyer's a-coming!" someone shouted, and there was an immediate excitement in the waiting room and a general exodus, as nearly everyone hurried outside to line up on the platform.

Hawk didn't stir, but Gladney, feeling a bewildering anticipation as he realized that he would be seeing Rebecca in a few minutes, began to fidget. It has only been two weeks since he had seen her, yet it seemed far longer than that. He just this minute realized how much he had missed her.

"Why don't we wander outside and wait?" he said casually.

"Anxious, are you?"

"Yes," Gladney admitted. "Yes, dammit, I'm anxious to see her!"

The station platform was crowded with people waiting for the train, and the children kept darting out toward the track, leaning over to look down the rails for the approaching engine. One foolish youngster of about twelve jumped down from the platform and stood in the middle of the track with both hands on his hips, as if challenging the engine to run him down.

"Billy!" a woman beside Gladney screamed. "You come back here!"

Gladney noticed that she had two younger ones with her. He said gallantly, "You stay put, ma'am. I'll fetch the lad for you."

He jumped down onto the tracks, catfooted up behind the boy, looped an arm around his waist, and slung him over his shoulder like a sack of potatoes. The startled boy yelped, and as laughter swept the platform, he began to beat furiously on Gladney's chest with his fist.

"Now you behave, lad," Gladney said in a low voice, "or I'll paddle your butt until you won't be able to sit right for a week."

The boy immediately subsided. Gladney deposited him on the platform beside his mother, then vaulted lithely up onto the platform, waving off the woman's thanks.

The chugging sound of the approaching train grew louder and louder, and the smoke boiled up from the stack, climbing high into the sky. Finally the engineer began blowing his whistle, and the children squealed in delight and made their own whistling sounds, trying to mimic the train whistle.

The engine roared past, with its huge driver wheels pounding furiously at the track. Then came the tender, the baggage car, a special horse car, and three passenger cars. By the time the last passenger car was even with Gladney and Hawk, the train, with squeaking brakes and hissing steam, had come to a full stop.

Steven was the fourth person to step off the last passenger car. He stopped at the foot of the steps and turned to offer his hand to Rebecca, who accepted it demurely as she descended. To Gladney, this seemed uncharacteristic of Rebecca, and something about it disturbed him, though he couldn't quite put his finger on what it was. Then Rebecca saw them, and she waved, smiling.

"Grandfather!" she said, rushing up to give him a hug and a kiss. "Oh, thank you for talking me into staying. It was good to meet Grandfather Stanford, you were so right about that." Her gaze moved to Gladney. "And Gladney, it's good to see you here, too. Have you and Grandfather been having a grand time?"

Rebecca's manner seemed sincere enough, and she

appeared genuinely glad to see him. As she stuck out her hand, Gladney was strongly tempted to push it aside and grab her and kiss her in welcome but, recalling her fury when he kissed her in the restaurant in Cairo, he decided against it. Instead he took the hand she offered him and shook it.

"Steven," she called back over her shoulder, "look who is here! Isn't this nice? We shall all be together again."

"Yes, of course." Steven's dark face wore a complacent grin. "Well, Glad. How are you?"

"Oh, I'm fine. I see you've healed pretty well from the mauling."

Steven nodded. "Pretty much. The doctor says that I can ride again."

What is it? Gladney was wondering. *What's wrong here?*

Indeed, nothing seemed amiss on the surface. And yet there were subtle undercurrents which were just out of tune. The way Rebecca had allowed Steven to help her down from the train. The almost proprietary way she had said, "Steven, look who is here," as if Gladney's presence had been an intrusion into their world. And last, the total absence of banter. Neither Steven nor Rebecca had directed a sarcastic remark at him. In fact, they were almost patronizing.

And then he knew. Steven and Rebecca had become lovers since the last time he saw them. That knowledge lodged as solidly in his mind as if they had told him in so many words. Gladney got a cold, hollow feeling in the pit of his stomach, and he turned and walked away without a word.

"Gladney, where are you going?" Rebecca called. "Aren't you going out to the track with us?"

He didn't answer, nor look back. Instead, he increased his pace, shoving his way rudely through the crowd, so that by the time he was at the far end of the platform, he was very nearly running.

"Now, isn't that odd?" Steven said. "Did you say something to him, Rebecca?"

"Of course not," she said, both baffled and a little hurt by Gladney's abrupt departure. "Grandfather, what's wrong with Gladney?"

"Why ask me?" Hawk said. "Ask me anything about a horse, and I can probably answer it. But the human animal, that's something else again."

"It's just that I don't understand why he behaved like that. We've done nothing to make him angry."

"In fact, we went out of our way to be pleasant to him," Steven said.

With that remark, Rebecca thought she knew what it was. Why would they go out of their way to be pleasant to Gladney if they didn't have something to hide from him? She sensed that Gladney had guessed their secret, and she was ashamed. It was illogical that she should feel shame because Gladney Halloran had guessed at her relationship with Steven—and yet she *was* ashamed.

"Steven, would you help Grandfather with Prince and Paddy Boy?" she asked. "I'm going after Gladney."

Steven scowled. "Why should you run after him? He's the one who was unpardonably rude!"

"It's something that I must do."

"Then I suppose there's nothing I can say. Except this: I don't agree with it, and sure as hell don't approve!"

"I wasn't aware that it was necessary for me to ask your approval, Steven Lightfoot!" she said coldly. In fact, her voice was much colder than she intended, but she was disturbed by Gladney's reaction, and she felt she must do something to appease him.

She started off without another word, moving quickly through the crowd, trying to search him out. She strained for the sight of the mustard-colored coat he was wearing, and once she even climbed on a box to look over the heads of the crowd. She couldn't see him anywhere.

After a bit tears came to her eyes, and her throat hurt as she fought to keep the sobs in check. She had hurt him, and she had hurt him badly. Somehow, he knew that she had been intimate with Steven. How could he have guessed? Was it because she and Gladney, like Jean and Paul, had already developed a level of conversation so private that they could read each other's thoughts? It was hard for her to believe, yet it must be so. Otherwise, how had he been able to read her mind enough to sense that she had let Steven make love to her? And how had she realized that he knew, and that he was sorely hurt?

She had to find him and explain to him. That thought gave her pause. Explain what? Explain that Steven had discovered a passion in her that she wasn't aware she had? And also explain that her feeling for Gladney was as strong as for Steven?

Her own thoughts were such a tangle! If she couldn't sort them out, how could she explain to him? It seemed an impossible task. Yet she had to try. She had to find him and try to explain!

But Rebecca was searching in vain, for she had already passed the Railroad Bar without looking in, knowing that no decent woman would enter such a place. However, since the Railroad Bar was the first bar Gladney came to, it was the one he went in.

He had already gulped two strong drinks. Now he gripped the empty glass in his hand and threw it directly at the mirror behind the bar. Everyone in the saloon ducked away from the flying glass splinters. A few jagged shards of the mirror still hung in the frame, and their dagger-like slivers reflected the face of Gladney Halloran, contorted in hurt and anger.

A bar girl, her eyes and lips heavily painted, swished over to him.

"What ails you, mister? Whatever it is, did that get it out of your system?" she said, jerking her thumb at the shattered glass. "If it didn't, we'll have to sic Big Ben on you. We can't have that," her full lips curved in a derisive smile, "this is a respectable place."

Gladney looked at the woman for a moment without saying a word, then picked up the bottle, found a new glass, and poured himself a drink. "I've lost her," he said morosely.

The woman shrugged. "Is that all? Well, there are other fish in the sea. Me, for instance. Why don't you buy me a drink? I'll help you forget her, whoever she is."

"I should have gone to Oak Valley as soon as I learned she was there," he muttered, ignoring the woman.

She shrugged and turned to leave. Gladney's hand shot out and clamped around her wrist. "Where do you think you're going?" he demanded. "You're acting like all the other women in the world. Stay here!" His voice was raw and savage.

She studied him warily. There was something about Gladney Halloran in that moment that was frightening, and his friends, who knew him to be easygoing, would have been astounded.

"All right," the girl said, trying to smile. "I'll stick around, if you promise to behave and forget about that other girl."

Gladney stared at her; then he smiled for the first time since coming into the saloon. But it was a smile from his lips only, for his expressive eyes still mirrored his hurt and anger. "I'll try to forget her. I might as well, anyway." He poured the bar girl a drink. "Maybe you *can* help."

"I'll try. That's what I'm here for." Her smile became provocative. "A little money might help me try harder."

"A little money?" he said vaguely.

She tossed the drink down, then put her hand on one hip, which she had thrust out proudly. "I'm worth it, sugar. Really I am."

Gladney looked startled, becoming really aware of where he was for the first time. He relaxed with a short laugh. "Yeah. Why not? After what she's done, why should I care?" He took a ten-dollar bill from his pocket, folded it twice, and stuck it down the top of her dress. He could feel the warmth of her breasts as he brushed them with his fingertips.

"I have a room upstairs," she said. "It's the first door on the right at the top of the stairs. Go on up, I'll be along in a little bit. I have to take care of a few things down here first."

"All right," Gladney said, flashing his crooked grin at her. He picked up the bottle, took one long pull from it, then started up the stairs.

He pushed the door open and stepped into the little room. There was a bed and two chests, one of which had a mirror. The room was lighted only by the bars of sunlight which spilled in through the slats of the window shutter.

He stood very still for a moment, wondering what he was doing here. He was not adverse to bedding a whore—sometimes it could be a joyless encounter, but at other times a paid woman could ease a man's loneliness. What the hell! Right now he was sorely in need of solace and forgetfulness.

He heard the door open behind him, and he whirled, thinking it was the bar girl. Instead, he saw a much older woman, with stringy gray hair and skin like a dried prune. She was carrying a pitcher, bowl, and towel.

"You'll be needin' these things, I reckon," she said tonelessly. She plunked the bowl down onto one of the chests and poured water into it from the pitcher, then set the pitcher and the folded towel beside it. The whole procedure was so impersonal, so . . . sordid, that he almost bolted then and there.

"Millie will be right up," she said, backing out of the room with a face totally devoid of expression.

"So her name is Millie, is it?" Gladney said aloud.

He took another swallow from the bottle. By now he could feel a lightness throughout his entire body, and he was drinking just to maintain that feeling. If he went too long without taking a drink, he would back away from the edge, but if he drank too much, he would go over it. It was a delicate balance, and he was maintaining it with an almost scholarly approach. And the last drink made up his mind for him—he would stay. After all, he had already paid, and as he often said while running a con game, "You pay your money and make your choice, friend."

He sat down on the bed and removed his boots. He heard a quiet knock on the door.

"Come in!"

Millie stepped in, then pushed the door closed. She stood with her back against it, smiling at him.

"Have you started to forget that girl yet?" she asked.

"What girl?" Gladney said, taking another drink.

Millie reached for the bottle and took a drink, then handed it back. "That's what I thought," she said with a wink.

"Get undressed," he said thickly.

Millie undid the ribbon which held her hair, then shook her head so that her fair hair fell to her shoulders in a tawny tumble of curls. Then, looking at Gladney through eyes the color of wood smoke, she began to unbutton her blouse, gradually exposing her breasts. They were firm and round, tipped by red nipples drawn suddenly tight by their exposure to the cold air.

Gladney shucked his own clothes quickly and stood there naked as he watched Millie continue to undress.

Her every motion was calculated. She was a woman who knew how to arouse men, and she knew instinctively that the ritual of undressing was as important as any other aspect of making love. She folded her clothes neatly and placed them on the chest near the water basin, then turned to face Gladney once more. The sun-splashes painted her body with brown and gold stripes, and the area at the junction of her thighs was a shadow, dark and mysterious.

"I think you've done this before," Gladney said gravely.

"Hush," Millie scolded goodnaturedly. "Don't talk. A man either talks too much or not at all, and always at the wrong time."

Though Gladney had merely been going through the motions of the ritual expected of a man in such situations as this, Millie's erotic skills were beginning to arouse him, and he felt his need growing very strong.

Millie lay back on the bed and stretched her arms up above her head. The motion raised the nipple of one breast into a bar of sunlight, highlighting it in its pink eagerness.

"Besides," she said, "I didn't think we came up here to talk. Did we?"

He went to her, and they kissed. Gladney felt her

229

breasts stiffen and rise against him. He took her then, quickly and violently, and afterward they lay together side by side, touching but not talking.

After a time, in the closeness of the little room, as the smell of her musk and sweat overpowered the cheap, sweet scent of her perfume, desire returned, and Gladney took her again. This time it started slow, and there was more tenderness than he would have thought possible with a professional woman. There was nothing fancy about it, and no conversation accompanying it, just her little whimpers into his ear, and her arms around him, and his around her, and the straining of their bodies together until they could come no closer. Then came the culmination; a pounding in his temples, a moment of suspension, then a quickly fading crescendo, until they were once again lying apart and yet together, her hair brushing his face, his hand resting on her breast.

"She's a very foolish woman," Millie said after a prolonged silence.

"What?" Caught in a slight doze, he started, turning his face toward her.

"The woman who hurt you," Millie said. "She's very foolish, whoever she is."

Rebecca may not have been foolish, but she was certainly confused—about a number of things. She had given up the search for Gladney and returned to her room at the hotel. She stood staring at her own image in the mirror. *How had Gladney known?* she wondered. Was there a big red letter A on her forehead? She'd read once that there was a time when adulteresses were so branded. Was she an adulteress then? No, no; for adultery to take place, one of the parties had to be married.

But she certainly wasn't married to Gladney, and

she owed him nothing. If she had committed a sin, she hadn't committed it against him. Then why did she feel so guilty about it?

A knock on the door interrupted her musings.

"Who is it?"

"Rebecca, it's me, Steven. May I come in for a minute?"

"Uh, Steven, I'm really worn out from the train ride."

"Just for a few minutes," he insisted.

Rebecca sighed. "Very well." She opened the door and stepped back to allow him to enter the room.

He peered closely at her. "Are you all right?"

"Of course I'm all right," she said irritably. "Why shouldn't I be?"

"I don't know. It's just that running off like that . . . Rebecca, I hope you'll forgive me, but you seem overly concerned about Glad, and I can't figure it out."

"Can't you?"

"No."

"Gladney knows," she said simply.

"He knows? Knows about what?"

"He knows about us. He knows that we . . . that I let you make love to me."

"How could he know?" He frowned. "Did you tell him?"

"No," Rebecca said. "I wasn't able to find him. He's disappeared somewhere. But I could tell he knew when I saw him at the train station. Couldn't you tell?"

"Of course I couldn't, and neither could you, Rebecca. How could you have?"

"Well, I did. I saw it in his eyes. The moment he saw us, he knew."

"So why should that upset you? I say it's good that he knows."

She stared. "Good?"

"Yes. Now there will be no misunderstanding. Gladney knows just where he stands, and just how everything is."

"And how is everything, Steven?"

It was his turn to stare. "How is it? I thought that was all clear. You are going to marry me. Gladney might as well get used to it now as later."

"How do you expect Gladney to get used to it, when I haven't yet?"

He frowned. "Rebecca, don't play games with me."

"I'm not playing games," she said with a sigh. "How many times do I have to tell you that I won't make a decision until after the Kentucky Derby? Nothing has changed. Don't you listen to what I say?"

"Oh, I have no doubt what your decision will be."

His confidence was infuriating. "Steven, you can be very annoying at times!"

Unabashed, he said cheerfully, "I figure if I keep at you, you'll have to consider my proposal more seriously. Besides," he gestured, "now that Gladney knows the truth, you shouldn't have any problem choosing between us."

She peered at him suspiciously. "Why do you think I'm making a choice between the two of you? I don't recall telling you that!"

"Oh, well." He looked off. "I just guessed."

"No, you didn't," she said accusingly. "Jean told you, didn't she?"

"Well . . . she may have mentioned it in passing."

"One thing I'm learning about your sister—she's not one for confiding secrets in." She gave an exasperated sigh. "Sometimes I wish I had never met either of you.

My life was so simple before the pair of you came along. I knew exactly what I wanted. I wanted to win the Kentucky Derby and start a thoroughbred farm with Grandfather. A clear-cut goal, not muddled up by other things."

"You can still have that as your goal," Steven said. "In fact, if you want me to, I won't even enter Bright Morn in the Derby."

"What?" She made a sound of disbelief. "Steven, why would you make such an offer? Winning the Derby means just as much to you as it does to me. I know it does."

"But winning you as my wife, Rebecca, means far more."

"I don't care. I won't hear of you pulling Bright Morn out of the Derby!" she stormed. "Don't you realize that I don't *want* to win that way? Besides, if Prince doesn't win, I would rather see Bright Morn come in ahead of the field than any other horse. Especially if it meant that Oscar Stull would otherwise win with Bold Diablo."

"All right, then I'll leave Bright Morn in the Derby. Whatever it takes, Rebecca Hawkins, I will do. I just want you to know that."

She stared at him a little sadly, shaking her head. "All I'm asking is that you just be a little patient with me."

"Patience is a hard thing to ask of a man as much in love as I am. But I shall try, Rebecca. I shall try and have the patience of Job, if that's what it takes."

"Will you stop saying that!" Then she shook her head in exasperation, and tried to smile. "Thank you, Steven, for understanding."

He smiled then. "I said I would be patient, Rebecca. I didn't say that I would understand."

At that very moment Oscar Stull and Red Parker were in Bold Diablo's stall out at the racegrounds. The stall gate opened and closed behind them, and Stull turned to see Mr. Mercy.

"Well?" Stull demanded.

"He's here," Mr. Mercy said. "The Lightfoot horse is entered in the thoroughbred race."

"Goddammit!" Stull swore, kicking angrily at a pile of hay. "How did they ever get that animal out of that burning stable?"

"I don't know," Mr. Mercy said tonelessly. "But the animal is here, and so is Rebecca Hawkins. Maybe we should have stayed around that barn a while longer, to make certain that everything went as planned."

"We couldn't have stayed any longer," Stull snarled, "without getting killed."

"Don't worry, boss, I'll beat the half-breed this time," Parker said cockily.

"Oh?" Stull sneered. He fingered the scar on his cheek. "You couldn't beat him back in Cape Girardeau, not even when you had help."

"That was different," Parker said defensively. "I was depending on someone else. This time I won't be depending on anyone but me, and I'll do what needs to be done myself."

"I wish I could be certain of that."

"There's one way you can be certain," Mr. Mercy said.

Stull turned his head. "How?"

"By taking Lightfoot's horse out of the race." Mr. Mercy reached into his pocket and took out a small brown paper bag. He delved into the bag and took out a handful of clear, colorless crystals. "This would do the trick, you can be sure."

"What is it?"

"Chloral hydrate. All I have to do is mix a little with olive oil, pour it in Bright Morn's oats, and he won't be running any race at all."

"What is that stuff? That chloral hydrate?" Parker asked.

"Have you ever heard of a Mickey Finn?"

Parker grinned his evil grin. "Yeah, who ain't?"

"This is what makes a Mickey Finn."

Parker gave voice to a high-pitched giggle. "I've never heard of a Mickey Finn used on a horse before. This I've got to see."

Mr. Mercy was looking at Stull. "Should I proceed?"

Stull kneaded his scar furiously. Then he gave a curt laugh. "Yes. But be careful you're not caught."

"I'm always careful," Mr. Mercy said calmly. "While I'm about it, should I also eliminate the Hawkins horse?"

"No," Stull said. "No, I think not. If two horses came down with the same symptoms, it might strike people as a little suspicious."

"Then what are you going to do, boss?" Parker asked. "The word is that the Hawk has bought a new sulky. With a new sulky and a good horse, I don't know if I can beat them."

"They need more than a sulky and a horse," Stull said slowly. "They need a driver as well."

"What you gettin' at, boss?"

"Just this. Mr. Mercy, after you have taken care of the breed's horse, I have one more task for you to do. I want you to find out who the Hawkins driver is, and where he is, and then eliminate him."

"Do you mean kill him?" Mr. Mercy asked expressionlessly.

"Yes," Stull said without hesitation.

"Very well," Mr. Mercy said. "I will see to it. Now, if you will excuse me."

"Mr. Stull?" Parker said uneasily, after Mr. Mercy had departed.

"Yes, Parker? What is it?"

"Is he . . ." Parker cleared his throat. "Is he really going to kill the Hawkins driver, just like that?"

"Mr. Mercy always does what I say, without fail. Not like some men I can mention." Stull pinned the little man with a baleful glare, running the ball of his thumb delicately along the length of his scar. "Do you have any objections?"

"No, no," Parker said hastily. "None a-tall. It's just that I ain't never seen anyone who could just kill, like that." He snapped his fingers, making a sound like a dry stick breaking.

"Well, you've seen one now," Stull said. "And also, you've seen how Mr. Mercy always obeys me without questions. It'll pay you to keep that in mind, Parker, in case you ever get any ideas about shirking your duty to me."

"I'll remember it, Mr. Stull, you can depend on me," Parker said fervently.

"See that you do remember. For if you should ever forget, you could end up as dead as the driver of the Hawkins sulky is going to be!"

Chapter Thirteen

"Becky, you must wear a white sash and a white cap for your drive today," Hawk said.

"Why?"

"The Cherry Hills Farm has an entry today, and their colors are the same shade of red as ours."

"Then why don't they change *their* colors?"

"Because they have an earlier registration date, so we have to change ours, with a white sash."

"Oh, very well," Rebecca said. She opened the traveling trunk and began taking out the things she would need. She said diffidently, "Have you heard anything from Gladney, Grandfather?"

"No," Hawk said. He paused. "Becky, he knows you are our driver."

"What?" She stopped to stare. "How does he know that?"

"He figured it out," Hawk said. "And when he faced me with it, I was unable to lie myself out of it."

"Will he let the secret out?"

"No," Hawk said. "At least I don't think so. And yet, I am worried. I can't account for his strange behavior since you came here. I know he was anxious to see you. What could be the matter?"

"I don't know," she said evasively.

"Are you sure you don't have some idea?" Hawk peered at her suspiciously.

Rebecca sighed, and faced him squarely. "Perhaps I do know, Grandfather." She hesitated briefly. "Steven has asked me to marry him, and I think Gladney knows it."

"I see," Hawk said slowly. "I can see why he might be a mite upset by that. And what was your reply to Steven?"

"I haven't given him an answer yet. I asked him to wait until after the Derby," Rebecca said. "I want to be absolutely certain before committing myself."

"That sounds sensible enough," Hawk said. "Did you tell Glad that?"

"No. That's just it. I haven't told him anything, because I haven't seen him, except for those few short minutes right after I got off the train."

"Then how does he know about you and Steven?"

"He appears to be a man of acute intuition," Rebecca said, again on the defensive. "How else could he have known that I was our driver?"

"He's a sharp one, right enough." Hawk started out of the hotel room, then paused, leaning against the door jamb with his arms folded. "Could it be that you feel something for Glad as well? Is that why you put off accepting Steven's proposal?"

"Yes," Rebecca admitted. "That is possible."

She looked at Hawk for a moment, then ran to him and let him put his arms around her and hold her close, as he had when she was a litttle girl. "Oh, Grandfather! I don't know what to do! I don't want to hurt Gladney, and I don't want to hurt Steven!"

"Seems to me you've got yourself into a dandy situation. But you're not the first girl faced with such a decision."

"Can you help me?"

He grinned. "Now how could I do that, girl?"

"By telling me which one I should accept."

238

"Oh, no! That would be just dandy, now wouldn't it? You're asking me to pick the man I think you should live with for the rest of your life. It's not my decision to make, Becky girl."

"But there are parents who do it," she insisted.

"Yes, and grandparents as well, I'm sure," Hawk said. "But I don't happen to feel that it's the function of any girl's folks to pick out a husband for her. If you really want someone to tell you what to do, ask your other grandfather. He's been known to have a few opinions in that direction."

"Grandfather, that isn't fair!" Rebecca protested. "In the first place, as you said, that was something between Grandfather Stanford and Mother, and I'll not get into it. And anyway, he's changed. I'm sure he'd be the last one to try and influence me one way or another."

"But if it was up to him to make a choice between the two young men, who do you think he would choose?"

"Oh, there's not much question about that," she said. "It would be Steven."

"Why do you say that?" Hawk said interestedly.

"His own grandson, my cousin, is marrying Steven's sister, and the marriage has Grandfather Stanford's approval. And I happen to know that he likes Steven."

"Even though Steven is involved in racing?"

"He has mellowed on that subject," Rebecca said. "In fact, he said that he had every intention of attending the Kentucky Derby."

"Imagine that now." Bitterness edged Hawk's voice. "It's just too bad that he's changed his mind too late to do your mother and father any good."

"I'm sure he'll always regret that. Anyway, it's not the same. Dad was totally dependent on horses for his living, and I think Grandfather Stanford may have thought that a bit too risky for mother. Steven, on the other hand, has a large family fortune to fall back on. I think Grandfather Stanford is impressed by that."

"Oh, I'm sure he is," Hawk said dryly. "I'm impressed as hell myself."

"Yes, but not in the same way," Rebecca said. "Grandfather, wealth doesn't seem as important to you as it does to most people."

"Well, girl, I've never had all that much, so I can't really say," Hawk said in the same dry voice. "But how about you? The Lightfoot money impress you?"

She kissed him on the cheek, just a peck, and walked away a few steps, head down in thought. "You know, I've had that dream of a thoroughbred farm for so many years, and I still have it. But I'm sure it wouldn't mean the same thing if I just married into it. I would much rather get it the way we have planned for so long. Perhaps that is your influence working on me, Grandfather, but somehow I don't think that the wealth itself is nearly as important to me as the dream."

"That's my girl," he said approvingly. "But that doesn't help much in making your decision, does it?"

"Not much, no."

"What do you feel in your heart?"

"That's just it, I don't know," Rebecca said. "I truly don't know."

"Then my only advice to you is to make no decision until you do know. That's where you'll find your answer, darling. For once you do make your decision, you'll have to live with it for a long, long time," Hawk said. He pulled his watch from his pocket and consulted it.

"It's not long until post time," he said. "I'll hustle over and get the sulky hitched up. You'd better finish getting dressed, Becky."

"Yes, I will."

Rebecca waited until her grandfather had left, then started getting dressed. This time, when she began to bind her breasts, she was struck by something different. No longer were hers the breasts of an innocent young girl, but rather those of a woman who had been loved. These very breasts had been caressed and kissed by her lover.

That was the part that she couldn't tell her grandfather. Since discovering that she was a woman of deep passions, she had begun to wonder if only Steven was the key to that passion. It wasn't only her heart that she would have to answer to. She would have to consider her own passionate nature as well. And that was something she could not explain to Henry Hawkins. Or to anyone else, for that matter.

Mr. Mercy lurked quietly in the shadows of the stables. He had taken care of one half of his assigned task—he had laced Bright Morn's oats liberally with chloral hydrate, and already the horse was beginning to show the effects. Now he had only to take care of the second half of his assignment, and in attempting to do so, Mr. Mercy almost made a mistake. He saw the Hawkins horse being taken out for a warmup trot, and when it was brought back to the stable, Mr. Mercy reached into his pocket and closed his hand around the pistol there as he walked toward the animal. But at the last minute he noticed that it wasn't the driver but old man Hawkins himself who was driving the sulky, so before Hawkins could see him, Mr. Mercy melted back into the shadows to watch and wait.

It was not that Mr. Mercy had any compunctions about killing Henry Hawkins. If Oscar Stull had ordered him to kill Hawkins, he would have done so.

241

It made no difference to him. It was merely another job.

Mr. Mercy had killed his first man in Norfolk, Virginia, when he was only fourteen years old. He had been sitting on a nail keg on the waterfront, watching a warehouse fire, when a hulking dockworker, deciding he wanted the seat, cuffed the youngster on one side of the head, knocking him off the keg.

Mr. Mercy—in his mind he called himself Mr. Mercy even then—left without a word, his ears ringing. He sneaked into a hardware store whose owner was lounging outside, watching the blazing warehouse. Inside the store, Mr. Mercy stole a handgun and a box of shells. He returned to the area near the nail keg, waiting patiently until the fire died down and the curious crowd began to break up. His gaze never left the dockworker. Then, when he saw the man get up from the keg and start down an alley, he hurried between two buildings to find a place to cut the dockworker off. He found a place in a doorway and waited. Already he could hear the heavy footsteps of the big man. As the footsteps neared, Mr. Mercy stepped out in front of the dockworker, the loaded pistol held down by his side.

The dockworker skidded to a stop. "What's this? Boy, what you doin' back here? Does your mama know you're out?" He laughed raucously. "Hey," he leveled a finger, "I know who you are. You're the youngster who gave me his seat." He laughed again, mockingly. "You get it, kid? I said you *gave* me your seat."

Without a word, Mr. Mercy raised the pistol. Holding it in both hands, he aimed it at the man's head.

Fear flared in the dockworker's eyes. He held up his hands. "Hey, wait now! You wouldn't shoot me over a little thing like that!" He began to backstep frantically.

Mr. Mercy pulled the trigger and the bullet sped true, blowing a hole in the man's forehead, splattering his brains all over the alley wall.

Mr. Mercy stood over the dead man for just a moment, but not looking down at him. He had his head cocked like an animal, listening for some outcry. None came; apparently the gunshot had gone unnoticed.

Mr. Mercy calmly stuck the pistol in his belt and walked away. No sense of guilt, no remorse, not even elation—he felt none of these things. He did it because he thought it should be done.

Mr. Mercy rarely bothered to analyze his emotions. Yet he did admit to himself that the act of killing another human being gave him a sense of power. The knowledge that he had the power of life or death over another person made him feel superior to other, lesser beings; it gave him the feeling that he was invulnerable even to death itself.

It didn't take him long to discover that the ability to kill dispassionately and cleverly was the key to a lucrative occupation. Most people were reluctant to take another's life, even if the provocation was severe. But though many were hesitant to take a life on their own, there were many, a great many, who would pay to have someone killed. Since men like Mr. Mercy were rare, he could command huge fees. So he found a ready market for his unique services.

He had been sought out by Oscar Stull several years ago when Stull needed a man killed. Mr. Mercy had performed well, and Stull was so pleased that he offered something no one else ever had: he offered to place Mr. Mercy on a retainer, at an ample yearly stipend. Mr. Mercy's needs were few, so he accepted the proposition, simply because he would not have to kill for others. Many people who hired him showed contempt for him after the job was completed and his fee paid. In Stull he had found a man who admired him for his peculiar skills.

Mr. Mercy was jerked out of his musings by the sound of footsteps, and he leaned forward to see someone approaching the Hawkins sulky. This time it had to be the Hawkins driver. Mr. Mercy knew that, because the small man stopped to pat the Hawkins horses, then he stood looking at the sulky. And to clinch the identification, the driver was dressed in the Hawkins colors—the same cherry-red sik that Mr. Mercy had seen him wearing in Cairo.

Mr. Mercy catfooted out of the shadows and right up to the driver. The driver was somewhat startled by his sudden appearance, but recovered quickly.

"Isn't this a beautiful sulky," the driver said, turning away from Mr. Mercy to caress the graceful little rig.

Mr. Mercy didn't answer. Instead, he placed the muzzle of the pistol to the back of the driver's head and squeezed the trigger. The driver died without ever realizing what had happened. The pistol was a small caliber, and made very litttle noise. Mr. Mercy put the weapon away and left the stable before anyone saw him.

Gladney was sitting in the saloon just across the street from the race track, trying to decide if he should go to the race or not. After all, he may have just imagined that Rebecca and Steven were lovers. He certainly had no proof. But from the moment that Steven Lightfoot had emerged as a rival for Rebecca's hand, Gladney had experienced pangs of jealousy as painful as physical blows.

And anyway, what if they had been intimate? They weren't married yet, so it wasn't too late, no matter what might have happened. Gladney, who had lived his entire life by his wits, was not one to quit easily. Not only that, but he was no paragon of virtue himself. Witness what had happened with Millie only a short time ago!

He'd be damned if he was going to let Steven win Rebecca by default. He would go to the race, and he would fight for her!

"Hey!" someone shouted from the saloon entrance. "Hey, guess what just happened! The Hawkins driver has been shot dead!"

"What?" Gladney shouted, bounding to his feet and racing across the room. He seized the man by the shirt front and jerked him forward until their faces were only inches apart. "What did you say?"

"Hey, mister, take it easy. I didn't do it!" the man said, trying in vain to pull out of Gladney's grasp.

"Did you say that the Hawkins driver was shot?" Gladney asked in a choked voice.

"That's what I said. He's been shot and killed!"

"Oh, no, my God! It can't be!"

Gladney shoved the man aside, so hard that he fell. Fighting and punching his way through the crowd around the saloon doorway, he ran toward the stables with a sense of horror ripping at him. A great wind seemed to howl around him. He had never felt so desolate and alone.

It can't be true, he told himself. *Please, dear God in heaven, don't let it be true!*

He ran until his heart pounded like a hammer and his lungs labored painfully for breath. When he reached the stables, he found a large crowd staring in morbid curiosity at the pitifully small figure that lay sprawled in death beside the gleaming new sulky.

"Oh, my God, no! It *is* true!" Gladney gasped out, seeing the flash of red and recognizing it as the blouse Rebecca wore when she was driving.

"Gladney, over here!" a voice called. "Gladney, I'm over here!"

Gladney whirled toward the sound of the voice and saw Rebecca standing with Hawk.

He blinked for a moment, sure that he had taken leave of his senses. Then she beckoned, and it was Rebecca! Alive and well and heartbreakingly beautiful. He stumbled toward her. Stopping before her, he reached out tentatively to touch her cheek. She was real, flesh and blood.

"But I thought, I heard . . ." He stuttered to a stop, looking at her and then at the dead driver. Rebecca was wearing a dress.

"That's Tom Corwin," Hawk explained to the puzzled Gladney. "He's a driver for Cherry Hill Farm. They have the same colors we do. In fact, today we're supposed to wear a white sash across the front. Or we *were* supposed to. Now I guess it doesn't matter."

"But I don't understand," Gladney said. "What happened?"

"Someone killed poor Tom," Hawk said sadly. "And as he was wearing our colors and was found beside our sulky, everyone naturally assumed that it was our driver."

"Rebecca, thank the Lord it wasn't you!"

"Shh," Rebecca held a finger to her lips. "Glad, please don't say anything that will give me away."

"I won't, don't worry," Gladney said. "But you can't stop me from feeling relief."

"I wonder why anyone would want to kill Tom?" Hawk said. "He was a real nice young fellow who didn't have an enemy in the world."

Now that the shock was past and he knew Rebecca wasn't dead, Gladney's wits started functioning again. "Perhaps they weren't after him."

"Well, then who . . ." Hawk stared. "Now wait, you don't mean Becky!"

"Everything points to it. Whoever it was thought he was killing your driver."

"But nobody knew about Becky," Hawk protested.

"That only makes my point," Gladney retorted. "They were after your *driver*, and they made the same mistake everyone did."

"But why?"

"There can only be one reason: to take you out of competition."

"Grandfather, what he says may be true," Rebecca said bleakly. "Don't forget about the fire."

"What fire?" Gladney demanded.

"The barn at Oak Valley farm burned down," Hawk explained. "They were lucky to get most of the animals out. Steven thinks the fire was set."

"It *was* set," Rebecca said emphatically. "And it was set by Oscar Stull."

Gladney said, "You know that for a fact?"

"No, but it stands to reason. Who else would be so evil?"

"True, but . . ."

"We know it was set, because somebody locked me in the burning barn and then took a few shots at Steven when he tried to get me out."

"That settles it," Hawk said abruptly. "No matter who's behind it, too many things are happening that I don't like. I'm scratching Paddy Boy."

"No, Grandfather, you can't do that!" Rebecca said in dismay. "Not now, not when we're getting close to Derby time. We've got a good chance to win here, and we need the purse."

"We don't *need* anything," Hawk said. "Least of all, we don't need you being put in danger, girl. You know

247

that Steven's daddy offered me the job of training his horses. I've just decided. I'm going to take it!"

"Grandfather, no! I won't let you do it!"

"Girl, you don't have any say in the matter," Hawk growled. "My mind is made up. There will be no more racing."

"Then you are doing just what you said you wouldn't do," she said scornfully.

He scowled at her. "Careful of your tongue, Becky! You may be a woman grown now, but I can still whale the tar out of you."

"Grandfather, don't you see? If you take that job, then that will deny me an independent choice. We won't be on our own anymore, we'll be dependent on Oak Valley."

"I should think you would be in favor of that," Gladney ventured.

Her head swung around. "Why?"

"Isn't it obvious? Haven't you and Steven come to some sort of accommodation?" Despite himself, Gladney couldn't keep a bitter edge from his voice.

"No," Rebecca said curtly. "No, we haven't reached any *accommodation,* and if you had the sense God gave a rabbit you would realize that. Now, I intend Paddy Boy to run today. If either of you do anything to prevent it, then I'll never speak to you again. And Grandfather, you know that I have enough of you in me to do just what I say I'll do."

"But Becky, I'm only worried about your safety," Hawk said. He wore a baffled look.

"I mean it, Grandfather." She crossed her arms over her breasts.

He stared at her for a long time. "Come along, son," he said with a sigh. "We're not going to be able to change her mind. I learned that long ago."

Gladney walked off with Hawk, more confused than

he had been at any time since having met the Hawkinses. Perhaps all was not lost. Certainly, if she was leaning toward Steven, this would have been the perfect opportunity to get it all out in the open. Yet she was fighting fiercely for her independence. That could only be because she hadn't made a final choice, and if she had not done that, it meant that he, Gladney, still had a chance with her.

And he remembered something. Just now she had called him Glad! It was the first time she had done that.

"Where is Steven?" he asked Hawk.

"I don't know." Hawk shrugged. "He's probably with Bright Morn. The thoroughbred race is scheduled for right after the harness races. Why do you ask?"

"I need to talk with him. There are a few things we need to straighten out between us."

They walked along for a few moments in silence. Then Gladney halted the older man with a hand on his arm, and faced him fully. "You know, I've been acting like a damn fool lately. Maybe it's time I grew up."

Hawk's smile bloomed, and he clapped Gladney on the shoulder. "Now you're talking! Come along, young fellow. Nothing's hard when you have a friend siding you."

Hawk's support buoyed Gladney's spirits considerably, and as he walked through the milling crowd with Hawk, who limped along on his bad leg, Gladney hoped that, whatever the ultimate outcome of his relationship with Rebecca, he and Hawk would always remain friends, for he truly liked the old gent.

Steven, when they finally found him, was highly agitated and concerned over Bright Morn. It appeared

249

that he had reason for his concern, because Bright Morn was moving about on very wobbly legs. Once or twice the horse even fell to his knees. A veterinarian was giving Bright Morn a thorough examination.

Finally the veterinarian stood back and gave his verdict. "This horse has been given some sort of draught."

"Draught?" Steven said. "What do you mean?"

"Recently I read a very interesting paper," the veterinarian said somewhat pompously. "It was titled 'The Effects of Chloral Hydrate on Horses.' Now, from the way your horse is acting up, I would have to say that is exactly what has happened here. Some villain has given the animal enough chloral hydrate to keep him out of the race."

"Will it do any permanent damage?" Steven asked worriedly.

The veterinarian stroked his chin. "It all depends on how much of the potion he was given. If the amount was too great, the damage could be permanent, I'm sorry to say. Otherwise, he should be all right in time."

"In time? How long a time?"

"Again, that's hard to say. He may feel the effects for a week or two."

"A week or more? That's great!" Steven said in despair. "The race is about three hours from now."

"Three hours from now, this horse will be fortunate if he can even stand on his four feet. There is no way he will be in condition to race for more than a week."

Gladney and Hawk had arrived to overhear most of the conversation, but had stood quietly by. Now Hawk said, "What's wrong here, Steven?"

"Look," Steven said morosely, pointing to Bright

Morn. "Look at him. Someone poisoned him. Who could do such a thing?"

"Perhaps it was the same person who murdered poor Tom Corwin," Hawk said heavily.

"Tom Corwin?" Clearly, Steven hadn't heard the news. "Tom Corwin was murdered?"

"Yes," Hawk said.

"But that can't be true! I was just talking to him only a couple of hours ago."

"It just happened," Hawk said.

Steven ran his hands through his hair and gazed blankly at Bright Morn. "Poor Tom," he said. "Here I was so concerned with Bright Morn that I haven't paid any attention to what's been going on around me. Tom was such a nice fellow. Why would anyone want to kill him?"

"Why indeed?" Hawk replied. "Unless they thought they were killing my driver."

"What do you mean by that, Hawk?"

"As you know, Tom was driving for Cherry Hill farms. Their colors are exactly the same as ours. In fact, we were going to have to modify our silks with a white sash in order to race today. And when Tom was found, he was lying beside our new sulky. Steven, I think that whoever killed Tom thought he was killing my driver."

"Think, hell!" Gladney spoke for the first time. "All of us here _know_ that Oscar Stull is the culprit!"

"You're probably right, Glad," Steven said slowly. "He poisoned Bright Morn for the same reason. To get your driver and my horse out of the races."

"That's what I'm after thinkin'," Gladney said, his brogue suddenly thick.

Steven nodded thoughtfully. "It seems we come up against Oscar Stull everywhere we turn."

251

"I agree with both of you," Hawk said. He sighed. "I only wish we had some way of proving it."

Steven nodded at Bright Morn. "The next three hours with my horse are critical. If I didn't have to stay with him, I would pay a call on Mr. Stull, proof or no proof."

"Well, I don't have a horse to worry about," Gladney said. "I'm going to call on him now." He started off.

"No, boy," Hawk said in distress. "Don't take any chances like that."

"Hawk's right, Glad. It isn't your fight anyway, so why risk it?"

"He tried to kill—He tried to kill Hawk's driver, and that makes it my fight."

Steven frowned. "I can understand your indignation, but what does the death of Hawk's driver have to do with you? Is he somebody you know?"

Gladney ignored the question. "What are we going to do, stand around with our hands in our pockets and let that blackguard do as he pleases?"

"Son, please be careful," Hawk said. "Stull can be a dangerous man."

"Maybe not so dangerous, if I can catch him without his watchdog close at hand. It's my hunch that Stull's had this Mr. Mercy doing his dirty work for so long, he may have softened up a mite. Anyway, I'm going to find out!"

Gladney strode away, his anger propelling him. He pushed his way through the throng of people milling about in the paddock. The paddock was always crowded with pre-race spectators and handicappers, but today it was more crowded than usual because of the excitement of the murder. Gladney made his way through the crowd until he reached Stull's sulky. Red Parker had just finished harnessing the sulky and was

252

about to climb in. Stull was standing nearby, smiling expansively, telling all who would listen that they were looking at the best pacer in America. A quick look around told Gladney that Mr. Mercy was not present.

"And I have the best thoroughbred as well," Stull was saying. "Bold Diablo will win handily later today."

"Stull, I'll be havin' a few words with you," Gladney said, his brogue thick in anger.

"Well, Mr. Halloran," Stull said blandly. "Having trouble finding victims for your con games, are you?"

"I'll admit to bein' a bit of a con artist," Gladney said. "But I'm not a cheat, a liar, and a murderer, and that's more than the likes of you can be sayin'!"

The crowd gasped, and the smile disappeared from Stull's face. It was not much of a change, for the smile had been without humor anyway. It was merely a subtle realignment of a few facial muscles.

"Mr. Halloran, I would be more careful if I were you, making such wild accusations," Stull said, caressing his purple scar with the handle of his riding quirt.

"'Tis the truth I speak and you know it, deep in your black soul," Gladney said tautly. "For it was you who killed Tom Corwin. Or had him killed. Of course, I'm sure the wrong person was killed, you had in mind someone else. But that doesn't help poor Tom, now does it?"

The crowd gasped again, and buzzed with excitement. An open accusation of murder! Such a remark could not be passed off lightly.

Stull's face was livid. "Sir, I am warning you!"

"And I say again—you are a liar, a cheat, and a murderer, and you'll answer for your deeds!"

Stull laughed harshly. "And how do you believe that will come about? You have no proof, Halloran, or have you forgotten that such charges need proof? Now get out of my sight before I lose my temper with you, sir."

"Lose your temper, bucko," Gladney said. "Yes, that is exactly what I want you to do. Lose your temper, Stull. Or maybe you're a coward as well as all those other things I named you?"

Without warning Stull lashed out with his quirt, opening Gladney's cheek like a knife slash.

"Perhaps you do need a lesson at that," Stull said, grinning wickedly.

"Fight, fight!" someone yelled.

Within minutes everyone in the paddock area had converged, forming a ring for the two combatants. At first the crowd was noisy as they shouted and jostled one another for the most favorable position from which to view the fight, but soon they grew quiet as they grasped the deadly purpose of the two men.

Gladney and Stull circled one another, Gladney holding his hands out, palms open, waiting for a chance to grab the quirt, and Stull looking for an opportunity to use it again.

Then Stull thought he saw an opening, and he lashed out a second time with the quirt, which cut through the air with the speed of a snake striking. But Gladney was waiting this time and was quick enough to grab the quirt and jerk it cleanly from Stull's grasp. He tossed it back over his shoulder into the crowd, and the watchers laughed and cheered him on.

Stull smiled cruelly. "I was going to take it easy on you, Halloran. I was just going to flay your hide a bit with the quirt. But it seems I shall have to teach you a needed lesson with my fists."

Now both men doubled their fists in front of them and resumed circling warily, moving in and out, each teasing the mettle of the other. The crowd watched in silent interest.

Stull was a huge brute of a man with great strength, but Gladney was wiry, quick, and extremely agile.

Also, as he had shown on more than one occasion, he packed a punch with power far out of proportion to his size.

Stull swung first, a clublike swing which Gladney leaned away from and then counterpunched with a fast jab. It was a good blow, and it caught Stull flush on the jaw, but he just laughed it off.

As the fight continued, it developed that Gladney could hit Stull almost at will, but since he was always in motion he couldn't get set for a telling blow; and his punches didn't seem to bother the other man a great deal.

Gladney hit Stull several times in the stomach, hoping to find a soft spot there. None developed, so he abandoned that and started sending his fists at Stull's face, enough to keep the other man occupied until an opportunity for a telling blow developed. It occurred when he saw an opening to Stull's nose. It wasn't much of an opening, but for someone with Gladney's quickness and superb reflexes, it was all he needed, and he zinged one in, feeling Stull's nose flatten under the grind of his knuckles.

Stull's nose started bleeding profusely, and a scarlet ribbon trickled across his teeth as he continued to grin his evil, mirthless smile. Gladney calculated that the nose was his best bet, and he tried for it again and again. But Stull grew cautious, and began protecting it much better as the fight wore on.

In retaliation, the big man was throwing great, swinging blows, but Gladney managed to evade most of them. He knew that if one connected solidly, it would probably be enough to finish him.

Gradually, as he dodged the swinging blows, he began to see where his best opportunity lay. After each of Stull's sweeping punches, there was an opening for a telling counterpunch, but it would have to be timed perfectly. He set himself, trying to lure Stull into putting everything into one swing, thus throwing himself off-balance. If Gladney wasn't able to win this way, the fight would soon be over, with disastrous results for one Gladney Halloran. But if timed just right . . .

Oscar Stull took the bait and sent a whistling round-house right, just missing Gladney's jaw. Quickly, Gladney stepped in and threw a straight right, aimed for the place where he thought Stull's nose would be, and he put all his strength behind it. The blow went true, and he had the satisfaction of hearing Stull bellow in pain. It was a brutal and telling blow, but not without some cost to Gladney, for he felt his knuckles go; and he winced as a sharp pain stabbed through his hand.

A dismaying thought passed through his mind. His right was the hand he used most to manipulate the walnut shells.

He ceased using his right hand then, and went back to jabbing with his left, holding the right ready for one more punch, realizing that one was probably all he had left in that hand. He was getting weary now, his arms and legs feeling heavy, and he was moving less quickly. He noted that his right hand was beginning to swell, and he wasn't sure he would be able to deliver a knockout punch, even if the opportunity should present itself.

Apparently Stull realized that he had the advantage now. He began to close in, rushing Gladney, swinging with both fists. It was all Gladney could do to parry the blows and try to stay out of the other man's reach. Even the blows he managed to parry had a damaging effect. His upper arms and shoulders began to pain from all the punishment they were absorbing.

Suddenly, Stull managed to land a straight, short

right hand to the head. It wasn't a wild, swinging punch, just a straight punch, and he wasn't even positioned, so much of the force was lost. Even so, it smashed into the side of Gladney's head. Lights danced before his eyes, and he dropped to the ground.

Shaking his head groggily, he still had enough sense of survival to roll over twice and get to his hands and knees. Stull ran at him and drew back his foot. Through a haze Gladney saw it coming, and was able to roll to one side just in time to avoid Stull's foot, which had been aimed at his rib cage. Had it landed he would certainly have suffered broken ribs and perhaps even a punctured lung.

Failure to make contact threw Oscar Stull off balance for just a moment, and Gladney rose up on one knee and drove his fist directly into Stull's groin.

Stull yowled in agony, and doubled over, his hands protectively cupped around his genitals. Painfully, Gladney climbed to his feet. He brought his right hand up from his toes, and smashed it into Stull's already broken nose. Gladney's hand felt as if it had come into contact with a sledgehammer, but it was worth it, for Stull fell to his knees, the fight gone out of him. Gladney stood swaying, staying on his feet with an effort, laboring for breath, holding his right hand cradled tenderly in his left.

Stull raised his head. His eyes blazed with venom. "You . . . have . . . made a . . . fatal mistake," he gasped out. "No one does . . . this to me! Do you understand! No one! You will . . . pay very dearly . . . for this!"

"I think I just did," Gladney panted, gritting his teeth against the pain in his hand. "But maybe this will make you think hard before trying your dirty tricks again! If you do, sir, I shall come after you again. You have my promise on that!"

He turned and started to trudge away, the crowd parting to make way for him. Congratulations echoed in his ear, and several men gave him a clap on the back.

As he broke free of the crowd, he stopped short. A few feet away stood Mr. Mercy, arms crossed over his chest. His face was without any expression whatsoever, but his eyes were cold as winter ice.

The two men locked stares for a long moment, neither speaking. Then Gladney strode on. He could feel the probe of those cold eyes in his back.

He knew that the time would come when he would have to deal with Mr. Mercy as well. And when that time came, Gladney knew, one of them would die.

Chapter Fourteen

Paddy Boy won the first race going away, by nearly eight lengths, and he set a new track record in doing so. The purse was more than two hundred dollars, the largest purse Rebecca had ever won.

But there was little joy in Steven's heart, for he had just been informed by the veterinarian that Bright Morn should be taken home and allowed to rest and recuperate.

"The quicker you get him in restful, familiar surroundings, the quicker and more complete will be his recuperation," the veterinarian said.

"Do you think I should take him out on the noon train?" Steven asked.

"I would," was the reply. "Otherwise, your horse will have to spend the rest of the day here and then ride the train tonight. It would be exhausting for him, and only weaken him all the more. Yes, I think you should get him home as soon as possible."

"All right, Doc, if you think so," Steven said with a discouraged sigh. "I'll go make the arrangements right now."

He left his ailing horse in the care of the veterinarian, bought a ticket for himself and a shipping order for Bright Morn, and arranged to have someone load the animal onto the train. While he was still in the main part of town, he went in search of Rebecca to tell her where he was going.

But she was not in her room, nor her grandfather's room. He left the hotel, puzzled, and returned to the stables, hoping that she might have returned there for some reason. He found Henry Hawkins rubbing down Paddy Boy, humming happily to himself.

In answer to Steven's question, Hawk said, "Nope, Becky isn't here, boy. But I reckon she'll be around here before too long. She'll be wanting to watch the thoroughbred races, I'm sure."

"I won't be here then," Steven said.

"You won't be watching the races?" Hawk straightened up in surprise.

"No," Steven said. He quickly explained about having to take Bright Morn home to Oak Valley. "That's why I wanted a word with Rebecca. I wanted to tell her where I was going . . . and ask if she wanted to go with me."

"I see," Hawk said. He went back to rubbing down Paddy Boy.

"Mr. Hawkins, I love your granddaughter," Steven said formally. "I want to marry her."

"Yep, I know," Hawk said. "Becky told me that you asked her."

"Well?"

"Well what?"

"Well, what do you think about it?"

"Boy, what I think doesn't matter," Hawk said. "It's what Becky thinks that matters."

"She loves me, I know she does," Steven said confidently. "But she wants to wait until after the Derby before she makes the decision."

"Why do you suppose that is, boy?"

"I don't know. I think that she had some crazy notion of winning the Derby so that she won't need me, or something like that. I'll be honest, Hawk, I can't figure out why she wants to wait." He shrugged helplessly. "Women are such strange creatures."

"Now that I won't argue against. But did you ever think of this?" He squinted at Steven. "Perhaps she is just trying to make up her mind."

Steven frowned. "Make it up to what?"

"Steven, you aren't the only young man interested in Becky, you know."

"Are you talking about Gladney?"

"Yes."

Steven laughed, but there was a sound of uncertainty about it. "You can't be serious! Glad?"

"I'm quite serious," Hawk said. "Glad is in love with Becky, and she knows it. I think she feels a duty to herself to give long and careful thought to the question before she makes up her mind one way or the other."

"One way or the other? But surely there can only be one way," Steven said. "Hell, I like Glad, I always have. It's hard not to like him. But he's a man with no roots. What can he offer Rebecca? He's a con man, for God's sake! Some day he's going to end up in jail. Then how would Rebecca feel?" He looked at Hawk intently. "Surely you, Hawk, can see my side. Surely you'll support me?"

"You're right about one thing, boy. You don't know much about women. All those things you said about Gladney may be true, but they don't mean much to a woman if she loves a man. But yet, I can see your side all right."

Steven relaxed with a broad smile. "Then I can count on your support?"

"Now that I didnt' say. I said that I can see your side. You said that you love my granddaughter, and I feel that is a fine thing. In fact, it is the most important consideration as far as I'm concerned. But Glad loves her too, and thus is just as deserving of my support. I can't give one of you my support and keep it from the other. So I won't openly support either one of you."

"But surely, Hawk, in your heart you have made a choice?"

"Boy, it isn't *my* heart that matters."

"But in your heart, you *do* have a choice?" Steven insisted. "Am I right?"

"Steven, you are a dandy gent, and any man would be proud to have you as a son-in-law, or grandson-in-law, whatever. But my preference has no place here, and I intend to remain completely out of it. That's as it should be. If, on the other hand, Becky should choose you, you will have my blessing. Besides," Hawk smiled wryly, "you seem to forget one thing here. Either that, or you don't know that girl very well yet. In the end, Becky will make up her own mind, and I won't have one dad-blamed thing to say about it."

Steven stared at the older man for a long time, then smiled, a slow, pensive smile. "When you see Rebecca, tell her, please, that I have gone to Oak Valley. And tell her that I will see her at the Derby, if not before."

"Now that much I can do."

The whistle of an approaching train in the distance was heard, and Steven looked back toward town. "I have to go now."

"Have a nice trip, son. Tell your daddy hello for me."

"I'll do that, Hawk," Steven said warmly. "I want you to know that whichever way this thing goes, I consider you a gentleman of class. And a friend for life, I hope." He put out his hand to take Hawk's in his, in a hearty clasp.

"That you can depend on, Steven," Hawk said sincerely.

The train whistle blew again, and Steven, with a grin and a half wave, turned and began walking rapidly toward town and the train station.

Hawk watched him go, then went to work on Paddy Boy. He wondered if he should have told him that Rebecca was in Gladney's room.

No, he decided; he was right in keeping quiet. It would only have stirred up more trouble.

Rebecca squeezed out the rag, twisting it tightly until the last few drops of water fell into the basin. Then she used it to bathe Gladney's shoulders and arms.

"Just look at yourself," she scolded. "Men! Why must you always be fighting each other? You're fortunate you don't have any broken bones."

"I know," Gladney said ruefully, holding up the swollen knuckles of his right hand. "Ah, but I tell you, lass, you should have seen it! 'Twas worth it, to beat Oscar Stull. Now don't be after telling me that you're not a wee bit pleased that Stull got a little of his own back?"

"You were foolish to fight him," Rebecca said. But even as she scolded, her eyes reflected a certain pride in him and her voice was soft, muting the cutting edge of anger. "Oh, just look at the bruises," she said, with a clucking sound.

And indeed Gladney, who was shirtless, had bruises all over his face, shoulders and arms.

"Lass, you'll not be carrying a grudge forever now, will you?" he said in a teasing voice.

"Look who's talking about carrying a grudge!" she retorted. "When I greeted you at the depot, you were so angry you ran off."

"I know, I'm sorry for that," he said soberly. "It was a childish thing to do, I'll confess to you. But when I learned you'd spent so much time with Steven, my heart ached worse than from any of Oscar Stull's blows, though he does hit like a sledgehammer."

"You don't own me, Gladney Halloran," she said heatedly. "Nor does Steven Lightfoot. I am my own woman."

"Oh, there's little doubt in my mind of that now," he said with a twinkle. "But you see, I have no wish to own you, darling Rebecca. Just to love you."

The words were softly spoken, and Rebecca continued to bathe him with the wet cloth while avoiding his glance. She said nothing for a little.

"Did you hear my words, Rebecca Hawkins?"

"I heard them," she said.

"I said I love you. I love you, and I want you to marry me."

Rebecca felt a lump rise to her throat, and her eyes misted over. She blinked them several times, but was unable to hold the tears in check, and they began sliding down her face. She threw the wash cloth into the basin and walked over to stare out the window.

"Will you be givin' me an answer, lass?"

"Steven has asked me the same question," Rebecca finally said softly.

"I figured as much." His voice was subdued, and he was silent for a moment. "And what was your answer to him?"

"The same as I'm giving you. I've not answered him, nor will I, until . . ."

"Until?"

"Until I know what the answer is myself," she said fiercely, whirling to face him. "Glad, you and Steven, you think that all you have to do is tell me you love

264

me and want to marry me, and I'll fall all over myself saying yes."

"I expect nothing of the sort. Not if you don't love me. But I'll accept nothing less, if you do."

"Well, I . . . can't give you an answer now, because I simply don't know."

Gladney grinned crookedly. "Then I take it I still have as much of a chance as the Indian?"

"Yes . . ." she replied.

"But?" he prompted.

She looked at him with a frown. "But what?"

"Your yes had an implied but. I have as much of a chance as Steven. But what?"

"I'm sure I don't know what you're talking about," she said almost angrily.

She turned back to the window and looked out. A train was just pulling out of the station, and the engine was puffing mightily, throwing a pillar of smoke into the sky. The chugging sound of the engine filled the town. Rebecca felt a pull of sorrow, as if someone she knew well was on that train. A ridiculous thought . . .

Behind her Gladney said, "I think you do know, Rebecca."

Rebecca hung her head and wept again. Gladney got quickly off the bed and went to her. He put his arms around her and pulled her to him, cradling her head on his bare chest.

"It may be," she said in a muffled voice, "that I don't have any choice in the matter. In the end I may have to marry Steven."

"Now, that's the most ridiculous remark I've ever heard you make!" He held her back to stare down into her wet eyes. "You mean because he made love to you?"

"Then you *do* know?"

"Of course I know," he said crossly. "I knew the minute I saw you together at the depot. It stuck out a country mile."

Rebecca nodded unhappily. "I am so ashamed," she said. Her voice was so soft that he could barely hear her.

"Why should you be ashamed?" he asked. "Rebecca, look at me." She continued to look down, and Gladney put a finger under her chin and tilted her face up so that he could look into it.

"You have nothing to feel ashamed of," he said. "And don't think you have to marry Steven because you have some foolish notion that you have been compromised. I am not a virgin, either—"

"But it's different for a man!"

He rode over her words. "But I have no intention of marrying the girl with whom I had my first experience. It is not an evil thing to do, I don't even consider it sinful. I don't see how anything which gives two people pleasure can be sinful. So don't hang your head in shame around me, because I won't allow it!"

"Then why were you so angry at me, if you didn't feel betrayed?"

"Let's keep things in their rightful place, Rebecca. I'll admit to being sick at heart because I thought that the Indian had gotten the jump on me. But it was mostly because I was jealous of him, not because I was angered by what you and Steven may have done together. As far as I am concerned, you're the same girl now as you were when I first met you."

"You mean it doesn't bother you?"

"I didn't say it didn't bother me," Gladney said with a rueful laugh. "But I can live with it. I'm a realist, if nothing else."

"You're only making me more confused." She gazed

up into his face, blinking away the residue of tears. His face was very close, his breath warm on her cheek.

Then he bent down to her. It was a kiss of incredible tenderness, his mouth touching her lips as softly as the brush of a butterfly's wing, yet there was a promise of passion that could soar like an eagle. His lips were steel encased in velvet, and fire trapped in ice. He demanded nothing, but he could have had her surrender.

Rebecca's heart raced and her head spun. Finally the kiss ended, and Gladney raised his face and looked at her with a quizzical half-smile on his lips.

"Please," she said in a whisper.

"Please? Please what?" he asked. "Please let you go, or please kiss you again?"

"Please, let me go," she said. But there was no conviction in her voice, and even as she spoke she felt herself raising her mouth to his.

The second kiss was as thrilling as the first, and Rebecca felt herself spinning on a giant wheel, growing giddier and giddier, losing control of the moment and the place. She knew only the white heat of their kiss, for the tenderness now had been burned away by the quick, erupting fire in her body, and the kiss, the clinging of their lips, was the only contact she had with reality.

All of a sudden there was a loud, demanding knock on the door, and from somewhere outside her private world, Rebecca could hear someone calling her name.

"Becky! Becky, are you in there? Open the dad-blamed door!"

"Grandfather?" Rebecca said dazedly, as she slowly surfaced from the rapture of Gladney's arms. "Grandfather, what is it?"

Gladney strode over to the door and swung it open. "Hawk, what is it? Is something wrong?"

267

"I'll say something's wrong!" Hawk said forcibly.

He was so upset that he seemed not to notice that Gladney was without a shirt. He didn't seem to notice Rebecca's flushed face and agitated breathing.

"It's Black Prince!" he announced.

"What about Black Prince?" Rebecca said, fully alert now.

"He's gone," Hawk said grimly. "He's gone, girl. He's been stolen!"

"Stolen? Oh, Grandfather, not Prince! But who—?" She broke off, her glance going to Gladney.

He nodded bleakly. "Oscar Stull, of course. Who else would have any reason?"

It had been amazingly easy for Mr. Mercy, following Stull's instructions, to spirit Black Prince out of the stables.

Stull had a special wagon which he used to transport his horses from the train depots to the tracks, and from the tracks to the depots. Thoroughbreds were often too high-strung to risk walking them back and forth. Mr. Mercy simply loaded Black Prince into the wagon and drove it out of the track area, and no one questioned him. And when Stull put the Hawkins thoroughbred on a train bound for Bowling Green, Kentucky, he listed the animal as his. Thus, even as a frantic search was going on for the horse, the thoroughbred was headed south on the train, ironically passing less than a hundred yards from the racetrack barns.

They had searched everywhere for Black Prince, with no success. It appeared that the very earth had opened up and swallowed the thoroughbred without leaving a trace.

Fighting back tears of despair, Rebecca asked, "What are we going to do?"

"I don't think there's anything more we can do at this point," Hawk said despondently. "I've notified the police and the track secretary. Wires have been sent to other tracks and stables all over the country. There is no way Black Prince can show up anywhere without being seen and recognized. I guess we'll just have to wait now."

"Waiting is going to be hard," Rebecca said. She shook her head in frustration. "I wish there was something we could do!"

"There is something," Gladney said. "I don't intend to wait."

Rebecca stared at him, a faint hope kindling in her breast. "What are you going to do?"

"I'm going to find your horse, Rebecca."

"Glad, don't tell me that just to get my hopes up. What can you do?"

"And what's wrong with raising your hopes, lass?" Gladney tried his usual crooked grin, but it didn't quite come off. "If we just wait around twiddling our thumbs while we wait for the police to come up with something, what will that accomplish? Nothing, I'm afraid."

"But the police are trained for things like this."

"They'll be looking for your horse, not Oscar Stull. Sure, we told them we *think* Stull is behind it, but we had no proof to offer. Only the remarkable coincidence that Stull mysteriously vanished from town at the same time as Black Prince."

"But, like I said, son, all the tracks will be notified to watch out for Black Prince. He can't race him anywhere without being found out."

"Have you stopped to consider the fact that Stull may have no intention of racing him?"

Rebecca said, "But if he doesn't intend to race Prince, what does he want with him?"

Gladney hesitated before saying slowly, "I believe he just wants him to be out of competition, so he won't have to race against him in the Derby."

"Oh!" She clutched at his sleeve. "Glad, you don't think he would *hurt* Prince, do you?"

"Well, no . . . I doubt that even Stull would go that far. Even if he can't race Black Prince, he would still be of value. He can use him for breeding stock."

"What good would that do him?" Hawk wanted to know. "He would never be able to list Black Prince in the pedigree."

"He probably wouldn't even try. But think about this. If he could get a really good colt out of Black Prince's line, Stull would simply substitute another sire for Black Prince in the papers. If the colt then goes on to become a champion, he would establish his own worth."

"That's possible," Hawk admitted reluctantly.

"And remember, Grandfather, Stull did mention that he would like to use Prince for breeding," Rebecca said. "When he challenged us to a match race."

Hawk scrubbed his chin. "That's true, he did. Perhaps you have a point, Glad."

"So now, what we have to do is learn what farm he's taking your horse to," Gladney said. "Then we'll go there and pick him up."

"You make it sound as easy as if you were going to the store to make a purchase," Rebecca said.

"Sounds that way, doesn't it?" Gladney's grin was more convincing now. "The faith of the Irish. We're all cursed with it. The doing will be harder than the saying, I'll admit. But I'm convinced it can be done, and by the good Lord, I'm going to do it!"

270

Hawk peered at him closely. "What's your plan, son? Just how are you going about it?"

"I figure we have one big advantage over anybody else looking for the horse. There is no doubt in our minds as to the culprit. So it comes down to finding Oscar Stull. I'm going to track him down."

"And I'm going with you," Rebecca said.

"No," Gladney said firmly. "You're doing no such thing."

"Oh, but I am," she said just as firmly. "After all, whose horse is it?"

"Rebecca, this could be dangerous. You already know how ruthless the man is. Besides, you might get in my way."

"I will not get in your way. I must be there when you find Prince. God knows how they may be treating him," she said in a choked voice. She looked into his eyes without flinching. "I'm going with you, Gladney Halloran. Nothing you can say will stop me!"

"Hawk, do something. Can't you convince your granddaughter how dangerous this may be?"

"Becky is a girl with a mind of her own. You should know that by now." Hawk shrugged. "No, son, I'm afraid there is nothing I can do, either. If she's made up her mind, I imagine she'll tag along with you."

Gladney sighed, then tried one last ploy. "Rebecca, how about Paddy Boy? Surely you can see how important it is that you stay with him. Who'll look after him?"

She studied him with her head canted to one side. After a moment a slow, almost sly smile played about her lips. "Maybe you're right, Glad. Maybe I am being selfish in insisting that I go with you. I do owe it to Paddy Boy to look after him while you're gone."

Gladney heaved a sigh of relief. "I thought you would see the wisdom of staying behind."

"Besides," Rebecca said guilelessly, "it will be nice to get back to Oak Valley for a few days, and have a nice visit with Steven."

"Oak Valley? Steven?" He scowled fiercely. "What the devil are you talking about?"

"A visit to Oak Valley. Paddy Boy needs a few days of rest, and there's no better place that I know. Steven and his father assured me that I'll always be welcome there."

Gladney's scowl blackened, and he glared at her. Finally he made a sound of exasperation. "You're a contrary, tricky wench, you know that." Then his crooked grin flashed. "You've got a touch of the con in you, you know that? That's as slick a sting as I've ever come across."

"Sure, Gladney me lad, and I've no idea of what you're after tellin' me, and that's a fact," Rebecca said in a fair imitation of his occasional brogue.

"Oh, yes, you do," he said glumly. "You know damned well. You can go along. I give up."

"Sure, and I was thinkin' you'd see it my way."

"All right, you can knock it off now. You've got what you wanted. I just hope you realize what you may be getting into."

"No more than what you're getting into," she said with a shrug. "And don't tell me it's different for you, being a man."

"It is different, in that I'm sure they wouldn't hesitate to kill a woman as soon as they would a man. They've already tried to kill you once, remember?"

"I remember," Rebecca said with a sudden shiver. "But even so, I'm going. I have more at stake in this than you do, Gladney. I'll take my chances along with you."

* * *

"Mr. Mercy," Oscar Stull said to his stone-faced seatmate as the train rolled southwest away from Lexington, "I think you are going to enjoy what I have in mind."

Mr. Mercy looked at his employer with a tiny flicker of interest in his otherwise dead eyes.

"Yes, sir," Stull said expansively. "I am almost positive you are going to like what I have planned." Stull laughed cruelly, caressing the scar. "As soon as the Hawkins pair figure out what happened to their pride and joy, they'll come for him. I've made no effort to hide our trail, so they'll be along. And when they do catch up to us . . . Well, I won't spoil your anticipation, Mr. Mercy, by telling you now what I have planned. But you can be sure that it involves your own pleasure. Oh, yes, indeed it does!"

Chapter Fifteen

Rebecca returned to Gladney's hotel room from the train depot after she had seen her grandfather and Paddy Boy off to Oak Valley, and told Gladney unhappily that the ticketing agent would give her no information at all.

"What did you ask him?"

"I asked him if he could remember selling a ticket to Oscar Stull. I described Stull perfectly, scar and all; there's no way he could not understand who I was talking about. But he would tell me nothing. Then, when I asked if I could see his shipping billings, he wouldn't let me do that either. He said it was against company policy."

"Stull probably bribed him to keep his mouth shut," Gladney said absently. "Anyway, that 'company policy' line is all to the good."

"Good?" Rebecca stared at him in astonishment. "What's good about it?"

He grinned crookedly. "If he said it was against company policy, that means he's a company man, and he's bound by all the red tape. A person whose mind is occupied with red tape has no mind of his own, and is easy to deal with."

"How is that?"

"Watch and see," Gladney said. "Now, let me see, where did I put it?" he asked, more of himself than of Rebecca, as he rummaged through his suitcase. "Ah!" he finally announced triumphantly. "Ah, here it is!"

He took a small case out of the suitcase and dumped its contents onto the bed.

"What in the world?" Rebecca gasped. On the bed, in glittering silver and gold, was a pile of badges.

"Now, do I want to be a sheriff?" Gladney asked, picking up a badge and holding it over his heart. "Naw," he said, tossing it aside. "How about a U.S. marshal? No. Ah, here's the one! Interstate commerce inspector. Nothing better for a railroad agent."

"Where in the world did you get all those badges?" Rebecca asked in awe.

"Oh, here and there," Gladney said offhandedly. "They come in handy in my profession." He pinned the badge to the inside of his coat. "Now, you just relax here for a short spell, and when I get back, we'll know Mr. Stull's destination.

Gladney winked at her and started out the door. Two seconds later he stepped back inside.

"Did you forget something?"

"Yes," Gladney said. "I'll be needing this for luck."

He kissed her quickly and lightly on the lips, then before the surprised Rebecca could say anything, he winked, and left a second time.

Fingers to her lips, Rebecca stared blankly at the door for several moments, and then sat in a chair by the window. She could see the street below, and a moment later she saw Gladney walking jauntily up the sidewalk, headed for the depot. He smiled and tipped his hat to ladies he met, spoke to the men, and shouted to the children.

He was, Rebecca realized, a man who took great joy in being alive. How could such a person be a con man?

She compared Gladney with Steven Lightfoot. Steven had everything—good looks, athletic ability, and wealth. Gladney also had good looks. Perhaps he was not as classically handsome as Steven, but he was very goodlooking, nonetheless. Gladney wasn't so graceful as Steven either, nor did he have the social presence that Steven possessed. And Gladney didn't have money, because he lived a hand-to-mouth existence, sustaining himself by his own wits.

The two men were very different, and yet they were friends. Their friendship had been tested by her arrival in their lives, she realized, but insofar as she could tell, the friendship had survived intact.

Why *were* they friends?

Rebecca pondered the question, and she decided that they were friends because, for all their differences, they were alike in one very particular way. They were both basically good men, with a feeling of concern for others. That, she decided, was the strongest character trait of each man, and that was why she could be drawn to both of them, despite their differences. All the other differences paled into insignificance when that similarity was considered.

Yet she had responded ardently to Steven's lovemaking. Surely such a strong response meant that she was in love with him, and only him. For to respond in such a manner to a man she didn't love could not speak well for her own moral fiber.

Steven had asked her to marry him; perhaps it would be the best thing for all concerned if she accepted his proposal. What if they never found Black Prince? Oscar Stull had a long head start on them, and despite Gladney's breezy confidence, it could well be that they would never find the animal. And if she couldn't ride Prince in the Kentucky Derby, what was the purpose in postponing her answer to Steven?

Then a tiny voice inside her head asked: what about Gladney? Wasn't it possible that she was in love with him? She had to admit that his kisses excited her tremendously. And if his kisses aroused her to such a fever pitch, what would it be like making love to him?

Rebecca felt herself blushing. She was actually daydreaming about making love to Gladney Halloran!

She couldn't believe she was doing this! She made a scornful sound in her throat and got up from the chair. She prowled the small room restlessly for a moment or so, then picked up yesterday's newspaper from the bureau and began to read determinedly, in an attempt to put her emotional problems aside.

She had been reading the newspaper for twenty minutes or so, without any clear recollection of what she had read, when the door opened and Gladney came swinging in, whistling between his teeth.

"Our man went to Bowling Green," he said jauntily. "And he shipped three horses on the same train. Bold Diablo, Lucifer, and Lazy Lindora."

"That's his colt, pacer, and filly," Rebecca said in discouragement. "He doesn't have Black Prince then."

Gladney smiled broadly. "I *thought* you said he had a filly."

"Of course, Lazy Lindora. I undestand he hasn't had too much success with her." She looked at him narrowly. "What have you got to grin about, Glad?"

"According to the shipping document I, ah, persuaded the ticketing agent to show me, Lazy Lindora is *not* a filly."

"Of course she is . . ." Rebecca stopped, her heart beginning to pound. "Stull passed Prince off as Lazy Lindora!"

"That has to be it."

Almost jumping up and down in her excitement, she said, "What do we do now, Glad?"

"Now we go to Bowling Green, Kentucky," he said. He took a pair of tickets from his pocket and dropped them onto the bed.

Rebecca scooped them up and held them to her breasts, whirling around the room. "Oh, won't Mr. Oscar Stull be in for a surprise!"

"Well, I'm not too sure about that." He scrubbed at his chin, frowning.

"What do you mean?"

"Somehow, it was all too easy to suit me. It's entirely possible he *wants* us to follow him. So we'll have to be doubly careful. Anyway, there's something else we have to find out."

"What?"

"We have to find out where Stull keeps his horses. Have you ever heard it mentioned?"

"No. Gladney, I never met Oscar Stull until that day when he challenged us to a match race. I know very little about him."

He said thoughtfully, "There's one thing we might do while we're still here."

"And what is that?"

"Ask a few people. Ask other owners, trainers, drivers, and jockeys. Of course, a lot of them are already gone, but some are still around. See if any of them know the location of Stull's horse farm, if he has one."

"All right."

"The train doesn't leave until nine this evening. You check with the horse people—"

"*Horse* people?"

"No offense intended." He grinned disarmingly. "But the name fits, you'll have to admit. Anyway, you talk to them. They're more likely to talk freely to you. I'll scout around and see what I can learn. We'll meet back here at the hotel in a couple of hours."

"In two hours. Right."

Rebecca left the hotel with lightened spirits. Perhaps it would all come to naught, but the fact that she was doing something helped ease the deep depression she had experienced when Black Prince was discovered missing. At least now they had a direction to follow, and it seemed clear that their hunch had been correct. Oscar Stull did have Black Prince. What they would be able to do when they finally ran him to earth was another matter.

However, her hopes were dampened after two hours of trudging around town and talking to various people, asking questions. Oscar Stull, it seemed was a very private man. He confided in no one. She knew little more when she returned to the hotel than when she had left.

Gladney had come up emptyhanded as well. After they discussed it gloomily for several minutes, Gladney's face suddenly brightened. He snapped his fingers. "Wait a minute! What about the track rules booklet? It seems to me it has a clause in it about having to register your horses. Do you have one?"

Rebecca nodded and opened one of her bags. She had packed earlier and left her bags in his room. She took a small blue booklet from the bag and gave it to Gladney. He leafed through it quickly.

"What are you looking for?"

"Here it is!" he said excitedly. He read from the booklet published by the Lexington Racing Association: "Registration Papers required: The Registration Paper of every horse starting shall be in the possession of the Racing Secretary at the time of entry, or not later than scratch time on the day of the race."

"I'm afraid I don't understand," Rebecca said. "How does that help us?"

"Don't you see? If the secretary has to have that information, he must also know what farm the horse comes from. Now all we have to do is pick his brain."

"Just how do you think you're going to get the secretary to give out that information?"

Gladney grinned. "Sure, and 'tis most likely that the boyo would want to get publicity for his track in the New York papers, now isn't it?"

The racing secretary of the Lexington Racing Association was named Seth Johnson. He was a tall, thin, cadaverous man with a white goatee, perfectly trimmed to a point. His office was dominated by a large walnut desk and a huge, dark green safe. The name "Standard" was printed across the front of the safe in old English lettering. On the wall behind the desk was a calendar which had only the racing days listed, and a list of races for each day.

"What newspaper did you say you represent, sir?" Johnson asked.

"The New York *Ledger*," Gladney said blithely. "Without doubt the finest newspaper in this country, or any other. I'm sure you will agree. The Honorable Mr. Wiggins, once a member of the Congress, you know, is the gentleman who publishes my paper."

"I see," Johnson said doubtfully.

"I have interviewed the young lady's grandfather, Henry Hawkins," Gladney said, by way of explaining Rebecca's presence. "Who, as I'm sure you also know, was a famous jockey in England not too many years ago. His horse, Paddy Boy, won the harness race. But Mr. Oscar Stull left town before I could interview him. As his horse won the thoroughbred classic, it would flesh out my story as well to interview the man. I thought possibly you might tell me where I could locate him."

"I'm afraid I can't do that," Johnson said. "Though I can tell you that he will be racing in Louisville. As I understand it, he intends to enter his horse, Bold Diablo, in Colonel Clark's new running for three-year-olds. Clark is calling it the Kentucky Derby." Johnson tugged at his goatee with a scornful gesture. "It is my opinion that Clark has grandiose ideas. Nothing like his proposed Derby will ever become popular here. The moods of the public change too rapidly. No, it is much better to maintain a flexible racing meet, where rules may be changed from race to race to accommodate the whims of the public."

Gladney blinked, taken aback by this rapid flow of opinion. "I must say I agree with you, sir, and I will include your opinion in my newspaper article. But I would still like to interview Mr. Stull." He scratched his chin. "Perhaps we could figure out where he went with a look at his registration papers. The papers should list his farm."

Johnson leaned back in his chair, holding his hands together in a prayer-like attitude, and said righteously, "Oh, I'm afraid I can't allow you to see those papers. The rules forbid it. They are quite confidential, you know."

"I see," Gladney said. He cleared his throat, and assumed a worried look. "This puts me in a bit of a spot, Mr. Johnson. My publisher, Mr. Wiggins himself, has sent another reporter to Louisville to cover the Kentucky Derby. If Mr. Stull gets to Louisville before I get a chance to interview him, that would mean I've lost the interview, for I couldn't go to Louisville where the other reporter is. Gladney heaved a sigh and leaned back in his chair. "In that case, it's likely that all this work would go for naught, and not one word I've writen would ever see print. No one will ever hear of the Lexington races."

"Here now!" Johnson leaned forward, scowling. "Why should that be?"

"It was only my own efforts which got me the assignment in the first place," Gladney said. "My publisher is convinced that the future of horse racing lies in the Kentucky Derby. If I don't get a story quickly, he'll kill this one, and give all the space to the Kentucky Derby."

"But that's preposterous!" Johnson looked pained. "I've already told you that the Kentucky Derby will never catch on. And you can quote me on that Seth Johnson. That's S-e-t-h J-o-h-n-s-o-n." He spelled out the name carefully.

"Oh, it's not that I don't agree with you, Mr. Johnson. But the problem, you see, is convincing my employer of that. Now, if I could manage my interview with Oscar Stull, I believe that would clinch it."

"I see," Johnson said in some agitation. He stood up and walked over to look out the window for a moment.

Gladney winked at Rebecca, and it was all she could do to keep from bursting into laughter.

All of a sudden, Johnson pulled down the shades and locked the office door. "It is not a good policy to make our records available to just anyone, you understand," he said pompously. "But considering that this is all for a noble cause, I'm certain that I am doing the right thing."

"Oh, I am certain it is the right thing, sir," Gladney assured him.

"Well, here is the pedigree chart on Bold Diablo. His breeder was H. B. Townes, and he is out of Lazy by Leamington."

"Lazy?" Rebecca sat up alertly.

"That's right, madam."

"Glad, of course that's it!" she said excitedly. "His filly is out of Lazy by Virgil. I remember hearing Stull's comment on that, because William Astor's horse, Vagrant, has the same bloodline."

"Ah, Vagrant. Now there is as fine a two-year-old as I have ever seen," Johnson stated. "I'm certain that William Astor would be a good man for you to interview for your newspaper. He is the son of John Jacob Astor, you know, and one of the wealthiest men in the world. His participation in our classics certainly does put a feather in our cap."

"I'm sure it does," Gladney said. "Is he in Lexington now?"

"Uh, unfortunately, no. Mr. Astor is in New York. His trainer has left for New York as well, but perhaps you would like to interview Mr. Townes."

"H. B. Townes? Exactly who is he?"

"Like I said, he is the breeder of Vagrant, and of Bold Diablo also. His farm is in Bowling Green. That may be farther away then you wish to go for your story."

"Bowling Green, you say?" Gladney's interest quickened. At last they were finally getting somewhere!

"Yes. He owns Townes Farm, one of the finest thoroughbred farms in the country, in my estimation. It is a beautiful place and well worth the visit."

"Do you know where the farm is located in Bowling Green?"

"I most certainly do. I have been there any number of times. It is exactly six-and-one-half miles west, on the Russelville Road. I'm certain that he can put you up, because he has guest cottages right on the grounds for visiting owners and trainers. Here," Johnson said, tearing a piece of paper off a tablet and scribbled on it. "Here is his address, and an introduction from me.

You really should take the time to look over his operation there. I think that would make an excellent story for your readers."

"Thank you, Mr. Johnson," Gladney said, standing up to take the paper.

"Don't forget now. That's S-e-t-h J-o-h-n-s-o-n. Not Johnstone. Many people get the two names confused."

"Oh, I won't forget. J-o-h-n-s-o-n-e."

"No!" Johnson shouted. "No *el*"

"I'll remember, Mr. Johnson," Gladney said with a straight face. "No *e*."

Once outside the office Rebecca let her laughter go. "Gladney Halloran, you are a terrible man!" she said, with mingled admiration and disapproval.

"I'm sure I don't know what you mean, lass," he said artlessly.

"You know perfectly well what I mean. That whole elaborate tale!"

Gladney grinned. "I thought I made a pretty good newspaper reporter."

"But that poor man back there will be waiting for a story to come out about him. Don't you feel bad about that?"

Gladney shrugged. "In this life, we have to learn to take the hard knocks as well as the good. Besides," he gave her a sidelong look, "Don't you feel good about us now having a lead on Black Prince?"

"Well, yes," Rebecca admitted reluctantly.

"Then I go with the way it balances out."

"In other words, the end justifies the means?"

"Something like that, yes," he said. "But only if the end *really* justifies the means. Otherwise, you are lying to yourself to justify deceit."

"As you do, when you con someone?"

"Sometimes," Gladney said wryly. "But never purposely to hurt anyone. That man back there . . . how's

285

he going to be hurt by any of this, except maybe a blow to his ego, when he doesn't see his name in print? On the other hand, if this helps us to recover your stolen horse . . . Balance, Rebecca, balance!"

Gladney and Rebecca took their luggage from the hotel down to the train depot, where they were informed that the train would be an hour late. It was now scheduled to leave at ten P.M.

"And what time will it reach Bowling Green?" Gladney asked.

"Seven-fifteen A.M.," the station master said, consulting a complicated-looking traffic and time schedule that he had unfolded.

"I see," Gladney said. "Tell me, sir, are there any private sleeping accommodations left?"

"Oh, indeed there are!" the station master said, his eyes lighting up. "Shall I reserve one for you and the missus?"

"We aren't married, not yet," Gladney said with a smile. "Just reserve a sleeping room for the lady. I'll just keep my seat."

"Very good, sir," the station master said. "Just a moment, I have to get the proper ticket stub."

The station master left the window and went through a door which led off the ticket room.

"Glad, I can't let you do that," Rebecca said.

He grinned wickedly. "I'll be happy to give up my ticket and move in with you."

"I can't let you do that, either," she retorted, yet she had to laugh.

Gladney was pleased to see that she didn't attempt to fake an indignant anger at his suggestion.

"Listen, don't worry about it," he said. "I sleep very comfortably in the seats. I've done it many, many times in the past. In fact, I've slept *under* the cars. Anything inside is a luxury, believe me."

She stared at him in disbelief. "*Under* the cars?"

"Yup, what we call riding the rods. I've also ridden in empty freight cars, cattle cars, any place I could ride for free," he said jauntily. "You see, I haven't always been as well off as I am these days."

"Well off! I'll bet it took just about all your money to pay for these tickets."

"That's close to true, darlin'", he said cheerfully. "Just so long as people don't know that, it's all right." He placed his finger alongside his nose and looked wise. "The secret of a successful con man: never let the mark know that your wallet is flat!"

Rebecca was laughing helplessly as the station master returned. "Here you are, sir, all ready," he said, handing a new ticket to Gladney.

"Thanks," Gladney said, and paid for the ticket. "Would you see to it that our baggage is loaded?"

The station master said, "Oh, absolutely, sir! I will see that it is taken care of."

"And now, Miss Hawkins, perhaps I could interest you in some supper? I'm starved."

"So am I," Rebecca said, suddenly realizing that it was true.

They ate in the restaurant across the street from the depot. It wasn't anywhere nearly as elegant as the meal on board the riverboat had been, nor, of course, could it compare with the dinner the Lightfoot family served in Oak Valley. But in its simple and tasty fare, there was a degree of intimacy that Rebecca had never before felt in a shared meal. That was because the other meals had been luxurious, all-out affairs, and the personalities had gotten lost in all the trappings. This meal was for the express purpose of satisfying hunger, and that gave it a functional aspect.

After all, Rebecca reasoned, when a woman gets married and spends the rest of her life with a man, not every meal can be a catered affair.

There I go again, she thought in disgust; *I'm thinking marriage, and I'm looking at this man across the table from me as a prospective husband.*

How *would* Gladney be as a husband? She had to wonder. And she looked at him, squinting her eyes, trying to picture him thirty years from now.

"Did you get something in your eye, lass?"

"What?" Rebecca said, startled by his remark and embarrassed over being caught. "No, no, just the bright lights in here."

"The gas lamps are very bright," he agreed solemnly. "It makes you wonder how we've managed to get along for so long on candles and kerosene lamps, doesn't it?"

"Yes," she said cautiously, wondering if he was making sport of her. She was never *quite* sure . . .

"Well," he said, looking at his pocket watch. "Our train will be pulling in in about a half hour. Would you like to go over to the platform and wait?"

"Yes. There is something exciting about a night train, don't you think?"

"Absolutely," Gladney said. "I hope that I never grow too old or too jaded to enjoy watching a train arrive or depart. Of course it always makes me feel a little sad watching a train depart, because I'm not on it."

Gladney lit a cigar, and they strolled arm in arm back to the train depot. There was a large crowd on the platform, milling about, laughing and chatting. At first, Rebecca thought they were all waiting for the train, but it soon became clear that the majority were there to watch the train arrive.

There was a group of people clustered around one

end of the platform, and they went over to investigate. The source of the excitement was a patent medicine man conducting his pitch. They watched in amusement.

The medicine man was tall and thin, wearing a black suit that was badly in need of a cleaning. His long, bony forefinger jabbed at the air as he spoke.

"Yes, ladies and gentlemen, I come to you from Boston, New York, Philadelphia, Washington City, and other points east, to relate to you the benefits of a wonder drug recently discovered. It will cure all illnesses. If you suffer from ulceration of the kidneys, loss of memory, weak nerves, hot hands, flushing in the body, consumption, torpidity of the liver, costiveness, hot spells, bearing-down feelings, or even cancer, this marvelous Indian extract will be your salvation. If you have dyspepsia, debility of thoughts, or fluttering of the senses, take this marvelous Indian extract, and all will be saved."

"That sounds like a marvelous extract," Rebecca said with a smile.

Gladney grunted, blowing cigar smoke. "There are all sorts of cons, Rebecca, and his is one of the crudest. And, I might add, one of the more harmful. That stuff he's peddling wouldn't cure gas pains. Unfortunately, the people who buy it will go home thinking it will."

In the distance Rebecca heard the lonesome whistle of the approaching train. It was a mournful wail that sent a shiver down her spine.

"Here she comes!"

Many of the medicine man's audience deserted him, as did Gladney and Rebecca, as they gathered close to the edge of the platform. Excitement grew as they waited. Soon, far down the track, a huge, wavering, yellow disc came into view. Shortly after, Rebecca could hear the hollow sound of puffing steam and see sparks whipping up into the night sky from the black smokestack.

The engine finally reached the platform, slowing, but pounding on past, and Rebecca could feel her body throbbing in rhythm with the engine's powerful beat. Now sparks flew up from beneath the wheels as steel ground on steel, and glowing embers dripped from the fire box. Then came the yellow squares of windows as the coaches slid by, just before the train came to a halt.

Once the train had stopped, the doors to the coaches started popping open, and the arriving passengers stepped out of the lighted cars onto the crowded platform, then began searching the crowd for a sight of those who had come to meet them.

"Board!" the conductor shouted, and Gladney guided Rebecca over to the mounting step, then up into the coach.

Rebecca could feel a throbbing beneath her feet as the engine's pulsing rhythm was transmitted throughout the coaches. She walked down the aisle of the coach and showed her ticket to the conductor, who smiled at her. Then he escorted them to the pullman coach and opened a compartment door. Inside was a cushioned seat, a table, and a water basin.

"Would you like your bed made right away?" the conductor asked.

"No," she replied. "This is fine. I'll take care of it myself later on. Thank you."

"Very good, miss," the conductor said, and with a half salute, he backed out of the compartment, his glance lingering curiously on Gladney.

"Sit down," Rebecca said after the conductor was gone. "We can visit for a spell."

"Thank you," Gladney said.

There was a kerosene lantern on the wall of the

compartment, but it wasn't lit, so as they sat in the lone seat they could see through the window without having their view impaired by their own reflections staring back at them from the glass.

"This is nice," Rebecca said contentedly. "I've never had a private compartment before."

"I suppose people like William Astor can afford their own private cars," Gladney said idly. "Even private trains, as far as that goes. To someone like that, this wouldn't be very much."

"Well, it is to me. And I do appreciate your thinking of it."

The whistle blew, and there was a loud hiss of escaping steam, then the train jerked several times and started to move slowly. Outside the window, the lights of the station house began to slide by, and they could see the reaction of the crowd as they pulled away.

A moment later, the station house was left behind, and they were crossing Main Street, looking down its length at the brightly lighted saloons and restaurants. The train rumbled out onto a trestle, and the lights of the city were played out below them, winking gaily as the citizens of Lexington enjoyed their night life.

"It's a pretty sight, isn't it?" Rebecca said.

"Yes, it's a very beautiful sight," he said.

It was a moment before she realized that he wasn't looking through the window at all, but was looking directly at her.

"I love you, Rebecca," he said in a low voice.

And the simple directness of his statement, made in the warm closeness of the small compartment, moved Rebecca more deeply than the most eloquent declaration.

Gladney turned to her, and she knew that he was

going to kiss her, and she knew that she wasn't going to resist. In fact, she welcomed it, and she stretched to meet him halfway, opening her lips to receive his kiss.

It was a kiss of hunger and urgency, and it set her head whirling. She felt his tongue brush across her lips, gentle and rough, tentative and demanding, enticing and commanding. Rebecca let herself go limp against him, and for the first time Gladney put his hands on her body. He touched her breast gently, then moved his hand up to lay it against her cheek.

"Becky, take off your clothes," he said huskily. "I want to make love to you."

Here it is, Rebecca thought.

Now was the time for her to face the truth about herself. For on both occasions when Steven had made love, *he* had removed her clothes. She had been able to satisfy a small corner of her conscience by telling herself that since Steven had removed her clothes, she was caught by an event and was helpless to resist, but hadn't actually assisted. It was an evasion of the worst sort and now, in the moment of truth, she knew it. Now Gladney had told her to remove her clothes, and if she did so, that was the first overt move toward being a willing participant. No longer would she have a ready-made excuse to trot out when her conscience prodded her.

That last artifice of her self-delusion crumpled as she willingly, even eagerly, began to undress. As she did so, Gladney secured the latch on the compartment door and began removing his own clothes.

Unashamedly nude, Rebecca opened out the bed and lay back to receive him.

Gladney joined her on the small bed. He kissed her again, and again placed his hand on her breast, but this time she could feel his touch with her naked skin. His hand burned a searing path down her body and across her stomach, finally coming to rest at the nexus of her thighs, at the center of all her turbulent feelings.

Rebecca floated in the stupor of languorous sexual arousal. Her blood was hot, and there was a sweet agony of want in her loins, and her body trembled with fire under Gladney's artful and tender ministrations. Ablaze with need, she plucked at him with urgent fingers. "Gladney?"

"Yes, my darlin' Becky! Yes!"

He moved over her, then into her. Rebecca experienced the most exquisite pleasure—silken sensations unlike anything she had ever felt or dreamed. Not even her experience with Steven could equal this.

She gave as well as took, and as she had become a willing partner, she was now more than a participant, she was an aggressor. She felt the building up of pleasure inside her, a tensing of potential, like a race horse just before the start; then, feeling herself approaching that magic moment, she abandoned all thought save her desperate quest for culmination.

She rushed to the precipice, there to hang balanced precariously for several timeless moments. During that time of rapture, she was able to experience not only her own sweet pleasure, but she could feel through Gladney the muscle-jerking spasms of bursting passion which was his release as well. The pulses of pleasure which swept over Gladney moved into her own body, so that his rapture and hers became a conjoining of ecstasy.

As Rebecca coasted down from the soaring of her sensations, she fell, not like a stone, but rather like a leaf, meeting new eddies of pleasure which would buoy her back up for a moment. Finally, after all the peaks and valleys had been explored, and there was nothing left but the contented warmth of what had been a blazing fire, Gladney disengaged himself and lay beside her, so that he could cradle her head on his shoulder.

Rebecca fell asleep that way, and she slept for several hours. She awoke once, and was momentarily shocked to discover that she was nude, and lying in the arms of Gladney, who was also nude. But memory flooded back with all its remembered sensations, creating a warm, almost giddy feeling, and she snuggled closer to him. She was rewarded by an affectionate squeeze, even though Gladney was asleep.

Beneath the bed, the wheels clicked out a lulling melody against the rails. She could see a silver moon hanging high in the midnight sky, and she watched the hills and trees flowing past the train. She wished there were some way to capture this moment and hold it locked forever in her heart.

Chapter Sixteen

Rebecca heard a distant knocking, and she turned over, burrowing into her pillow, hoping that the sound would go away. But as she turned over she realized that Gladney was gone, and with the realization she came quickly and fully awake, feeling a pull of panic. Where was he?

The train was still moving, so he couldn't have gotten off. The knock sounded again.

"Who is it?"

"Becky, it's me. Get dressed quickly, lass, and we can have a bite of breakfast before the train reaches Bowling Green."

"What time is it?"

"It's past six-thirty already."

"Six-thirty!" she wailed, burying her head again in the pillow. "Go away, Glad, it's too early."

"It's not all that early. We'll be pulling into Bowling Green before too long." His low laughter sounded. "Wake up, sleepyhead. I'll be waiting out here in the corridor. Now, please hurry."

She sighed and sat up, yawning. She looked out through the window and saw the sun, a blood-red ball in the winter sky, just barely above the tree line. Sleep still weighed heavily on her, but she knew that Gladney was right; she would have to dress quickly if they were to have time for breakfast before reaching their destination.

Suddenly, Rebecca realized that she was nude, and at the same time she remembered the night before in full detail. On the morning she had awakened after making love with Steven, she had blushed in quick shame, but this morning her reaction was totally different. This morning she felt only joy!

"Glad?" she called.

"I'm still here. I haven't moved an inch."

"Is anyone out there with you?"

"Well, of course not! What the devil! Who would be with me at such a time?"

She padded to the door and opened it just a crack. She peered out and saw Gladney leaning back against the window at the end of the coach. His arms were folded, and he looked at her with a crooked grin on his face. She looked the other way and saw that the corridor was indeed empty, all the sleeping compartment doors closed.

"Why did you leave the compartment?"

"Now wouldn't it be a fine thing, lass, for the conductor to find me still in your compartment this morning?"

"Have you seen him?"

"Aye. I had a cup of coffee a while ago in the dining car."

"Then it wouldn't seem quite so suspicious if you came in now, would it?"

"Perhaps it wouldn't, no," he said gravely. "You're inviting me in, is it?"

With an expression as solemn as his, she stepped back and opened the door as wide as it would go. It was a wicked thing for her to do, for in doing so she was exposing herself. If anyone happened along the corridor at that particular moment, they would have received quite a shock. But she didn't care, she didn't care!

"Becky, are you daft this morning?" Gladney asked, with a look of shock.

Wordlessly, she reached for him and pulled him into her embrace. She pressed the full length of her body against his and kissed him passionately.

"Becky, we shouldn't be . . ." But again her mouth found his, quieting his protest.

There was the sound of a door slamming at the far end of the coach, and then the voice of a woman and a child as they started along the corridor. Undoubtedly they were bound for the dining car. Their footsteps came closer and closer; soon they would be abreast of the door.

Without breaking the kiss or taking his arms from around her, Gladney managed to kick the door shut just before the pair outside could see inside the compartment.

Rebecca murmured, "Do you really want to have breakfast, darling?"

"Not any more," he said, laughing deep in his throat. "I seem to have suddenly lost my appetite."

"For food, you mean?"

"For food, yes. Oh, yes!"

He took the initiative now, kissing her, and she thrilled to the texture of his mouth on hers. Her lips opened hungrily. She was a little frightened by the intensity of her need, but she let everything go out of her mind and sagged against him.

In a moment they were on the bed, locked together in a feverish embrace. Rebecca gave herself to him without reserve, feeling once again the delight of his hands wandering over her body. They were familiar with each other's needs now, and arousal was quick and full. He rose over her, and they joined together.

Rebecca's breath left her with a sigh as she welcomed his entry, and she matched him move for move.

In a small part of her mind Rebecca wondered how she could be this wanton. She had invited—no, she had urged him into the compartment to make love to her. But most of the wonder sprang from the fact that she felt no guilt or shame. She felt nothing but joy and delight, and as he loved her, she was lifted once more to the dizzying heights of sensation, going from peak to peak with such rapidity that it was impossible to tell when one was left and another attained.

Finally, a shuddering moan of pleasure from Gladney told her that he had joined in this maelstrom of sensation, and she locked her arms around his naked back, holding him close to her, as they blended into one entity in the final, shattering moment of ecstasy.

A few moments later, with the pleasant weight of Gladney lying on her, Rebecca became aware enough to realize that the train was slackening speed. She turned her head toward the window and saw houses passing. They were entering Bowling Green!

"Gladney," she said urgently. "Reach over and pull the shade down!"

He looked toward the window, and then began to laugh.

"Don't laugh, damn you! Pull down the shade! Please!"

Still laughing, he complied, turning the compartment dim. She saw the humor of the situation, and she joined in the laughter as they got off the bed and quickly dressed.

The driver of the carriage for hire agreed to take them out to the Townes thoroughbred farm. He asked, "Will you be going to the main house, or to the stables?"

Gladney scrubbed his chin. "Why, aren't they together?"

"No, sir," the driver said in reply. "The stables, they're more'n a mile from the main house. H. B. Townes, you see, he has trainers that live the year around on the place, and he has living quarters for them at the stables, out of the way of the main house."

"Then I suppose you'd better take us to the stables," Gladney said.

"You going to buy one of H. B.'s horses? He sure raises some champions out there."

"We may," Gladney said cryptically.

Rebecca leaned back on the black leather seat, her hand snuggled in Gladney's, and watched the countryside roll by. She suddenly realized that spring was at hand. The hills were alive with dogwood blooms and azaleas, and the pleasant odor of honeysuckle scented the air. Cardinals and bluebirds flitted from tree to tree.

She had no idea of what lay in store for them when they arrived at their destination, but for the moment she was content. She scratched a fingernail against Gladney's palm, and he closed his hand convulsively around hers. She looked over at him, and he winked at her.

"There it is!" their driver said, pointing to a large sign across a gate: "H. B. Townes: Thoroughbreds Sold."

The farm was bordered by neatly built stone fences which snaked out over the hills, dipping down into valleys, pushing through flowering trees and across green fields. As their carriage turned onto the lane starting beneath the overhead sign, the road forked, with another, smaller sign, indicating the main house in one direction, the stables the other.

Their driver took the stable fork. "What did I tell

you?" he asked a few minutes later, as they approached a neatly kept row of stables and saw a man walking toward them. "I told you that H. B. Townes would likely be down here."

The approaching man stopped and waited for them. He was short and plump, Rebecca noted, with deep-set brown eyes which twinkled with the love of life, and she sensed that here was a man who enjoyed what he was doing. He wore chin whiskers, and he combed them with his fingers as Gladney and Rebecca got down and walked over to him.

"Good morning, and welcome to the Townes Thoroughbred Farm," he said jovially. "I am H. B. Townes. Are you folks looking for a horse?"

"We are," Gladney said.

Townes beamed. "Good, good. You've come to the right place then."

Gladney said, "I hope so. Is there a Mr. Oscar Stull around?"

"You just missed him," Townes said regretfully. "He was here, yes. In fact, he spent the night here. But he left on an early train this morning, he, Mr. Mercy, and his horse, Bold Diablo. I believe he's headed for Louisville. He told me that he was going there to take care of entering the Kentucky Derby."

"You say he took Bold Diablo along with him," Rebecca said eagerly. "Did he leave any horses here, Mr. Townes?"

"As a matter of fact, he did, yes. He left Lucifer, and . . ." He suddenly stopped and smiled broadly. "I'll wager I know who you are, young lady. You must be Rebecca Hawkins, Hawk's granddaughter. Oscar Stull said you'd be around."

"Yes, you're right. I am Rebecca Hawkins, and this is my friend, Gladney Halloran." As the two men shook hands, Rebecca said with a puzzled frown, "I'm afraid

300

I don't understand, Mr. Townes. Why would Oscar Stull expect me to come here?"

"Why, to see to your horse, of course. You have come to make arrangements for Black Prince, haven't you?"

"Yes!" Rebecca said excitedly. "You mean Prince is here with you?"

"Of course he is here," Townes said with a look of astonishment. "Didn't you expect him to be?"

"Yes, but . . . Well, we thought he would be here, but . . ." Rebecca broke off, looking at Gladney for help.

"What Rebecca means, Mr. Townes, is that we didn't expect anyone to admit the animal was here."

Townes was shaking his head. "Now you have me thoroughly confused. You didn't authorize Stull to transport your horse here? You didn't tell him you intended boarding Black Prince with me?"

"We did not, sir," Rebecca said. "As far as we are concerned, Oscar Stull stole our horse. We had to track him down to your place."

"I see," Townes said, combing his beard. "Or rather, I don't see. This is odd, very odd indeed."

"We were fortunate to find out that Stull came here," Gladney said. "If we hadn't, Rebecca's horse might have been lost forever."

"No, no, that wouldn't have happened," Townes said emphatically. "I sent a notification to Hawk in care of the Louisville Jockey Club, telling him what my boarding fees were. The first time your grandfather visited the club, Miss Hawkins, he would have received the notice."

"But that might not have been for days, at least a couple of weeks," Rebecca said in dismay. "Probably not until Derby week—"

"That was Stull's idea, Rebecca," Gladney broke in.

"By the time you or Hawk found out where Black Prince was, it would be too late to enter him in the Derby."

Townes said, "The Derby? Are you planning on entering the horse in the Kentucky Derby?"

"Certainly," Rebecca said. She added vehemently, "We not only intend to enter him, but we intend to win!"

"I see," Townes said with a sigh. "Miss Hawkins, it would seem that I have somehow been made a party to Stull's chicanery. I have never liked the man, but I never dreamed that . . . I resent being used in such a manner, and I shall send him a letter at once, a letter of protest, and demand that he remove his other animals from my care at once. I beg of you, please accept my apology for any trouble or distress that I may have caused you."

"You don't have to apologize, Mr. Townes," she said. "As you say, you were victimized by Stull, just as Grandfather and I were."

"You are most gracious, Miss Hawkins. In the meantime, please accept my hospitality. And naturally, you will not be charged one penny for Black Prince's board."

"Thank you." She looked at Gladney. "We must send a wire to Grandfather, telling him we have found Prince. He is worried sick, I know."

"You can do that from Bowling Green, of course," Townes said. "I'll loan you a pair of horses to ride into town with."

"Uh . . ." Rebecca glanced sidelong at Gladney. "Do you have a buckboard instead?"

"Certainly. You two wait right here. I'll have one hitched up for you."

Gladney opened his mouth to protest, a little upset

that Rebecca should seek to protect him. Then he thought better of it. After all, it was quite a ride into Bowling Green, and he hadn't exactly mastered horsemanship during his stay in Clarksville.

As he had promised, H. B. Townes brought a buckboard out to them shortly. They drove into town and sent the wire to Henry Hawkins. They discussed Stull's motives in abducting Black Prince and then making no attempt to hide his trail.

"The only motive I can see is that he simply hoped to prevent Hawk from entering the Derby," Gladney said.

"I really don't care too much, so long as we got Prince back safe and sound."

"But Stull should be made to pay for it," Gladney said grimly.

"Glad . . ." She placed a hand on his arm. "We have Prince back. Let's forget about it for now, and enjoy our time together."

"Now that, lass," he said with his flashing grin, "is something in which I heartily concur."

H. B. Townes was still at the stables when they returned, and he invited them to spend the night. "We have a fox hunt scheduled for early in the morning. Maybe you two would like to participate?"

"Oh, that would be marvelous!" Rebecca clapped her hands. "I haven't hunted since we left England! Glad?"

"I don't think so, Rebecca. It's not a sport I'm mad about." He grinned. "My sympathy is always with the poor fox."

"Glad, you don't have to be embarrassed. Not everyone can ride to the hounds."

"Certainly not, Mr. Halloran," Townes said. "As a matter of fact, I won't be riding to the hunt myself.

But there is so much that goes on that I'm sure you'll enjoy yourself without actually riding in the hunt."

"Please, Glad?"

"All right." Gladney capitulated with a shrug. "As long as I don't have to ride a horse over a fence."

"Fine," Townes said. "We'll have a hearty breakfast, and be off shortly after dawn."

"That's the way to do it," Gladney said in Rebecca's ear. "Sneak up on the little bugger while he's still asleep."

"Hush now!" she whispered back with a little laugh. "You'll have a fine time, I promise you."

Although H. B. Townes had cottages on the grounds for horse buyers to stay in while they examined his stock, he insisted that Gladney and Rebecca spend the night in the main house. "I feel bad about what has happened, and I feel partially responsible. This is little enough to do."

In an aside to Rebecca, Gladney murmured, "For my part, I'd rather he let us use a couple of the cottages. Then we could," he leered, "visit each other during the night."

It was still dark the next morning when a servant walked down the upstairs corridor, knocking on all the doors. At each he announced, "Mr. Fox has done had his breakfast. Now it's time for you-all to have yours."

Rebecca had been loaned a riding outfit, and when she had put it on and stepped out into the hall, she found Gladney waiting for her.

"What do you think?" she asked, turning to model it for him.

He grinned lazily. "I'll tell you what I think. If men saw women in trousers often enough, I doubt they'd ever let them into dresses again."

"Glad, you're awful!" she said in a scolding tone, but she was inordinately pleased.

He offered her his arm. "Are you hungry?"

"Not really. I'm too excited. Gladney, I do wish you could ride. You're going to miss out on all the sport."

He made a face. "I can do without the contrary beasts, thank you very much. Besides, Mr. Townes has assured me that I will enjoy myself. And I fully intend to, if it is only in seeing so many good-looking women in trousers." He ran a hand caressingly over her bottom.

"Gladney, don't do that!" She stepped away from him. "What if someone saw you?"

"They'd be envious, if it was a man. All right, all right!" He held up his hands. "I'll behave myself."

There were some twenty people, both men and women, around the table in the dining room when they entered. It was quite a feast, for a breakfast. On the table were calves' brains, steak, Virginia ham, buckwheat cakes, roasted potatoes, light bread, and strong coffee. And even though the hour was early and everyone was talking animatedly about the coming fox hunt, appetites were hearty, and within a short time most of the food was consumed.

The familiar hunter's bugle sounded outside, and a servant hurried in to whisper something in the ear of H. B. Townes, who was seated at the head of the table. He smiled, dabbed at his mouth with a snowy-white linen napkin, and got to his feet.

"Ladies and gentlemen, that is our call to the hunt! The fox is about ready to be turned loose, and your mounts are saddled and ready. Shall we get on with it?"

There was a concerted rush for the front door, and the fox hunters mounted the horses lined up outside. It was full daylight by this time, although white

305

clouds of mist still sulked in the meadows, and patches of it were impaled by the trees, stretching out like long, lacy streamers.

An ancient black man, with white hair and a white beard, walked along before the mounted hunters and held up a wooden cage for everyone to see. Inside the cage, a small, red-orange fox darted back and forth nervously.

Gladney, standing beside H. B. Townes, with a cigar trailing smoke, shook his head pityingly, and looked at Rebecca with accusing eyes.

"Our quarry, ladies and gentlemen," Townes announced. "Good hunting!"

He motioned for the fox to be released. A red-orange flash sped across the well-kept lawn, darted through a hedgerow, then scurried across the meadow. Not until the fox had disappeared into the tree line on the far side of the meadow were the dogs released. They had been baying loudly and tugging impatiently at their leashes.

The dogs, nearly two dozen by Gladney's estimate, exploded across the lawn, already in full cry. The horn sounded again, the signal for the mounted hunters to ride after the baying hounds. Gladney winced as the hedgerow was cleared in a graceful leap, the horses almost in an even line, and within a very few minutes the thunder of their hoofbeats had receded.

Gladney stood with Townes, watching the red-jacketed riders vanish one by one into the woods. He had to admit that it was a colorful sight, although it still struck him as a cruel sport.

"Come along, Mr. Halloran," Townes said. "We'll ride along after them at a more sedate pace."

For the first time Gladney noted that Townes had had two more saddled horses brought around. His mind flooded with dismay as he realized that one was for him. Well, there seemed no help for it. Be damned if he would disgrace himself in front of Townes by refusing to ride!

Gritting his teeth, he reached up for the saddle horn and pulled himself into the saddle. The horse was a well-trained animal, and he made no violent response to Gladney's swinging up onto his back. Maybe it wouldn't be so dire, after all.

"Let's go!" Townes said, and he slapped his legs against the side of his mount, urging him into a quick gallop.

Without any signal from Gladney, his horse broke into a gallop after the Townes's horse. Gladney seized the saddle horn in a death grip. But after a few moments he began to relax. Amazingly, he hadn't tumbled off, and after a little while he was even able to adjust himself to the rhythm of the galloping horse.

Gladney smiled, then laughed aloud to himself. What the hell, in time he might even come to like it!

Townes led the way into a wide, open meadow, and then stopped his horse there. Gladney sawed back on the reins and his mount halted alongside the other one. He smiled again, feeling a sense of accomplishment.

"They'll be coming back before long," Townes said. "The fox has been treed. Didn't take long this morning."

"How do you know they treed the creature?"

"Listen to the hounds, my boy."

Gladney cocked his head, listening. He realized that Townes was right; the braying of the pack of hounds had increased in pitch. Just then a bright-jacketed rider broke out of the woods and came racing toward them. The rider reined in before them with a flourish.

"We caught him!" the man exclaimed, red-faced with excitement.

Now other horses and riders emerged from the woods and collected around Townes, their voices rising and falling in excitement. It was a few moments before Gladney noticed something that sent a chill of alarm through him—Rebecca wasn't with them!

He waited for a few moments, his apprehensive gaze on the line of trees. She didn't appear. Gladney kneed his horse over to Townes and got his attention. "Mr. Townes, where is Rebecca? She hasn't come back!"

Townes's gaze passed over the group of riders. "Why, I do believe you're correct. That is strange." Raising his voice and motioning for quiet, he said, "Miss Hawkins isn't among you. Does anyone know her whereabouts?"

The hunters looked at each other, and then one by one shook their heads. Townes asked, "Who remembers seeing her last?"

The man who had ridden up first said, "I recall seeing her off to my right just before we ran that fox to ground. She was almost out of sight in the trees, but I forgot about it when the hounds told us they'd found the fox."

"Well, she may have gotten lost, being unfamiliar with the terrain," Townes said. "We'll go look for her. Mr. Halloran, you remain here, just in case she shows up before we get back."

"I should help you look . . ."

Townes shook his head. "No, it's better you stay here. You're a stranger here as well. We don't want you getting lost as well." His laughter sounded rather forced. "We'll find her, never fear."

The red-jacketed hunters strung out in a thin line and rode back into the woods. Gladney remained in the meadow, his glance constantly raking the line of trees, expecting any moment to see Rebecca come riding toward him, to tell him some humorous story of what had happened. Maybe she had fallen off her horse. Now that *would* be humorous—if she wasn't hurt.

She did not appear. The sun rose higher and higher, and the woods echoed with the voices of the hunters shouting Rebecca's name over and over.

Gladney tensed as he saw a flash of scarlet in the woods. But it was two men, H. B. Townes and one of the hunters.

Townes's face was unduly grave as he rode up to Gladney. "Mr. Halloran?"

"Yes?" Gladney said tightly.

"There's something I think you should know. This is Rod Wayne." He indicated the man with him. "Go ahead, Rod, tell him what you told me."

"Well, I didn't think much of it at the time," Wayne said tentatively. "Not until I got to talking to H. B. here as we looked for Miss Hawkins. He told me that this fellow Oscar Stull pulled a dirty trick on Miss Hawkins."

"That's true. But what has that to do with now?"

"Well, it just might figure."

"What might figure? What are you getting at, man?"

"It was my understanding that Oscar Stull and his sidekick left for Louisville yesterday. I was given to understand that. But today, during the hunt, I saw him back in the woods there." He jerked his thumb over his shoulder. "Like I said, I didn't think anything of it at the time . . ."

Gladney strained forward. "You saw Oscar Stull?"

"Nope, not Stull," Wayne said. "It was that queer sidekick of his, the one they call Mr. Mercy. Strikes me as a strange name for a man like that. He gives me the shivers just looking at me."

"You saw Mr. Mercy this morning, during the hunt?"

"I could swear I did. And it struck me at the time that he was watching Miss Hawkins pretty close."

Chapter Seventeen

Her surroundings were so strange, and the circumstances of her being there so unclear, that for moments after Rebecca awoke she couldn't be certain whether she was conscious or dreaming. She opened and closed her eyes several times, and in so doing she ascertained that she was indeed awake.

She didn't know where she was, or how she had come there. She remembered riding through the woods, the hounds bellowing full-throatedly as they treed the fox; and she remembered riding through a hedgerow, and sensing rather than seeing a horse moving toward her in the shadows.

Rebecca had thought the other horse carried another hunter, and she had not been alarmed. Then an arm clamped around her neck from behind and a hand held a wet, sweet-smelling cloth over her nose and mouth. Rebecca fought for breath. Her throat and chest burned, and brilliantly colored lights danced before her eyes. She tried to cry out, but she couldn't, and finally she felt herself slipping into unconsciousness.

Now, Rebecca realized that she was tied, spread-eagle fashion, on a hard pallet on the floor of a small room. On one wall there was a window which seemed to be covered by an isinglass curtain, and the distorted sunlight which came in through that window was the only illumination in the room. She could hear flies buzzing. One landed on her leg and walked up toward her thighs, and feeling it on her skin Rebecca realized that she was totally naked!

She jerked convulsively, trying to shoo the fly away; its presence was not only irritating, but it struck her as the final indignity. The fly did leave her thigh, only to land on one of her bare breasts. She raised her head as high as possible and blew a stream of air toward it, forcing it to buzz away a second time.

Rebecca looked down the length of her naked body. Her legs were spread open, and ropes went from each ankle to posts set in the floor several feet apart. Her arms were lashed to posts in the same manner. She knew that in such a position she was absolutely defenseless, and she wondered with a feeling of panic if the person who had done this had not already taken his pleasure with her. But, she reasoned, if he had, surely she would have known, and it didn't appear that she had yet been violated.

The fly landed on her another time, and walked down her pelvic bone, across the most tender and sensitive portion of her skin, just before it dipped into the intimate patch of hair. Rebecca moved again, thrusting her hips up to throw the fly off.

She sensed someone's presence. She strained to see who it was and finally had to twist around to look back over her shoulder. That was when she saw her captor for the first time.

It was Mr. Mercy!

"What is the meaning of this?" Rebecca demanded.

She was so frightened that her throat was tightly constricted, and her voice sounded weak and strange to her own ears. "What do you want?"

Mr. Mercy walked around her, keeping some distance away, just staring at her with those dead eyes.

312

She had to twist her head around and strain to keep him always in view. Now his eyes began to glow with a hot, smoky look, and Rebecca felt her skin crawl.

Then the gray man stopped at her feet.

"Why am I here?" she asked.

"Mr. Stull ordered me to bring you," Mr. Mercy said tonelessly. "We knew you would come after your horse, and I was to wait until you both got there. You got there sooner than we thought you would."

"That still doesn't tell me what you want with me!"

"If something happens to you, your grandfather will be too upset to enter the Kentucky Derby, even if he does get his horse back. And Mr. Stull figures that the Indian is sweet enough on you so that he also might be too upset to enter. That would leave the field open for him."

"But what is going to happen to me?"

Mr. Mercy dropped to his knees, right between her spread legs, and looked at her with those cold, gray eyes.

"Mr. Stull left that up to me," he said. For the first time she saw the shadow of a smile on his thin lips.

Rebecca felt a chill race over her body, as if someone had run a splinter of ice down her spine. She strained against the ropes, arching her back up and thrashing her legs as much as the ropes would allow. She realized almost immediately that this was a mistake, for he enjoyed this immensely, and he continued to watch her with his cold, fish-like stare.

She went very still. "Please go away," she cried hopelessly.

She might not have spoken, as Mr. Mercy evinced absolutely no reaction to her words. He just looked at her, staring at the juncture of her thighs with such intensity that Rebecca could imagine herself being seared by his gaze. She felt her throat begin to clog with cold tears of fear as a wave of despair washed over her.

"We'll go out again in the morning," H. B. Townes said to Gladney that evening, after the hunting party straggled in after a fruitless search that had lasted the entire day.

"I'm going out there myself, tonight," Gladney said determinedly.

"But you can't find anything at night," Townes protested. "Besides, you're on your own, and you don't even know this part of the country. It would be foolish to look for Miss Hawkins at night."

"I'm always on my own," Gladney said doggedly. "I've been on my own all my life. Until now . . ." His throat closed up for a moment. Then he continued, "I intend to keep looking until I find her."

"But you have to rest," Townes said. "And you've got to eat."

"I can't help but wonder if Rebecca is getting any rest," Gladney said tightly. "Or anything to eat."

Townes sighed. "Mr. Halloran, I can sympathize with you, believe me I can. It's just that I think you're being rash. I don't see how you can hope to accomplish anything at night."

"Will you loan me a horse, sir?"

"Of course I will, my boy. Gladly. And if you'll take the time to eat a quick meal, I'll draw you a rough map of the surrounding countryside. You realize, of course, that we have no assurance that Mr. Mercy is still in the neighborhood."

"He can't be too far away. It's obvious, to me at least, that this whole thing was planned, from the moment Stull took Black Prince. I'm sure there must be a house, cabin, a shack of some kind, not too far

314

from here, and that's where this blackguard has taken Rebecca."

Townes ran his fingers through his hair in deep thought. "I can't think of any such place offhand, but at least I can draw you a map."

Townes worked on a crude map while Gladney wolfed down some food, not tasting a thing he ate. Townes drew in the roads, most of the nearby farms, and last of all the railroad track, meandering through hills and valleys and over creeks and rivers. When he was done, he had drawn the entire area for a radius of three miles around his own farm.

He finally straightened up with a sigh. "He may have gone well beyond this area, but if you are determined to continue the search tonight, I imagine this is about all the area you will be able to cover."

Gladney studied the map intently. "We can eliminate this area right away," he said, placing his hand across the eastern quadrant of the map.

"How do you reach that conclusion?"

"He had to have knocked her out in some way. And he couldn't very well carry an unconscious woman back this way, which comes close to Bowling Green, without someone seeing him and getting suspicious. And your place is here, so with all the fox hunters looking for Rebecca through the woods in here, we also know he didn't come through there either." Gladney pointed to the southern quadrant. "Your house is here. I doubt he'd come through here either. That leaves the most logical direction to take her." He indicated the western section of the map.

"There is nothing in that direction but meadowlands and woods," Townes said thoughtfully, "until you get over as far as Buzzard Knob."

"Buzzard Knob? What's that?"

"It's a mountain. Well, not much of a mountain," Townes smiled sparely, "but what comes closest to being a mountain around here. It's overgrown with trees and underbrush."

"Anything on it?"

"Not that I know of. I understand there were once some moonshiners on the mountain, but not any more. It isn't even a good picnic area."

"In other words, no one ever goes there?"

"A few hunters maybe, but there's no reason for anyone else to traipse up there."

"Yet there's a railroad track running through here," Gladney said tapping the map with his finger.

Townes nodded. "I just drew that in so you would have a reference point. That line was abandoned some time back, when the Hopkinsville line was completed. I don't imagine there's been a train on that in five years or more. Weeds have grown over it, and a man would almost have to know it was there to find it. In fact, now that I think of it, I *know* no engines have been on that line for a long time, because they have abandoned the turntable at the end of the line up here." Townes indicated the spot where the hatchline he had drawn ended.

"A turntable?"

"Yes, you know, so the engine could be turned around to come back the other way."

"Yes, I know how they work. But they have a small switching house, don't they?"

"Well, yes, I seem to recall that there was one there. It wasn't much bigger than a tool shed, and it's deserted now. Quite likely it's fallen to ruin after all this time."

"How far is it from here?"

"Oh, four, maybe five miles. I didn't draw it on the map, because I didn't think of it, but it would be here, at the end of the line." He drew a little square at the end of the railroad line.

Gladney nodded, lost in thought. "Thank you, Mr. Townes."

"Do you think that may be where she is?"

"How can I know? But at least it strikes me as good a place as any to start looking."

"If she is there, and you being alone . . ." Townes was frowning. "Perhaps it wouldn't be a bad idea to send along some of the others with you."

"I don't agree, Mr. Townes. If I'm wrong, if this is a wild goose chase, I'll be wanting all the help I can get in the morning. They'll be better able to help for a good night's rest. I think it's better that I scout this shack, if it's there, on my own."

"Well, whatever you say." Townes walked across the room to a desk and opened a drawer. "Here, I think you should take this along."

He held out a pistol, holding it with his thumb and forefinger as if it might explode and rupture his hand.

Gladney started to reach for it, then drew his hand back. He shook his head. "No, Mr. Townes. Thank you very much, but I'd rather not."

"You're unfamiliar with guns?"

Gladney gave a short, mirthless laugh. "I was in the war, sir. Let's say I am *too* familiar with them. I'd rather handle this without a gun."

"Suit yourself," Townes said with a shrug. "I don't much like guns myself." He returned the pistol to the desk and closed the drawer with a crash.

The ancient black man who had released the fox early that morning had come silently into the room, and now stood just inside the door. Townes looked around and saw him. "Yes, William?"

William said, "We have that horse saddled and ready for Mr. Halloran."

317

"Good. Come along, my boy, I'll walk outside with you."

Outside the house a brisk breeze had come up, blowing from the southwest, carrying with it the smell and feel of rain. Clouds obscured the moon and the stars, and there was only the light from the house to see by.

"It's coming on to rain," Townes said in dismay. "You still want to do this?"

"I'm going," Gladney said grimly.

Without being told, William produced a poncho. Gladney thanked him, and looped it over the saddle horn.

"It'll be darker than tar out there," Townes warned.

"I'm going to find the abandoned railroad tracks, and follow them to the end. I can't get lost that way, no matter how dark it is.

"You'll find the tracks down this field road, about a mile, more or less." Townes pointed to a faint road that went south behind the house. "Just stay on the road until you hit the tracks, then ride west, to your right."

"Thanks again." Gladney turned for his first good look at the horse. It struck him as being meaner and bigger than the one he'd ridden earlier, and the instant Gladney put his hands on the saddle to mount up, the animal took two quick steps to one side.

"Lobo may be a touch skittish at first . . ."

"Lobo?" Gladney said in alarm.

"The name doesn't mean anything," Townes said with a chuckle. "He doesn't live up to his name, believe me, and he's a good animal. He never seems to tire."

"Glad to hear it," Gladney said dryly.

He drew a deep breath, then swung up into the saddle in one quick motion. As Gladney's weight came

318

down into the saddle, Lobo danced sideways several steps and stiffened as if he was about to buck. Instead, he performed a couple of quick corkscrews.

"Lobo!" Townes said in a scolding tone. "You just be nice and settle down now."

Gladney patted the horse on the neck, thinking how ineffective that probably was, but the horse finally seemed to settle down. Gladney sighed in relief and gathered up the reins in one hand.

"Good luck, my boy," Townes said.

Without once taking his gaze from Lobo's bowed head, Gladney gave his host a little wave. He clucked at Lobo, and the animal started at a trot down the road Townes had called a field road.

The rain held off until Gladney finally came across the disused railroad tracks. He reined Lobo in long enough to untie the poncho and put it on, being very careful with it for fear he would spook the horse. Then he turned the animal down the tracks, riding along the ties between the rails.

It was more than just a rain; it was an electrical storm, and the sky literally came alive with jagged bolts of lightning. Thunder cracked like cannon fire. Gladney was afraid that the lightning and thunder would frighten Lobo, but the animal appeared undaunted by the storm.

During the war, the men in Gladney's troop had always been cautioned to stay away from railroad tracks, because the rails would, as his sergeant once put it, "Draw lightning quicker'n a dog's tail!"

Yet Gladney knew that he had no choice. If he abandoned the rails he would surely lose his way. Lobo seemed to have some instinctive sense of danger about the rails, because he kept trying to leave them. Each time Gladney hauled him back between the rails. It became a contest between man and animal, and Gladney wondered how long he could keep it up.

The rain continued to fall. It slashed against him and ran in cold rivulets off the folds and creases of the poncho. It blew in sheets across the railroad tracks, and drummed wickedly into the wind-whipped trees to either side. The lightning, when it flashed, lit up the countryside in stark, harsh white. It was followed immediately by thunder, snapping shrilly at first, then rolling through the valleys, picking up the resonance of the hollows and becoming an echoing boom.

Rebecca was cold and damp, but more than that, she was terrified. She was so frightened that her fear kept her from really feeling the discomfort she was experiencing. The rain was blowing in through the cracks and holes of the little shack, and by now there was a puddle on the floor. The pallet on which she was lying was about six inches high, and the water had risen to a depth of two inches, so that she was not lying in water. But she was drenched and thoroughly miserable.

"Mr. Mercy, please let me go," she pleaded one more time. But Mr. Mercy, as he had done virtually all day, remained silent. He was sitting on an up-turned box on the far side of the shack, completely motionless. When it had grown dark he had lighted a lantern, but it was turned low and he sat mostly in shadow. She could see him fully only when he was exposed by the lightning flashes, which occurred at a frequency of every minute or so.

Mr. Mercy had not raped her—not yet. He had watched her the entire afternoon, and now into the night, staring at her with those flat, dead eyes, so that her flesh crawled and her stomach heaved, and she wanted to vomit in fear and revulsion.

Once he had taken out a gun, and using the barrel

of it he had traced her whole body, running the cold steel across her breasts, around her nipples, down her stomach, and had paused there. At that point Rebecca had closed her eyes, fearing the worst, but after a moment the gun barrel had traveled on, onto her thighs, down one leg and up the other, coming back to her pubic mound again, this time without stopping, the icy steel creeping on up her stomach, across her breasts, up her neck, then stopping right under her nose. Mr. Mercy had cocked the pistol, and Rebecca heard the terrifying click of metal on metal and saw the cylinder turn. She could see through the cylinder opening the blunt silver end of the bullets, and she knew that one of those bullets was lined up with the barrel, waiting for the hammer to fall.

Rebecca had closed her eyes and said a quick prayer, regretting that she had not been a more religious person, but hoping that God would measure the quality of her faith, if not the quantity. Finally, Mr. Mercy had let the hammer back down slowly, and gone over to sit on the box near the wall.

He had been there ever since, unmoving, staring at her until the light failed, stirring only to light the dim lantern; and even now, when a lightning flash lit up his face, she could see that he was still in the same position. She wasn't even sure that he blinked. He appeared to have the same lidless stare as a snake.

Rebecca heard a squealing sound, then a splashing, and a scurrying of tiny feet. She looked toward the half-open door of the shack and saw three enormous rats. They had evidently been driven inside by the rain, and they were looking around with bright, beady eyes.

Rebecca had always felt a revulsion for rats, and the thought that they might cross to her was mind-numbing.

321

"Dear God, please!" she whispered. "Please, God, please, don't let them come near me. Oh, please, don't let them!"

The rats squeaked among themselves, and two of them climbed up the slanting wall to the rafters of the shack, but one of them leaped out into the puddle of water, and swam toward Rebecca.

"Please, no, no!" Frantic, she struggled against the restraining ropes, but as before, she was unable to free herself.

"Mr. Mercy," she called. "Mr. Mercy, do something! For God's sake, do something about the rats!"

Mr. Mercy remained motionless, a dark, unmoving shadow in the corner of the room. For all the reaction he showed, he hadn't even heard her.

Rebecca turned her face to look at the rat, and saw it still advancing inexorably toward her.

"No!" she moaned, clenching her eyes shut. "Somebody stop it!"

There was another flash of lightning, and this time it was so close that the thunder sounded right on top of the flash. Concurrent with the lightning and the thunder there was a gush of wind, and a fresh torrent of water rushed in through the door. The water washed the rat away just before it reached the raised pallet upon which Rebecca was tied, and, squealing, it pulled itself up at the opposite end of the floor. Dripping, it scurried up a leaning board, then scampered across a rafter to hunch in the comparative dryness of the roof alongside the other two.

The lightning bolt may have struck the rails. Gladney knew only that there was a ringing in his ears, and he saw a dull blue glow spread out from either side of the rail on his right. But the flash also revealed a small shack off to the left. He reined Lobo in, then urged him off the track over to a stand of trees about thirty yards from the railroad shack. He tied Lobo to a tree, then went at a crouching run toward the shack. The night was black between lightning flashes, but Gladney saw a faint glow of light coming from the shack. His pulse began to pound. He flattened himself against the wall by the door and peered inside. What he saw almost made him ill. Rebecca was naked and spread-eagled on the floor!

The sight was enough to make him disregard caution. He pushed the door open and barged inside. "Rebecca! Dear God, who did—?"

"Gladney!" she screamed. "No! Get away, quick!"

Belatedly, Gladney realized how rashly he had acted. He whirled just in time to see Mr. Mercy standing up. Light glinted off the gun in his hand, which was pointed straight at Gladney.

Gladney had no time to think. Instinctively, he kicked out with one foot. His boot hit the puddle and sent a spray of water into Mr. Mercy's face.

The man fired his pistol, but the shot went wild, the water having thrown his aim off. Gladney leaped to one side and shouted angrily, drawing another shot. This one went awry, too. In a flash of lightning Gladney saw that Mr. Mercy was pawing at his eyes with his free hand.

Gladney charged him, seized the gunhand wrist in both of his, and wrenched it upward just as the gun was discharged a third time, the bullet singing through the roof.

Now, with the gun momentarily neutralized, Gladney managed to bring enough pressure to bear on Mr. Mercy's wrist to squeeze the pistol out of the other man's hand. Gladney heard the gun drop. He let go of Mr. Mercy's hand and hit him hard, a hammer blow on the side of the man's head. Mr. Mercy was driven back by the blow, and Gladney, yelling with rage, closed in and hit him again, knocking him back against the wall.

"For what you've done to Becky, I'll kill you with my bare hands, you monster!" Gladney bellowed.

Mr. Mercy glanced around desperately. He spotted an iron rod leaning against the wall near his hand; it was a rusty piece of a switching lever. He snatched it up and swung it hard just as Gladney charged into him. The blow caught Gladney on the shoulder, and because his footing in the mud and water was precarious, he went down with a mighty splash. Mr. Mercy swung at him again, but Gladney managed to get out of the way just in time, rolling quickly across the muddy floor.

Mr. Mercy started toward him, the rod raised up over his head. Then he stopped short, and Gladney saw him actually smile, a cruel smile totally devoid of humor. Then he stooped down and scooped up the pistol. Now he had a definite advantage, for Gladney was all the way across the room from him, still on his hands and knees on the floor.

Mr. Mercy aimed the gun at Gladney, then shook his head, lowering it.

"No," he said in a colorless voice. "I think I'll do this first." His lips peeled back in a grimace that was more a snarl than a grin. "I'll let you watch, con man."

He swung around to stand over the pallet. He pointed the gun at Rebecca's head and pulled back on the hammer.

"No!" Gladney bellowed.

"Oh, I'm not going to kill her . . . yet. I'm going to have her first, while you watch, con man," Mr. Mercy said in a voice thickened by lust. He fell to his knees between Rebecca's outspread legs. As Gladney started to scramble through the water, the pistol swung his

324

way. "You can either stay over there and watch, or die right now!"

Gladney halted, staring into the muzzle of the gun. Then Mr. Mercy began to fumble at his breeches with his free hand, and Gladney's mind went blank. Disregarding the pistol aimed at him, he scrambled like a crab on his hands and knees, intent on throwing his body across Rebecca's in protection. He saw Mr. Mercy and the pistol through a red mist. A distant part of his mind expected a bullet any second, but he kept coming, determined that not even a bullet would stop him.

Then he heard a high, squealing sound and saw something that stopped him. Three huge rats had dropped from the rafters in the roof and landed on Mr. Mercy's head, sinking their claws and teeth into his flesh and hair the instant they landed. Mr. Mercy screamed, a high-pitched sound of terror and hysteria. With his free hand he clawed at the rats, but they clung like leeches. Then he began to beat at them with the gun. Taking advantage of the man's inattention, Gladney hurriedly scrambled through the water until he could cover Rebecca's body with his, but his fascinated gaze never left Mr. Mercy and the rats.

Mr. Mercy screamed again, and suddenly the pistol was discharged. Before his eyes Gladney saw the top of the man's skull disintegrate. Later, he concluded that in his panic Mr. Mercy had inadvertently pulled the trigger at a moment when the gun muzzle was against his temple. He flew backwards.

Gladney was on his feet immediately, standing over the body. Mr. Mercy's eyes were open and staring, truly dead now.

The three rats still busily swarmed over his head. With a sound of disgust, Gladney kicked them loose and stomped on them until all three were dead.

As he finally stopped, breathing heavily, his stomach heaving with nausea, Rebecca spoke behind him. "Gladney, are you all right?"

He spun around. "Am I all right? I'm fine—now. The question is, are *you* all right?"

"Oh, Glad, it was horrible!" Tears filled her eyes and ran down her cheeks. "If you hadn't come when you did, I don't know what I would have done!"

Gladney was already fumbling with the wet knots of the ropes binding her. Looking up, he said hesitantly, "He . . . he didn't . . ."

"No, he didn't touch me. I don't know why. I was sure he was going to fall on me any second."

"He's a crazy. Who can figure out men like that? He probably got more of a thrill out of seeing a woman going mad with the waiting than in actually doing the deed."

He had her bonds loose now, and Rebecca sat up into his arms, weeping freely.

"There, Becky. There, lass," he said soothingly. "It's all over, darlin'. Sure and 'tis all over, I promise you."

She shuddered again and again. "Please, Glad, find my clothes," she said with a whimpering sound, "and get me out of this horrible place!"

Chapter Eighteen

The first pink fingers of dawn tentatively touched the flowing dogwood and white oak trees, and the light was soft, the air cool. Gladney liked being in the woods at this time of the morning. He was camped in the shadow of a range of low-lying hills along the banks of the Ohio, just west of Louisville. The last morning star made a bright pinpoint of light over the blue mountains lying in a rolling line to the south.

The coals from his campfire of the night before were still glowing after he had swept away the ashes, and Gladney threw several chunks of dry wood onto the bed of coals. He stirred the fire, nursing it into crackling flames which danced merrily against the bottom of the suspended coffee pot. The whirring knock of a woodpecker challenged all the other creatures of the forest, as a rabbit bounded swiftly from one clump of bushes to another.

Gladney smiled at the rabbit, then poured himself a cup of coffee and squatted down to drink it. It was black and steaming, and he had to blow on it before he could drink it. He watched the sun climb slowly, turning from red to orange, from silver to white. He watched it until it was so bright that he could no longer stare at it.

He turned his thoughts to Rebecca. After he had rescued her he had taken her back to the Townes farm for a good night's rest. Then she and Gladney had put Black Prince on the train and returned to Louisville. Steven and his sister Jean, Rebecca's cousin Paul Stanford, and both of Rebecca's grandfathers met them at the depot in Louisville. It had been a grand and happy reunion . . . and Gladney had felt out of place and superfluous.

Jean's wedding to Paul Stanford was set for this Sunday, and the Kentucky Derby was a week away, on Monday, May 17th. Rebecca was to be maid of honor at Jean's wedding, and Jean had invited Gladney to attend.

But Gladney begging off, explained that he had some urgent business to attend to. The truth of it was, he felt that he would be an unwelcome intrusion at the wedding, and such a feeling made him uncomfortable. Also, he knew that Rebecca had a decision to make. She had to decide between him and Steven, and since she had promised an answer after the Derby, she didn't have much time to make up her mind.

Every instinct in Gladney told him to remain by Rebecca's side, so he would be a constant reminder of what had happened between them. But the gentlemanly thing to do was to absent himself for a few days. If nothing else, it would eliminate the tension and bickering that would probably develop between him and Steven.

Gladney laughed aloud. Gentlemanly! If any of his racetrack friends heard the word applied to Gladney Halloran, they would hoot in disbelief!

At any rate, he had declined the wedding invitation, and decided to do something that always relaxed him. He would camp out for the few days until the Derby. He had told Rebecca that he would see her at the Churchill Farm Race Track either on the day of the Derby or a few days before.

So he had a couple more days of solitude. Jean Lightfoot should be married by now, and within a few days Gladney would find out whether or not he was to be married also!

He stood up and stretched to work out the kinks produced by sleeping on the ground. He cleaned up his few breakfast dishes, then lit a cigar and strolled about, going over in his mind a plan he had formulated these past few days. It was a scheme that was brilliant in its simplicity—at least Gladney thought so. What was important, if it worked, it would teach Oscar Stull a much needed lesson.

"Miss Hawkins, Miss Hawkins!" a voice called from just outside Rebecca's door.

"Yes?" Rebecca responded.

She was standing before the mirror, studying her reflection in the glass, trying first one earbob, then the other. She wished that Jean had loaned her only *one* pair of earbobs; then it wouldn't be so difficult to make a choice. Now, she couldn't decide which pair she liked best.

The door opened, and one of the Lightfoot house servants, a large, heavy-set black woman, stuck her head in. "Miss Hawkins," she said, "Miss Lightfoot wants to know, can you come down the hall to her room. I suspect she's in a fix."

"Oh?" Rebecca turned. "What's wrong, Doney?"

"You ask me, I say it ain't nothin' but a fine case of the jitters," Doney said with a grin. "I seen it happen many times with a bride just before she gets hitched up."

Rebecca smiled. "All right, I'll be right there."

She went down the long hall to Jean's room. Most of the wedding guests had already arrived, and their laughter poured up the stairwell to the second floor.

Rebecca had been downstairs earlier to look at the decorations. The house was festooned with fresh flowers and greenery, and an orchestra had been hired to supply music for the entertainment of the guests. The dining room furniture had been pushed to one side, and a large glass bowl containing a fruit punch liberally laced with Kentucky Home bourbon sat in the center of the table. The farm workers, grooms, trainers, and other Lightfoot employees had been clustered around the punch bowl, drinking and exchanging self-conscious jokes about their unaccustomed suits. Occasionally, one of them would pull his collar away from his neck as if trying to get air, and the others would laugh at him. It was just such a burst of laughter that Rebecca heard now as she stood outside Jean's door.

She knocked. "Jean?"

"Come in!" Jean said.

Rebecca opened the door and stepped inside. As she closed it behind her, the noise from downstairs quieted somewhat.

"Jean, what is it?" Rebecca said in alarm.

Jean was sitting in front of her mirror, already dressed in her white wedding gown, breathtakingly beautiful, and crying.

"I can't go through with it," Jean said.

"Whyever not?" Rebecca said in astonishment.

"Rebecca, what if I'm not doing the right thing?" Jean said despairingly. "Marriage is a pretty big step, you know. I'm going to have to live with Paul for the rest of my life, once I marry him!"

Rebecca bit back a smile. "Do you love him?"

"Of course! At least, I think I do. That is . . . I know I do. But still . . . Marriage!"

"Then it's simple. Just don't go through with it," Rebecca said gravely.

"What?" Jean stared. "You can't be serious! All those people down there—I couldn't do that to them!"

"They aren't going to live your life for you, are they?" Rebecca pointed out.

"Well, no."

"Then you don't have to answer to them, do you? You don't have to answer to anyone but yourself, Jean."

Jean breathed deeply a few times, then she said curiously, "Paul's your first cousin. Wouldn't you hate me if I hurt him?"

"You would hurt him far more if you married him and found out later that it was a mistake."

"I believe you really *would* be on my side if I did such a thing!" Jean said incredulously.

"Absolutely."

"Thank you, Rebecca." Jean gave a sighing laugh. "Do you know what I'm going to do now?"

"Yes," Rebecca said, smiling. "You are going to go downstairs and marry Paul Stanford and live happily ever after."

Jean laughed outright. "You're right," she said. "About the first part anyway. I guess I just needed someone to assure me that I was doing this because I wanted to, and not because I had to."

"They say bride jitters are perfectly normal."

Jean stood and put her arms around Rebecca, hugging her warmly. "Oh, Rebecca! I'm going to adore having you as a relative! Whether it's as a cousin or a sister-in-law."

"Now, you must hurry," Rebecca said. "The vicar is here already."

"I'll be right down," Jean promised.

Rebecca gave her an affectionate and reassuring squeeze, then stepped back out into the hall. She saw

Steven coming toward her. Formally dressed in a cut-away jacket and tails, he was heartbreakingly handsome.

"Is anything wrong with Jean?" he asked anxiously.

"No, not really," she answered with a smile. "Just the last minute jitters, is all."

"Oh," Steven said. He looked at her closely, then gave a low, appreciative whistle. "Rebecca, I've never seen anyone as beautiful as you are." He took her hand. "Just say the right word, and we can make this a double wedding."

"Steven . . ." She snatched her hand from his, then sighed. "Even if I was ready to marry you this very minute, I wouldn't think of making this a double wedding. This is Jean's day, and I wouldn't think of making her have to share it."

"Now it's my *sister* you're using as an excuse!" he said with a wry smile. "Anyway, you can't blame me if I hope that her wedding gives you ideas. Come along now, it's about time for things to get underway. That is, if you're certain that Jean is all right?"

"Your sister is fine, believe me. Yes, let's go down."

Steven offered his arm and she took it, then walked down the stairs with him. She saw both her grandfathers looking up at her, both beaming proudly, and the expressions upon their faces made her feel warm and loved. She gazed around the house, at the elegant setting and at the handsome young man with her, and Rebecca knew that she could very happily and easily fit into this life. She could marry Steven, and it would be a good marriage.

But what of Gladney? a voice inside her asked.

Ah, Glad! He was a sweet, even an exciting man. On the other hand, he was a man who lived by his wits, existing hand to mouth, living the same sort of

332

nomadic life she so longed to escape. Here, with a man who loved her, and in an environment which was right for her and her grandfather—and for her children when they came along—she could find true, lasting happiness.

Yes, Gladney had excited her tremendously when they made love, but then so had Steven. Besides, Rebecca was now almost ready to admit to herself that it wasn't Gladney or Steven who had shown her the heights of rapture when they made love, but her own nature finally given free rein. Such a nature, Rebecca had about decided, would allow her to enjoy lovemaking with anyone—it was the act, and not the actor, which thrilled her so.

But Gladney had saved her life. Didn't she owe him a debt of gratitude, a genuine affection? Maybe even her love? Still, a lifetime could not be structured around gratitude. Even though the very life she was now enjoying might be Gladney's gift to her, she knew that he hadn't saved her just to possess her. He would understand if she chose Steven.

Wouldn't he?

"Here comes the bride!" someone shouted.

Everyone turned to look up at Jean descending the stairs. She was carrying a bouquet of garden roses and a small white Book of Common Prayer. She looked at Rebecca and smiled, and Rebecca thought that she had never seen anyone as radiantly beautiful.

The assembled guests parted, and Mr. Lightfoot, waiting at the foot of the stairs, stepped up to take Jean's arm. He escorted her to the other end of the room, where Father Jackson, the Episcopal priest of St. Paul's Church in Louisville, was waiting for them.

Rebecca saw Paul Stanford standing near the priest, smiling foolishly as he watched Jean approach, and

Rebecca knew in that moment that this was what she wanted as well. She wanted the sancitity of love—but with the man she loved.

That, of course, was the agonizing question. Which man did she truly love?

Father Jackson began, "Dearly beloved, we are gathered here in the sight of God, and in the face of this company . . ."

Chapter Nineteen

Gladney had never seen anything quite like it before. None of the many fairs, race meets, carnivals, and circuses he had attended had been anything like this. The atmosphere seemed more like that of one huge party than the gathering of people for a sporting event. Yet the program in his hand indicated beyond a doubt that it was indeed a sporting event, and in Gladney's estimation it was a sporting event such as America had never seen.

"Program—First Day, Monday, May 17, 1875."

The first race was an Association Purse Race, with three hundred dollars added to the regular purse. But it was the second race of the day that attracted the avid attention of the entire country, and that had drawn this large and enthusiastic crowd. The second race was called "The Kentucky Derby." The purse had an additional thousand dollars added.

After scanning the program, Gladney worked his way through the milling crowd, heading for the club-house. Behind him he could hear a band playing "My Old Kentucky Home." He smiled to himself. It was probably about the tenth time he had heard that particular melody today. He had heard other songs, of course; stirring marches, and numbers like "Home, Sweet Home" and "Dixie." "Camptown Races" was

335

also a popular favorite. But nothing was requested of the bands as often as "My Old Kentucky Home."

Flags fluttered from the tops of the twin towers that dominated each end of the grandstand, and bunting hung from every vantage point on the grounds. Women in brilliantly hued dresses, carrying brightly colored umbrellas added to the chromatic swirl. The men were dressed in equally colorful costumes, and here and there Gladney spotted men in full formal dress.

Police were in abundance, helping to control the crowd, which Gladney had heard estimated at ten thousand people. The police were harried by lost children crying for their mothers, and by boisterous celebrants who had already consumed too many mint juleps; but the police generally maintained their good humor, and the crowd, though lively and loud, was friendly and cooperative.

Steven Lightfoot was the first person Gladney recognized in the crowd, and he yelled at him, breaking into a trot.

"Hey, Indian! Wait up!"

Steven halted, turning. "Hello, Glad," he said with a warm smile. "I'm sorry you missed Jean's wedding. It was quite an event."

"I'm glad it went well for her. Have you seen Hawk or Rebecca?"

"Not since we came down early this morning, but I would imagine they are with Black Prince." Steven was wearing the blue and gold silks which were his riding colors. "That horse of theirs is really looking good," Steven added glumly. "The auction pool odds have him way down because he is an unknown, with no track record, but I'm telling you that Black Prince may just be the best horse here today."

Gladney arched his eyebrows in surprise. "Don't tell me you're rating Prince over Bright Morn."

"I really don't know, to be honest, Glad. Bright Morn would have been a challenge to Black Prince before he was drugged. Now I just don't know. I'm not sure he's a hundred percent recovered."

"How does he look now?"

"In the workout this morning he looked pretty damned good. If he holds up that well in the race, he'll run a good race."

"Any word of Oscar Stull?"

"Not a peep. He must be around somewhere. Maybe he's afraid to show his face without Mr. Mercy here to protect him. Glad . . ." He touched Gladney's shoulder. "I don't know if I thanked you properly for saving Rebecca. If not for you, God knows what would have happened to her."

"Riders, to the paddocks, please! To the paddocks, please!" The call came from a uniformed ponyboy. He was riding a horse through the crowd, holding a megaphone to his mouth. Gladney could see several other ponyboys scattered throughout the huge throng.

"Well, it's time," Steven said briskly. "I have to get Bright Morn out and parade him around. Come along, Glad. I'm sure Hawk and Rebecca are down there by now."

The two men started at a brisk pace toward the paddocks.

Gladney said, "Steven . . ." He looked embarrassed and cleared his throat before going on. "I want to wish you good luck in the race, Indian."

Steven looked over at him with an amused expression. "Good luck in the race, you say?"

"Aye. What else could I have meant?"

"Oh, I don't know," Steven said negligently. "With Rebecca perhaps."

"Sure and you'd not be wanting me to be a hypocrite now, would you, bucko?"

Steven doubled up with laughter, and he was still laughing when a groom came running up to them.

"Mr. Lightfoot?" the groom said breathlessly.

Steven sobered. "Yes, what is it?"

"Mr. Lightfoot . . ." The groom looked away. "I have to say that I'm sorry."

"Sorry? Sorry about what, man?" Steven said with a puzzled frown. "Bright Morn? Has something happened to my horse?"

"I'm sorry, Mr. Lightfoot. He's dead," the groom said miserably. "I went to check on him a few minutes ago, and found him dead."

"Dead?" Steven cried in horror. "But he can't be! I was with him not an hour ago. What happened?"

"I don't know," the groom said helplessly. "I just don't know, sir."

"Out of my way!" Steven shouted.

He shoved the groom out of his path and started at a dead run for the stables. He ran blindly, angrily, knocking people out of his way. Gladney ran after him, yelling at him to slow down. But Steven ran on, unheeding.

By the time Gladney finally caught up with him, Steven was in Bright Morn's stall, on his knees beside the horse. The animal's sides weren't moving, and Gladney knew that he was dead.

Gladney said, "Steven, my God! What a terrible thing! I can't tell you how sorry I am."

Steven twisted his head around. His dark eyes swam with tears. In a choked voice he said, "It has to be Oscar Stull behind this."

"I agree. It couldn't be anyone else."

Steven surged to his feet. In a quiet, deadly voice, he said, "I'm going to kill the sonofabitch!"

338

"No, Steven. That would be a mistake. You could be charged with murder, since we have no proof of his skullduggery yet. With Mr. Mercy it was different. I caught him in the act."

"I don't care, I don't care about that," Steven said, his eyes wild now. "Don't you understand? I loved that horse, he was part of my life!"

"I know all that, but this isn't the way to do it."

"What other way is there? He's done anything he pleases to me, to Rebecca and Hawk, and gets away with it. If I kill him, he'll trouble none of us again!"

"But you could hang for it. Is his life worth yours? You're not thinking, man!"

"I don't care! If a man ever needed killing, it's Oscar Stull. Now get out of my way, Gladney. Don't try to stop me!"

He gave Gladney a hard shove and started off. Gladney recovered in time to bound after him and grab him by the shoulder. Steven turned on him in a blind fury. So enraged was he that it was easy for Gladney to ram a hard blow through his guard. The blow landed flush on the chin. Steven's face went blank and he slowly crumpled to the ground.

Gladney stood over him, breathing hard. "I'm sorry, Indian. It's for your own good."

The groom had approached silently. Now he said, "What are you going to do with Mr. Lightfoot now?"

Gladney stooped, picked Steven up, and threw him over his shoulder. "I'm going to tote him to the Clubhouse. Hopefully, he'll have enough of a headache when he wakes up that he'll forget all about this foolishness."

"I hope so," the groom said. "Mr. Lightfoot is too nice a man to get into trouble over the likes of a scoundrel like Oscar Stull."

With the groom making a way for him through the

339

crowd, Gladney transported the unconscious form of Steven Lightfoot to the Louisville Jockey Clubhouse, located just north of the grandstands.

The bugler called the first race to the post, and five horses paraded down to the starting line. Gladney saw them out of the corner of his eyes, but this wasn't the race he was interested in. He was interested in the second race only, mainly because Black Prince would be one of the entries.

But even as he was carrying Steven into the Clubhouse, he saw Black Prince's name being scratched from the big slateboard outside.

Gladney found a settee on which to place Steven, then he hurried back outside to the slateboard where all the horses were listed.

"Why was Black Prince scratched?" he demanded of the man at the slateboard.

"Ask inside," the man said with a shrug. "I just do what they tell me."

Gladney went back inside, and he found Hawk, his face pale and drawn with disappointment and frustration.

"Hawk, what's this all about? Why was Black Prince scratched?"

"Ask Colonel Clark," Hawk said bleakly, jerking his head at the Association President standing nearby.

"We have just discovered that Black Prince was to be ridden by a woman," Colonel Clark explained stiffly. "I'm sorry, Mr. Hawkins, but you know that the rules plainly state that only men can ride."

Gladney said, "How did you find out that the rider was a woman?"

"We were informed by Oscar Stull," Clark said. "We didn't pay too much attention to this at first, but when I asked Mr. Hawkins if it is true, he confessed that it is."

340

"Where is Rebecca?" Gladney asked Hawk.

"She's outside," Hawk said.

"I'll go have a word with her." Gladney started for the door, then stopped and looked back. "Colonel Clark, for your information, two of the horses which were most likely to defeat Stull's own horse have now been eliminated. Some unknown party killed Bright Morn and now, if you ask me, that same person has managed to get Black Prince disqualified. Doesn't that smell a little to you? If I were you, I'd caution Mr. McGrath not to allow Stull around Chesapeake, as Chesapeake seems to be the only horse left with any chance of beating Bold Diablo."

"Did you say that Bright Morn is dead?" Hawk said in dismay.

"Aye," Gladney said. "That bastard killed him. Or had him killed."

"That's a serious charge, Mr. Halloran," Colonel Clark said. "Can you substantiate it?"

"No, I can't substantiate it," Gladney said bitterly. "If I could, I'd have his arse in jail. But I'd caution McGrath to be on the alert, nevertheless."

Gladney pushed his way through the door and walked out onto the front porch of the Clubhouse, barely managing to control the anger that boiled inside him. Maybe the Indian had had the right idea after all, maybe the way to rid the world of scum like Oscar Stull was to kill him outright.

He lit a cigar and stood looking over the milling crowd. He saw the ponyboys riding through the crowd, calling the jockeys to weigh in, and then he remembered the plan that he had dreamed up during his campout. He jumped down off the porch and made his way to the stables as fast as he could. At this very moment, with one race in progress, and the jockeys

341

weighing in for the Kentucky Derby, there might be an opportunity for him to . . .

Reaching the stables, he saw that there was still time. If he worked fast, he could do it!

A short while later Gladney was back in the crowd, searching for Rebecca. He finally found her at the rail of the first turn, and he went over to her.

"I'm sorry, Becky," he said lamely.

Rebecca looked around at him, and her eyes were rimmed red from crying. "I wanted to ride in this race more than I've ever wanted anything in my whole life," she said. "And now, just because I'm a woman, I can't. It's just not fair!"

"I know, Rebecca, and I agree. It isn't fair. But that's the way it is."

"Everything that we have worked for is gone," Rebecca said in a choked voice. "Everything!"

"At least you still have Black Prince," he said. "That's more than Steven can say about Bright Morn."

She looked alarmed. "Has something happened to Bright Morn?"

"He's dead, Becky. He was poisoned. At least, we think that's what happened."

"Bright Morn is dead? Oh, Glad, how awful for Steven!" Tears flooded her eyes again. "How selfish and unthinking of me to be upset because I was disqualified when poor Steven has lost his horse. Where is he now? I should go to him."

"You won't be able to do him much good at the moment," he said, looking off.

"Why?" She peered at him suspiciously. "What are you talking about?"

"I, uh, had to knock him out."

"You *what*? How could you?"

"Becky, he was out of his head with grief. I couldn't

reason with him. He was going to hunt Stull down and kill him!"

She nodded sadly. "You did the right thing. Although, and may God forgive me, I must confess to having the same feeling when I learned that he was responsible for me being disqualified."

"How did he ever discover you're the Hawkins driver?"

"He saw me with Black Prince, dressed in my riding silks," Rebecca said despondently. "It was early this morning, and I thought no one was around. It was a stupid thing for me to do. I hadn't even pinned up my hair."

"Christ, I *am* sorry about that, Becky."

The bugle sounded the call to the post for the second race of the day—the first Kentucky Derby.

"There goes the parade of horses," Rebecca said sadly. "And I am not there. I guess I never will be now."

The first horse in the parade, a chestnut named Verdigris, wore the number three, and the rider wore blue silks with a white cap. The second horse, also a chestnut, by the name of McCreery, wore the number four. The third horse, wearing the number five, was named Enlister, and the rider was dressed in blue and yellow.

"There he is," Rebecca said suddenly, pointing to the fourth horse in the parade.

It was a big, prancing black horse, with the number six on the blanket just behind the saddle. The jockey, Red Parker, was wearing yellow and black, and a flickering, evil grin.

The horses continued to parade before them, until fifteen in all had come by, ending with a horse called Ascension, wearing the number forty-two and carrying a rider who was dressed in red with a white sash.

343

"Oh," Rebecca said vehemently, as the outriders and the others got the horses lined up. She crossed her fingers behind her back. "I hope Bold Diablo loses."

"He will," Gladney said smugly.

"I wish I could be as sure as you sound."

"Take my word for it, lass. Red Parker will not win this race."

"I don't like the sound of that," she said, giving him a searching look. "You aren't going to do anything foolish now, are you?"

Gladney smiled innocently. "Becky, my darlin', sure and I promise I'll not be leavin' your side for the whole race."

"When you go into that Irish brogue, Gladney Halloran, something's up and I know it," Rebecca said sharply.

"You're too suspicious by far. It's not becoming for such a pretty lass."

"Glad, you're up to something. I know you are!"

"Hush now, the great race is about to begin." He smiled winningly and leaned on the rail to watch.

The riders sat quietly astride their mounts, waiting for the starter's whip to snap behind them. A stillness fell over the huge crowd, as everyone on the infield moved to the rail to watch. Then the starter snapped his whip and they were off!

The field was away on the first attempt. Volcano went to the front immediately, followed closely by Verdigris, Aristides, and McCreery. Chesapeake was away poorly.

"Oh, no!" Rebecca exclaimed in dismay. "Look at Chesapeake. What's wrong with him?"

"Never mind Chesapeake, look at Bold Diablo," Gladney said gleefully, and as the horses pounded around the first turn, beginning to string out, Rebecca could see that Bold Diablo trailed the pack.

344

On the backside the horses began changing positions. Aristides moved into second place and hung into position. By the end of the mile Aristides had moved into first place.

"Look at Aristides," Gladney said, pounding on the rail with his fist. Usually Gladney didn't get too excited over a horse race, unless he had a wager on the outcome; but there was something about this one, the first Derby, that caught him up, generating its own excitement.

Beside him, Rebecca said, "Look at Bold Diablo."

Gladney looked, and saw that Stull's horse was now trailing by three lengths and losing ground rapidly. It was all Gladney could do to restrain his glee.

Now Aristides began to increase his lead, though Volcano made a game effort to stay in the running. The rest of the field was strung out for one hundred yards behind, with Bold Diablo now running dead last.

As the horses came around the stretch, H. P. McGrath, his corpulent form clearly identifiable, stood just inside the rail waving his jockey on. Lewis, the young black jockey, was stretching out over his horse's neck, laying on the whip, and Aristides was running with long, smooth, powerful strides, hanging onto the lead despite a determined effort by Volcano. Artistides crossed the finish a winner, leading Volcano by a length. Verdigris was third and Chesapeake, the posttime favorite, was eighth. Bold Diablo came in last.

"Glad," Rebecca said, "what happened to Bold Diablo? Why did he do so poorly?"

"How should I know, lass? You're the horse expert here. Come on, let's wander back to the stables. The only satisfaction coming to us from this race is seeing Oscar Stull's face when he learns he's lost."

Gladney and Rebecca encountered Hawk as they headed for the stables, and the trio made their way through the press of people to the stables. The crowd there was large also, with people gathered around Aristides, talking with McGrath, the horse's trainer, Andy Anderson, and the jockey, Oliver Lewis. There was a conspicuous absence of people around Bold Diablo's stall.

As they came up, Red Parker was whining, "I'm telling you, Mr. Stull, there's something wrong with the horse! I laid the whip to him real good, but I couldn't get anything out of him!"

"You are a stupid incompetent who couldn't win a race if you had Pegasus to ride!" Stull raged. "What good did it do to dope up Chesapeake? You didn't take advantage of it. After all the trouble I went to, what good did it do me?"

"I swear to you, it wasn't my fault! You know as well as I do that a jockey can only do so much. Anybody will tell you that winning a race is ninety percent the horse, ten percent the rider!"

"Don't feed me excuses, Parker! A loser always whines that it isn't his fault."

"Wait a minute!" Red Parker held up his hand and stared at the horse's left foreleg. "Mr. Stull, this isn't Bold Diablo!"

"Are your wits addled now as well?" Stull massaged his scar angrily. "Of course it's Bold Diablo!"

"No, sir, it ain't," Parker insisted. "Just look at his left leg there. Where's the scar?"

"What scar? What are you yapping about?"

"Yes, sir. Don't you recall? Bold Diablo got a scar there when he was in Cape Girardeau, and it ain't quite healed. There ain't no scar on this horse!"

"But that can't be." Stull dropped to one knee, and stared at the foreleg, running his fingers over it. "Goddammit, you're right! I don't understand what's going on here!"

From where they had been silent onlookers, Gladney said, "How does it feel being a loser, Stull? We just thought we'd drop by and tell you how happy we are for you. There's nobody I can think of I'd rather see come in last."

Stull shot to his feet, face purpling. "You! You're behind this, damn you!"

"Behind what?" Gladney said innocently.

"You know what! Somehow, you managed to run a ringer in on me." Stull took a step forward, hands clenched. "Where is Bold Diablo?"

Gladney's eyes narrowed. "You accusing me of stealing your horse? I'd be careful about throwing accusations around, especially since your henchman, Mr. Mercy, is no longer around to protect your hide."

A voice hailed from outside the stable, "Mr. Stull? Are you in there?"

"Yes, blast it!" With an angry glare at Gladney, Stull stormed toward the stable entrance.

Gladney and the Hawkinses trailed after him. Outside, they saw a ponyboy reined up. Beside his horse ranged another—sleek, black, and huge.

The ponyboy said, "Is this your horse, Mr. Stull?"

"Yes, it is!" Stull gaped at Bold Diablo. "Where did you come across him?"

"I found him in Raven Wing's stall, chomping oats. I'm sorry, Mr. Stull." The ponyboy looked embarrassed. "Your horse and Raven Wing look so much alike . . . Well, I'm afraid the track groom must have made a mistake."

"A mistake?"

"Yes, sir. Of course your entry fee will be returned. And the bets on Bold Diablo will be adjusted. I am sorry, sir."

"Yes," Stull growled. "I'm sure you are. But little damn good that does me now."

347

The ponyboy turned Bold Diablo over to Red Parker, fetched Raven Wing from the stable, and left with him.

Gladney was laughing openly. "It seems things aren't going so well for you, are they, Stull? First you lose your pet killer, Mr. Mercy, and now this. Take heart, Stull. Some days are like that."

"Mr. Mercy is no concern of mine," Stull said tightly. "When I discovered that he lied to me when he told me that Mr. Hawkins here wanted his animal boarded at the Townes farm, I discharged him. What happened after that has nothing to do with me."

"Oh, of course not," Gladney said sarcastically.

Stull stared at him hard. "And I still think you're behind this switch today."

"But you heard the ponyboy," Gladney said blandly. "He said a mistake had been made."

"Whatever mistake was made, you were behind it. I'm sure of that." Then he dismissed Gladney with a contemptuous gesture, and turned to Hawk. "Mr. Hawkins, I made this offer before, but with my other thoroughbred. Now, I make you another offer. Neither of our horses got to run in the Derby today. I challenge you to a match race between your horse and Bold Diablo. The winner takes the horse of the loser. What do you say, sir?"

Sudden interest sparked Hawk's faded eyes. He rubbed his chin, and said slowly, "Well now, I don't know . . ."

"Go ahead, Grandfather," Rebecca said quickly.

His head swung around. "I thought you were against it, Becky?"

"Everything is different now. We were barred from the Derby. Something that Mr. Stull is responsible for," she stared coldly at Stull, "and this will give us a chance for Prince to win *something*."

"Very well," Hawk said crisply. "We agree to the match race—on one condition."

Stull said suspiciously, "What condition is that?"

Hawk placed his arm around Rebecca's shoulders. "That Becky be allowed to ride in the race."

"What?" Red Parker snorted derisively. "You can't be serious?"

"I'm perfectly serious," Hawk said. "I think my granddaughter to be one of the finest riders I have ever seen race. And if we are to put Black Prince on the line, only Becky will be riding him."

"Take him up on it, Mr. Stull." Parker snorted again. "If he thinks she's the best he's ever seen, I'd like to show this old coot what a real rider can do!"

Oscar Stull motioned Parker quiet. He still seemed dubious. "I don't know about this. It could be a trick of some kind."

"Don't use your own motives, Stull, to judge others," Gladney said.

"No tricks," Hawk said stoutly. "I simply want Becky to ride. Otherwise, it's no race."

"It doesn't matter anyway." Stull shrugged. "The rules don't allow a woman to ride."

"This race will be between us, Stull. We make our own rules," Hawk retorted. "Besides, the official rules stipulate that in a special race, with the agreement of both parties, any rule or law laid down by the Association may be temporarily suspended. And as one party I certainly agree to suspending that rule. It's up to you."

Stull stared at Rebecca. A slow grin spread his lips. "Why should I balk? If you're willing to risk your horse on a girl riding him, I certainly can't object." He held out his hand. "You have yourself a match race, Mr. Hawkins."

"No, sir." Hawk made a show of putting both hands

behind his back. "I only shake hands with gentlemen."

Stull's face reddened, and he rubbed furiously at his scar. "I'll ignore that insult, and get my revenge in the race. When shall it be?"

"I happen to know that there is a slot left in the schedule tomorrow for just such a special race. If it is all right with you, I'll go make the arrangements now."

"That's fine with me. I'm looking forward with relish to the race." Stull's mouth stretched in a wolfish grin.

"Stull," Gladney said harshly, "speaking of trickery —in case you get any more ideas, I intend to sleep in Black Prince's stall tonight with a pistol in my hand."

"And so do I," said another voice.

They all glanced around to see Steven Lightfoot behind them.

Rebecca hurried to him. "Oh, Steven, I'm terribly sorry about Bright Morn."

"So am I," he said, his hard gaze on Stull. "But between us, I think Gladney and I can see to it that nothing untoward happens to Black Prince."

Stull shrugged negligently. "Suit yourselves, gents. But if I were you, Mr. Hawkins, I'd worry about an Indian half-breed and a con man sharing the same stall with my horse."

Steven tensed, taking a step toward Stull. Rebecca placed a hand on his arm, and he held still.

Stull turned away with a contemptuous gesture. "Come along, Parker. We have a race to run tomorrow. And this one," he looked coldly back over his shoulder at Rebecca, "I fully intend to win. Nothing will stop me."

Chapter Twenty

Headlines from the Louisville *Courier-Journal* of Tuesday, May 18, 1875:

DERBY DAY!
*A brilliant inauguration of the
Louisville Jockey Club Association!*

*The day a great success at every
point, and the promise of the
future assured!*

*McGrath's Aristides the winner
of the Great Event yesterday,
taking down the Derby purse!*

Rebecca sat in her hotel room, reading the story of the very first Kentucky Derby. The story told tho amount of the purse, $2,850, gave the Auction Pool at $105, and made much of the fact that Aristides won, although another horse belonging to the same owner had been favored.

Rebecca was in a pensive mood. All her hopes, dreams, and ambitions had been tied up with that race, only to have a tragic and frustrating set of events occur, which had changed things drastically. Now, it all came down to a match race between Black Prince and Bold Diablo. Already she was having second thoughts about urging Hawk to accept the challenge. A horse race could be decided on many things, often things that the rider had no control over. And if they lost, Rebecca knew that her heart would break at having to turn Prince over to Oscar Stull. Giving him to anyone would be bad enough, but to Oscar Stull!

At least, she thought, she would be able to ride this race proudly, without subterfuge. With Stull's agreement to that condition, it had already been announced publicly that the rider of Black Prince would be a woman.

As she leafed through the newspaper, she came across a story that dealt with the match race being run today, with a headline in somewhat less bold type:

MATCH RACE!
By special permission from the Association, one rider in the match race will be female. A first in racing history! Rebecca Hawkins, disqualified jockey of Black Prince, in the Derby, to face Red Parker, on Stull's Bold Diablo. Post-time at 2:30 P.M.

"Becky," a voice said, and Rebecca looked up to see her grandfather sitting across from her, studying her gravely.

"I didn't even hear you come in, Grandfather!"

"I know you didn't girl," Hawk said. "A cannon could have gone off in your ear, and I don't think you would have heard."

He got up and crossed to her chair. He took the newspaper and tossed it onto the bed, then knelt down, taking her hand in his.

"Becky . . . I want you to listen to me, girl, and heed my words."

"Yes, Grandfather," she said meekly, wondering why he seemed to be so concerned.

"Today, when you and Black Prince were ready to take the track, it was going to be a team effort, am I right? Black Prince needs you as much as you do him. Am I right?"

"Yes, of course," she said, still puzzled.

"Then you must understand my meaning when I tell you that I think you're letting him down. Right now, Becky, you are letting him down."

"Grandfather, how is that?"

"How? I'll tell you. You are flat, Becky, flat as a day-old pancake. I've been watching you all morning. You're sighing around, mooning over first one thing, then another. In other words, you have no competitive fire! That won't do. You've got to be razor sharp, and nothing on your mind but winning this race. You've got to be ready to win! Do you realize what will happen if you don't? We lose Black Prince!"

"Grandfather, I know all that. I do want to win. Do you think I want to lose Prince, and to *that* man?"

"You may not *want* to lose," Hawk said. "But that's not enough. You have got to want to win. It has to be there, that feeling of wanting to win, until you can think of nothing else. It has to fill every nook and cranny of your heart and soul. That means you put everything else out of your mind!"

"I'm trying, Grandfather," she said unhappily. "But it isn't all that easy. So much has happened, so many things have turned out so differently from what I had hoped for, or had imagined would happen."

"Dandy! Then let's talk about those things. Say them. Let's get it all out in the open, here and now. If you don't, say goodbye to Black Prince!"

She stirred uneasily. "I don't think it's all *that* bad."

"Well, it so happens I do," Hawk said grimly. "Now spit it out."

"For one thing, I can't help but feel sorry for Steven," Rebecca said. "I know what he thought of Bright Morn, and to see him poisoned on the very day of the race! How awful that must be for him! And then for me to be disqualified. What makes it so bad, Grandfather, is that it was my own fault. I should have been more careful. I had no idea there would be anyone around to see me, let alone recognize me. I was just careless, that's all, and there is no excuse for it."

"But those things have happened, girl," Hawk pointed out. "They are behind us, and all the worrying and fretting in the world won't change that. It's wasted effort, don't you see?"

"But there is something else," she said. "Something that is *not* behind me."

"What's that?"

Rebecca sighed and got up from her chair, then walked over to the window and looked out. From her hotel room, she could see the Ohio Riverboat Club. A group of laughing, hand-waving men and women were filing onto a riverboat for a day's excursion on the river.

Briefly, Rebecca wished that she could change places with one of the women down there. Any one of them, she thought. Then the weight of all her recent problems wouldn't be on her shoulders. She saw one young woman in a blue dress, and she closed her eyes and thought very hard, speculating as to who the girl was, wondering what it would be like to be her, right now, with nothing before her but the promise of a day without anything to worry about. Rebecca could almost feel the cobblestone levee under her feet, so hard did she imagine her transposition into the body and soul of the young woman in the blue dress.

"You didn't answer me, Becky," Hawk said patiently.

"What?" Rebecca whirled, feeling herself being jerked back into the hotel room, back into reality, back into the middle of her trials and tribulations.

"I said, what else is there to worry about?"

"I promised Gladney and Steven that I would make a decision after the Derby. I promised to make a choice between them. Well, the Derby was yesterday!"

"And have you made a decision?"

"I think I have," she said slowly. "But it was such a difficult decision, Grandfather. You see, I love both of them."

"You can love both of them," Hawk said. "But you must love one as a husband, and the other you must love as a brother."

"But the one I love like a brother will be hurt when I tell him," she said bleakly. "And I can't stand to think of hurting him."

"You have no choice," Hawk said firmly. He peered at her curiously. "Which one did you decide on? No!" He held up his hand. "No, don't tell me!"

She smiled palely. "I didn't intend to, Grandfather."

He was nodding. "Yes, you have to keep that decision to yourself until after the race. You musn't let anything distract you now. If you do, you will surely lose."

"You're right," Rebecca said. "But even if we win the match race, we are very little ahead of where we are now. The purse will be small, Grandfather, save the winning of the other horse. And we've no money to bet with. What will we have accomplished?"

"We will have accomplished justice," Hawk said sternly. "Becky, Steven's horse being poisoned, your being kidnapped and almost killed, then your disqualification from the Derby, all of our problems over the past few weeks can be traced back to one man—Oscar Stull. If you beat him soundly today, he may withdraw from the racing scene entirely. He's a man who hates to lose, we already know that. I think losing literally makes the man sick. Think how much better off racing would be without him. *There* is your accomplishment!"

Rebecca smiled suddenly, a smile almost carefree. "You're right. You *are* right, Grandfather. It's worth winning, just to be rid of him, once and for all."

"Oh, that's dandy!" He brightened. "That's what I wanted to hear. Now, come along, we have to get down to the track."

It may have been a carryover from the enthusiasm of the day before, or it may have been the idea of watching a woman jockey compete against a man. But for whatever reason, the track was as crowded as it had been on Derby Day. Thousands of people were there, many of them enjoying a picnic on the infield before the race. The mood was very festive.

Newspaper reporters were present as well. Many had learned of the event when they came to cover the Kentucky Derby, and remained over for an extra day, for this promised to be a drama of human interest to their readers, especially since one of the riders would be a woman. The fact that she was also the granddaughter of Henry Hawkins added an extra element, for every racing fan in America knew of the Hawk.

Hawk allowed the reporters to photograph and question Rebecca for some time, but he finally called a halt, asking if they wouldn't leave so she could get prepared for the event, and all did so willingly.

Bold Diablo was already saddled, and Red Parker was up. He paraded the big horse up and down the paddock area, waving jauntily to the crowd and promising to prove once and for all "why women shouldn't be allowed to compete against men." Evidently there were many who felt as Parker did, because the odds were twenty to one against Rebecca, not only because she was a woman jockey but because Black Prince was an unknown horse. He had never raced, and thus had no history. Bold Diablo, on the other hand, had twenty-two wins out of twenty-six starts, and by now everyone knew about the mixup—that Bold Diablo had not been the horse which had run so poorly the day before. And of course, those who had lost money on him had been refunded their money, so now they were willing to wager on him again.

From Black Prince's stall, Hawk and Rebecca could hear Parker's loud, boisterous claims as he paraded around the paddock area. Rebecca, dressed in her silks, but this time allowing her hair to hang naturally to her shoulders, stood by Black Prince, caressing him affectionately on the neck.

"Bold Diablo is a good and experienced horse," Hawk was saying. "He could probably run this race without Parker, he's that intelligent. Black Prince has never run one, so it's now up to you, Becky. You can't give away any ground and hope to win. You can't make *any* mistakes. Black Prince has heart, we know that, and he has speed and stamina. But he lacks experience, so he has to depend on you for the brains and strategy."

"I know, Grandfather, and I will do my very best," Rebecca promised.

The door to the stall swung open and they glanced around to see Gladney and Steven standing there together.

"Hello," Rebecca said, her smile blooming. "I was beginning to think you two had deserted me."

"Not very damn likely, lass," Gladney said.

"Rebecca," Steven said, "we have something—Glad and I, we have something we want to say to you . . ." He stopped, clearing his throat.

"What?" she asked, intrigued by the utter seriousness of his face.

"Well, we . . ." Steven floundered again, and glanced over at Gladney. "You tell her, Glad. You're the one with the silver Irish tongue."

"It's just this, Becky," Gladney said. "The Indian and I are both in love with you, but we've both agreed that we also want what's best for you. We know you promised us an answer after the Derby, but we don't want you to even think about that until this race is won."

"What we're saying is," Steven broke in, "we want you to go out and win this race. Forget everything else until that is accomplished."

"That's the truth of it, lass," Gladney said with his crooked grin. "And when you do make your decision, we want you to know this, too. We know you can only choose one. And we've decided that whichever one of us is the unfortunate one, why, we've been fortunate to have had the privilege of knowing and loving you for a little while. So Becky, you do what you have to do, and we'll abide by your decision."

Steven nodded. "That's right."

Rebecca smiled tremulously, and tears came to her eyes. She walked over to the two men and kissed them both, full on the lips. "You're both fine men, and I know I can have only one of you," she said. "But at least for the duration of this race, I have the love of both of you, and that's all Prince and I need to win."

Outside, the bugler blew the familiar notes, calling the horses to the post.

"That's it, girl," Hawk said quickly. "Get mounted."

Rebecca went over to Black Prince, and her grand-

358

father gave her a boost into the high-stirruped saddle. He then took the reins and led the horse out for the parade.

"Indian, you know horses better than I do," Gladney said, as they watched Black Prince leave the paddock. "Does he have a chance?"

"It's hard to say. He's never been in competition," Steven said thoughtfully. "And so much always depends on the competitive edge. But I've seen him run, and he may be one of the fastest natural runners I've ever seen."

"I hope you're right," Gladney said fervently. "I hope to Christ you're right!" As he spoke, Gladney subconsciously fingered the spot where his diamond stickpin would have been, if he had been wearing it.

"Ladies and gentlemen!" one of the officials near the starting line shouted through a megaphone. "Yesterday, one of Kentucky's most beloved statesmen, John C. Breckinridge, died. In honor of his memory, we are going to lower the flag to half-mast before this race begins."

Although his voice could only be heard by those nearest the starting line, the word was passed through the crowd by others until everyone was aware of the solemn pronouncement, and they all stood silently as the flag was lowered to half-mast. During the ceremony, Rebecca and Red Parker sat on their mounts, side by side.

Parker leaned toward her. In a low, vicious voice, he said, "You ever feel a whip in the face, girl? Because if you get too close to me that's exactly what's going to happen to you. You just think about that and stay out of my way, or you'll be sorry.

"You can't frighten me, Parker," Rebecca said steadily.

The flag-lowering ceremony was completed, and the

starting official walked over to the two waiting horses. "Gentlemen, uh, that is, lady and gentleman," he corrected himself. "Are you both ready?"

Rebecca leaned over Black Prince's neck, holding the reins loosely in her hands, and poised herself, feeling every muscle in Black Prince tense in readiness. She fought against the fluttering in her stomach and said, "I am ready, sir."

"Miss Hawkins, the signal to start will be the crack of my whip," the starter said.

Rebecca already knew this, of course, and she was tempted to tell him so in no uncertain words. Instead, she merely nodded and waited. She had long ago learned the art of projecting a victory, and before any race she pictured in her mind the finish line with her crossing it first. It was a mental and emotional trick that helped set her mind to the task before her. That picture was in her mind now.

The whip snapped crisply.

Parker used his whip from the very start. Bold Diablo shot forward like a bullet, and was immediately steered to the rail. He was a full length ahead of Black Prince as they passed the first furlong, and increased his lead to two lengths before reaching the first quarter. Then Black Prince, under Rebecca's urgings started to move up with his long, rhythmic strides. The horse reached full speed and gradually closed the gap, and at the half-mile post the two horses were running head to head, close together.

"Back off!" Parker shouted.

He reached across and lashed out at Rebecca with his riding quirt. Rebecca, seeing it coming, held her own quirt up and fended him off, much as if they were fencng. Even so, the tip of his quirt stung her sharply across the knuckles.

Bold Diablo was a fine, noble horse, and when he

saw Black Prince closing on him, his competitive spirit came into play, and he refused to allow Black Prince to pass. However, Black Prince was a game horse too, with an inbred competitive spirit which made him hang in. As they reached the mile post, both horses were still giving it all they had, while their riders continued to fight with each other. Finally, with only a furlong to go, Black Prince began to ease ahead, inch by inch, then foot by foot. Parker, realizing what was happening, stopped trying to use his whip on Rebecca and began using it on Bold Diablo, lashing his flanks in furious desperation.

Bold Diablo responded nobly to the urging, and began taking some of the lead back from Black Prince, so that Black Prince's lead was by a neck, half-a-neck, and then only by a nose. But now the last bit of Bold Diablo's reserves were used up. Try as he might, he could not pick up that last inch.

Both horses flashed across the finish line to the deep-throated roar of ten thousand frenzied fans, and Black Prince, by the length of a nose, was the winner!

Rebecca allowed the horse to stretch out his run until she could pull him up. Then, acknowledging the cheers of the crowd, she returned to pull down the purse, which in this instance was three hundred dollars put up by the Association, plus the titles to both horses.

Hawk, Gladney, and Steven had already rushed out onto the track by the time she trotted Black Prince across the finish line. They were shouting and laughing, cheering hysterically. Rebecca swung off the horse, and all three men rushed to give her a hug and a kiss of congratulations.

Oscar Stull came charging up. "So you've won my horse, have you?" His face was purple with rage, and the scar on his face was never more visible. "Well, you can have him!" Stull snarled. "But by the time I get through with him, he won't feel like running ever again!"

Stull stormed toward Bold Diablo, now standing just across the finish line with Red Parker sitting quiet and dejected up on his back. Stull raised his whip toward the horse as he began to run toward him, screaming in a blind rage.

"Stull, hold up now!" Hank bellowed, starting toward the man. "That's my horse now, and I'll not have you beating him."

Stull, if he even heard, ignored Hawk's voice, and within two steps he had reached Bold Diablo and slashed his whip across the horse's face.

Bold Diablo's competitive spirit was still sharp, and this was not the first time his owner had whipped him. The animal gave one warning neigh, but Stull lashed out at him again, and when he did, Bold Diablo reared high on his back legs, spilling Red Parker to the ground. The horse neighed again and then came back down with both hooves flashing toward Stull. One hoof caught Stull on the shoulder, breaking it. But Stull didn't even feel that one, because at the same time, the other hoof had caught him in the head, crushing his skull and killing him instantly.

There had been quite a mob around the finish line when Oscar Stull was killed. But his attack on the horse had been witnessed by all, and an impromptu meeting of the judges absolved Bold Diablo of any blame, due to the fact that he had been sorely provoked. Therefore, the Association posted no sanctions against the horse, and Hawk and Rebecca were allowed to lead him away to their stall.

Red Parker suffered a wounded dignity and, because of his unsportsmanlike use of the whip against Rebecca, he was barred from riding in all future events at Churchill Track. Spewing obscenities at the dead Stull, he was escorted from the grounds by two policemen.

And now, more than an hour later, in the upstairs observation room of the Louisville Jockey Club House, which had been turned over to the Hawkinses for their victory celebration, Rebecca waited alone. She had asked her grandfather to bring Steven and Gladney to her. It was time for her to make her decision known.

She stood at the window looking over the track. There were still several hundred people milling about, but the major portion of the crowd had departed by now. Rebecca felt proud of her race and proud of Black Prince. She wished that she had been able to ride in the Derby, because she had a strong feeling that the Derby would one day be the greatest event in thoroughbred racing, but, as Hawk had told her, there was no sense in worrying about what was past.

There was only the future now, and that she was about to take care of. She felt a strange mix of emotions as she waited for her grandfather and the two young men. On the one hand, she felt sadness for the one she would have to tell no. But having made the decision, she also felt an immense joy over the prospect of sharing her life with the man she now realized she loved more than any other. There was no longer any doubt in her mind as to her choice, for once arrived at, it was a choice she knew was right.

The door opened behind her, but Rebecca continued to stare out at the track.

"Becky girl," Hawk said. "They are here."

She turned slowly. The expressions on both faces were almost childlike in their hope and anxiety, but behind the anxiety their eyes spoke of their determination to accept her decision graciously.

"Well," she said with a sigh. "I suppose the time has come."

"Yes," Steven said.

"And I'm ready," Gladney said quietly.

Rebecca drew a deep breath, then took two quick steps and kissed Steven on the mouth.

Gladney tried to hide his quick look of pain, and started to turn away.

"No, Glad," Rebecca said softly. "Wait, please."

She stepped back from Steven and looked at him pensively. "Steven, you are a fine man, and you will make someone a wonderful husband. But that kiss was just my way of saying goodbye to you."

Steven returned her look, and she could see the hurt and sharp disappointment in his eyes. However, true to his promise, he made it as easy for her as he could. He smiled painfully, then reached over and seized Gladney's hand, pumping it vigorously.

"So it's you she's chosen," he said. "Congratulations, Glad, but don't expect me to say that the best man won."

Gladney stared at Rebecca in momentary disbelief, then he whooped with joy, grabbed her and swung her around, before kissing her soundly.

"Well!" he said. "For once in my life I'm almost speechless. Almost, I said."

"If you ever mistreat her, Glad," Steven said sternly, "I'll come back and finish the licking I was giving you in Cairo." Then he smiled again, with less effort this time. "I'll be on my way, I reckon. I know you two have things to talk about, plans to make, that sort of thing, so I'll just leave you alone together." His gaze shifted to the track outside, his face settling into lines of sorrow. "Besides, I have to find myself a horse somewhere."

"You don't have to look very far," Hawk said gravely.

"Now what does that mean?"

"It means we've decided to give you Bold Diablo," Rebecca said happily. "To replace Bright Morn."

He looked bewildered. "But you don't have to do that."

"I know we don't *have* to," Hawk said.

"But we want to, Steven," Rebecca said. "That was our plan all along."

"Well, let's just say," Hawk looked wryly at his granddaughter, "that it was Becky's plan all along." He added hastily, "But I didn't give her much of an argument."

He handed Steven the title papers to Bold Diablo, and Steven saw that the papers had already been adjusted to show him as the horse's owner.

"And Black Prince will gladly grant him a re-match," Rebecca said. "Any time you think he's ready."

"Well, I just don't know what to say," Steven said, bouncing the papers in his hands. "Except thanks, to both of you. And now I guess I'd better go get acquainted with my new horse."

Steven started through the door, paused and turned back, as if to say something. Then with a small, rather melancholy smile, he waved and left.

"Well, girl, I guess we're about back where we started," Hawk said. "We've got a pretty good thoroughbred, that we know now for a fact, and a pretty good pacer. And that's it. I guess we'll soon have to hit the racing circuit again."

"We aren't *quite* back to where we started," she said, smiling at Gladney. "We have Glad." She reached out to take his hand.

"That's true, and I think that's dandy." Hawk

grinned as he shook Gladney's other hand. "And let me tell you, boy, that I couldn't be happier for you."

"Sure, and aren't we all bein' a bit down about our finances now?" Gladney said in his thickest brogue. "When there's nothing to be after worryin' about. Nothing at all."

"Glad!" Rebecca said sharply. "Glad, I don't like it when you fall back into that brogue of yours. It usually means that you're up to something, and I want it understood right now that your con days are over. Do you understand me?"

"You mean you'd not let me work a con, even if it meant putting a bit of bread on our table?" he said, his eyes dancing with mischief.

"We've eaten for many years without the need of a con," she said.

"Then it'd take more than the need for food before you'd let me work at my chosen profession?" he said, feigning a hurt look. "But if the end justifies the means, then it'll be all right?"

"Now, I didn't say that."

"But we'll leave the door open, is that it, lass?"

She had to laugh. "I do believe you've just conned me again."

"We'll see, we'll see," he said cryptically. "In the meantime, perhaps I've a bit of good news for the pair of you."

"And what might that be?" Hawk asked.

"I managed to scrape together a few dollars, and I placed a little wager on Black Prince."

Rebecca said tartly, "At least for once you bet on a winner."

Gladney was grinning, "I put it down in the name of Mr. and Mrs. Halloran, lass."

"You did what!" She glared at him. "Of all the gall!

366

You didn't know I would agree to marry you." She hesitated. "Did you?"

"Now that's something I think I'll let you wonder about for a spell," he said artlessly. "Maybe I just figured that if you knew the only way you could get the money would be as my wife, it would help my cause."

Rebecca was outraged. "You actually thought I'd marry you for the money?"

"No, not really," he admitted shamefacedly. "But I guess it does look that way, and I do apologize for that, darling."

"I accept your apology," she said, mollified. Her curiosity got the better of her. "How much did you—" She laughed. "How much did *we* win?"

"I haven't figured it out yet. Let's see now, the odds were twenty to one when I made the wager . . ."

"Twenty to one?" Rebecca said indignantly. "You mean there was that little faith in Black Prince and me?"

"Don't scorn it, lass," Gladney said. "It served us well in this instance."

"Yes," Hawk said with a chuckle. "I guess it did. Say now, at twenty to one, a twenty dollar bet is— what? Four hundred dollars! Good Lord! Boy, how much were you able to get down?"

"Well, it was a little more than twenty dollars," Gladney said, grinning hugely.

"How much more?" Rebecca demanded. Her heart began to beat rapidly and she awaited his answer with bated breath.

"Five thousands dollars. We won one hundred thousand dollars."

Hawk put his hand over his heart and dropped down into the nearest chair. "One hundred thousand!

I don't believe it! Great God almighty. Becky, that's enough to buy the horse farm!"

Rebecca had something else on her mind at the moment. "Glad, where did you get that much money to wager?"

Gladney grinned and held his finger up, wagging it at her. "Now, lass. Do you recall the pea and the walnut shell? You wanted to know how I did that, didn't you? There are some things that are best left a mystery, don't you think? For example, wasn't it a mystery now how that ringer got run in on Bold Diablo yesterday?"

She gasped. "You mean Stull was right? *You* were responsible for that?"

Grinning, he took her into his arms. "You know what they say," he said softly. "Now you see it . . ." He brought his mouth down on hers, and Rebecca closed her eyes in expectation of his kiss. Just before their lips met, Gladney finished, "And now you don't."

Patricia Matthews

...an unmatched sensuality, tenderness and passion.
No wonder there are over 14,000,000 copies in print!

40-644-4 LOVE, FOREVER MORE $2.50
The tumultuous story of spirited Serena Foster and her determination to survive the raw, untamed West.

40-646-0 LOVE'S AVENGING HEART $2.50
Life with her brutal stepfather in colonial Williamsburg was cruel, but Hannah McCambridge would survive—and learn to love with a consuming passion.

40-645-2 LOVE'S DARING DREAM $2.50
The turbulent story of indomitable Maggie Donnevan, who fled the poverty of Ireland to begin a new life in the American Northwest.

40-658-4 LOVE'S GOLDEN DESTINY $2.50
It was a lust for gold that brought Belinda Lee together with three men in the Klondike gold rush, only to be trapped by the wildest of passions.

40-395-X LOVE'S MAGIC MOMENT $2.50
Evil and ecstasy are entwined in the steaming jungles of Mexico, where Meredith Longley searches for a lost city but finds greed, lust, and seduction.

40-394-1 LOVE'S PAGAN HEART $2.50
An exquisite Hawaiian princess is torn between love for her homeland and the only man who can tame her pagan heart.

40-659-2 LOVE'S RAGING TIDE $2.50
Melissa Huntoon seethed with humiliation as her ancestral plantation home was auctioned away, suddenly vulnerable to the greed and lust of a man's world.

40-660-6 LOVE'S SWEET AGONY $2.75
Amid the colorful world of thoroughbred farms that gave birth to the first Kentucky Derby, Rebecca Hawkins learns that horses are more easily handled than men.

40-647-9 LOVE'S WILDEST PROMISE $2.50
Abducted aboard a ship bound for the Colonies, innocent Sarah Moody faces a dark voyage of violence and unbridled lust.

40-721-1 LOVE'S MANY FACES (Poems) $1.95
Poems of passion, humor and understanding that exquisitely capture that special moment, that wonderful feeling called love.

Buy them at your local bookstore or use this handy coupon:
Clip and mail this page with your order

PINNACLE BOOKS, INC.—Reader Service Dept.
2029 Century Park East, Los Angeles, CA 90067

lease send me the book(s) I have checked above. I am enclosing _____ (please add 75¢ to cover postage and handling). Send check r money order only—no cash or C.O.D.'s.

Mr./Mrs./Miss _____

ddress _____

ity _____ State/Zip _____

Please allow four weeks for delivery. Offer expires 1/1/81.

The Windhaven Saga
by Marie de Jourlet

Over 4,000,000 copies in print!

☐ **40-642-8 WINDHAVEN PLANTATION** $2.50
The epic novel of the Bouchard family, who dared to cross the boundaries of society and create a bold new heritage.

☐ **40-643-6 STORM OVER WINDHAVEN** $2.50
Windhaven Plantation and the Bouchard dream are shaken to their very roots in this torrid story of men and women driven by ambition and damned by desire.

☐ **40-242-2 LEGACY OF WINDHAVEN** $2.25
After the Civil War the Bouchards move west to Texas—a rugged, untamed land where they must battle Indians, bandits and cattle rustlers to insure the legacy of Windhaven.

☐ **40-348-8 RETURN TO WINDHAVEN** $2.50
Amid the turbulent Reconstruction years, the determined Bouchards fight to hold on to Windhaven Range while struggling to regain an old but never forgotten plantation.

☐ **40-499-9 WINDHAVEN'S PERIL** $2.50
Luke Bouchard and his family launch a new life at Windhaven Plantation—but the past returns to haunt them.

☐ **40-722-X TRIALS OF WINDHAVEN** $2.75
Luke and Laure Bouchard face their most bitter trial yet, as their joyful life at Windhaven Plantation is threatened by an unscrupulous carpetbagger.

Buy them at your local bookstore or use this handy coupon:
Clip and mail this page with your order

PINNACLE BOOKS, INC.—Reader Service Dept.
2029 Century Park East, Los Angeles, CA 90067

Please send me the book(s) I have checked above. I am enclosing $_____ (please add 75¢ to cover postage and handling). Send check or money order only—no cash or C.O.D.'s.

Mr./Mrs./Miss _____

Address _____

City _____ State/Zip _____

Please allow four weeks for delivery. Offer expires 1/1/81.

Announcement

LOVE'S BOLD JOURNEY
by Patricia Matthews

This will be the tenth novel in the phenomenal best-selling series of historical romances by Patricia Matthews. Once again, she weaves a compelling, magical tale of love, intrigue, and suspense. Millions of readers have acclaimed her as their favorite storyteller. In fact, she is the very first woman writer in history to publish three national bestsellers in one year . . . two years in a row!

Patricia Matthews's first novel, *Love's Avenging Heart*, was published in early 1977, followed by *Love's Wildest Dream*; *Love, Forever More*; *Love's Daring Dream*; *Love's Pagan Heart*; *Love's Magic Moment*; *Love's Golden Destiny*; and *Love's Raging Tide*.

Now that you've finished reading *Love's Sweet Agony*, we're sure you'll want to watch for *Love's Bold Journey*, which will be published in October 1980. It is the story of Rachel Bonner, an independent and resourceful young woman who marries a man she doesn't love. Driven by misfortune to open a brothel tent for the men working on the railroad, she falls deeply in love and is drawn into the intrigue of corruption surrounding the construction of the Union Pacific Railroad. Will the bonds of love be broken by villainy and scandal? Or will Rachel and the man she loves be able to overcome the threats to their happiness?

As in all novels by Patricia Matthews, the storytelling is exciting, the characters memorable, and the ending a satisfying experience.

Watch for *Love's Bold Journey* in October, wherever paperbacks are sold.